DAUGHTER OF THE PINES

MARIA A EDEN

For Tommy.
Dad, you never got to read this, but you live between the pages.

...and for all the children of the Pine Barrens who spent summer nights on dirt roads, daring their friends to turn out the lights.

A MESSAGE TO
THE READER

Daughter of the Pines is a romantic fantasy that's intimately influenced by the story of the Jersey Devil and the New Jersey Pine Barrens. Every character is fictional, and even though the Ledes family pays homage to the real family that inspired the folklore, there is no intentional description of anyone, dead or alive, in this work of fiction.

The story is a gaslamp tale, which means it's a reimagination of a real place and time, retold through the lens of magic. This story is *not* a historical retelling, and even though the town of Galloway exists in our realm, the Galloway described in the book is another version from another realm.

If you're reading this story to gain an accurate historical and geographic representation of the Pine Barrens in colonial times, you will not find that here.

My goal was to paint the Pine Barrens landscape in a haunting, otherworldly way. Because, as anyone who regularly spends time in the Pine Barrens will tell you, the place is supremely haunting. If you haven't been lucky enough to visit the Pine Barrens, you should make it a priority. To those who love the real Devil who lurks in the pines as much as I do, I hope you enjoy an escape within these pages that feels like coming home.

–Maria

The Ledes Family Tree

The Triplet Lords

The Ledes Cousins

Aaron — Beatrice

Bain — Patrice

Cade — Sarah

1 Paxton

2 Brannon

3 Samuel

5 Jackson

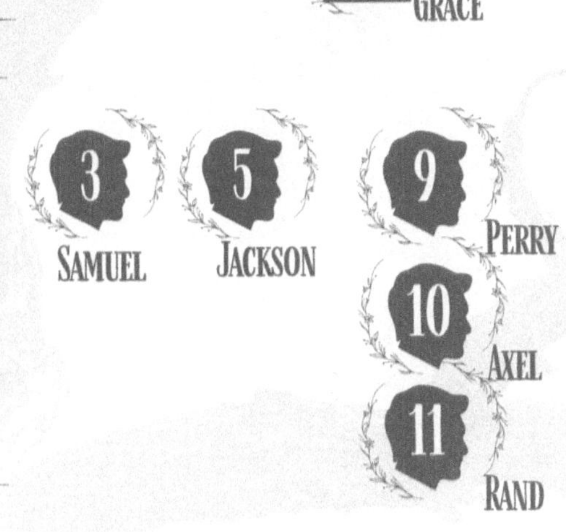

6 Mira

7 Anna

8 Grace

9 Perry

10 Axel

11 Rand

4 James

12 Harper

PROLOGUE

There are many thin places in this realm, but none so much as the Barrens.

Nobody understood how the trees took root in the arid, sandy earth. Each inexplicable summer came with the threat of fire as searing rays of sun bathed the boughs in heat.

Trees burned to ash in the sand, leaving expanses of charred wood. The master of the fire realm stoked his flames, stretching his legs and arms, sparking his fingers in the soil.

One such summer, the Lady Ledes of Galloway was heavy with child when a heat wave struck the Barrens. Blazes licked the ground just outside the village as the weight of labor fell upon her.

That night, the Ledes triplets were born. The more the babes wailed, the more the raging fire in the pines quelled, as though the triplets absorbed the flames. Magic is born with the souls that hold it, and the triplets were born with the gift of fire, so bright it could snuff out flames.

A magic so strong in triplicate, it could close the thin place in the Barrens.

The villagers rejoiced. Indeed, the birth of the triplet boys must be a gift to Galloway, their magic the key to keeping them safe. As the last embers died away, a woman emerged from the soot and dust. Some villagers claimed they had seen her roaming the woods before, content to live in the thickest part of the Barrens with nothing but shadows to speak to.

The woman approached the manor where the triplets lay sleeping and asked to speak to the lord. When the lord welcomed her in, surrounded by the protection of his royal guard, she dropped to her knees.

She explained to him that she could speak to demons. When the babies were born, their cries carried between the trees. The master of the fire realm, the king of all demons, had heard them, and he had whispered in her ear. He knew of the fire magic born to the babes. When the fire died, the thin place vanished, closing the gateway between realms with the power of three.

"The king of demons spoke it to me, my Lord," the woman rasped, her withered hands shaking. "Their power is born to them like all magic, but their birth has sealed the thin space and separated our realm from the very depths of hell. When your sons have their thirteenth child, the Devil will take it as his own—payment for stolen flames. The thirteenth Ledes child will be a devil unto themself. Only then will the demon master return to these Barrens."

The Lord of Galloway pulled out his iron sword, ordering the shocked soldiers to restrain her. The mysterious woman sobbed and pulled at her gnarled hair, but by the time the men reached her, she had disappeared into nothing more than mist and an empty cloak.

PART ONE

CHAPTER

ONE

The man in tweed held the winning hand.

Voices carried above the sound of dice clattering on felt tables and cards being shuffled. Aromas of lemon, whiskey, and pipe smoke filled my nose. I tapped my cards on the sticky wooden table, waiting to win.

Despite the noise, my mind was mercifully calm. Open.

I purposefully picked at the lace hem of my dress while the man in tweed set his cards face down.

Two pairs, tens and jacks.

I ran my thumb over my cards and scraped my lower lip with my teeth as I considered my hand—also, two pairs, but only fives and tens. I lowered my head, keeping a thoughtful pout on my lips and a scrunch of confusion in my brow.

I had been watching the man in tweed for days.

He was a lucky bastard.

But I didn't need luck, thankfully. Three coins hit the table beside me, gleaming in the lamplight.

I had recognized the woman who placed the bet the moment she bought into the game. She also frequented the

9

tavern, and I had seen her before, taking her fill of ale and whispering in men's ears. She recognized me, too, but she didn't acknowledge it.

For that, I was grateful.

I counted my coins. Twice. I matched her bet, letting my uncertainty waft to the others around the table as I twirled a strand of midnight-black hair around my finger.

The woman had the losing hand, but she wasn't playing to win—at least not at cards. She angled her head toward the man on my right, tracing the delicate trim on the neckline of her dress like a cat considering a bird. Her target, a handsome man with a strong jaw, wore a militia uniform with infantry badges on the arm.

His leathers creaked as he puffed out his chest, tossing down his coins, betting them all on his pair of queens.

"Double or nothing," he said. He leaned closer, crossing his thick arms across his chest. "And I'll sweeten the deal. If I win, I'll buy you ladies a drink."

I pushed away the magic that swam toward me from the woman's mind as she eyed the guard. His thoughts, however, were too strong and confident to block out, and I held back a flush when his mind wandered to taking both of us home with him.

The man in tweed huffed, placing a hand over his winning cards. "I fold."

What an idiot.

I tried not to let triumph show on my features just yet. The guard revealed his hand first, arcing an eyebrow. The woman put down her measly pair of fours, exhibiting no disappointment in her loss.

"Well, darling," she purred at me. "Will you and I be drinking for free tonight?"

I exposed my hand, allowing my gaze to sweep the cards around me as though I were trying to figure it out. As though I hadn't known from the beginning that I would win.

My words were slow, churning. "That's two pairs, but your queens are higher."

"Two pairs beat a single pair, no matter the highest suit," the man in tweed stated. He shook his head before gulping down the remaining dregs of liquor in his glass. "Take your winnings, young lady."

He muttered something about beginner's luck as his empty glass thudded on the table.

I scooped my winnings into my hand with glee, playing the part, and slipped them into the secret fold Maggie had sewn under the lace hem of my dress.

The woman slipped into the guard's lap, consoling him with a pat of her hand on his stubbled cheek. Despite his defeat, something victorious gleamed in his eyes.

I stood to leave, avoiding eye contact with the familiar man behind the taps.

The last thing I needed after a win was a lecture.

I was so close to getting out of Galloway I could taste it. We could afford to sublet the flat in Delphi with only five hundred more shillings. If I kept winning like this, my brother and I would be out of this miserable place by the solstice. James, of course, didn't know I was cheating at cards to achieve our goal, but what kind of sister would I be if I didn't at least try?

Flames flickered in the glass orbs of the wall sconces as I pulled open the massive, wooden side door and ascended the ivy-covered stairwell back into the eerie comfort of the mist. I pulled the hood of my cloak over my head and slunk around the tavern, keeping to the shadows. A few black tendrils unfurled from my braid, whipping in the cold air.

The mist was always thicker at night.

It had been a comfort as a child, peering out into its dense grayness, knowing it would always be there to cover me. It used to remind me of sliding between two cotton sheets—that fleeting moment after you get into bed, but your body hasn't warmed the fabric.

Only the mist held a chill that never seemed to thaw, and now that I was grown, that ice had crept into my bones.

I would miss the mist, strange as that might be, when I finally escaped this place. As I carefully strode over the cobblestones with a hand over my coins to prevent them from jingling, I could have sworn the air around me let out a sigh.

It was too late to be spotted alone on the street, especially this close to the triplet lords' manor. The enormous estate could be seen from almost anywhere in Galloway, haloed by torches alight with fire magic.

The magic of the triplet lords—a magic so unlike my own, despite my blood relation. I glanced up and down the street, struck by the energy it must take to illuminate the lamps. My father and his brothers were ever-present in the flames.

I ducked down a partially concealed alleyway between two buildings, my favorite shortcut. My feet wobbled a bit on the wavy stones, but I hummed to myself, trying to drown out the whispers that seemed to creep from the darkest corners.

Things only I could hear. Maybe the musing of a spirit, perhaps an echo from somewhere on the other side of the wall. I tried not to think about it as I approached the end of the alley that led to my street and the row of humble brick townhomes—an almost comical contrast to the ornate manor that loomed behind me.

The enormous building was always watching me, silently judging for my father's refusal of it.

A hushed breath whooshed over someone's teeth from down the alley, and I froze, hoping the shroud of thick air was enough to hide me.

Gooseflesh erupted on my skin as a broad shadow appeared at the end of the passage. I turned on my heel, only to find myself face to face with a man dressed in embroidered leather. His uniform was adorned with the same crest that decorated the walls of our townhome. The same crest that flew from the flag in front of the manor.

My heart hammered, and panic surged in my blood. I didn't attempt to use my magic to read his intentions. Magic meant nothing when every cord of muscle in my body begged me to run.

I lurched forward, but someone tugged at my arms from behind me, and ropes tightened around my wrists. "It's a bit late for you to be out unaccompanied, *Lady Harper.*"

CHAPTER

TWO

I spun to face my captor, and he glared at me with icy blue eyes. The man before me was tall with sandy hair that gleamed in the flickering lamplight. His features were sharp, calculating, as he fastened a knot around my wrists.

Fear melted into fury. "What are you doing? Untie my wrists." I glanced at the Ledes militia crest stamped on the leather strap of his uniform. *My crest.* "Right now. I command you to let me go."

My captor's accomplice, a lanky man, just as tall but with wavy black hair, jogged to my side. When he saw my wrists, his shoulders slumped. "I thought we agreed not to use the ropes, Logan."

"I thought we agreed she's a flight risk," Logan hissed, and the ropes tightened. "Captain."

Captain?

"She is a flight risk," the dark-haired captain said. "But you can't tie her wrists. If one of her uncles found out, they'd have you hanged."

I bit my lip. The man was likely correct, but that depended on which one of the triplet lords was doling out the punishments. "Untie me, or I'll prove what a flight risk I am and run right into the manor to report you."

Words spoken with forced bravery. I cursed my magic for seizing up, as it tended to do, in moments like this.

Running was foolish. The men would likely catch me on my trembling legs. I wasn't very fast, even with more ideal footwear and unbound arms. I had dressed like an ordinary villager this evening. A simple, homespun linen dress. Dark gray to blend into the shadows under the black wool of my cloak. Unfortunately, the boots I wore had a heel.

A damned heel large enough to slow me down, but not high enough that the two large men didn't make me feel small. It didn't matter. I inclined my chin, summoning all the height of my average-sized frame.

"Untie me," I said, forcing my words not to tremble. "Now."

The man with the rope loosened the knot and scrubbed a hand through his straw-colored hair. "Fine, but you're coming with us. We need to discuss something with you."

A part of me wanted to scream for my father, but another part of me, perhaps a more cowardly part, didn't dare to. I couldn't exactly explain to Father that I had snuck out after supper to cheat in an illegal game of cards.

My eyes adjusted in the shadows, and I squinted at the militia badges on the man named Logan's broad chest. A silver bar gleamed under the crest of arms.

A lieutenant. I had somehow found myself trapped in an alley with two high-ranking militiamen, and there was no way I could outrun them. They didn't seem at all bothered by detaining a daughter of one of the lords, either.

The triplet lords had their roles in Galloway. My father, the most academically inclined, was responsible for record-keeping and financial matters. Uncle Aaron, fair and level-headed, led the police. Uncle Bain oversaw the militia.

Bain was the most fearsome of all three lords, and this lieutenant answered to him.

Nausea bubbled in my stomach, and acid rose in my throat. "My Uncle Bain won't look favorably on this meeting, Lieutenant. Besides, it's late. I need to get home. My father—"

"Doesn't know you're not tucked snugly into your bed, does he?" The way the lieutenant purred the words into my ear sent a chill down my spine.

"Logan, cut the tough-guy act, okay? This is Harper Ledes, not some criminal we're taking into the station." The dark-haired captain appeared weary as he crossed his arms.

"Ledes or not, what she was doing in that tavern is illegal," Logan returned. "You should know the law, Miller."

I tried my best not to react, but the muscles in my face betrayed me with a nervous twitch. Miller. *Uncle Aaron's new militia police captain.*

The tall, dark-haired man uncrossed his arms, revealing the gleaming badge under his cloak.

Jacob Miller, the new police captain, had just seen me emerge from an illegal gambling hall. An illegal gambling hall that my cousins had been operating for two years. If Uncle Bain found out about this, all of us would be sent beyond the wall.

If we were lucky.

My eyes widened at Captain Miller, but his return stare was soft, pitying even. He grabbed my elbow and led me through the alleyway to a door propped open behind a storefront, then ushered me inside.

When we entered the dark room, the captain lit a candle and placed it on a small table.

"Where are we?" I asked through gritted teeth.

"I'm not quite sure," Miller admitted, rubbing his chin. "The door was open when we staked out the alley. I think it's the back room of one of the shops. The tannery, maybe, based on the smell."

I surveyed the men in the candlelight. They had to be about my age. Early twenties, perhaps.

"We couldn't bring you to the manor or the barracks," Logan said. "This discussion needs to be discreet. Please, sit down."

I swallowed a lump in my throat as Miller offered me a chair. The two men before me were formidable, but Captain Jacob Miller had a relaxed stance as he leaned on the table. His tousled hair was almost as dark as mine. He stared down at me, studying me like a lost kitten.

Logan wore the fighting leathers of the upper-level militia, and I wondered how many demons a man had to battle outside the wall to rise to that rank at such a young age. A scar through his left eyebrow reflected the candlelight with a silver-blue hue.

There was only one kind of creature that could leave a mark like that. Only a being meant for the devil's realm, a demon, could mar a human's flesh with silver. He met my gaze with his cold blue eyes, and I shivered.

Logan's hand rose to his brow before he spoke. "We've been watching you in the tavern for weeks. You seem to always win at cards. Why is that?"

My mouth was dry, words sticking to my tongue. "I'm good at cards."

"I'm sure the mindspeaking helps," Jacob said, shrugging.

My lip quivered, betraying me, and the two men exchanged a knowing glance at my reaction.

Even though I was the one who could mindspeak, they were reading me like a book. Nobody had ever suspected anything before. How could these two strangers know just by watching me from afar?

The only person who knew about my mindspeaking was James, and I trusted my brother to the ends of the realm.

I brushed my magic against the walls of the police captain's mind, but there was an impenetrable barrier there.

"I don't know what you're talking about," I said, willing my voice not to shake. "My father and his brothers are fire wielders, not mindspeakers. I didn't inherit any of their magic."

"Yes. Mindspeaking isn't common in the Barrens," Jacob said, inspecting his fingernails. "But your mother, Sarah, was from York, wasn't she? It's not as uncommon up north. I should know. That's where I'm from originally."

My jaw fell open. Captain Jacob Miller might have been a high-ranking official, but some things in Galloway were off limits. Sarah Ledes was one of those things.

A fresh wave of anger rushed over me, washing away any dregs of fear. "Don't say my mother's name. You have no right to speak of her, and you've no right to accuse me of something like that."

Unlike elemental magic, which was considered useful, mindspeaking was viewed as an unfavorable intrusion.

My magic flared again, pushing against the wall of his

mind. He had to be bluffing. There was no way he could know this about me. Perhaps I'd been less discreet than I thought in the tavern. Maybe I had revealed my hand during the card games. I silently cursed myself.

There was no way I would admit this to him, not when I was so close to getting out of the Barrens. So close to escaping a lifetime of suffocation and giving my brother an escape from a tragic betrothal. I opened my mouth, but I was interrupted by a flood of magic curling into my mind.

"*I'm not accusing you. I'm telling you,*" Jacob said into my head. "*I know you can mindspeak. Because I can, too.*"

CHAPTER

THREE

"You can mindspeak?" I asked out loud.

The remnants of his magic reverberated in my head, overwhelming all noise. My voice was a shadow, an echo of his own.

"Nobody knows, do they? Not even your fun cousins who operate illegal gambling rooms out of their tavern," Jacob said. "Except, of course, your brother, James. Because he can do it, too. It must have been hard for your father to realize his children didn't have his fire magic. Of course, the citizens of this town don't know if Sarah had magic at all. Because nobody's allowed to talk about her, right?"

Heat flooded my skin. It was one thing to question me, to bind my wrists, to entrap me in this dark, stinky room and threaten me, but to disrespect my mother's memory—I wanted to turn the table over and shove the smug police captain into the wall.

"I'm warning you," I said, trying with all my might to summon a flame from my father's bloodline. "Don't say my mother's name aloud again. Why did you bring me here,

Captain Miller? If you're going to arrest me, then do it. Don't bring my family into this."

Jacob and Logan exchanged a dark look.

"We're not going to arrest you. We need your help," Jacob explained.

"You expect me to help you? After treating me like a criminal?" I asked.

Logan rolled his eyes. "You are a criminal. But there's something much more serious going on. There've been multiple raids on the armory. Captain Miller has been trying to use his *gift* to investigate who the thief is, but everyone in the militia suspects his magic. They know where he's from, and he was promoted to his position for a reason. We think someone on the inside is stealing, and we've come up short."

My brows furrowed. The thefts at the armory had been mentioned at family dinner. Uncle Bain had said several of their most prized weapons, swords forged from iron, the only material of this realm that could kill a demon, had been stolen over the past fortnight. The smiths were working overtime to replace them.

Jacob's calm exterior broke for a heartbeat, a muscle in his jaw ticking. "We need someone from outside the militia or the police to help us."

I drummed my fingers on the table. "So. You're not arresting me?"

Jacob held a hand over his heart. "Arrest a lady? I would never dream of it. Especially a lady so willing to help. So willing to avenge the Ledes name. Someone who cares about Galloway's safety above all. I'm humbly asking for your help."

He was humbly blackmailing me.

Logan scoffed. "I'm more than happy to arrest you, for the record."

The lieutenant was just as arrogant as his companion, but there was something stonier about him. I inclined my chin. "Who are you anyway? How are you involved?"

"My name is Lieutenant Logan Greer," he said, putting his hands on the table to speak eye-to-eye with me. "I'm here because I'm the arms lieutenant. Whoever's stealing the irons is stealing directly from me."

I met his stare, taking in his gaze, and something in his resolve flickered, coating the air with a subtle hint of his desperation. Logan Greer didn't seem like the kind of man who liked to be challenged. He didn't seem like the kind of man who tolerated one of his subordinates stealing from him, either.

I reached for my magic, beckoning it to snake into his mind, but something about this man unnerved me. My magic retreated.

Logan Greer certainly needed my help, so I stared back at him with narrowed eyes. "Why didn't you ask James? If you're so sure that both of us can mindspeak, why not ask my esteemed brother?"

Logan's lip quirked at the corner, illuminating a dimple on his cheek, and I almost laughed at how such a delicate divot could mar such a flawlessly handsome face. "Because people are more likely to let their guard down in front of a lady, especially a lady who doesn't have *the brand.*"

My throat constricted. At the mention of the brand, the magical numerical imprint bestowed on the Ledes children at birth, any morsel of mindspeaking energy I had left ran dry.

It had always been this way. Intense emotions, especially

fear, drained my abilities. There was nothing that evoked stronger emotion than the brand. My cousins had been given their brand, painlessly at birth, as a way to mark them. How many times had I fantasized about burning the number twelve into my skin, even if I didn't have the luxury of magic protecting me from the pain? I pushed away the words in my mind.

Brand. Brand. Brand.

Shame. Shame. Shame.

"I may not have a brand. It doesn't make me any less of a Ledes." My voice sounded small, the same way it had when my cousins had teased me about my naked forearm as a child.

James had a brand. Number 4, after Paxton and Brannon, Uncle Aaron's oldest sons, and Samuel, Uncle Bain's oldest son. My arm should have been marked with the number *12*, but I was never given the chance. It didn't change anything. I was still the youngest Ledes cousin.

Jacob swallowed, casting his gaze to the ceiling. "You'll draw less attention," he said. Despite my inability to read him at that moment, I knew he felt pity for me.

"The brand doesn't matter," I whispered. Words my father had repeated to me like a mantra in my childhood. I never got a chance to be branded, not after what happened to my mother. Some family members thought my lack of a number made me less of a Ledes.

Less noble somehow.

I crossed my arms. "What if I say no?"

"Then you're under arrest," Logan returned, shrugging.

Jacob sent him a warning glance. "We'll escort you to the armory first thing in the morning," Jacob said, not giving me a chance to object. "I've already sent a letter to your maid,

Maggie. I explained that your services were needed at head-quarters."

"What could you possibly need my services for at the barracks?" I'd never ventured into the part of town that housed the militia before, nor had I ever gone that close to the wall.

Logan's lip twitched again, along with his infuriating dimple. "We know many things about you, my lady, especially what a talented artist you are. That's why I'm commissioning you to add a mural to the part of the wall surrounding headquarters."

He had to be joking. "You want me to paint the wall?"

Logan's expression cracked. "I assure you. You'll be perfectly safe." A bold statement from someone with a demon's mark on his brow.

I glanced out the window, where the mist had grown ever thicker, an ominous reminder that a stone wall was the only thing between Galloway and whatever had given Logan Greer that scar.

CHAPTER

FOUR

I couldn't sleep that night. My dreams, when they did drift into my mind, were the kind that jarred me awake the moment they took root.

It was the wall I saw, over and over. Getting near the stone barrier that protected the village from the Barrens was a terrifying prospect, let alone painting it. I eventually fell into a deep sleep amid nightmares of claws scraping on stone behind the strokes of my brush.

When Maggie burst into the room, peeling back my midnight blue damask curtains with enough force to kick up a cloud of dust, I sat up and rubbed my face.

I groaned in annoyance, and she bristled.

"There's a very handsome militiaman wearing a lieutenant's badge waiting for you downstairs, Harper Josephine." She said my name like I had just stolen a taffy from her secret jar.

Maggie bustled to my armoire and began throwing my frocks onto the bed before I could even slide my legs out from underneath the warm comfort of my wool blanket.

I grumbled something about being insufferably early, and Maggie stopped dead in her tracks, my undergarments dangling from her arms. "You knew he was coming early. It woulda been nice if you told your poor maid." She huffed a breath and furrowed her brow. "Now look at me, rushing you into undergarments without even a cup of coffee to warm your belly."

"I don't need anything to warm my belly," I said, shivering. It was a lie. Coffee would be a necessity. "Maybe you can tell the lieutenant I've fallen ill and can't honor my commitment today."

Maggie turned toward me, my dresses tumbling out of her arms. Her usually plump, rosy cheeks were pale and hallow, and her eyes were frantic.

Nobody liked being caught off guard less than she did, and guilt washed through me when I realized that, thanks to my unexpected plans, she would likely need to spend the whole morning reworking her schedule and menu.

She raised her brows at me. "Have ya fallen ill?"

"Not physically," I said, biting my lip.

Maggie only tutted in reply, so I pulled my stockings on before allowing her to tie the laces of my corset. I peered out the window.

It was always dreary in Galloway, thanks to the mist, but I welcomed the gloom. It matched my mood most of the time.

Maggie had chosen a black dress trimmed in gray with a collar that fit smartly up my neck. She smoothed my ebony hair into a low bun, allowing enough room for my cape and scarf.

She hastily powdered my nose, which did little to cover the freckles on my otherwise pale skin. Then she dipped a brush into the powder and swept my lower eyelids with a deep blue kohl.

Maggie usually enjoyed painting me like a porcelain doll, but we were rushed. I didn't object like I usually did. The light blue shade did bring out the blue undertones in my gray eyes. A dusting of blush made me less pale, but I resented the rouge for making me appear cheerier than I felt.

"It will have to do," Maggie said, holding my shoulders at arm's length. She spun me, stuck a bejeweled pin in my bun, and pulled it a little more taut than usual.

"I do love you, you know," I said, twisting my mouth into a pout.

The usual cheerful flush rose to her cheeks as she ushered me into the hall. "I'm afraid I know you do, my lady."

Lieutenant Logan Greer was waiting at the bottom of the stairs, his hand tucked into the leather strap of his uniform. From afar, the man could have been mistaken for the statue of some self-important war hero—broad-shouldered, tall, and stonelike.

He tipped his head toward us as we descended the stairs. "Good morning, my lady. I hope you don't find it burdensome to depart so early."

I inclined my chin, holding onto his stare. "No better way to start a burdensome day."

Maggie nearly choked. After clearing her throat and shooting me an emphatic stare, she said, "May I offer you something to eat, Lieutenant? I'm afraid Miss Ledes hasn't had anything for breakfast."

Logan glanced at the clock alongside the stairwell. "I suppose we can spare a few moments."

Maggie's shoulders slumped in relief. "I have biscuits and

butter for you, my lady's favorite breakfast. Please sit in the parlor, and I'll bring you the tray. Would you like a coffee?"

"I prefer tea, if it's not too much trouble," he said.

I rolled my eyes. This man was the living embodiment of too much trouble. Of course, he preferred tea.

Logan gestured to the nearby door, inviting me into a room in my own home like a true, pretentious gentleman. An amused smirk curled on his lips, and I knew he was enjoying torturing me. I straightened my shoulders before striding to my favorite chair beside the fire.

I had settled into the seat when the front door opened, and James entered the hall, still dressed in his riding clothes.

Pins and needles brushed over me as James raised his brows. My brother knew I had been scheming to get the money we needed for our new flat, but I had been vague about how I was earning it. My heart hammered as I realized that all my plans were falling apart.

I was kidding myself. There was no chance now.

James and I would never get out of here. He would be forced to marry someone he could never love. What's worse, our greater plan would never come to be. My father would have eventually come with us. Cade Ledes would have followed his children to the ends of the realm, probably out of the colonies and across the ocean. He would have never left Galloway on his own, but if both of his children were gone, his brothers would never fault him for following us.

I seethed at the thought of the arms lieutenant obstructing the only way for our family to escape two decades of misery and entrapment in this miserable village. Twenty-one years shrouded by a mist that was dense with nothing but grief and regret.

And now, for James, heartbreak.

Logan stood at once and bowed. "Master Ledes, good morning. Lieutenant Logan Greer, of militia arms. At your service."

James, always noble, stuck out his gloved hand to shake Logan's. "Lieutenant Greer, to what do we owe the pleasure of your company this morning?"

"We have heard about the *talent* your sister has..." Logan began, turning to me with a mischievous grin. "With her brush. The new police chief, Captain Miller, has commissioned Lady Harper to paint a mural on the wall facing the armory." He began to share his grand vision for boosting militia morale.

"*What the fuck did you do?*" James projected into my mind, smiling and nodding at our guest.

I grabbed my cross stitch and stabbed the needle into the fabric. "*Do you want the good news or the bad news?*"

"*For fuck's sake, Harp.*"

"*The good news is I won three hundred shillings last night. The bad news is I was caught cheating during an illegal poker game at the tavern. The new chief of police questioned me and accused me of mindspeaking. Now I'm being blackmailed to help them solve some mystery at the armory under the guise of painting the wall.*"

A muscle ticked in James's jaw. He and I were skilled at having two conversations at once. "Yes, Harper's florals are particularly beautiful. That's one of her paintings above the mantel."

Logan nodded at the painting, appraising. "Stunning."

"*How did he know you were mindspeaking?*" James asked me.

"The new police captain, Jacob Miller, can mindspeak, and he's been watching me."

James ran a hand through his dark, wavy hair, listening patiently to Logan, but I knew he was counting to ten in his mind to prevent himself from throttling the man before him. I tapped my finger on my stitching frame, hoping the numbers would lose their game.

If James didn't punch Logan Greer by the end of this morning, I would happily do it myself. I narrowed my eyes at the lieutenant, who leaned on the mantel like he and my brother were old chums.

This man had threatened me, not only by revealing my magic, but also by forcing me to go near the only thing keeping a restless pack of demons from infesting this town. Only to meet his ridiculous needs. My blood boiled like an unwatched kettle as the haughty lieutenant spoke pleasantly with my brother.

If anyone found out about the gambling operation at the tavern, there would be three more Ledes cousins in hot water.

Maggie rushed in with a tray teeming with much more than biscuits and tea, and it took everything in me not to leap onto the table and pile my plate high with fruit and pastries.

But a lady doesn't scarf down her breakfast, or so I had been told many times over the past twenty-one years. I folded my hands and waited until the two men were seated before I reached for my plate. James, bless him, filled one and handed it to me.

"I'll fix this. I'll go to the manor as soon as you leave. Our uncles would flip if they knew you were going that close to the wall," James said as he bit into his scone.

"Absolutely not. I'm doing this. We're so close to getting out of here. If I don't help them, they'll arrest me, and we'll lose everything we've saved. I need a few hundred more shillings to afford the sublet. I won't let them force you to—"

James turned toward me, cutting me off with his physical words. "Although I'm sure Harper's talent would have the desired effect on the wall, I do worry about her being there. It's too dangerous, I'm afraid. I'm sure the lords will agree."

I sighed into my coffee. My father and his brothers would undoubtedly agree it was dangerous to get near the wall, let alone stand by it for hours and paint.

Uncle Aaron would probably try to negotiate an alternative location.

Uncle Bain would threaten to rip Logan's throat out.

I considered how satisfying the latter would be as I tapped my nails on my mug. But then I pictured how Uncle Bain would react if he knew the truth about what was going on in the tavern his sons owned.

My father would be the most reasonable. Calm and level-headed. He always was. Father would be supportive if I told him I wanted to paint the wall. When I was a teenager, attending lessons with my cousins had been torturous. My cousin Mira and her triplet sisters would tease me if I didn't know the answer or if I was caught doodling.

When I'd told my father about it one night as he tucked me into bed, he'd asked me what I thought we should do about it—together. Uncle Aaron would have lectured, anxiously planning my return and making peacekeeping provisions. Uncle Bain would have yelled, first at me for being weak, then at Mira for being cruel. But Cade Ledes always just listened.

Trusted that I could figure it out myself.

"James, you're ruining an opportunity for me," I said, glaring at him. He was ruining an opportunity for himself, but I didn't feel like having that argument again. "I'm a grown woman, and if I'm not scared, then you shouldn't be either. I'll talk to Father tonight, but I've already held Lieutenant Greer up enough this morning. We should be on our way."

So, I followed Logan Greer out the front door and into the mist, each step feeling like the period on the end of a sentence.

Each step closer to what lurked behind that wall.

CHAPTER

FIVE

The lieutenant cleared his throat. "So, when did you get interested in painting?" Our townhouse wasn't a far walk from the militia headquarters.

"I don't remember a time when I didn't paint, to be honest. When did you get interested in blackmail?"

Logan's shoulders stiffened, and his steps quickened. "I'm trying to be civil, Miss Ledes. There's no need to be oppositional."

He was oppositional—to me living my life in peace—but it was still too early in the morning, and I hadn't had enough coffee to continue this argument. "What would you like me to paint on your precious wall?"

"Jacob thought it might be nice to paint something bright, maybe a forest scene in the springtime," Logan said.

In the Barrens, nothing was bright, and spring hadn't sprung here in decades. I tried to sift through my memory for something to paint that fit that description. The idea of something bright and cheerful didn't sit right with me. Not

33

when the other side of that wall was plagued by beings as dark as possible.

"It might be hard for me to paint springtime when I've never seen it," I reasoned. The truth stung a place deep in my chest.

"You've never been outside of Galloway, have you?" Logan said.

No. I had never traveled outside the wall. Had never seen the sea, even though it was only a short ride away from the eastern gate. Sometimes, if I concentrated, I could almost hear the waves crashing on the shore, could imagine the ships sailing from harbors across the sea where kings still reigned.

"One day, I'd like to see it," I said. "But it isn't safe for a lady to travel. Not when demons roam the Barrens and news comes from all over the colonies, whispering of revolution."

Logan's arrogance melted away to pity. "It is perfectly safe to travel with the right equipment. Perhaps one day Lord Cade will feel comfortable."

I pulled my magic back, not wanting to detect the bitter sting of his sympathy.

"Not yet," I said. "But when I get enough money, James and I are leaving for good. Moving to Delphi."

Logan angled his head toward me. "You're leaving your father?"

I regretted telling him immediately. There was no way to explain this to him without betraying James. "My father needs to get out of this village more than anyone. If James and I leave, he'll follow us. We've wanted to live in Delphi since we were children. James will study at the university, and I already have my portfolio ready for the art conservatory."

My heart cracked at the thought of it. I imagined what my studio space might have been like at the conservatory, smeared with color and teeming with canvases of clear skies and lush blooms.

"Lord James is betrothed to Emelia Hern," Logan said, wrinkling his brow. "Wouldn't that complicate things?"

It would simplify things, but I could hardly explain it to him.

"It isn't a union of their choosing," I said. "If my brother moves out of town, she'll find a new suitor."

"From what I hear, the Herns are quite happy with their match," Logan said.

The lieutenant was seemingly fond of gossip. I was accustomed to everyone in this village knowing our business, but the thought of people chattering about my brother's love life struck an angry chord.

James was unhappy with their match, but no one had asked for his opinion. No, my family had decided what was best for him, even if he did love someone else.

I stopped walking. "You don't know what you're talking about, Lieutenant. Besides, we wouldn't be the first Ledes cousins to leave Galloway. Samuel and Jackson have been gone for years. Ana and Grace have been boarding at the music conservatory in Lawrenceville for months. Why would it be any different for James and me if we wish to go?"

Logan pressed his lips into a straight line. I could tell he was mulling over a clever response, but when he turned toward me, something had softened in his eyes. Men like Logan could never understand. The militia members pledged their lives to fight for this village, but I had been born with obligations I had never asked for.

"I'm sorry to be impertinent, my lady," Logan said, gazing at the cobblestones beneath our feet.

I huffed an impatient sigh. "If you're going to be bold enough to tell me how to live my life, you can cut the 'my lady' bullshit." I trudged ahead. "Just call me Harper."

"Fine," he said, his voice sharpened by annoyance. It didn't shock me. I had that effect on people. "Harper," he emphasized the *R*. "When we get to headquarters, you should act like you have a vision for this mural, even if you don't."

But a painting was already unfurling in my mind, fresh with the promise of escaping this place, brush strokes of red, embers of gold. The demons that lurked beyond the wall were cold and icy. The mist that blanketed this town muted Galloway, dulled everything meant to be colorful, but I would paint the opposite of mist on the wall.

"What makes you think I don't have a plan?" I asked, charging ahead.

I had many plans, in fact, but they were all falling apart.

Logan Greer tugged on the leather straps of his uniform before he fell into stride beside me with the gait of a soldier. Despite the gloom around us, his sandy blond hair shone in the dregs of sunlight, the only bright thing in all of Galloway, it seemed.

"Enlighten me," he said, pulling his collar around his neck.

"I'll paint fire. It will be a great homage to the Ledes brothers."

When my father and his brothers were born, a fire had ravaged the Barrens. This was long before the mist, during an era when robust sunlight filtered through the canopy of pine boughs to the forest floor. Some say the Devil himself claimed the Barrens as his playground, allowing his fires to spill into this realm from his own.

The midwife who delivered them, Raina, had been a powerful mystic. She had felt great power even before they were delivered. The pines had erupted in flames the night they were born, and the triplet lords had been bestowed with fire magic. Legends say their cries snuffed out the fire for good as their magic took root, strengthened by the power of the number three.

Of course, the Ledes family boasted magical ancestors, but the magic had lain dormant for generations until Aaron, Bain, and Cade entered the world.

There hadn't been a fire in the pines since.

James and I had heard the story when we were children. Maggie had tucked us into our beds with the tale, but we knew we couldn't speak it to our uncles, especially not in front of my father.

Not when the midwife who had birthed them had ushered my mother out of this realm.

If speaking my mother's name was taboo, saying the name of her murderer was a punishable offense. Even uttering Raina's name in my mind made me shiver with guilt. Not even Mira would dare to say that name in front of me, fearful of what her father would do if he heard of it.

Logan nodded in approval. "Your uncles will be pleased."

"I expect so will their sons," I returned.

Three sons of the triplet Ledes had inherited fire. Nobody had been surprised when James didn't. My brother and I had kept our mindspeaking a secret from everyone. Not even our father knew the truth. Uncle Aaron's eldest twin sons, Paxton and Brannon, had inherited his power.

Only one of Bain's sons had inherited fire, but Axel had never been proud of it. Axel and his triplet brothers' talents were in merriment, which made them perfect tavern owners.

It never seemed to bother my father that we didn't inherit his magic. He had always spoken of his magic with such disdain that James and I had the impression he was glad his "gift" hadn't been passed to us.

"You have none of his magic, then?" Logan asked. "Many in town have speculated that you do, after what happened..." His voice trailed off.

I shot him a warning glare, and he squared his shoulders. He had already spoken of my mother. Surely, he didn't dare to speak of her murder, too. I was aware of what was whispered about me in Galloway.

I was the baby who was found, safe and sound, born to a mother who didn't survive the flames. My mother had been murdered with the very element her husband could wield. The midwife had fled the scene before my brand could be given.

I'd often wondered why Raina hadn't branded me with my *12* before she ran. A chill ran through me when I considered that perhaps...she had hoped I wouldn't survive.

I wouldn't need a brand if I were dead.

We reached the barracks just in time. I had suffered through enough of Logan's prying questions. The field was already teeming with men training in combat, sharpening their iron blades, and mounting their horses for patrol. Beyond them, the barracks were divided into zones. The brick sleeping quarters were on the periphery, and the militia police building was in the center.

The militia army patrolled outside the wall. Militia police patrolled within it.

Closest to the wall, the stone armory building was a fortress, bedecked in iron gates, through which the swordsmith's fires smoldered.

The wall stood beyond it all, tall and foreboding. I hadn't been this close to the ominous stone structure in my life. Most residents in Galloway preferred to stay away from the wall. It was as tall as two men, built from the sturdiest stone from the banks of the Rancocas. The pines were eerily still beyond it, shrouded in a mist so dense that only the thickest boughs could be seen.

I had never dared to ask James if he could also hear whispers beyond the wall. As a child, the sound would drown out my thoughts whenever I went as close as the park by the eastern gate. I wasn't sure if I was hearing something solid or if perhaps the thoughts of those around me echoed in the mist.

Logan held his head high as we entered the barracks quadrangle. When the men saw him approach, dressed in his lieutenant uniform, they straightened, and those idling sprang to their feet. Logan nodded to them, his jaw firm. He said nothing until Jacob Miller strode out of the militia police offices to meet us.

"Captain Miller," Logan greeted, saluting. Jacob outranked him despite their alliance in this ordeal, and he made a good show over it. "I present Miss Ledes, who has volunteered her talents to paint the wall."

"Miss Ledes, how selfless of you," Jacob said, smiling down at me with a curt nod.

I nodded tersely at the man who had pulled me off the street less than twenty-four hours ago. I built a wall in my mind, thicker and more robust than the one surrounding us.

I let anger swirl until it was unreadable, even by his magic.

Jacob smiled at me, and I wondered if he had sensed my wall or tried to project his words into my mind, only for them to echo back.

"On your feet," a deep baritone voice called through the quad, instantly alerting everyone around me. The torches flickered with fire magic as I turned on my heel. I recognized the voice that kindled that flame.

My eldest cousin Paxton stopped suddenly when his gaze landed on me, and his expression morphed from stern to shocked. I couldn't stop my feet from flying across the mossy ground. I ran and didn't stop until my cousin folded his arms around me.

CHAPTER
SIX

"I didn't think you would be back for another month, Pax," I said, squeezing the air out of him.

"Our mission was cut short," he explained, hugging me so hard my feet lifted from the floor. It had been months since Paxton and Brannon had left for Delphi. Galloway always felt a little safer when they were here, holding down the barracks, acting as the militia's flames. Relief rolled off my shoulders, and the air seemed a little lighter.

Logan and Jacob were at my heels in an instant, saluting the general with stiff hands to their brows.

"General Ledes," Jacob said, "We didn't think you would be back until the end of the month."

Paxton's lips straightened into a hard line as he nodded at the captain. "The plan changed. Do either of you care to explain to me what my cousin, the baby of the Ledes family, is doing this close to the wall?"

Logan's face paled, and it took everything within me not

to smirk. "Miss Ledes has volunteered to paint a mural," he said.

Paxton arched his brow. "No."

Jacob and Logan exchanged a worried glance, making me wonder if Jacob was projecting words into his lieutenant's mind.

"When she suggested it, we thought it would boost morale, General," Jacob said, fixing his features into cool stone.

When she suggested it? I stared hard at Jacob, ensuring he sensed the heat of my anger wash over his mind.

Paxton shook his head. "I don't want her that close to the wall. Find another spot to paint your mural, Harp."

Brannon, just as broad and tall, a near-identical mirror to Paxton, strolled over. His head dipped low as he studied a map. "Pax, I found the best route to Long Beach if we take the northern trail."

Paxton nudged his twin hard in the ribs, prompting him to look up. "Harper?" He, too, pulled me into a confused hug.

"So glad you're back, Brannon," I said.

Paxton and Brannon weren't identical twins, but most people who didn't know them well had difficulty telling them apart. Brannon, the softer of the two, often wore his glasses to curb some of the confusion. The brothers made perfect militia generals, confident Paxton and cunning Brannon. I beamed up at Brannon as he squeezed my shoulder.

"Wait a minute, why are you here?" Brannon asked, narrowing his eyes at me.

"I was wondering the same thing," Paxton said. He rolled up his sleeves and crossed his forearms, exposing the brand on his muscled arms.

Number 1.

Uncle Aaron was the first of his brothers to have children, and nobody was surprised when Aunt Bea had twins. I always wondered how Paxton and Brannon could be so warm and kind when their sisters were so vile.

Jacob chimed in. "We were considering alternate locations for Miss Ledes to paint her mural. Perhaps she could adorn the side wall of the tavern." He tapped on his chin, daring me to object.

I fought the flush creeping up my cheeks, and a part of me wanted to scream every expletive I knew into his mind.

Paxton and Brannon were unaware of the illegal casino operations Perry, Axel, and Rand had been running in the cellar of their tavern. The twin generals cocked their heads toward me, gauging my response to the suggestion.

I was between a stone and a wall, and I didn't want to bring anyone else down with me. Flames would have curled out of my nostrils if I had even an ounce of my father's magic. Jacob smiled back at me, so smug I could have smacked him.

"You two don't need to fuss over me, Bran," I said, patting him on the arm right over his branded number *2*. "This is the most protected place in Galloway. I would be surrounded by a whole militia the entire time I worked. I want to do this for the officers. But now that I'm closer to my canvas, I realize the wall is too bumpy to paint a scene. The entire area needs fresh stucco before I start."

I shot Jacob a sweet smile.

"Fine," Paxton said. "Under one condition. Harper will have a personal guard at all times." He nodded to Logan. "Lieutenant Greer, I assign you to be Harper's guard."

Logan's jaw tightened, and his blue eyes swept over me

like I was a bug on the bottom of his shoe. "General, it would be my honor, but the armory has been vulnerable. I've had three irons stolen in the past week, ten in the last month—"

"We know," Brannon said, arching a brow. "That's why we came back."

Logan was walking too quickly for me to keep up with him on our journey back to the townhouse. I attempted to catch my breath as we trudged down the cobblestone streets of Galloway, away from the wall and back to—I hoped—an ornate lunch spread from Maggie.

"Your family dynamics are too difficult," Logan said, tucking his hands into his jacket.

"What's so difficult? Three triplet lords, twelve cousins."

"I'm going to be your guard. I need to know the ins and outs," he said, his words cutting through the mist.

"Why are you taking this so seriously?" I asked. "You don't have to guard me. This is all for show, right?"

He spun, and I almost ran into his chest as he stopped in my path. "I do have to guard you. I have a direct order from the generals."

I rolled my eyes, and he turned on his heel, continuing his too-fast pace as though he couldn't wait to deposit me back home.

I sighed. "Fine. Our family dynamics are simple. All you need to know is that Pax and Bran are the oldest and act like big brothers to all of us. James already wants to kill you. Perry, Axel, and Rand are the closest in age to me, and all they want is a good time. Mira is the princess. The rest of my cousins don't even live in Galloway anymore, so there's nothing else you need to know about them."

Pretty soon, James and I wouldn't live here either if I could get Logan and Jacob off my back and go back to reading minds in the tavern. Samuel and Jackson, Uncle Bain's two eldest sons, lived in Delphi. I had written to both, inquiring about the best neighborhoods in the city.

I combed my brain for other ways to make money if the tavern was out of bounds. Could I offer psychic readings and read my patrons' innermost desires?

No. I wasn't a mystic and couldn't pretend to be.

I could set up a side gig as the town matchmaker. It was easy enough to figure out who desired whom. It made the manor's parties loud and tiresome. James usually feigned a headache to get out of going, but a small part of me liked to know people's secrets.

"If you'd involved Paxton and Brannon in this from the beginning, you would've never needed me," I said.

"Do your cousins know you can mindspeak?"

My throat tightened. "No."

"Do they know you routinely break the law?"

"No. What do you think the generals would say if they learned one of their lieutenants threatened and coerced their baby cousin?"

His broad shoulders stiffened.

I scanned the man walking two paces ahead, trying to crack through a wall in his mind, but there was nothing but blankness. For some inexplicable reason, it was difficult for me to break into Logan's mind, and my pulse quickened every time I tried.

He halted, and I swore I could see the hair stand up on

the back of his neck. Did he feel me trying to read his emotions?

Logan turned, and this time, I collided right into his chest, a broad wall of muscle and leather. "We are not coercing you. This is an alliance. You're helping us solve a crime."

I swallowed hard as I angled my chin to meet his stare. "That's bullshit, and you know it. If you want me to take this seriously, then you need to be realistic. And civil."

The stern line of his mouth curved into a forced smile, illuminating that maddening dimple on his left cheek. I was so close that I could see the stubble peppering his chin and the fine line of his cheekbone as it melted into his temple.

"I have been a perfect gentleman," he said, challenge in his eyes.

My throat bobbed. "Perfect gentleman, my ass. If you want to make this more difficult, that's your problem."

"I'm not the one making this difficult," he said, his eyes darkening. "I have a serious problem here. It's up to me to run that armory, and those weapons are being stolen on my watch. I'm up for promotion at the end of the month, but that's never going to happen if I don't put a stop to this. I don't know if my men are stealing them or..."

His gaze darted to the wall. There was no need for him to finish that sentence. I knew exactly what he left unsaid. I couldn't help but glance at the silvery blue scar through his left brow. My lips parted, but no sound came out.

"You're obstructing justice. Not being ready this morning when I came for you. Getting the generals involved." His jaw tightened. "Demanding stucco for the wall. I could have arrested you yesterday. I could have shut that tavern down. But I didn't, and it had nothing to do with blackmail. I assumed you'd be willing to help. This is your village—your family—at risk."

There was much more at risk than foolish weapons, but I could hardly tell Logan that.

I didn't let the guilt build up to more than a pang. If I were arrested, we would never get out of this place, and James would be resigned to an unhappy life. None of my cousins were betrothed yet. It made little sense to me why James, the fourth born, was the first to be considered for marriage.

The Hern family was wealthy. Mrs. Hern had been widowed several years ago, inheriting a sizable fortune from her late husband's family, and a part of me wondered if my father had been keen to ensure James had a comfortable life.

Once Mrs. Hern accepted the arrangement, there was no going back. But if we were to leave—explain that James must move to Delphi to advance his studies—Emilia would never be expected to leave Galloway to come with him.

Living outside of the manor cost my father. He had used some money to purchase the townhome, while my uncles could make better investments. But it would've been too complicated for my father to continue to live where my mother had once lived. It wasn't fair to ask him to be reminded of that without reprieve. His brothers had understood.

"I had a good reason to be playing cards last night," I said through gritted teeth.

The dimple deepened as a grin spread across his face. "Of course, *my lady*."

"I'll help you," I said.

"Thank you." He paused, meeting my stare. "Harper."

I cursed myself for how my stomach twisted when

Logan Greer said my name, low and sultry, like he had rolled the word in honey. I darted around him, resolved to be the one walking fast now.

A soft chuckle behind me made me ball my hands into fists.

I allowed Logan to follow me until we reached the town-house door. I grasped the handle and leaned my weight against it, ensuring he knew he wasn't welcome inside.

"Seven o'clock," he said. "The stucco should have plenty of time to dry by morning."

CHAPTER

SEVEN

Logan arrived the following day, promptly as promised. This time, to Maggie's relief, I was ready for him. She woke me with the first muted sunrays, content as usual to primp me. She started by combing my hair and braiding the ebony strands into a neat coronet. Again, I allowed her to paint rouge on my cheeks after she worried that nearing the wall would make me more pallid than usual.

I had already finished breakfast when Logan arrived, but that didn't stop Maggie from inviting him to eat with us. To my relief, he declined, and the two of us were on the street before James returned from his morning ride.

We didn't speak as we walked to the barracks, and a part of me wondered if Logan felt guilty for arguing with me after receiving his command from my cousins. I opened my mouth more than once, but swallowed down the words before they came out.

I hadn't spoken to my father about the mural yet. I'd had an opportunity the previous night, but I had taken my

49

supper, along with my pride, up to my rooms and gone to bed early. Father wasn't the kind of man to pry, even when something weighed on his heart, but I couldn't help but feel uncomfortable keeping this from him. I knew word would eventually spread about the mural, especially with Paxton and Brannon back in town.

He would worry, but he wouldn't tell me what to do. Father was the peacemaker in the family and had always been. Even though he had lost more than anyone, he managed to somehow be the one to pick up the pieces for everyone else.

When we finally reached the barracks courtyard, Logan broke the silence. "Jacob will be on duty for the day," he informed me. "I'll stand guard when you paint, but if anyone suspicious enters the barracks, I may ask you to accompany me as I investigate."

I swallowed the lump in my throat and nodded. Scanning the crowds outside didn't reveal Paxton or Brannon. My cousins were nowhere to be seen as I followed Logan into the armory.

A fire surged in the forge at the center of the room as the smiths warmed their tools, and one man was already working the iron into a blade, his hammer clanking off the anvil in sharp bangs that echoed through my bones. I watched for a moment, mesmerized by the flames licking over the metal and sparks flying from the hammer.

There was something so beautiful about the way the iron glowed. I had never seen anything so bright, so vibrant. I burned the image and the color into my mind, eager to capture it with paint.

Logan cleared his throat, releasing me from the fire's

thrall. He led me to a small desk in the corner, adjacent to the rows of blades, axes, and chainmail.

He sat down and began leafing through some paperwork. He didn't look at me as he said, "I need to run through inventory before we start. I gathered supplies for you yesterday. Let me know if anything is lacking."

He gestured to a trunk nearby. I approached it and began to paw through the contents—glass jars of paint in various hues, brushes, palette knives, oils, and turpentine. Some of the brushes were too small for mural work, but I decided I had enough supplies and didn't want to risk the ire I would receive for more requests.

I closed the trunk and sat upon it, not knowing what to do with my hands as the smiths moved about the armory. Metal clanged against metal, the kind of noise I could feel in my teeth. It made me wonder how Logan could remain at that desk all day or if perhaps he'd learned to drown out the din after a while.

Logan's head was bent over his work, his quill scratching on the parchment. His hair cascaded over his forehead as he wrote, and I studied the strands, long at the top and cropped on the sides. As the smell of turpentine wafted into my nose, I wondered what it would be like to paint him.

It wasn't unusual for my mind to turn every scene into a painting, but something about depicting him on canvas made me ache. My brushstrokes would need to be measured and careful around the fine angles of his jaw, and I was quite sure I wouldn't do justice to the slopes of his cheeks and the curve of his mouth. It would be impossible to capture the shimmering, silvery hue of his scar.

Logan's scar made me uneasy. It was too unearthly for poetic justice on a canvas.

He had one of those faces. Even if I had spent every spare moment of my time since he'd escorted me home from the barracks fantasizing about punching that face, I couldn't deny the beauty in it.

I forced my gaze away from him and blamed the terpenoid fumes for making me delirious. After a few moments, he stood, and I started inspecting the axes on the rack nearest me.

"Time to paint some stucco," he said, lifting the massive trunk.

I nodded, following his lead into the quad.

Every step we took toward the wall was heavier, as if the mist were settling into the space around my knees. When I was ten yards away, it was like I was walking through water. When I was near enough to see the swirls of the stone, a buzz settled into my ears. There were spells on the wall, wards designed to keep out all that lurked in the pines, cast by mystics and woven into the stone so deeply that nothing but death could unravel them.

I was sure it was the voices of those mystics that were humming in my head as I approached.

My breath quickened with the beat of my heart, and I stopped a few paces away from the expanse of fresh stucco, my new canvas, unsure if I could go any closer.

I had forgotten Logan was there with me until I heard his voice. "It gets easier," he said.

I spun, startled by the deep timbre of his voice over the high-pitched buzz.

"The more you go near it, the less buzzing you'll hear."
"You hear it, too?"
He nodded, his shoulders slumping. "The first year I did

patrols on the other side of the wall, I felt the vibration in my sleep. Even when I was far away from the wards."

Shadows darkened his face as he peered at the top of the wall. He would have had to use a ladder to see over it, but his gaze tore through the stone.

"What is it like?" My voice was a whisper, muted by humming.

He bit his lip, his stare unwavering. "Cold. The things that lurk out there are not of this realm. Most of them leave humans alone, but—" His brow furrowed, making the scar on his forehead bunch in thought. "Some of the creatures are violent. They don't like to be provoked. Thankfully, we have this."

He gestured toward the wall, strong and tall, devoid of cracks. Every day, the masons patrolled the inside, searching for leaks through which the mist was curling too freely. Patrolmen guarded the wall on the other side as well. Close enough to the wards to retreat, if necessary, but always in danger of becoming ensnared.

Logan patted the iron sword strapped to his hilt. "Don't worry. We're perfectly safe as long as I have my iron."

The polished blade somehow reflected the sun's light despite the mist, all the thicker this close to the Barrens. It had been dense in the last year, even in the middle of town. Iron was the only thing that could repel a demon, and Maggie had told me once that the mystics had used iron to make the wards on the wall.

As Logan held his blade, the mist retreated in its presence, leaving a halo of thin air.

I nodded, opening the trunk and examining my paint. I had sketched a few ideas last night before bed, but now that

I was there surveying my canvas size, I knew which composition felt right.

The turpentine swirled in the jar as I diluted dark brown paint, ready to outline. I glanced up from my crouch on the floor to find Logan staring at me, his arms crossed and feet spread wide.

"What are you doing?" I asked, standing.

He huffed a breath. "Guarding you."

"You don't need to stare at me to guard me."

"Yes, I do."

I glared at him.

He stared back like our eyes were sparring. "How can I guard you without looking at you?"

I rolled my eyes. "You can face that way, and if I'm in trouble, I'll say something."

"A guard doesn't face in the opposite direction of the thing he's guarding," Logan said, his words becoming clipped.

Heat boiled into my face, making me wonder if my father's fire magic would surface after all. This man had no shortage of arrogance. "I'm not a *thing*. And if you stare at me, I can't paint."

He cocked his head. "Why?"

"Because it's hard to do something well when someone's staring at you the whole time. I might make a mistake." I crossed my arms.

"That's not true. I spar very well, and we always have an audience when we train," he said.

"That's different," I said, grabbing my brush and waving it. "I'm not throwing a sword around. Painting takes patience. You need to be very exact with how you move your brush." I shook my head and huffed a breath.

"It's a delicate skill. I shouldn't have assumed you could relate."

"I have many delicate skills, my lady." He fought back a smile.

I plopped my paintbrush into the oil and swirled it a bit too enthusiastically. "Then you won't mind if I stare at you the next time you're doing something *delicate?*"

He pursed his lips, considering. The way the dimple on his left cheek hollowed out made me want to fling paint into his face. I huffed and went to work, content to let him stare if it meant he would stop speaking.

He laughed. "If it pleases you, I'll shift my attention to the right and watch you in my periphery."

I shot him a sinister smile. "Nothing you do pleases me, Lieutenant, but that sounds fine."

His fist rose to his chest, and he blew out a breath, as if he were wounded. He held my stare for a moment before adjusting his stance and focusing on a spot ten feet away.

I went to work, outlining the shapes of my composition across the canvas, stepping back to survey the scale. This was a much larger working area than I was used to, but there was great satisfaction in painting broad, elongated strokes.

Before long, I became lost in the work, the scrape of the damp brush over the wall, getting used to how the paint played with the hard surface. My body and mind had relaxed, and the hum had melted into the background.

"What are you doing so close to the wall, Harper Ledes?" A raspy, male voice slithered through my mind.

Palpable fear rushed through me. I glanced over to Logan. He had apparently not heard anything at all.

I had always heard whispers when I neared the wall. Incomprehensible and muffled, like listening through the plaster walls of the townhouse. Nobody had ever addressed me by name.

My brush trembled, but I continued working not to raise Logan's alarm. Despite my initial panic, a strange sense of calm gripped me, allowing my magic to flow freely.

"*Who are you?*" I spoke into the creature's mind.

"*I should be asking you the same question,*" the creature replied.

"*You seem to know who I am. Harper Ledes, daughter of Lord Cade, the twelfth child of the triplet lords.*" I didn't know why I had responded with my formal title, but something about this creature felt noble as well.

A soft chuckle. "*Harper Ledes. Daughter of Sarah. I've been waiting many years for you to venture near the wall.*"

The pit in my stomach deepened with my mother's name. "*Why? Who are you? We are not to speak of my mother. Surely you know that.*"

"*I am beyond the laws of your village. Tell me, Harper. Can your brother mindspeak through the wall?*"

My brush continued to undulate over the stucco as my hands trembled. "*I never asked him. How can you mindspeak?*"

"*I'm not mindspeaking. I am speaking. But the guard at your side cannot hear me.*" The creature let out a sigh that almost sounded human.

"*What do you want?*" It would have come out as a whisper if I had spoken aloud.

The creature slithered away, and I sensed it as clearly as I heard his words ricochet through my mind.

"*I want you to understand. Things in Galloway are not as they seem. Start asking questions, my sweet. Until tomorrow, Daughter of Sarah.*"

CHAPTER

EIGHT

Our old rooms at the manor always smelled a little musty, even when Maggie came ahead to open the windows and start the fires before our weekly family dinners.

I stared at my reflection in the vanity mirror, the creature's voice beyond the wall rumbling through my thoughts. Surely, it had been my imagination. Perhaps the stress of these past few days had gotten the best of me.

The manor had always felt like a second home, even though I had never lived there. James remembered when he, my father, and my mother occupied these rooms. For me, it was a place to rest between parties and balls. A respite that was warm and familiar, even though the rooms themselves saw very little use.

Somewhere I belonged but was never a part of.

After painting, Logan had escorted me a short distance to the manor, and I had immediately run to the library. If there was any place in Galloway where I could get answers about the voice, it was in those shelves. The manor had the most extensive collection of books in the village, probably in the south of Jersey. But I hadn't found any books about demons as I walked the dusty rows.

Several volumes outlined the history of the Barrens, so I had borrowed them, hoping for some mention of the demons that dwelled here. Skimming through them had revealed nothing, but I reasoned there would be plenty of time to comb through them when I escaped the party tonight.

It was nearly evening, and I still hadn't seen my father, but I was sure the news of the mural had reached him by now.

His days had been full, especially since taking on the duties of wedding planning. Picking out table linens and place settings was usually something the mother of the groom would fuss about, but my father had been enthusiastic about the preparations.

Father had never shied away from being a different kind of parent. He had taught James and me how to ride and hunt, but he had also learned how to braid my hair when I was young, just in case Maggie was unavailable. I sat at my vanity, my memory swimming with all the times my father had sat behind me, patiently brushing out my knots after parties.

All because my mother couldn't.

How many times had my mother sat in this very chair? Aunt Patrice stood behind me now. Her reflection was composed as she worked a brush through my long, dark strands. I knew she was thinking of my mother as well. Waves of nostalgia and whispers of her name wafted from her mind as she pulled the brush methodically up and down.

"My lady," Maggie asked, hands clasped before her chest.

"Would you like me to style Miss Harper's hair for dinner? I'm sure your maid is awaiting you."

Aunt Patrice smiled at Maggie. "You know how much I like to fuss over my niece, Maggie. I want to give the bun a try this time. You can fix any loose strands."

I nodded in the mirror, wondering how someone so soft and mild could have been paired with my gruff Uncle Bain. James spread out on the settee behind me and smirked at my reflection. I didn't have to read his mind to know he was wondering the same thing.

Aunt Patrice and Uncle Bain had five boys, all men now. It was some cruel trick of the universe that my sweet, gentle aunt had no daughters while my shrewd, cold aunt had spawned triplet terrors. Aunt Beatrice had raised her daughters to be haughty, power-hungry, and self-important. Even though my father and his brothers considered themselves equal in nobility, Aunt Beatrice acted as if marrying the oldest triplet made her a queen, not just a mere Lady of Galloway.

It didn't help that her sons were branded with the numbers *1* and *2*. But Paxton and Brannon had never been boastful of their positions. They never made me feel like less of a Ledes, even without a brand of my own.

"When will you get dressed, James?" Aunt Pat asked, her fingers dancing through the midnight strands of my hair. "This party is for you, after all."

James turned his gaze to the floor. "It won't take me long to get dressed, Auntie. I don't have nearly as much hair as my sister."

"Harold has fallen ill, but Uncle Bain said he'll send Benjamin up for you as soon as he's available. It shouldn't take him long to dress Bain."

I stiffened, witnessing the color wash from my brother's cheeks.

James stood, perhaps a bit too quickly. "If Harold is ill, I can dress myself. Please tell Uncle Bain not to fuss over me."

Aunt Patrice tutted. "Nonsense. It's no fuss at all. Benjamin will make quick work of Uncle Bain. He's not the star of the evening. You are, dear."

Before my brother could object, there was a soft knock on the door.

"Come in," Aunt Patrice said with gentle authority.

Benjamin entered, bowing low to my aunt before turning his attention to my brother. "Mr. Ledes, I shall dress you for dinner if you are ready."

A fissure cracked through my heart. My brother's jaw was fixed in a firm line, raw devastation in his eyes.

"*Tell him you don't need a valet,*" I pleaded into my brother's mind.

"*I can't do that to him,*" he returned. "*It would disgrace him.*"

"*What's worse?*" I hissed back.

Benjamin's stare tore into James, his face impassive. He didn't so much as raise an eyebrow. I didn't have to read my brother's mind to know he was having an internal war.

Send him away, and Benjamin must explain his dismissal to my uncle. Accept him, and both men would suffer through the agony of this engagement party, as servant and master.

"How are you enjoying being a valet, Benjamin?" I asked.

My brother gave me a grateful smile for buying him time.

Benjamin had been promoted to the coveted position

less than a month earlier after years as a horse handler. This was the first time I had seen James and Ben interact inside the manor itself.

The valet regarded me with kind, blue eyes, and his freckled nose wrinkled into a grateful smile. "It suits me very nicely, my lady. Thank you for asking."

"I suppose my uncle smells a great deal better than the stables." From the corner of my eye, I saw Maggie's fingers raise to her temples.

Benjamin fought a smile. "A great deal better," he said.

Aunt Patrice snorted. "Benjamin, you give the man a bit too much credit."

At this, the valet beamed and turned back to my brother, whose shoulders had loosened.

James almost smiled. "Come to think of it, I'll get dressed before my sister insults me next." He considered the man with longing in his eyes, his chest heaving a sigh. "I'm ready."

"*Thank you, Harp.*" His words hugged my mind.

"*Good luck, James.*"

CHAPTER

NINE

The dining room at Ledes Manor was bedecked in rare flowers that must have been imported from a place where sunlight reached the ground. Beside me, Emelia Hern stood wide-eyed as she took in the massive dining hall.

She wore a stunning blush-colored dress. Her hair was styled in perfectly plaited braids, and a sweep of gold rouge shone on her rich, brown skin, highlighting the apples of her cheeks. Emelia was easily one of the most beautiful women in Galloway, regal and poised on the outside, but based on the flurry of thoughts that bounced into my brain, she was successfully concealing her nerves.

"I've never seen such a table in my life," she said in an awed voice.

"Well, triplets and twins run in our family." I smiled at my future sister-in-law, failing to mention that the colossal table sometimes felt cramped when this crowd sat around it. Emelia seemed just as nervous about this union as James did.

When my brother was announced in the dining hall, a

flush colored his neck. Although he was impeccably dressed, there was something ruffled about him. He had taken his time coming downstairs, and a part of me wondered if he and Benjamin had used the stolen time to comfort each other.

I took a large sip from my wine glass as I did the mental calculations. We would have had the funds to leave if I had played three more winning hands. The apartment in Delphi, the chance at the conservatory, all that had offered us an escape from this engagement was no more than a fantasy now. I hadn't dared to return to the tavern now that Logan and Jacob knew about it. Besides, now that I had made an appearance at the wall, the militiamen who frequented card games would surely recognize me.

James had money of his own, but Father had moved it into a fund for Emelia's dowry.

I had considered asking for payment to paint the wall, but Father was in charge of the village coffers. He would never give his own daughter money from the town's funds.

James and I could have lived in the smartly appointed yet modest flat. We could have hired Benjamin as our butler, and my brother wouldn't have to live in misery.

Once this engagement party was behind us, Aunt Bea and Aunt Patrice would set the wedding planning wheels in motion.

I did a double-take as James walked through the crowd, accompanied by the cheerful lords of Ledes Manor. My chest cracked open when I found my father.

Smiling.

Not just smiling—*beaming* as he entered his son's engagement party with Mrs. Hern on his arm.

The triplet lords were not identical, but they had the

same bone structure. I had always thought my father's face was perhaps a little longer than Bain's or Aaron's, but as I beheld the grin on his face, I realized it wasn't longer at all. It was the shadows that usually darkened his features, wrought with grief and longing for something that was long gone.

James must have noticed it, too. He shook Mrs. Hern's hand with the vigor of a determined man, seemingly fueled by the rare smile that reached our father's eyes.

I combed my memory for the last time my father had seemed happy, but I came up blank. This party was one of many held here in the dining hall since my mother died. Birthdays, promotions, and anniversaries were celebrated around this table. What about James's betrothal could have brought my father so much joy?

I jumped at Emelia's voice, having forgotten she was there.

"Will you introduce me to your father?" she asked, her voice an octave higher than before.

My magic recoiled with her anxiety. She worried, loud enough for me to hear, if she would fit into the family.

"Oh, right. I suppose I should introduce you." I took her by the arm and escorted her to my brother's side.

James bowed. "Miss Hern," he said, raising her gloved hand to his lips. "It's a pleasure to see you again." He sent her a smile that almost convinced me he was attracted to the woman.

My brother was smooth. Nobody could deny him that.

"A pleasure, my lord," she said, a flush rising to her cheeks. As she curtsied to my father, she bit her lip. I was used to people fawning over my father and my uncles. All three brothers were well respected in Galloway, and to meet them was an honor, but Lord Cade was by far the least imposing of the three.

After several agonizing moments of small talk, I backed away from the conversation, muttering an excuse about refilling my glass. The butler's pour was generous, and I took the opportunity to slink to the furthest corner of the parlor.

I leaned against the wall, my dark gray dress blending with the stamped wallpaper. The soft glow of the candle sconces, lit with fire magic, cast enough shadow on the wall to conceal me further, and I melted contentedly into the darkness.

From afar, I watched my brother smile at his bride-to-be. Emelia was beautiful at his side. I wondered for a moment what their children might look like.

Tendrils of magic swirled from my mind, reaching out to my future sister-in-law. *Excitement, trepidation. He's handsome. What do I do with my hands? Should I have worn my blue dress? It would have matched his eyes.*

A strong shoulder bounced against my own, causing me to nearly spill my precious drink. When I saw who had nudged me, my muscles relaxed.

"Didn't mean to scare you. Harper," Rand said before extending his drink to mine in a toast. "Don't be so glum. The fun cousins have arrived."

I winked at him and clinked our glasses together. "Now the party can start."

Axel appeared through the door, a near-mirror image of his triplet brother. "It seems you're already a glass of wine ahead of us. Don't let my father hear you slurring your words like that." He raised his eyebrows, mischief dancing over his face.

It was true. Uncle Bain disapproved of overindulging, even if we had heard many stories of the debauchery of his youth through the years. I shrugged, knowing it would be worth a lecture on a night like tonight. "I do what I need to survive. Where's Perry?"

"He drew the long straw and stayed at the tavern tonight," Axel said. He took a deep swig of his drink. "Lucky bastard."

"Skipping family dinner? What will Uncle Bain think?" I asked, arching a brow.

Rand put his hand to his chest in mock offense. "We're businessmen, Harper. What would you have us do? Those drinks aren't going to pour themselves."

I snorted into my wineglass. It was rare not to see all three of them at the tavern, but family dinners were taken very seriously in the Ledes family, especially celebratory ones like this.

"Where were you last night?" Axel asked. "I must admit, our patrons were much happier in your absence. Some of them have never had the chance to actually win at cards."

A big part of me wanted to unload the stress of the past few days on my cousins, but I couldn't fathom accomplishing that without telling them about my mindspeaking. I knew they would never judge me, but I wouldn't want them to bear the burden of my secret. James and I had always agreed it was best to keep it to ourselves.

Something about it felt dangerous.

My gaze shot to the portrait of my mother on the other side of the parlor. One of the few pieces of Sarah Ledes that Aunt Pat had begged to keep in the manor.

Mother's hair had been a shade lighter than mine, but I

shared her slim nose and proud mouth. James had inherited our father's blue eyes, but my eyes were as gray as the mist that shrouded this town.

Another feature my mother had passed on to me. Had she passed along the ability to mindspeak, too?

Daughter of Sarah. Had that creature near the wall somehow known my mother? I tried to push away the tingle of unease that had clung to my skin since I heard the creature's voice. The wall's buzz seemed trapped within my ears.

I drained my glass.

Perhaps I had inherited my mother's eyes and her magic, but I had gained my tendency to push down my feelings directly from my father.

"I've been trying to cut back on the gambling," I returned, clearing my throat. "It's not considered very lady-like." I nodded toward my father and James, who were deep in conversation with Emelia and Mrs. Hern.

"I guess you're right," Rand said, crossing his arms. "I feel bad for you, Harper. This is going to be your life until the wedding. One stuffy party after another. Reputations to uphold."

My shoulders sagged with the weight of my failure. James and I had been so close to getting out of this mess. Moving away from this cursed, mist-shrouded town. This party was the final nail in the coffin, holding us here. A nail that confined James to a lifetime of pretending to be someone he wasn't.

My heart cracked for James and Ben.

"One day, you two will be up there, parading around your betrothed," I said.

Axel nearly spat out his ale. "Nobody will go through

this kind of trouble for us, Harp. We're the pariahs of this family, remember?"

He had a point. Uncle Bain's face always twisted in disdain whenever someone inquired about the tavern, and with their older brothers, Samuel and Jackson, in Delphi, the triplet misfits bore the brunt of my uncle's temper. Aunt Pat kept Lord Bain in line well enough.

Rand nodded. "The best I can do is find a match on my own and hope Dear Old Dad approves."

I nodded back. Perhaps James and I should have tried harder to fall out of our family's good graces.

Finding someone on my own had to be preferable to this ridiculous high society courting game our family had started to play, and poor James was the unlucky bastard to be subjected to it first. As the youngest Ledes cousin, it might buy me some time. Perhaps by the time my family considered me marriageable, they would have grown tired of all this.

James and I had always known we'd be subjected to courtship, but it had seemed like a distant threat. Marriages were arranged to uphold family bloodlines like ours. Aunt Patrice had always been forthcoming in her stories about how our grandmother had arranged her marriage to Uncle Bain. From what I could tell, my parents had been a love match, even if the family had arranged it.

I always hoped I'd be happy with my match. Father would choose someone compatible for me. Handsome, if I were lucky. But James and Ben couldn't speak of their love without scorn. How was Father to know of James's heart, even if he did want happiness for him?

Merry voices carried from the parlor, and everyone's attention turned toward Paxton and Brannon as they entered the room, decked in their militia finery. When I realized Jacob and Logan flanked them, also in their formal uniforms, I released a groan of annoyance.

Axel arched a suspicious brow. "Why is the new police chief here?"

"Probably to sniff around," Rand said. "Good thing we left Perry. If he'd seen all three of us here, he would've set his dogs on the tavern."

My brow knitted. "Have the police been giving you a hard time?"

"No, but that new chief knows things he isn't supposed to," Axel said. "I'm sure he's heard about what's going on in the cellar. For some reason, he hasn't investigated it."

A wave of guilt washed over me. Jacob did know about it, in good part due to me.

On cue, Jacob's gaze swept to us in the corner of the room. His eyes darted away when he spotted me. Walls were up in his mind, thick bricks that kept my magic away, but I couldn't help but catch a wave of emotion from him.

The chief of police was *overwhelmed*. Even though he was halfway across the room, I could see his chest heaving. His index finger grazed the cuticle of his thumb.

He's nervous.

Perhaps he hated parties like this as much as I did. As a fellow mindspeaker, I knew how exhausting it could be. Uncle Bain approached both men and shook Jacob's hand. The captain snapped out of it enough to smile.

Logan, on the other hand, wore a smug smile, as if he'd been attending parties like this his whole life. I had never seen him here inside the Ledes Manor before, but that didn't mean he hadn't been to previous gatherings. His shoulders squared as he scanned the room, his composure breaking a bit as he spotted me against the wall.

"That guy is staring at you, Harper," Rand said under his breath.

I scoffed. "I know."

"Friend of yours?" Axel asked.

"Hardly." I didn't appreciate my cousins teasing me, but I sure as hell didn't want them to leave my side. There was no time to explain the events of the last few days or the mural to them as Logan sauntered toward us.

"Lady Ledes," he said, nodding to my cousins. "A pleasure to see you off duty."

"Mr. Greer, these are my cousins, Axel and Randal," I returned, businesslike. "The lieutenant has been assigned to guard me at the wall while I paint a mural at the barracks."

My cousins exchanged a smirk as they shook Logan's hand.

"I know of your fine tavern, my lords," Logan said. "I owe you a debt of gratitude for many good drinks after a hard workday."

"If you've been tasked to guard Harper, we'll make sure to pour them extra strong for you the next time you stop by," Axel said.

Logan laughed, and the stupid dimple erupted around his smile. "I appreciate the gesture."

All I could do was glare at him as the dinner bell rang and the firelight dimmed and flared, a flicker of magic to signal the beginning of the feast.

Axel's arm wrapped around my own. "I'll escort you to your seat, cousin," he said, pulling me away.

"Thanks," I replied, squeezing his hand.

"I didn't know you had a big, strong soldier at your beck and call, Harp."

"He's a big, strong asshole," I said, glancing over my shoulder at Logan. Something in my abdomen dipped when I realized he had been watching me as I walked away.

"He seems like someone who likes to play with his prey, Harper," Axel said, his voice lowering. "Be careful."

CHAPTER

TEN

A breath of relief puffed through my lips when I saw that I had been seated between James and Brannon. Across from me, Paxton's sleeves were rolled up, displaying his *1*, as he spoke intently with Jacob about the border wall.

Logan had been seated next to Mira, who proceeded to thrust her cleavage out as far as it would go. My cousin twirled her hair around her pinky finger. The pink lace dress and her flouncing curls highlighted her beauty, but her coy smirk made her look like a wolf dressed as a lamb.

"My sisters have been at the conservatory," she said, loudly enough for all to hear. "I was also accepted to study there, but I chose to stay behind. There's much to attend to at the manor these days."

Mira had made it clear to Aunt Bea that she wanted to be the next Ledes cousin to wed, and being seated next to the handsome arms lieutenant must have scratched that itch.

I attempted to conceal my amusement, but the dark glare Logan sent me from down the table confirmed I was doing a poor job. He grumbled something, and Mira giggled in response. He took a deep swig of ale.

James had been seated next to Emelia, naturally. Uncle Aaron caught Emelia's attention with a few amusing stories, and James took advantage of the break in conversation to take a deep breath.

"*Are you okay?*" I asked my brother, mind to mind.

"*She's a lovely woman.*" His words were clipped, blunted by sadness.

"*That's not what I asked,*" I said, squeezing his forearm just above his branded numeral **4**. He gripped my hand with his own and gave me a grateful smile.

Across the table, Jacob's gaze flitted to my hand, focusing on the gesture toward my brother. He must have known the two of us were mindspeaking.

It felt like an invasion. The police chief's jaw worked as he looked away, and despite his steadfast walls, another wave of emotion, this time unreadable, wafted toward me. Perhaps the captain was remorseful for blackmailing me after all.

Dinner was a rather standard show for the manor. Opulent crystal stemware, fine silver, floral-embroidered napkins, and food my aunts had selected to please the crowd. The conversation flowed easily, and I found myself chatting with Emelia's mother, Bess.

Mrs. Hern had a dry, sarcastic sense of humor and told a few stories that even had my father chuckling. Something had come over him tonight, cracking through the reserved shell that usually cloaked him. He even gave a toast.

I let my magic approach my father from across the table. It was something I tried not to do. When we were children, James and I had promised never to use our magic to read our father's thoughts. It was a subtle feeling, but someone accustomed to it would have sensed the tendrils of power slithering into their mind.

We were unsure if our mother had been a mindspeaker, but we didn't want to risk our father's suspicion by allowing our magic near him.

I allowed my power to rest on the periphery, where only vague emotions swirled.

Contentment. Hope.

More than once, I caught Uncle Aaron and Uncle Bain watching their brother. They must have noticed the shift in him as well.

When Uncle Aaron stood and invited the men into the study for cigars, I rose and smoothed my dress. The women would move into the drawing-room, but I had no desire to listen to Mira's retelling of her conversation with Logan at dinner. Nobody would miss me if I slunk back to the townhouse and went to bed early, except perhaps Aunt Pat.

Besides, I had reading to do and intended to bring home the books I had borrowed from the library. I'd had too much wine at dinner, but I was sure nothing would sober me up faster than reading the historical records of Galloway.

It was as though the mist itself was slithering through my veins at the memory of the voice I heard behind the wall. I shivered, wondering if the thing could sense me this far away from the pines.

I slunk out of the dining room and entered the deserted manor halls, dark save for the candles illuminating the sconces. I passed painting after painting of my ancestors, all bedecked in finery in lush gardens. As a child, I would stare at the portraits for hours, wondering what it had been like to live in the Barrens in the years before the mist and the wall had blotted out the sun.

No such gardens would survive here now.

Our quarters were on the other side of the manor, but I needed to collect my things. Maggie was already back at the townhouse, but I was grateful to walk home alone, even if whispers lived in the shadows.

One foot was on the staircase when a thick hand clasped my shoulder. I turned to find the arms lieutenant one step behind me, severe lines etched on his face.

"May I help you?" I asked, pushing his hand away.

"Yes, you can," he said. His jaw was fixed in a firm line, but the effect of ale relaxed his words.

I didn't blame him one bit. I would have had to drink to stomach a conversation with Mira, too.

"Jacob just got word of another raid on the armory. He's taking the generals with him to investigate as we speak."

My eyes widened. "I'm sorry to hear that, but if the raid already happened, I'm afraid there's nothing I can do to help you."

"I need you to help me spy." A muscle on his jaw twitched as he peered around the foyer, assuring we were alone. "Now."

Shades of worry danced over his face in the glow of the lamplight, making his chiseled features appear even more striking.

Fear and a beat of excitement gripped me. "Fine. Follow me, then."

CHAPTER

ELEVEN

Logan had scoffed at me when I requested a moment to change out of my finery before investigating, but I hastily convinced him it would be a lot harder to creep around the barracks in a full skirt and corset.

He followed me to my rooms with stiff shoulders, and I heard the incessant tapping of his heavy boot from the other side of the door the entire time I changed.

I chose my riding pants and tunic and fastened a black wool cloak around my shoulders. When I emerged from my bedroom, Logan's shoulders stiffened, and the tapping stopped.

He cleared his throat as his gaze swept over me. "You're wearing pants."

Surely, a man so worldly could not be offended by the sight of a lady's legs. The more I got to know Logan, the more he surprised me.

"Does that not suit your taste, Lieutenant?" I cocked my head, ready for his snide retort, but his mouth opened without a sound.

He grabbed my elbow. "Come on, we've wasted enough time," he said, leading me to the door.

I slapped his hand away. "There's a faster way to get to the barracks," I said, smoothing my cloak. "I can take you there, but you'll have to trust me."

He rolled his eyes. "I certainly don't trust you, but I'll follow you if you know a shortcut."

I nodded and led him down the hall, cursing myself and this whole wretched situation. He didn't trust *me*? He was the one who'd pulled me off the streets and threatened me. Logan and Jacob had dragged me into this mess, and if it weren't for their meddling, I would be home by now.

Likely counting my riches and packing my trunk.

The staff entrance at the back of our rooms led to a dark, narrow hallway—vacant quarters for butlers and valets that Cade Ledes no longer needed after he moved his family out of the manor. Beyond them, a hidden door concealed a labyrinth of corridors behind the walls. As children, Axel, Perry, Rand, and I would spend hours exploring, eager to discover the best pathways to the kitchen. When we got older, we used them to sneak out of family dinners, but my favorite use of the secret passages was to gain access to the library.

Logan trailed me as I turned down the hallway toward abandoned rooms no one had used for decades. We passed several open doors that revealed simple beds and wooden dressers coated with a thick layer of dust.

Only family members and select house staff knew about the secret door at the end of the hall. I stopped in front of the darkened room where the staircase opening was tucked behind a wardrobe.

"If you tell anyone about this secret passage, I'll report

you to Uncle Bain for trespassing. I'd hate to see you punished," I said, inclining my chin. It was futile, trying to make myself tall next to his towering form. I'd had too much wine at dinner, but wasn't tipsy enough to give Logan this information without a threat of my own.

He smirked at the challenge, closing the distance between us. "Your secret is safe with me. Besides, I think you're forgetting I know some very specific information about you that could have *you* punished." The dimple on his cheek deepened. "My lady."

Hot anger flared behind my eyes, and for a moment, all I saw was flames. This man had a bottomless well of audacity. "Being here alone with you appears quite scandalous. If someone saw us, they might get the wrong idea." I raised my brows, hoping the threat of dishonor would make him reconsider taking me along.

His eyes narrowed. "I would never do anything improper with you."

I shrugged and let my magic snake over his skull, keen to figure out a way to break him down. My hopes of dissuading him from taking me along melted when the only emotion I found in Logan's mind was stubborn determination.

I stuck out my lower lip in a pout. "Slinking around up isn't very proper, though, is it?"

A flare of anger that matched my own surged from him, and I was startled by the thrill it gave me. I didn't usually enjoy using my magic to bait someone's emotions, but getting a rise out of Logan Greer was intensely satisfying.

Before Logan could reply, voices echoed from down the hall. He grabbed my hand, and a wave of warmth washed over my skin. I pushed him into one of the abandoned rooms. The door was ajar, but I dared not close it and risk a creak.

I shoved Logan into the narrow space behind the open door and the dusty wall. He pulled me up against him, his arm around my waist, and I found my face pressed up against his heaving chest.

A rush of heat pulsed through me.

How dare Logan Greer smell so good? I allowed my magic to retreat, not daring to read his emotions when our bodies were pressed together. My ear was flush against the linen covering his collarbone, so close I could hear his heart pounding through the thin fabric. My own traitorous heart sped up at the sound.

As they approached, I recognized Uncle Bain's gruff voice arguing with one of my cousins.

I must have been breathing too loudly because Logan put a finger to my lips. Musk and leather filled my lungs, and I reasoned the wine must have dizzied my head as I breathed him in.

I supposed even top-tier assholes could smell nice.

"*Logan.*" I was glad his mind was open, even if he did jump a bit when my voice projected into his mind. "*Don't move.*"

His chin jerked in acknowledgment.

"There was another raid, Paxton. Do you know what this means?" Uncle Bain growled.

"Enlighten me, Uncle."

Bain let out an exasperated grunt. "The mist has been getting thicker every day. Surely you've noticed."

I was going to pass out. The mist had been getting thicker, but I'd thought I had imagined it. My heart raced even wilder. Something had spoken to me from that mist this morning. Did the voice have anything to do with the raids?

Logan's grip around my waist tightened, and for the first time since I'd met the man, I was grateful for his presence as he kept me upright.

"Of course, I noticed it," Paxton said. "But what do the thieves have to do with the mist?"

"The demons in the Barrens can only be killed with iron, and the demons make the mist. The creatures are hovering around the wall. The sentries have seen them lurking between trees. The iron must be in the Barrens somewhere. It's angering them."

My legs began to weaken, but Logan's grip was steadfast.

"Brannon has been mapping their movements around the wall. Two sentries described something with horns a few days ago," Paxton said, his voice measured. Uncle Bain was prone to outbursts, and all the cousins knew to tread softly when he was stressed.

"A cryptid," Uncle Bain growled. The light from his lantern surged with his anger. "One has never been spotted this close to the wall. What would bring that creature here?"

"Perhaps the irons around Galloway have affected the entirety of the Barrens," Paxton reasoned. "Uncle, Brannon and I believe someone within the militia is stealing the irons."

Bain huffed. "Of course. Only someone from the inside would have access to the armory. What kind of motive would someone have to steal irons? None of the shipments or warehouses from the iron works in Batso have been threatened. The machinery at the Harrisville Mill remains untouched. They're only stealing from within our walls."

Their voices faded into the shadows as they disappeared through the passageway.

"It takes about two minutes to get through the tunnel between the manor and the barracks. We'll give them time to get out of earshot," I told Logan into his mind.

He nodded, his chin bobbing against my hair. He paused a moment before he asked, *"Can you hear me speak into your mind, too?"*

I stepped back, and he released his grip on my waist. It was strange to speak this way with anyone but James.

It felt—intimate.

I narrowed my eyes, studying his face in the dark. *"I can hear or sense anything I want, but I can hear full thoughts if you're directing them toward me. It's also easier for me to hear what someone is thinking when they're concentrating. That's how I cheat at cards."*

He shot me a satisfied grin. *"It would have certainly been scandalous to find us in here. You act like you don't mind being pressed against me."*

I rolled my eyes, regretting that I'd given Logan, of all people, instructions on how to mindspeak with me. *"Lieutenant Greer, you wound me. I'm an excellent actress."*

"Whatever you say, my lady."

I held in a growl, not wanting to make any noise, but a flush crept up my neck and into my cheeks.

Triumph flashed across his smug face, making me want to kick him. I closed the distance between us and pushed his shoulder against the wall again, harder this time, perhaps emboldened still by the wine in my veins. I stared him in the eye as I pressed the length of my body against him. His chest heaved, straining against his leathers.

"I'm the one who can mindspeak, remember? Reading

your emotions is far easier than reading your thoughts. I can sense just how much you *like it when I push you up against this wall."*

His eyes widened.

"Act your way out of that, Lieutenant."

I would have never said something like that to him aloud, and certainly not without the influence of alcohol. I cursed myself for not controlling my impulses.

A diabolical smile spread over his lips, punctuated by two infuriating dimples. *"Do you like the idea of me having dirty thoughts about you, Harper?"*

The way he said my name ignited me like a flame through a piece of parchment.

"Let's go," I said aloud.

I hadn't been in the passage to the barracks in years, and in our youth, we had only dared to make it part of the way down this particular hallway, knowing that every step brought us closer to the wall. Echoes bounced off the tunnel's stones, and I tried to soften my footsteps as I trotted along, Logan behind me. "The exit is up ahead."

"When we get to the barracks, I'll lead the way," he said. His tone was businesslike now, and I puffed out a breath, relieved that the moment of reckless flirtation was behind us.

Was it flirtation? No, he had been intentionally provoking me. It was all part of his arrogant attitude and his plan to keep me under his thumb.

Logan put his finger to his lips when we finally reached a door. We opened it and found ourselves hidden in a thicket of elm trees. He got his bearings in a moment and took my hand, pulling me toward a shed. His grip tightened as we ran to the back of the barracks, where a ladder leaned against the back wall.

He motioned toward it, and I climbed up on shaky legs. The roof was only slightly sloped, covered with slate shingles, and when Logan met me atop it, he crouched down.

"We can move to the front of the roofline, and you can tell me what's going on in everyone's heads below," he whispered.

I nodded. We slunk to the front of the roof on our bellies, clinging to the slate, and I was thankful for my decision to change into pants. The angle was perfect for spying, the slope just right. A few people were ambling about below us, and I watched them stiffen as Paxton approached, Jacob at his side.

Trepidation. Anxiety. Annoyance.

So many emotions bombarded me from the soldiers below, and it made me wonder how I would ever sift through all their thoughts. I cursed the wine in my veins as their emotions overcame my senses, and I tried not to let the nervous tension seep into my skin.

"If Jacob is with Paxton, don't you think the guards will have walls up?" I asked.

I could feel the emotions wafting from the crowd, but only snippets of their thoughts broke through the chaos. It was like trying to listen to a song while submerged underwater. The intensity of it made family dinners feel like a soft, pleasant conversation.

Logan nodded. "Jacob won't be there long. He's going into the pines to investigate."

I shivered. Going into the pines was dangerous at any time of day—but at night? I watched Jacob pace the ground, his dark hair muted in the moonlight, his face pale. A long sword, iron no doubt, was strapped to his back. I realized Paxton had a matching sword strapped to his own back, and my stomach churned with the realization that Pax was planning to accompany him.

"*Jacob is worried*," I said into Logan's mind. It was instinctual to speak this way to him when we were acting as spies.

Logan nodded. "*Do you see the man there? With the red tunic? Round belly, bald head.*"

I did. My focus shifted to him, and I closed my eyes, tuning out the physical and mental noise from the crowd. Mercifully, the man had no walls in his mind.

"*He was celebrating his daughter's birthday when the alarm went off,*" I reported to Logan. "*He's resentful that he was called away.*"

Logan's face softened with relief. "*Carl is a good man. I don't blame him for feeling that way. I'm glad to hear he's not the thief.*"

I scanned the men below us, one by one, and recounted their thoughts to Logan. He was right. All of them had their guard down and their minds open when Jacob walked away. The news about his mindspeaking abilities must have been common knowledge, but none of them knew another mindspeaker was hiding on the roof above them.

Many were irritated to be called away from their homes. A few were worried about being called into the pines, but none showed signs of guilt.

Logan scribbled in a notebook as I reported to him. After a while, the sentries left, either taking up an assignment or returning to the barracks for a few moments' rest. Before long, Logan and I were alone in the empty courtyard, monitoring nothing but swirling mist.

Less unease buzzed through my veins, but it still felt dangerous to be alone anywhere with this man. I played with the hem of my cloak in silence. It wasn't until several minutes passed that I dared to speak.

"Was that the first Ledes family dinner you've ever attended?" I asked him, gazing up at the sky.

He shifted onto his side, facing me. "It was. I quite liked it."

I scoffed.

Blue reflected in his eyes despite the mist that drowned out the moon, and the silvery scar in his brow gleamed as it arched at me. "You don't like family dinners?" he asked.

"Not usually. Especially not tonight," I admitted.

"Why?"

"Because I don't like the idea of my brother being forced to marry someone he doesn't love." I replayed the events of the night. Emelia's nervous smile, her mother's rich laughter as she sat at the table beside my father. The Hern family was lovely, that much was certain, but James and Benjamin deserved love. Real love. Not something fabricated or forced.

"I get it," Logan said, his face softening, and I wondered if the lieutenant was perhaps capable of feeling empathy.

"Did you enjoy sitting next to Mira at dinner?" I asked.

I regretted the question the moment it left my lips and cursed the wine that was undoubtedly still lowering my inhibitions and loosening my tongue. Although I had enjoyed watching him suffer through a conversation with Mira, the thought of my heinous cousin sinking her claws into Logan disturbed me. Anything Mira did disturbed me, and it had been that way since we were children.

He chuckled. "I'm no mindspeaker, but I could tell your cousin enjoyed my company."

I shook my head. "Don't be too surprised if you get an invitation to tea this week from my Aunt Bea."

Logan leaned closer, pinning me with his stare. "What should I tell her?"

I nearly blurted out a million reasons why Mira was awful, how she made me hate going to lessons and wish I had a different last name, but I bit my lip.

"Tell her whatever you want," I said, picking at the pits in the slate roof. Logan would be a perfect match for her. With her entitled nature and his arrogant ambition, they would be a force to be reckoned with.

"I saw you watching us at dinner," he said, the corner of his mouth twitching.

I propped my head in my hand. "Excuse me?"

"From across the table. You were watching me. And Mira."

I schooled my expression into indifference. It was nothing new. The mindspeaking gift had given me an innate curiosity about people's interactions, and knowing Logan was uncomfortable had been highly entertaining. "I was indeed. Watching you suffer, and I enjoyed every moment."

"Why?" His question hung in the air like it was suspended from the pine boughs.

Muted light from the torches below danced over his face, all sharp lines and soft divots.

I tipped my shoulder up. "Ever since you accosted me in the alley that night, my life has been unraveling. I liked watching you squirm, I guess."

Logan narrowed his eyes, and my skin prickled. In truth, I had enjoyed accompanying him on this spying mission. There was a thrill to it that I didn't hate. I felt important, like the main character in a suspense novel, having a dangerous adventure.

Logan considered me for a moment before he leaned

close enough to whisper in my ear, his mouth nearly grazing across the angle of my jaw.

I pulled in a breath. Leather and musk with a subtle hint of whiskey, the smell of pure sin, leeched into my blood.

"You know what, Harper?" His voice caressed my ear. "I think I like watching you squirm, too."

My eyes widened. His words vibrated through me and ratcheted me out of my drunken stupor. I reeled back, furious with myself for letting him get a rise out of me. Logan Greer had already blackmailed me. It had cost me everything. I would be damned if I let him play with my emotions.

I met his gaze, and for a heartbeat, it was as though the mist was swirling within his steely blue eyes. He blinked, and his stare shifted, fixing on my mouth. A flutter rose in my chest, and I fought the impulse to let my magic snake into his mind.

Because my prying, meddlesome magic desperately wanted to know what he was thinking at that moment.

Thankfully, my heart was smarter. I turned and forced myself to look away, swallowing down the urge.

"I'm growing tired of spying," I said. "I'm ready to go home."

His laugh cut through the mist like velvet smoke. "As you wish, my lady."

CHAPTER

TWELVE

James and Father had returned to the townhouse after the party, so I followed their lead. I had no desire to sleep in our chambers in the manor alone, especially after traversing the depths of the secret tunnel. Much to my annoyance, Logan had escorted me home, but I walked half a block ahead of him the whole way.

The feeling of his gaze on my back lingered, leaving a tingle over my spine that didn't dull, even when I retired to my bed.

It had been difficult to fall asleep. Every time I was about to drift away, a phantom whispered in my ear, the shadow of breath on my neck, and roused me. Logan Greer wasn't the only one who haunted me. The rasp of the mysterious voice from beyond the wall crept into my dreams.

I was sailing, riding between the pine boughs. Heavy hoofbeats pounded under me, and I was crying. Oh, I was crying so much, using all of my breath, but nobody was there. I was alone, cold, and covered with ash. The frenzied sound of a horse's braying tore through me, and I woke in the early hours, bathed in a cold sweat.

Start asking questions, Daughter of Sarah.

I had left the books I found in the library in my bedroom at the manor, but I was certain I wouldn't find what I was searching for within their pages.

From the stories I'd been told, the demons had always inhabited the Barrens, but they'd grown restless after my father and his brothers were born. All the residents of Galloway feared demons. I had never heard a conversation about them that wasn't hushed.

People dreaded their voices carrying over the wall. They were afraid of angering the things on the other side. But had voices ever come from that side of the wall before? The side shrouded in the shadows of the pines and covered by a mist so thick you couldn't see?

The voice I heard didn't feel malicious. My magic allowed me to pick up intentions within words. But I couldn't be sure my magic worked the same way on demons.

There had been a time when Galloway existed without a wall. Every dwelling in town had iron gates over the windows, shutters on pulleys and chains. If I were to pull the shutters closed on my own window, they would have creaked with disuse.

The wall had made this town safer—freer despite the structure that moored us within its borders.

Maggie appeared in my room hours after I had awakened, pleased to see me ready to dress. Her approval abated when I picked at my breakfast in the parlor, reluctant to put any food into my churning gut.

James rose to answer the door. I had been too distracted to hear the knock.

"Good morning, my lord." Logan's voice in the foyer was as smooth as black silk.

"Good morning, Lieutenant."

"*Tell him I'm dead,*" I huffed into James's mind.

"I trust you slept well after such a night of merriment," Logan said.

"*I don't have the energy for games today, Harper,*" James returned.

I plunged my fork into the slice of bacon on my plate.

"It was a wonderful evening," James replied. His words were edged with exhaustion, not at all the contented type.

The bacon sat untouched on my plate as I got up to rescue my brother. Logan's jaw tightened as I turned the corner, and I gave him a nod in greeting.

"Good morning, Lieutenant," I said, drawing my black cloak around the shoulders of my simple gray dress. Maggie had told me the color brought out my eyes, but all I hoped was that the muted shade would help me blend into the mist.

"We shall take our leave then, Mr. Ledes." Logan held the door open for me, and I didn't speak as I sailed through it.

I pulled the wool tighter around me in the cool autumn air. The haze was so thick that I could barely see the houses across the street, and I knew Logan wouldn't allow me to walk out of his line of sight.

Our boots echoed on the cobblestones for several moments before I heard him clear his throat.

He stopped, catching my forearm in his hand. "I would like to apologize for last night," he said. His hand rested above the line of my glove, and I marked the way his rough fingers slid over my wrist. "It was rude of me to be so..."

I pulled my hand away. "Bold?"

He took a deep breath, summoning strength. "Yes. It was quite inappropriate for me to act that way. I'm afraid the ale loosened my tongue. But that's no excuse. I'm your guard, and I assure you I will act as such from now on."

I nodded, inclining my chin. The air between us was thicker as we resumed our walk toward the barracks.

When we neared the quadrangle, I spotted Brannon barking orders to a group of men with irons strapped to their backs. They were going into the Barrens, likely to search for the source of the growing mist and the missing weaponry that was angering them. I nodded at my cousin, who nodded back in acknowledgment before strapping on his own weapons.

"What's a cryptid?" I asked Logan as we rounded the path to the armory.

His face paled. "It's a higher demon," he replied, scrubbing his hand through his hair. "They live in the caves at Atsion, and people in the village there spotted them a few times over the last decade. They're amorphous, but the form they usually take is horned and skeletal."

Gooseflesh prickled on my skin. "Uncle Bain said it compelled a sentry into the woods."

"They're known to compel or possess people. They can shapeshift into anything in your mind's eye." Logan nodded. "Anyone who falls under their spell thinks they're following something safe and familiar. If they survive to tell the tale."

I remembered everything the voice had said to me through the wall. Whatever spoke to me was likely not the cryptid—unless it had no desire to possess me. But why could I hear it in my head? He had asked about my brother, almost insinuating that he had been mindspeaking, but I hadn't dared to mention it to James.

My brother had enough on his mind. How did the demon know about James anyway? He and I had never ventured past the wall in our lives. How did the beast even know my name?

My mother's name?

I picked up my paint supplies with trembling hands as Logan hoisted the heavy trunk to his hip.

The mist was so thick I couldn't see the wall before me, and as Logan and I put down the supplies, the barracks melted into the haze. I focused on the sketch outlined in dark umber. Three hands clasped together, forming a bowl. Water dripped from between the fingers as flames crested over interwoven fingers.

Fire magic in the hands of the beholders.

A tribute to my uncles and father and everything this village was built on. Water for the magic of the shoreline. Fire for the magic that burned in my father's blood.

Logan took up his agreed-upon stance, looking at me yet away from me. I dipped my brushes into the paint and let it smooth onto the stucco in broad, sweeping strokes. I became so engrossed in my work that, after a while, I forgot he was there.

Buzzing drifted into the background. All I sensed was the breath in my lungs and the paint rubbing against the smooth stone.

Shadows erupted from my brush while highlights bristled over them, adding dimension to the forms before me.

I was my most authentic self with a brush in my hand. It was the only time I could escape the relentless flood of voices and emotions that poured from others' minds into my own.

My magic understood. It granted me a break, a respite while I was painting.

Logan's voice startled me. "How did you learn?"

My brush wobbled. I had forgotten he was there. "Learn what?"

"To paint," he said. "How did you learn to paint?"

"Oh." I dunked my brush into the terpenoid oil and wiped my hands on a rag. "When I was a child, I begged not to have music lessons with Mira, Ana, and Grace."

His jaw tightened at Mira's name, and I wondered if he had yet received a tea invitation from Aunt Bea.

"My father knew I loved art," I explained. "He hired a tutor. I was saved from music lessons and got to do something I loved instead."

Logan nodded. "Lord Cade seems fair and kind."

Tears rushed to my eyes, but I pushed them away. "My father is the gentlest, kindest man I know."

I picked at my cuticle. He was fair and kind. He was also fiercely devoted to his children and always put them first. James was so like him in this way, which was why my brother couldn't bear to tell our family he didn't want to marry Emelia, let alone any woman. Scandal aside, James would rather wallow in a lifetime of sadness than deny my father any happiness.

Planning this wedding made our father happy for some inexplicable reason.

My brother was a much bigger person than I could ever be.

But James was old enough to remember what it was like to lose my mother. He had been there through my father's breaking.

"Have you started asking the right questions, Daughter of Sarah?"

My body stiffened at the intrusion of the phantom voice, and blood drained from my cheeks. Had it sensed me thinking of my mother?

Logan narrowed his eyes at me. "What's wrong?"

I blinked at the wall, my brush limp in my hand. "I've been hearing whispers by the wall since I was a child. Yesterday, something spoke to me. I just heard it again."

The words tumbled out of me in a panic. I wasn't sure why I confided in him, but it felt right. Logan was insufferable, but he was tasked with protecting me from the other side of the wall, and I was beginning to feel vulnerable.

His attention shifted to the top of the wall as though he was listening. "What did it say?"

"It told me to start asking questions. Did you hear it? I think it's a demon, but it doesn't feel malicious."

He shook his head. "I didn't hear anything. All demons are malicious, Harper." He pointed at the scar above his brow.

I nodded and projected back toward the direction of the demon's voice, remembering my purpose. *"Who are you? Do you know anything about the irons that have been stolen?"*

"I have seen the comings and goings of the irons," the voice said, a cunning lilt to his words. *"I can take you to some of them, if you wish."*

My eyes widened. "He says he knows where some of the irons are," I told Logan. "He offered to lead us to them."

A muscle in Logan's jaw ticked. "It's a trap, Harper. Don't listen to it. Whatever it is."

"I don't sense any lie," I said, shutting my eyes. When a human lied, it washed my magic with a bitter sting. Could I read the same emotions in a demon? Would a demon even have emotions to read?

"It's trying to lure you into the Barrens," Logan said, his voice tense.

"*The arms lieutenant has every right to be distrustful,*" the voice said. "*Especially when the very beast that gave him that scar is in possession of the irons.*"

My blood ran cold.

"*Are you a demon?*" I asked the voice. Logan was beside me now, so close he could see the paintbrush trembling in my hand.

"*I have been called many things, Harper Ledes.*" His voice slithered through me. "*To many, I am a demon, but to Sarah, I was a friend. I am the Alister.*"

I backed away from the wall, fighting the sensation rising in my throat. If Logan hadn't put his hand on my back, I would have fallen.

"What do you want?" I asked out loud, projecting my voice over the wall.

The laughter in my head was soft, sullen. "*I want what you want. I want what your brother wants. I want to break free of this place, but above all, I want to restore what is right.*"

This was the second time the voice had mentioned James. Had he spoken with the demon as well? How could this man—this thing—possibly know what we've been working for?

My breath puffed like a cloud through the cold air. "*Are you trapped within the mist?*"

I could not help but pity the creature, knowing what it felt like to be trapped. The suffocation. The heaviness pressing through the air.

"Harper, my darling girl." His voice dropped to a whisper only I could hear. *"I am the mist."*

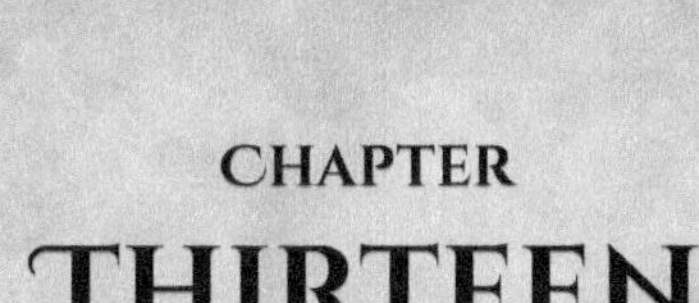

THIRTEEN

Logan and I argued about following the voice for at least ten minutes. He refused to take me into the Barrens, even though it could lead us to the stolen arms.

"The whole point of this is to find the stolen weapons," I said. "This may be our only chance." And as soon as we found those cursed weapons, I could focus on making all the mistakes of the last several days right again. There had to be a way to help James without compromising the secret of his relationship with Ben.

It was too late to get to Delphi, but if I could finish this mission and complete my mural, I could focus on fixing it. There had to be another way, and this voice had offered us our first lead.

Logan ran his fingers through his hair, tugging it at the sides with frustration. "I know what the whole point of this is." He huffed a sigh. "You don't even know half of what's at stake, Harper."

I gaped at him. What else was at stake that he was withholding from me? I opened my mouth to speak, but Logan put up a hand.

His shoulders softened. "I'll discuss it with Jacob," he said. "We'll investigate it a bit more before we decide. Your role is to investigate here, at the barracks, not in the Barrens."

"This is exactly what you wanted," I said. "My magic has led you to the answer you need, and now, you don't want to use the only information we have?"

Logan appeared to be waging an internal war. "I beg you to remember that I was also given an assignment directly from the generals to keep you safe. I will speak to my captain and let Jacob decide."

My muscles relaxed. He hadn't said no, and what he proposed was very fair. I glanced over my shoulder at the mural, satisfied with what I had accomplished, before the voice distracted me. I had mapped out the deep burgundy tones of the shadows in the dips and grooves of the hands, and although I hadn't yet painted the fire, the shape of the flames had started to take form.

Light built from dark tones.

I decided to withhold from Logan what the demon had called himself and that the irons were connected to something that had harmed him. After all, there was clearly something the lieutenant had been withholding from me. I had never heard of an Alister before, but I hadn't received a thorough education on the different types of demons.

The library was my only chance to find the answer.

I turned away from the mural to find Logan studying me, still as stone. In the thickness of the mist, I couldn't see a foot in front of me, but I could tell the sun was shining somewhere above us, illuminating the thick air like a white soup.

I tucked a strand of hair that had unfurled from my braid behind my ear. "How did you get that scar on your eyebrow?"

The Alister had told me the beast that marred him was with the irons, but how could such a demon endure being near them?

The furrow in his brow deepened, highlighting the bluish hue of the scar. "There's a demon in the pines that flies above the canopy of the trees. It has the body of a horse, but it's winged. Not wings like a bird, but like a bat. Scaley and leathery."

I took a breath, my lips parting.

Logan took a step toward me. "The beast is rarely seen, but we all whisper about it. I was new to patrol when I encountered a cluster of lesser demons in a thicket of pines. They were tree imps, small, nasty things with curled horns and sharp talons. I cut my iron into one of them, causing them to scatter. But one had been above me, ready to strike. It leaped out from the tree and latched onto my head. When I cried out in pain, they took it as a signal to attack. A dozen of them swarmed me."

"The imps did that to you?"

He shook his head. "No. Imps are lesser demons. They don't leave scars like this. When they swarmed around me, the winged horse swooped down from the sky. It clamped down on the imp that was attached to my head and threw it off me. Its mouth grazed my forehead, leaving a scar. Only a greater demon leaves a mark like this. I was in the infirmary for a week."

I cocked my head and stepped closer, staring at the ethereal mark on his skin. Logan had his own version of the brand, in a way. Only his had been earned by valor rather than by birthright.

"The winged horse saved you from the imps?"

He shrugged. "I don't know if it saved me. Perhaps it simply wanted to eat one of them. Or me."

My hand drifted to his forehead in awe, sweeping away a lock of Logan's blond hair to get a better look. I couldn't help myself, even though I knew I shouldn't touch him. Our drunken flirtation while spying on the rooftop replayed in my mind, and a thrill flickered through me.

My lips parted as I traced my finger over the ridge of iridescent skin, and a tingle ran up my arm. The silvery hue was familiar somehow. Like I had seen it in a recurring dream or mixed up the color on the palette for some long-forgotten painting.

"It's beautiful, the way it shimmers."

My eyes were drawn to his cold blue stare, and for a moment, I was frozen. The mark on his skin somehow made him even more striking to behold, the shining line cresting over the strong ridge of his brow like lightning forking through a cloudless sky. He swallowed, his jaw set in a firm line, and I let my fingers linger there before pulling away.

I caught a whiff of his cologne, spice and musk clinging to the leather of his uniform. I took a step back and smoothed my frock. "I think I've painted enough for one day."

He nodded, and this time, he had no retort. No smart remark as he helped me gather the jars into the trunk.

Logan walked beside me back to the townhouse, but neither of us spoke. When we reached the front step of the house, he nodded at me, a silent bid of good evening.

Dusk was settling in, casting the house in a pink glow as I slid through the doorway and leaned on the door. It clicked behind me, and I jumped when I noticed my father, reading a book in his favorite chair. I strode into the parlor and plopped onto the sofa.

He smiled at me over the pages—a Cade Ledes type of smile, so subtle, one saw it mainly in the curve of his cheek—before placing his bookmark and closing the pages. "There you are, Harp. I've seen so little of you these past few days. I was beginning to think you'd left town."

I laughed, wishing that he was correct. "Did you hear about the mural I was commissioned on at the barracks?"

"Hear about it?" My father chuckled as he shook his head. "Uncle Bain was furious. Aaron and I both thought he was overreacting, of course. Your uncle almost stomped down there this morning and demanded that you stop before we talked some sense into him."

I bit my lip, not at all surprised by Bain's reaction. "I'm painting a trio of hands holding flames. It's to honor the magic of the triplet lords."

"If Bain learns you're painting the mural in his honor, his opinion on the matter might soften," he said, rising from his seat to kiss my head. "Thank you, honey. That's such a beautiful gift to my brothers and me."

I wrung my hands. He was in an unusually good mood. I considered asking him the question that had been weighing down my mind like an overwrought rag. If I didn't ask him now, I would regret it for the rest of my life. So much had been left unanswered in the past few days, and I was beginning to think I had imagined my grand scheme to save my father and my brother.

"Father, can I ask you something?"

His soft, amber-brown gaze connected with mine, edged with concern. "Of course, Harp. You can ask me anything."

"If I decided to move to Delphi, would you come with me?"

His brow furrowed. "Is that what you want? You never mentioned it to me before. Why would you want to leave Galloway?"

"All the best art schools are in Delphi, and James wants to study literature. What if he applied to the university? What if I could study at the conservatory? I already prepared a portfolio. I could paint the sky and know how to capture the blues and the light filtering through the clouds. It's always been my dream." My words were coming out faster than I desired. I took a steadying breath. "There's nothing for us here. Nothing for me. Nothing for you. There has to be more than this. There has to be..."

My words got stuck in my throat.

What was I going to say next? *Freedom? Something better than being choked by the wall around this town?*

My thoughts halted when pain flashed in his eyes. "I never knew you wanted to leave, Pumpkin. I wish you had told me."

Pumpkin. My eyes widened. He hadn't called me that in years. "I just..." I stammered, unsure of which direction to take.

If Jacob and Logan hadn't interrupted my plans, I wouldn't have had to ask him this. He would have followed us.

He would have. All three of us would have been free.

I bit my lip and watched my father's face twist with confusion. Didn't he want to be free of the weight of this place? Didn't he feel the same way I did, living within the walls of this town and suffocated by mist? I pushed back a wave of shame when I considered that perhaps he had never felt that way at all.

I sighed. "I just think there's something better for us outside of Galloway. All of us."

He placed a steady hand on my shoulder, and my heart began to calm. "I would follow you to the ends of this realm, Harper. You're my daughter. My world. If you want to move to Delphi, we can consider it after the wedding. But I have my reservations. Our family is here. My brothers are here. And James has so much to look forward to. Can you imagine how it would feel to have children running around here again? I might become a grandfather soon."

My shoulders sank. He had become so invested in this union between James and Emelia. Getting us out of here would be next to impossible now, and if the union led to grandchildren...

"Where's James?" I asked.

"He should be home any moment. The Herns invited him to tea this afternoon."

"How is the wedding planning coming along?" Honestly, I didn't want to know, and I regretted the question before I was even finished asking it.

My father picked up his book again, a gleam lighting in his eyes. "I must admit, it's very enjoyable. Bess is so creative. She's made most of the decisions. I admit I'm mostly along for the ride, but I'm quite enjoying the ride."

I sighed. Bess Hern certainly seemed like a burst of positive energy, and Emelia was quite pleasant, too. If James had to be forced to marry someone he didn't love or feel attracted to, at least they were good people. I knew of other marital arrangements in which there was an understanding of the intention. Emelia seemed like the kind of woman who would be understanding and discreet.

The door creaked open, and a moment later, James joined us in the parlor, his face etched with forced smile lines. After receiving a rather generic update on teatime, our father excused himself to freshen up before dinner.

James sank into the couch cushion beside me, and I pulled out my book.

I pretended to read as I projected into his mind. *"How did it really go?"*

There were some things too private to say aloud. *"Oddly, I feel guilt both to Benjamin and to Emelia now. I can never love her, not in the way she deserves. She's a delightful woman. I can foresee us developing a friendship...in time."*

I sighed, turning the pages as James rested his head in his hands. There would never be a good time to ask my brother the question I needed to ask him.

"James, have you ever heard voices coming from the wall?" I asked, feigning nonchalance as I paged through the book.

He jolted out of his seat. Anyone who might have been watching us would have thought I pinched him. *"No, have you?"*

I closed my book, along with my eyes, and rested my head on the sofa back. *"Something spoke to me from beyond the wall today and yesterday. It was a male voice, but he told me he wasn't mindspeaking. Just speaking."*

When I opened my eyes, James looked like he was going to vomit. *"Harper, I don't want you going near the wall again. A demon was projecting into your mind. I'll deal with the police chief and the arms lieutenant tomorrow. This insane charade can't continue."*

I tapped my fingers on the sofa arm. *"Whatever spoke to me said he knew Mother—said he was friends with her."*

The color washed from his face. *"Harper. That's not possible."*

"The demon is an Alister. I'm not sure what that is. He alluded to the possibility that you would be able to hear him, too."

"I don't know much about the demon species." He shook his head. *"But I've never heard a voice from the wall, Harper."*

"Maybe you should come with me tomorrow," I suggested. *"He was very mysterious. Perhaps he would give you more information."*

He nodded. *"Of course, I'll go with you."*

"There's something else you need to know," I said, wincing. *"Logan knows about my conversation with the demon. By morning, so will Jacob."*

James rubbed his temples for a full minute before he got up from his seat and poured himself a dram of bourbon from one of our father's decanters.

"Make mine a double," I said aloud.

CHAPTER

FOURTEEN

Maggie bustled into my room at the usual time the following morning. The previous night's whiskey drinking had gone on a bit longer than I had anticipated, and by midnight, James and my conversation had evolved from worry into fits of giggles.

Absurd ruminations about the voice beyond the wall were the last thing we had spoken about before bed. James suggested the voice could have been the product of some psychotic break I was having. I mused that perhaps years of inhaling terpenoid fumes had finally gotten to me.

"Perhaps the voice was Bain in disguise," James had suggested between fits of laughter.

The thought of Uncle Bain crouching behind the wall, his mouth pressed to the stones while lurking under a cape, sent me over the edge, and I had laughed so hard I thought I would bruise my ribs.

Maggie exhaled a reproachful huff as she untied my nightgowns, and I wondered if she could sense the remnants of alcohol clinging to my skin.

My maid cocked her head with interest as she tied up the stays of my undergarments. "Don't you think it's curious, my lady? The lieutenant's scar being so like your own?"

I released a forced breath from her firm tug on the laces. "Excuse me?" Now I was truly hearing things. "I have no such scar."

Maggie bunched her brow. "You surely do, right over the middle of your spine."

I spun in a feeble attempt to contort my body to see the proof that she was wrong. "You must be hallucinating."

Maggie tutted. "I surely am not. Curious. I thought you knew about it, but come to think of it, how would you have ever seen that part of your skin before?" She snapped her fingers and grabbed my hand mirror. "Turn your back to the vanity glass and hold this."

I did as she suggested and positioned my bare back to the mirror, peering into the hand mirror from a position over my shoulder. Sure enough, the peachy tone of my skin was disrupted in a jagged line almost as wide as my hand.

Silver and catching the light with the same sheen as Logan Greer's eyebrow.

I stared at it, dumbfounded, until the sound of the front door sprang Maggie into motion. "Forgive me! Here I am dilly-dallying with a mirror, and you're barely dressed before breakfast."

My limbs were frozen, paralyzed by shock, as she hastily tied me into my dress. I continued to stare at the place on my back through the mirror, even though the skin was covered with fabric.

How long had that scar been there? How could I have never noticed it before?

Logan and James exchanged pleasantries as Maggie and I

descended the stairs. She bustled past me, asking for an extra moment to make me a plate. I simply shook my head. We didn't have time for biscuits, and the blow of seeing the scar left a pit in my stomach I was too nervous to fill with food.

"Don't lose sight of our task," Logan said in sharp tones as he walked through our front gate. His boots crunched over the cobblestones, splashing through the drizzle.

I stared at his scar as he held the gate open for me.

Eeriest blue. Mysterious. Inflicted by a demon so powerful that he was in the hospital for a week.

I was going to be sick.

"Do you think we can discover who the source of this voice is today?" James asked.

Logan nodded curtly. "I want to understand what this voice is, too, but more importantly, we need to find out who's stealing the weapons."

With every step, the skin along my spine stung, threatening to burn a hole straight through the fabric of my dress. I pushed down the sense of foreboding. Surely, I would remember getting an injury like that. *Wouldn't I?*

"What were its exact words again, Harper?" James said.

"The voice said he could lead me to who was stealing the arms," I said, trying to compose myself. "Maybe the thief lives within the pines."

What if this voice was the voice of a greater demon? What if *he* was the one who had given me the scar? Did this thing have something to do with my mother's death?

Logan shivered in the rain, pulling his cloak around him. "Perhaps the irons are being kept in one of the dwellings in the Barrens."

Only a few brave souls had set up homesteads in the pines outside of the towns, and their homes were heavily warded. There was only one such house I knew of outside of the walls.

The house where I had been born. Where all the Ledes cousins had been born.

The house where Raina had once dwelled.

"Maybe the thief is a demon," James said, his voice dropping low.

"You may be correct." Logan nodded to my brother. "I fear your presence near the wall will raise some suspicion of our investigation, my lord."

I rolled my eyes at Logan's formality. He treated my brother with the respect due to a lord or lady. Surely it was because James was much more noble in his mannerisms.

Logan was correct to assume James would cause a stir, though. When we arrived at the wall, heads snapped to attention at the presence of Cade's son in the barracks. Father didn't involve himself with the militia, preferring the more mundane tasks of law and record keeping for Galloway.

To have both of Cade's children in the barracks at the same time was highly unusual.

"I haven't visited the barracks in years," James said, scanning the quadrangle with interest. "Don't worry. I'll stick to the story. I'm here to admire my sister's progress on the mural. That's all. I won't stay long."

Jacob Miller made his way out of the police building and strode toward us. At the sight of James at my side, his spine stiffened.

"Good morning, my lord," he said, nodding to James. "I trust you've learned what happened yesterday."

James shot Jacob a distrustful glare. "I disapproved of Harper coming here in the first place, Captain Miller. I was distraught when I heard something was communicating with her."

"I assure you, Master Ledes," Jacob said. "Your sister will be well protected here."

"The voice told me that my brother would be able to hear him," I told Jacob.

He paled. Surely, Logan had not left out that part.

I nodded at James. "We've come to test out the theory."

James's gaze swept the quadrangle, assuring we were out of earshot. "My sister tells me you can mindspeak, Captain." His voice was razor sharp.

Jacob's gaze shot to mine, and something like guilt washed over him. Perhaps he was starting to regret the implications of blackmailing a Ledes.

"She's right," Jacob said, clearing his throat. "I'm originally from York. Harper mentioned some of your family is from there, too." He didn't dare mention our mother's name to James. "It's a common gift there, just as elemental magic is common here in Jersey."

James nodded, satisfied with the answer. Fire magic was unique to the Barrens. In shore isle towns, including the areas just beyond the wall, water magic was much more common, but I had never traveled past the wall to watch the water wielders sail their boats in Brigantine or Margate.

James tucked his hands in his pockets. "Let's see the mural, Harper."

My brother's expression softened as my rendering of the enormous hands cradling flame materialized through the mist. He looked back and forth between the wall and me, at a loss for words.

"It's for the lords," I said. "Magic as fire in the hands of the beholder. A tribute to their protection of the pines."

"Harper," James said, his voice filled with awe. "It's beautiful. Have they seen it yet?"

"No." I scoffed. "Are you kidding? It's not done. You can't see it through the mist unless you get close. I'll bring them here when I'm finished."

"This is also my first time seeing it," Jacob admitted. "Logan said it was spectacular, but his description didn't capture its beauty."

I glanced at Logan, and he immobilized me with his stare. "It's indescribable," he said.

His eyes did not stray to the mural.

I cleared my throat and turned to the wall, the three men trailing behind. Unwelcome visions flashed into my mind. I attempted to push away the memory of hiding with Logan in the passage, but the patch of skin on my back heated as I replayed the sound of his heart beating through his uniform. How good he had smelled. How his fingers had grazed the skin on my wrist.

"*The arms lieutenant is staring at you like you're a piece of meat,*" James snarled into my mind.

"*Mind your own business,*" I scolded. "*And be careful what you say. The captain may be able to hear us.*"

James turned to Jacob, who had schooled his expression into a cool mask. "*Well, Captain, can you?*"

Jacob's gaze shot up to the sky. A muscle in his jaw twitched before he said, "*I can.*"

Waves of remorse washed over me, emanating from his mind. Yes, Jacob must have begun to feel guilty about his approach to this mission. If he had asked me for help, I likely would have obliged, and it wouldn't have impacted my card games. By now, James and I would have had enough money to move into our new flat in Delphi.

I shook my head. "I'm going to call for the voice—erm—the demon."

But nothing seemed demonic about the voice I had heard on the other side of that wall. If I were to be honest, speaking to it—whatever it was—felt natural. Like I was chatting with James, mind to mind.

Somehow, the intentions of the demon felt right. Trustworthy. Thinking about it unnerved me.

"Friend? Alister, are you there?"

James stiffened at my words. He and Jacob exchanged a worried look. I had called the demon a friend, but it didn't feel wrong. If he had been a friend of our mother, how could he not be a friend of mine?

"Harper Ledes. You have returned," the demon crooned.

I motioned to James, gesturing toward the wall, but he stared back at me with confusion.

"I have been thinking about what you said," I continued. *"I would like to learn more about you. Can you tell me what it means to be an Alister?"*

I gestured again at the wall, but James shook his head. "I hear you, but I don't hear what you're speaking to," he said aloud.

The voice chuckled, low and silky, through my mind. *"Harper, you aren't alone."*

My heart raced, anxiety surging through my blood. *"I've brought my brother, James, with me. Lieutenant Greer and Captain Miller accompany us. I asked James about the voices through the wall. He cannot hear you. But I can. I've heard whispers for a long time."*

I held out my hands to James. Maybe I truly was losing my mind? "You really can't hear him?"

James shook his head.

I turned to Jacob, grabbing his hand. "Can you?"

Jacob stared at the wall like he had seen a ghost. "I'm sorry, Harper."

A sigh rumbled through my mind, and I could almost hear the vibration through the being's lungs. *"Your poor brother. He has many secrets."*

My racing heart stalled. How could this thing know about James and Benjamin? Was there anything he didn't know? He said he was the mist itself. Was he present everywhere the mist was present? How could the mist enter the wards of the wall?

"How much do you see?" I asked. My voice trembled despite the internalization of my words. *"How much do you know?"*

His voice was heavy when he said, *"I am the mist, Harper Ledes. I am the Alister. I see everything I touch."*

CHAPTER

FIFTEEN

I didn't have energy to paint that day. What I needed more than anything was time in the library. Logan, much to my surprise, had agreed to take a break from our time at the wall. Despite my protest, he insisted on escorting me to the manor. James decided to go home, and in my peripheral vision, my brother rubbed his temples all the way to the edge of the quadrangle.

Logan was uncharacteristically quiet as we strode up the walkway to the manor, and I hoped he was too lost in his thoughts to notice I was stealing glances at his scar. If there was any place in Galloway where I could find some answers, it was the manor library.

The vast collection of books was housed on the second floor, and because it took up so much space, there wasn't much else on that level of the manor. I had always thought it strange that the library was empty most of the time I visited it as a child, but I had sometimes found my father there, no doubt researching some law or village history.

"I thought you said we should be focusing on the

114

robberies," I said, keeping pace with Logan. The man was beginning to feel like my overgrown, surly shadow. "Why did you agree to come here?"

"Your link to this demon and the robberies are intertwined," he said, the muscles in his jaw tensing. "I'm your personal guard. If you're going to the library, that's where I'm most needed. We need to learn more about the demon before we trust any information it gives us."

I nodded. "I don't anticipate being attacked by a dictionary, but I appreciate your diligence."

The library was one of my favorite places, a sanctuary where I could escape Mira and hide from our lessons, nestled in the depths of a rich leather chair with a sketchbook and some charcoal. I would spend hours in my favorite corner, surrounded by the smell of musty parchment, light reflecting through the jewel-toned stained glass, making me forget it was dreary on the other side.

Logan followed me as I paced up and down the aisles of books, running my fingers along the spines, wishing they would speak back to me.

"What are you looking for?" Logan asked, his hands in his pockets.

I bit my lip. "A glossary of sorts, something that will explain the Alister. I don't know why something about him feels so familiar to me. Perhaps I read about a demon made of mist somewhere over the years."

I had decided to trust Logan with the name of the demon, even though the warning bells continued to chime in the back of my head. A strange part of me wanted to keep the Alister to myself.

"Listen, Harper," Logan began, fidgeting with the

leather cuff of his uniform. "I know you don't want to discuss your mother."

I held up my hand, stifling his words. "It's not that I don't *want* to talk about her. I'm not *supposed* to talk about her. It's forbidden."

"But *why* is it forbidden?" His voice was low, muted by the stacks of pages surrounding us. "I understand she died tragically, but why can't you speak of her? We've been communicating with a creature in the pines who claims he knew her, but we can't ask anyone about it."

I took a steadying breath. Logan said *we* as if we were a team. As if he would try to figure this whole thing out with me. What he said was true. I knew nothing about my mother except that her name was Sarah. James and I had always assumed she could mindspeak and we had inherited that magic from her, but I had never dared to ask my father about it.

Mindspeaking wasn't considered a favorable magical gift. Even if she did possess that kind of magic, it's possible she had never shared it with anyone.

There was nothing that belonged to Sarah Ledes in our townhome—not a book, not a diary, not even an old trinket or piece of jewelry. I knew this because, as a child, I would search for things. Every time I opened a box that had been untouched for a while or a book with a creaky spine, I hoped to find a little piece of her within it.

But all I ever found was dusty emptiness.

James was hesitant to speak about her, even in my mind. He had been young when she died, but I knew he remembered small things about her, some things that were too heartbreaking even to mention. Her portrait in the manor dining room was the only likeness I'd ever seen of her. Sometimes, when I squinted into the mirror and brushed my hair, I would pretend I was looking into her gray eyes instead of my own.

"I honestly don't know how she died," I said, picking at the hem of my sleeve. "But I know it was related to my birth, and I know the midwife was involved somehow. Even though I was never able to speak of it, there was always this understanding. My mother's death must have been tied to magic."

Realization flashed in Logan's eyes, and he nodded. Death tied to magic was not something to take lightly, and most believed speaking of it was akin to speaking a curse. Legends claimed that anyone who spoke of death by magic would be killed by magic themselves. I thought back to all the times Maggie had touched her lips and bowed her head when she had alluded to my mother in the past, fearful that uttering her name would conjure her demise. Maggie believed she herself would be ripped right out of this realm by the same force that took Sarah Ledes.

"So, nobody in your family speaks of her at all?"

I tapped my fingers along the spines of the books. "Well, some are more comfortable than others."

Indeed, one person had fought to keep that portrait hanging in the dining room. *Aunt Patrice.*

I pulled a few hefty tomes from the shelves and cracked them open at a table. The first book was a religious text focused on repelling demons, not on identifying them. The second was a lengthy historical account of an early settler in the pines, describing how the first villagers used iron stakes to repel demons. I knew it was wishful thinking, but I hoped to at least get a glimmer of information about wounds inflicted by higher demons.

But there were no mentions of a mist or the Alister.

Or scars.

I thumbed through a book that recounted the experiences of the early villagers. Did they realize they were building their homes in a thin space so close to another realm? Did they feel that connection to the fire realm and decide to take the risk? I wished with all my might that my family had never settled in this place, that they would have traveled east to the sea and crossed the bay to the isles. How different would my life be if my ancestors had kept walking?

"Did anyone in your family ever speak of the time before the mist thickened?" I asked Logan. He was seated in a leather chair, his broad shoulders lounging against the back as he propped a book on his crossed leg.

His brow furrowed. "My parents spoke of it vaguely, but I never asked much about it. I was a baby when the mist thickened. It was always a part of my life growing up. I can't remember a time it wasn't here."

"The triplet lords were born fifty-five years ago, angering the Master of the Fire Realm," I said. "This mist began to thicken twenty-one years ago, around the time my mother died. Perhaps her death disrupted the thin space the same way my father's birth did?"

Logan's brow furrowed. "Did your mother also have magic?"

I squeezed my eyes shut. "James was young when she died, but he remembers communicating with her in a very close way. As he got older and came into his power, well after her death, he realized some of their conversations could have been mindspeaking. We don't know if she had magic, but we suspect she did."

"Mindspeaking isn't a common gift in this area," Logan said.

No, it certainly wasn't. I didn't know much about magic, but I knew mindspeaking wasn't considered a gift. Many people were understandably disconcerted by the idea of someone slipping into their private thoughts.

It was taboo to have mindspeaking abilities, so much so that many kept it hidden. I shivered, wondering if there were more mindspeakers in Galloway after all.

"The Alister said he is the mist," I said, scanning through the book. "The mist came when my mother died, and he says he knew my mother."

"Do you think the Alister had something to do with your mother's death?" His words were hushed, swallowed by the darkness of the stacks.

My skin iced over. There was a possibility the demon had something to do with her death, but without knowing the specifics of how she died, how were we to figure it out?

"I also don't understand why the mist can slip past the wards of the wall and cover this town," I said.

Logan's voice lowered into a whisper so soft I could barely hear it. "Do you think the Alister knows..." He trailed off, hesitant. "The midwife?"

I was confident I could get Aunt Pat to share information about my mother, but it seemed unlikely she would be willing to discuss Raina. What had it been like for her, knowing the woman who helped bring all five of her children into this world was responsible for murdering her sister-in-law—her best friend?

"I don't know."

The little house where Raina had lived, the birthplace of all twelve Ledes cousins, lay outside the wall. When the wall was built after the mist appeared, my father ensured the house remained outside its protective barrier, condemning the burned ruins to exile. I often wondered whether the place was still intact or if the demons and the pines had taken it over.

"Let's do as much research as possible," I said. "Maybe we'll find some answers, and I won't need to ask the Alister about it."

I was quite certain the demon would answer any question I asked with a vague response anyway. The mist served its purpose in covering truths in a shroud.

When my eyes began to burn an hour later, I slammed my book shut with a definitive *clunk*. I had found several mentions of the demons, mostly in historical texts, but nothing about the mist or how it might be linked to one of them.

Logan jumped to his feet, his bleary eyes darting to the clock on the wall. "It's late, my lady. I'll walk you home before Lord Cade starts to worry."

I nodded and stood, smoothing my dress. Logan had spent far too many hours guarding me, and for what? What danger was I subjected to in this library besides a paper cut? Logan must have been dreadfully bored, and I knew he had better things to do with his time. I wondered what the arms lieutenant went home to at the end of his day.

Was there someone there? A family member? A woman to warm his bed? I pictured him complaining about me, the insufferable youngest Ledes cousin, as he pulled off his boots and loosened the straps of his leathers. Lamenting after a long day, while someone listened to his stories with a sympathetic ear. The thought made me irrationally sick, and I hated myself for it.

"May I ask you something?" I said. "You mentioned there was much more at stake for you than stolen irons."

Logan pressed his lips into a thin line, and I let my magic wash over him just enough to know that he was deliberating whether he should share this information with me.

He cleared his throat. "I was up for a promotion. Right before the irons were stolen, I was told of the generals' intention to advance my rank from arms lieutenant to infantry captain."

I raised my brows at him. He had already alluded to his promotion. "You mentioned this before. So, when Paxton assigned you to be my guard..."

"The generals are testing me," he said. "But asking me to be your guard was a vote of confidence. I can't be promoted unless we find the arms."

"I see." It made sense that Logan would want to help me figure out the demons. If we understood the messages the Alister gave us—if he kept me safe in the process—it could lead him straight to a promotion.

"There's more," he said. "My brother Michael is stationed in the branch of the infantry that's posted at the shore. If I get promoted to captain, he's next in line to take my place as arms lieutenant. The colonies are restless. Some even talk of a revolution."

I nodded. Even I had heard the rumors and seen the propaganda. Father had mentioned there were more and more boats off the coast these days, and some townsfolk had started to mutter angrily about the king who ruled from across the sea.

Logan pulled on his cloak. "Michael will be safer within the walls."

A lump of remorse rose in my throat, and I opened my mouth to speak, only to be silenced by Logan's voice.

"I fear Lord Cade will be worried for your long absence. I'll walk you home."

I glanced at the clock on the mantel. We had been in the library for hours, yet we had gained no useful information. By now, Maggie would have left my supper in my room.

"My father won't worry about me on a Wednesday evening. He plays cards at the manor with his brothers once a week. James is having dinner at the Hern house. Maggie is probably already retired for the night."

Logan's lips twitched into a smile, and that maddening dimple on his left cheek deepened. "Then allow me to take you out for a drink. It's a nice night to visit the tavern."

I ignored how my stomach dipped when he smiled at me, and I forced my gaze to the floor as I pulled on my cloak. "That would be fine. Besides, I'm famished."

The tavern. Why hadn't I thought about it before? So, Logan and I set out on the path to the tavern, to the very place I knew we would find Aunt Patrice on a Wednesday night.

CHAPTER

SIXTEEN

Perry was chatting with a gorgeous blond woman in an emerald dress when Logan and I entered the tavern. It was busy in the main room for a Wednesday night. Perry's head tilted up in response to the cool air wafting through the door, an automatic nod of greeting.

When he realized his youngest cousin was striding toward him, his smile broadened, but it melted away when he spied the arms lieutenant at my side.

He whispered something in the blond woman's ear that made her giggle before he turned to us. "Harper, I was beginning to think you'd found a better tavern to patronize."

My eyes rolled. There wasn't another tavern in Galloway, nor was there any other place where I could play my role as a card shark. "I've been busy, cousin. I was commissioned to paint a mural on the barracks wall. Surely, you've heard. The whole family seems to have an opinion about it."

Perry's smirk was feral as he raked his gaze over Logan. "I

123

heard my father wanted to gut the officers who commissioned your talents. Is this one of them?"

Logan paled a bit before clearing his throat. "Yes, my lord. Lieutenant Greer, at your service. Lord Bain may gut me if he wishes, but I promised the generals I would keep your cousin safe. I take my oaths seriously, I assure you."

Perry crossed his arms. "Do you take your oaths so seriously, Lieutenant, that my cousin can't have a pint of ale alone?"

My cheeks heated, and I hated myself for it. I knew what it seemed like, coming here with him tonight. He had asked me for a drink after a long day of work.

I should have said no. Logan Greer was not my friend.

But he had proven to be an ally, given his willingness to help me research the Alister.

None of that changed the fact that Logan had blackmailed me and threatened this very tavern. I began to regret agreeing to a drink.

"Lieutenant Greer is determined to be my shadow," I said. "Unfortunately. Maybe I should encourage my uncle to do his gutting after all."

Logan's eyes narrowed on me. "If you'd like me to take leave, my lady, I will." He turned to Perry. "What's the best exit for the barracks? Should I use the front door or the stairs to the cellar?"

Perry's jaw ticked, and his eyes narrowed. "The cellar stairs lead to nothing but storage."

Logan scoffed at that. "Of course, they do."

Perry rolled up his sleeves, his branded numeral *9* twitching over the muscles of his forearms. Uncle Bain's triplet sons hadn't inherited his upright views. Perry, Axel, and Rand were the jokesters of the family, the party boys, the ones dismissed with a wave of the hand. But Perry did inherit his father's hot temper.

Anger flared from my cousin and washed over my magic, searing my senses.

Perry opened his mouth to speak, probably to suggest to Logan which exit to take, when a soft voice interrupted him.

"Lieutenant Greer, what a pleasure to see you."

Logan stiffened and bowed to Perry's mother. "Lady Ledes, the pleasure is mine."

"Please call me Patrice," she said, her words loose with the effects of the wine sloshing in her glass. The smile lines around her eyes deepened as she winked at me.

I breathed a sigh of relief, and Perry's shoulders relaxed in his mother's presence. Aunt Pat allowed her sons to dote on her at the tavern on Wednesday nights, the one night of the week when Uncle Bain didn't worry about the tavern or whether his wife visited his rebellious sons there.

On more than one occasion, Aunt Pat had seen me slip down those cellar stairs, but she had never said anything about it. I had returned the favor by never mentioning to any of the lords of Galloway how tipsy she liked to get on my uncle's poker nights.

A hollow ache panged through me. Had she and my mother liked to have drinks together on Wednesday nights before my mother died?

Patrice reached up to pat Perry on the cheek. "Bring out one of your best bottles for us, Peridot."

I bit my lip at her use of his childhood nickname. Perry would definitely kick us out if I dared to laugh at him. He shot me a warning glare before tossing the bar rag over his shoulder and stalking through the crowd to the wine rack.

Aunt Pat took Logan's arm and guided him to the booth

in the corner where she preferred to sit, her wavy brown hair cascading behind her, unbound in her effort to relax and blend into the crowd. Despite her casual dress, people whispered as she passed, and a few bowed their heads in respectful greeting to the Lady of Galloway.

As an unspoken rule, nobody bothered Lady Patrice when she sat in the empty booth in the corner, but she gestured for us to join her. Usually, she brought a book with her as a companion, and tonight was no exception. Based on the gilded hearts on the cover and the silhouettes of a man and woman in embrace, it was likely one of the romances she favored.

"Oh, Logan, I was so glad to sit beside you at the engagement party." She turned to me. "Mira was talking poor Logan's ear off, and I did my best to be a buffer."

I tried not to replay the image of Mira patting Logan's forearm as she laughed, twirling her curly brown hair around a blood-red painted fingernail.

I sighed, wishing Perry would hurry back with my wine. "Mira loves the sound of her voice."

Perry appeared with an uncorked bottle that he plopped down on the table, followed by three glasses. He sneered at Logan as he walked away, looking for the pretty patron we had distracted him from, no doubt.

"I think Mira wants the next engagement party to be in her honor," Aunt Pat said.

I ignored the lump in my throat.

My aunt raised her glass. "The party was brilliant, though. To James and Emelia."

I half-heartedly lifted my glass to meet hers and caught Logan studying my face from the corner of my eye.

My brow furrowed under the concentration it took not

to meet his gaze. If I was ever going to get information from Aunt Pat, now was the time.

The door swung open at the entrance, and a swirl of mist trailed in behind a party of companions.

I shivered. "The mist has been getting thicker."

Aunt Patrice gazed out the window, frowning. "Uncle Bain is very worried about it."

"Why would the mist worry him?" Logan asked, leaning back in his chair.

"Before Bain and his brothers were born, the Barrens were a different place. Fires plagued our village until the space between realms thickened. The Devil was trapped within the fire realm when the triplets were born. Bain believes the mist is a foreboding harbinger of change."

"So, you believe the stories?" I asked, sipping my wine.

Aunt Pat's eyes widened. "Of course I do. Triplet lords aren't born with fire-wielding magic every day, Harper. It was their power, tied to the magic of the number three, that sealed the realm. I have family members who remember the days of the fires."

"I still don't understand what the fires have to do with the mist," Logan said, leaning on his elbows.

"The mist has been known to thicken in the presence of demons. The demons were trapped in this realm when the triplet lords were born. Bain believes the mist thickens as the demons grow increasingly restless. There's been an increase in sightings near the wall."

I trembled and refilled my glass, hoping the wine would warm my blood. "Nothing better to distract from thickening mist than a merry party. My father seems quite happy to be planning a wedding," I said. "James and I mused if he was even half as happy to plan his own."

Aunt Pat let out a wistful laugh and took another deep sip of the crimson wine in her glass. "I don't recall him being nearly as enthusiastic about choosing table linens when it was his wedding."

I allowed myself into the outskirts of Patrice's mind, just for a moment. Sadness, sodden with a layer of grief, overcame me like a bird watching windswept boughs through a gilded cage. She was thinking of my mother, the lacy gloves she'd worn with her wedding dress, and what it was like to stand beside her as maid of honor.

Not just a friend. A sister. I pulled away, magic threatening to suck air from my lungs with the intensity of her sorrow.

I had always pictured their friendship in terms of being married into the family. Had they been friends even before they were ladies of the Ledes family?

"Did you know her before they got married?" I let my words glide into a reverent whisper, barely audible over the chatter and clinking glasses in the tavern.

Logan glanced down at the table, feigning interest in the wood grain for a moment before excusing himself to fetch an ale from the bar. He mumbled something about not liking wine before leaving us alone at the table.

Death by magic was tied to a curse. Anyone who mentioned it was at risk of being pulled into the curse itself. But I was already linked to my mother's death. I had been there. Perhaps I was already cursed with mindspeaking.

Or speaking to demons, which seemed to be unique to me somehow.

Aunt Pat sighed into her wine glass, and tears welled in her eyes, glittering in the dim light.

When Logan arrived at the bar, she said, "Your mother

and I grew up next door to each other. Did you know that? Just west of the manor." Her eyes darted to the surrounding tables. "I was the one who introduced her to Cade."

I shook my head, my pulse quickening. We were *talking about her*. Not with meaningful insinuation or pointed nods of the head, but freely, with words aloud.

I swallowed hard.

Sarah and Patrice had been bonded long before they married into this family, and the fact that I was only learning this now felt unfair and wrong. It was an insult to my mother. I had no idea how she had met my father. Patrice had been her maid of honor. How much of my aunt had died that day? How much of her continued to fade away when she couldn't even say her friend's name freely?

I knew then why her sadness had been so crippling. She had never been allowed to grieve. Every memory was trapped within her, eating her alive.

I swallowed a wave of nausea. "I don't know anything about her."

We had come here tonight to learn about Sarah Lede's death, but within Aunt Pat's misty eyes, I was struck by how much I didn't know about my own mother's life.

"We were pregnant together, you know," she said. "Twice. Samuel was born a week before James. My triplets arrived just before you did, Harper."

I had known that part. Perry, Axel, and Rand always let me be part of their games and pranks growing up, and we always celebrated our birthdays together. *Nine, ten, eleven, and twelve.*

I glanced down at my unbranded forearm.

Patrice's eyes darkened as though sensing my shame. "I always thought the brands were ridiculous. It means nothing, Harper. You're the twelfth and final Ledes cousin. Brand or no brand."

I dared not bring up the midwife, but I needed to ask. "Why do you think I wasn't branded?"

My aunt bit her lip and lowered her voice. "I don't know what happened that day. There was only one thing we knew for sure. There could never be a thirteenth Ledes child. The brands were painted on our children's skin with magic as a promise. As proof that the thirteenth child would never be born."

A chill ran over me as the mist swirled on the other side of the windowpane. That promise had never been inked onto my flesh.

"Because of what the mystic said the night my father and his brothers were born," I said. "Do you believe it's true?"

Patrice nodded, the flame from the wall sconces flickering in the shadows of her amber eyes.

"Bain and Aaron had sworn to Cade that we wouldn't have any more children. He and—" Her lip quaked before she uttered her name. "—Sarah only had James at that time. Bain and I had tried to be careful. Not careful enough. When we found out Sarah and I were both expecting...we were terrified we might have multiples. We were dangerously close to thirteen."

Gooseflesh prickled my skin, but Aunt Pat's shoulders relaxed, as if saying Sarah's name had released a small part of the anguish locked inside her.

My mouth went dry. "I can't imagine. You must have been so stressed."

She nodded. "It was terrible."

They had come so close to fulfilling the Devil's promise. A vow he'd made the night the triplet lords were born. "She must have been relieved when she realized she was carrying a single baby."

Patrice nodded. "There were ways to tell how many babies were growing, but it wasn't until closer to the end that the *midwife* could tell." She said the word midwife like it was the foulest expletive, something disgusting and wicked. "I was terrified to learn I was carrying triplets, but Sarah was relieved to have only one. We knew then that we could have no more accidents. You were due to be born before the triplets, but they were born early. You came a few weeks later."

And then Sarah was gone, and Raina had fled.

Nobody knew for sure why she had run, but my mother hadn't survived. Had Raina killed my mother to ensure the Devil's promise would never come true? Was that what the Alister was trying to tell me? I couldn't bring myself to ask, but the dark look in Aunt Pat's eyes matched the dread in my heart. I took a deep sip from my glass, quenching my dry throat.

My birth was the end of so many things. The end of a promise made by the Devil. The end of my mother's life.

But it was the beginning of the mist—the beginning of the wall.

Aunt Pat must have read the hurt in my eyes because she grabbed my hand. My aunt's face was as pale as the mist-shrouded sky. "Harper, I need to tell you something."

I blinked. "Okay."

Despite all I had learned in the last few days, a part of me didn't want to know what my aunt was about to say.

"Before Sarah knew she was expecting one baby, I think the stress overwhelmed her. She wasn't herself toward the end. Every night, she would take long walks alone near the edge of town. This was before the wall was built, but the mist had just appeared."

My heart began to hammer, sending lightning bolts through my veins. The hum of the wall drummed through me, so close, despite being safely within the tavern's walls.

I steadied my breath enough for a few words to stumble out. "Did you walk with her?"

Patrice shook her head. "She insisted that she go alone, but some nights, I followed. She would walk the edge of town in the shadow of where the wall is now. Talking to herself."

CHAPTER

SEVENTEEN

All I could see was light. The only sound was air escaping my lungs. My aunt's voice was muffled. She must have said my name several times before I answered.

Talking to herself. Talking to herself in the mist.

"Harper, are you okay?" Aunt Patrice asked. As her face came into focus, her amber eyes were wide. "I'm so sorry. I should never have brought her up."

I lifted my hand. I could no longer accept that silence was the answer when it came to my mother's memory. How could I have accepted it all this time?

A part of me wanted to run out to the street and bellow the truth. That Sarah Ledes had spoken with the demon who made the mist, and now, so had I. The mist had thickened when she died. Surely there were secrets buried in the Barrens that only the mist could tell me.

"I was the one who brought her up. Thank you for telling me. I never realized how much I didn't know until

133

this moment. Talking about her feels strange, but it doesn't feel wrong."

Patrice bit her lip. "Please. Don't mention this conversation to Cade," she said.

I nodded in agreement. "I won't. Promise."

We kissed goodbye after I stood, explaining that I was exhausted and needed to get to bed. I walked like a phantom, propelled by limbs that weren't my own. I didn't wave to Perry as I stepped toward the door, but I found the back of Logan's head at the mahogany bar.

He was surrounded by a few men in uniform, holding pints and laughing.

Good. He had found some friends to drink with, and with any luck at all, he wouldn't even notice I had left.

The thick air wrapped around me as I opened the heavy tavern door, and the wind whispered in my ear. My mother had begun speaking to the Alister just before I was born. The mist had appeared just before I was born. Had Raina killed my mother to ensure the Devil's promise was never fulfilled? Had she tried to kill me, too? Why did she not turn on my aunts?

Why did I survive?

The demons answered to the Devil himself.

They were growing restless. *I was growing restless.*

Had my mother's death angered the demons somehow? The Alister knew the answer to these questions. I just knew it. Every word he uttered to me until now had been cloaked in a riddle, but that would end tonight.

I needed answers.

The Alister was a demon, but that didn't scare me. It should have. The wall should have been enough to scare me, but that wasn't enough to stop me from walking right toward it.

I pulled the black wool cloak around my shoulders, letting it cover me like a shadow, and stalked down cobblestone streets toward the wall. I took the path around the small park in the town center, walking in the darkness cast by the fence that separated the street from the grassy square within.

My steps were whispers on the cobblestones, and I kept my head bent in the hood of my cloak, allowing the hum of the wall to roar through me as I approached the gate. A long shadow appeared on the street beside me, and my breath hitched.

I quickened my steps, ducking into the park itself. I hadn't gone more than ten paces before a hand seized my shoulder and pushed me up against the iron gate.

"Where the hell are you going?"

I swore, shaking out of Logan's grip. His other hand rested on the iron behind my head, caging me in. "Why the hell are you following me?"

"I'm your guard," he snarled. "It's my job to ensure you don't do anything stupid."

I took a deep breath. We were so close that my cloak brushed against his leathers. "Who says I'm doing something stupid?"

"You're going to the wall."

"I'm going home."

A scoff. "Please, Harper. The only thing past this park is the wall. What did your aunt say to you?"

It was none of his business. Besides, this was his fault. If it weren't for him, I would've never heard the Alister's message. If he hadn't brought me close to the wall, I would have been free from voices and demons and family secrets.

My jaw clenched. "I need to talk to the Alister. Patrice said my mother spoke to something in the Barrens just before she died. I know she was speaking to him. He knows what happened to her. He knows why she died."

In the distance, a frantic whinny echoed from beyond the wall. The sound ricocheted through my chest, making my bones ache.

Logan winced, and his hand moved to the scar on his brow. My eyes widened. *Had he heard it, too?*

He shook his head. "You can't talk to a demon alone in the middle of the night. It's my job—"

"Your job," I said, pushing his shoulder, "is to guard me when I'm painting. You're off duty. Now leave me alone."

I didn't make it more than a few steps before he caught my forearm. "My job is to protect you, and you're not going near that wall right now. It's late, you could get—"

"Why do you care?" My voice rose. "You're not my protector, Logan. You forced me into your little detective game, remember? You're the reason I'm at risk. I never wanted anything to do with any of this. I should get someone to protect me from *you*."

His jaw tightened. "Right now, you need protection from your own foolish decisions. If you go near that wall at night, you might encounter something that will lure you into the Barrens. What if the cryptid is waiting for you on the other side of the gate?"

I shook out of his grip. "I can handle myself."

"Magic will only get you so far out there. What if it compels you to walk through the gate so it can tear you apart with its razor-sharp claws?" His brow knitted, highlighting the silver scar.

We were tucked in the shadow of a tall oak. All I could see was his face through the mist—his perfect, frustratingly handsome face. The light was sparse in the shadow of the tree, but it clung to the curves of his jaw, the sweep of his lip, and the flicker of blue in his eyes.

My fingers itched to touch all the highlighted edges, but instead, they tightened into a fist.

His breath quickened as his gaze dipped to my mouth. I could have kissed him then, and he would have kissed me back. If I had wrapped my hand around the base of his neck, he would have pulled me in with his fingers wrapped in my hair, and he would have pressed his lips to mine until the hum of the wall was drowned out by my pulse hammering for him.

But I didn't kiss him.

I pushed him. Hard.

And I hated how my hands marked the swell of his shoulders, the thick muscle under the leather of his uniform. I headed back to the street in the direction of home. "Tomorrow, I'm asking for a new guard."

"Good," he replied. He followed me to the gate of the townhouse, trailing ten steps behind me until I slammed the door and stomped to my room.

I watched through the lace of my curtains as he patrolled the street, walking back and forth, his shadow long in the lamplight. His pacing ceased, and I tightened my grip on the windowsill. His gaze flicked to the upstairs window. No candle was burning in my room, and I knew he couldn't see me, but it didn't stop my heart from pounding.

He ran his hands through his hair, muttering something to himself as he stalked away. I watched him until he turned a corner, disappearing into the haze.

CHAPTER

EIGHTEEN

The following morning, I woke with a searing pain in my back. I had dreamed of hoofbeats on the forest floor, and my muscles ached like I had been trampled in my sleep.

I spun in the mirror and twisted my arm to touch the scar over my spine, but I couldn't reach it. I didn't need to feel it to know it was the source of my pain.

When Maggie answered the knock on the front door, Logan's voice didn't echo up the stairwell. Instead, the voice that greeted her was softer, with York's subtle, rounded accent. I peered down the stairs to find Captain Jacob Miller, his shoulders stiff as he greeted Maggie.

"Captain Miller, what an honor to meet you," Maggie said, smoothing her apron. "Can I tempt you with a little breakfast?"

I slid down the stairs, dressed in all black from the lace collar of my dress to the ties of my boots.

As usual, I dressed to match my mood.

"Captain Miller, good morning," I said, giving him a

nod as I took him in. The captain had left the top button of his uniform undone. His wavy black hair was tousled and long enough to reveal a wave at the tips.

So different from the man he had partnered with.

"I would love something to eat. Thank you," he replied.

Maggie squealed in delight and bustled toward the kitchen.

"You just made her whole day," I said, crossing my arms.

He shrugged. "Usually, I eat at the barracks, but there was a change of plans this morning."

I steeled myself for the explanation. Logan had likely pleaded not to guard me, and I envisioned him and Jacob bickering over who would take on the unwelcome task. As a Captain, Jacob outranked Logan in the affairs of the militia, but the two men were equally invested in the stolen arms. One police chief focused on the crime, one arms lieutenant intent on recovering his weapons.

But no explanation came. Instead, the captain grew distracted, his eyes scanning the ordinary objects in the room with interest.

He cocked his head, studying a small, framed cameo that a local artist had painted of James and me when we were small children. "Did you paint this?" he asked.

"No. It was painted when I was a baby," I said, waving my hand. "Why was there a change in plans this morning? Did something happen?"

He blinked, refocusing. "There was another raid at the armory last night."

His lips tightened into a line as he raised his eyebrows, and despite knowing his defenses would be up, I let my magic reach for him. It was like running my fingers over worn brick on a winter's day—cold and rough.

I bit my lip. "Was it bad?"

He nodded. "Over a hundred weapons were stolen."

I gasped. There was no doubt that whoever had stolen the arms was working with an accomplice. A knot tightened in my gut. We had gotten no closer to solving the crime, and it was partly due to my resistance.

"You're not investigating it?" I asked him.

The muscle in his jaw ticked. "I will be investigating it, together with you, on the wall. Logan is neck-deep in it. He called the smiths to work overtime, reworking swords into daggers, trying to scrape out as many weapons as possible." Unease flickered in his eyes. "We need to figure this out. This investigation has been taking much longer than I anticipated. We've sent militia to the coast to recover some of their backup weapons."

Shivers of dread scraped through me at the thought of our militia out in the barrens, unarmed, when I could have done something to stop it. Logan must be terrified, knowing his brother was stationed at such a volatile shore point with the threat of dwindling protection.

Footsteps padded in the hall behind me, and my father came into view, straightening his sleeves as he pinned his favorite cufflinks. He looked up in surprise to find the police captain in his foyer.

"Ah, good morning, Captain Miller," he said, extending a hand.

Jacob's spine straightened. "Good morning, my lord."

Perhaps Jacob was still new enough in town that he didn't realize Cade Ledes was the approachable triplet lord. Not serious like Aaron. Certainly not hot-tempered like Bain. They did look nearly identical, but anyone could spot Cade for who he was.

"You're up late this morning," I quipped. After poker games, his version of sleeping in was akin to my version of waking early.

He shot me a wry smile. "Aaron won again last night. Bain kept challenging him, and by the time we looked at the clock, it was well past midnight."

And he was still up earlier than I had been.

"Hopefully, there isn't much on your schedule today," I said.

His face brightened, and he straightened his suit jacket. "Only pleasant things. Bess and I are going over the invitations today. As soon as James comes home, we'll be off to meet her."

On cue, my brother strode through the door, looking more flushed than usual. I didn't need to ask where he had been.

There was little doubt that he and Benjamin were together this morning. These morning rides were the only times they could see each other. Surely Uncle Bain didn't need his valet this morning if he was up late. It would have given Benjamin more time than usual to escape his duties.

James took one look at my father's cheerful face before a mask fell over his own, washing away the flushed longing and replacing it with a bland smile. "Give me a moment, Father. I'll be dressed shortly."

He shot Jacob a curt nod before bounding up the steps.

Jacob's face had gone utterly pale, and I felt a pang of remorse for the mindspeaking captain. I knew how hard it was being bombarded by everyone else's emotions, especially before breakfast.

Mercifully, Maggie ushered us into the dining room,

where my father small-talked with Captain Miller over eggs, biscuits, and fruits.

I held my coffee cup, inhaling the rich aroma of the only thing that made me act with any shred of civility in the morning. Jacob poured himself a large cup of his own.

"Can I offer you cream and sugar, Captain?" Maggie asked.

"No thanks," he said, taking a deep swig. "I take my coffee black."

Maggie chuckled. "Just like my lady," she said. "Ever since she was a young girl, Master James and I have joked that Lady Harper's coffee is as dark as her sense of humor."

Black and bitter.

Captain Miller shot me a bemused smile. "Lieutenant Greer warned me as such."

Great.

I rolled my eyes before excusing myself from the table. Maggie fussed over wrapping up an extra sandwich for Jacob before we set out into the mist, much later than my former guard would have allowed.

As we walked toward the barracks, it became evident that Jacob's work ethic was more relaxed than that of his partner. He strolled beside me, hands in his pockets, taking in the view from the street.

We passed a group of policemen on the corner, and they tipped their hats to him with genuine smiles. He tipped his back, offering casual greetings and calling each of them by name. If it weren't for the badge on his chest, he would have passed for their coworker, not their captain.

"Why are you so nervous this morning?" I asked Jacob.

He sighed. "This raid was catastrophic. Bain promoted

me quickly because of my abilities. If we don't fix this, the lords may regret their faith in me."

I scoffed. "I already regret my faith in you, but you and the lieutenant don't seem to care what I think."

Jacob bit his lip. "Logan warned me you might feel that way."

"What else did Lieutenant Greer warn you about me?" I asked tersely.

He twisted his mouth into a smirk. "Oh, not much. Just that you tried to approach the wall by yourself last night and attempted to slip away from him to do so."

I straightened my spine. "There was no chance in hell he would have accompanied me, so I took matters into my own hands."

"He takes his assignment very seriously." Jacob shot me a grin that made my blood boil.

I glared at him. "Let me remind you—yet again—that I'm helping you solve a crime. I didn't want to be a part of this."

Jacob sighed. "I know. When I came up with the idea to approach you, I wanted to simply ask for your help." The captain tipped up a broad shoulder. "But Logan began to watch you, and after some time, he assured me you wouldn't help us without some...encouragement."

I huffed a laugh. How long had Logan Greer been watching me? It probably wouldn't have taken him long to conclude that blackmail was the only way to persuade me. But I knew, deep down, that I would have helped if they had nicely asked. I pulled the wool of my cloak around my shoulders and draped the hood over my head as the vapor solidified into a steady drizzle.

As we reached the barracks gates, large droplets began to

fall, and despite the thick fabric of my warmest cloak, a chill whipped through me. Hurried shouts of men echoed through the humidity.

Horses, mounted by armed riders, trotted toward the iron gates of the wall as Paxton barked orders from the front. My cousin carried an iron shield strapped to his arm. Beside him, Lieutenant Logan Greer, armed with two long daggers strapped to his thighs, led the line.

CHAPTER

NINETEEN

The hum was a welcome distraction as Jacob and I approached the wall. Hoofbeats rattled the ground with their urgency. The sound vibrated through me and settled into the spot on my back that held my unreachable scar.

Deep within the recesses of my mind, an urgent gallop drummed through me, a memory from a forgotten day. The phantom beats pounded on a forest floor, and with them, a wail threatened to rip from my chest.

"You don't need to worry," Jacob said, shaking me from the memory. "Logan knows how to handle himself out there."

My jaw was clenched harder than I realized. Jacob had surely been reading my mind. I relaxed my muscles, cursing myself for having my walls down enough for Jacob to sense my emotions. I shook the memory of the horse from my mind, sure it was some nightmare.

I stared ahead at the lines of militia members marching

to the gates. "I'm not worried about Logan. This robbery feels like my fault. Paxton is going out there..."

Jacob held out his hand. "Trust me. This isn't your fault. And General Paxton knows better than anyone how to stay safe in the Barrens. They're merely going on patrol, sweeping the area for any clues. Logan asked to accompany them."

The lid of my trunk clicked open, and I allowed the heady, oily smell of the paints to wash over me. I took out my palette and started mixing a cerulean blue, content to paint what I pictured the sky might look like on the other side of the mist.

Jacob had a very different approach to guarding me as I painted. He paced for a while before settling on the wet ground beside the wall. When the rain stopped, he pulled out a book and started reading, scribbling some notes here and there in the margins. He was so engrossed I could have climbed the damned wall, and he wouldn't have noticed.

White and gray swirled off my brush, blending into the cool blue hues as I formed the clouds. As the wispy forms neared the ground, they thickened, taking on gray undertones.

The clouds had become foggy.

Misty.

I took a long stride back and inspected my work. Perhaps my eyes couldn't see clouds any other way, no matter how many descriptions I had read in books. Or how many paintings I had seen in our galleries at the manor.

Jacob stood beside me, cocking his head to the side.

"I don't know what the sky is supposed to look like," I said.

"You've captured it beautifully," he replied, his tone dripping with pity.

"Thank you." I began packing up my supplies. "I've been observing the men closely. Nobody has any ill intent or suspicious thoughts."

There was more motion around us than usual this morning, no doubt in response to the raid. Plenty of the men had been worried about their weapons. Some had been nervous about going into the pines. None had been plotting or scheming.

"I agree," Jacob said, closing his book.

"I'm starting to wonder if these raids aren't an inside job after all," I mused. "Do you think it's someone from out in the pines? Perhaps from a nearby town?"

"You may be right," he said, rubbing his chin. He stared at the wall, long and hard. "You didn't hear any voices from beyond the wall today."

It wasn't a question.

"No, I didn't." A part of me wanted to linger longer at my work and wait for the Alister, but I had a feeling the increased patrols around the wall had kept the creature away. Horses had passed by more than once throughout the morning.

"Can I ask you a question, Miss Ledes?" Jacob said.

I laughed. "For the love of the devil, just call me Harper."

His mouth curled into a bright smile, and a spark shone in his blue eyes. "Okay. Harper. Logan told me you were going to request a new guard today. Why didn't you?"

My shoulders stiffened. "I didn't have a chance to make the request. Paxton and Brannon have been busy all day."

"You could have made the request to me. I outrank Logan."

"I didn't realize he answered to you," I challenged. "Logan seems to call most of the shots in this mission."

He laughed, a teasing lilt playing on his lips. "If I may be so bold, I think you may still want him to be your guard."

Fire burned under my skin. "First of all, you may not be so bold. Second, you don't know what you're talking about."

He crossed his arms. "I can mindspeak, too, remember."

My cheeks reddened again as I struggled with a powerful urge to throw paint at the police captain. Before I could reply, a commotion from the far end of the barracks burst through the gates.

Horses barreled into the quadrangle, and Paxton's voice rang out above the clop of their hooves. "Bring in the rest of the men, now! Bring out the gurney and call the healer!"

We raced toward the sounds of my cousin's voice, and as the air cleared around him, I was terrified to see Paxton was covered in blood. I sucked in a deep breath, choked with mist, when I realized the blood splattered over the leather of his uniform was not his own.

Paxton held the reins to another horse that trotted beside him. Atop the mount, the rider was limp, lifeless as blood oozed from a large tear in the leather across his flank.

The rider's face was covered, but I recognized the golden hair that draped over his face. His arm fell away. Logan's eyes were closed, but the ethereal scar over his eyebrow shone in stark contrast to the pallor of his skin.

From beyond the wall, a panicked horse whinnied in the distance, and the sound sliced through me like a knife.

The earth spun below me, and my heart twisted along with it. The ground was being ripped from under my feet. A steady hand gripped my elbow—Jacob's hand.

It wasn't until I saw Logan's arm raise to cover his wound that the earth slowed down. He was alive, but—the blood.

Too much blood.

His uniform was ripped, exposing the flesh over his ribs and abdomen. Three deep gashes in perfect parallel arched over his flank. Only one weapon could inflict an injury like that.

Claws.

CHAPTER

TWENTY

The healer had slammed the door in my face, muttering something about needing to concentrate. Her apron had been covered in Logan's blood, and her face was wrought and weary. I don't remember if Jacob walked me home that night. Or if I said anything more for the entirety of the day.

When the sun rose the following morning, I woke with the first beams of light and paced in the parlor for several hours until I realized nobody was coming to escort me to the mural. When I finished my second cup of coffee, Maggie brought me extra biscuits, grumbling about tragedies and wounds under her breath.

When she tried to reassure me that the lieutenant would be okay, I didn't have the energy or will to retort that I didn't care.

Because I did care. Too much.

The fog outside the window was so thick I could barely make out the shape of the gate spires in the near distance.

151

"If you're off for the day, you're free to accompany me to the manor," James offered from across the breakfast table.

I nodded, shivering. I hadn't even realized he was sitting beside me until he spoke aloud. "Thank you. That may be a good idea. I've work to do in the library."

"What work?" My father was half-hidden behind an open newspaper, and until he uttered the question, I had also forgotten he was in the room.

"I'm... researching for the mural," I stammered, tumbling into the lie. "Cloud forms, sky images."

James raised his eyebrows. *"You look terrible, Harp."* He spoke into my mind.

I poked at my biscuits with the blunt tip of my butter knife. The image of Logan clinging to his horse as he bled was seared in my mind. My dreams had been haunted by the sound of claws against stone and hooves pounding over the pine needles.

I had been riding on the back of a black horse when I woke from my dream in a cold sweat. I had been falling.

Falling forever.

And the ache pulsing from the scar on my back had simmered into a constant burn.

James's eyebrows knitted together. *"The lieutenant was moved to the manor last night. He's recovering in the infirmary, expected to make a full recovery."*

My father peered over his newspaper. "I've heard the mural is coming along beautifully. James and I will have lunch with Aaron and Beatrice when you're done in the library. They want my opinions on the courting process and suggestions on who may suit Mira."

The biscuits I had nibbled on earlier became stones in my gut. The last thing I wanted to do was help Aunt Bea play matchmaker, especially when Logan's name was inevitably on her list.

Maybe he and Mira were a well-matched pair, after all.

Mira was beautiful. She was confident, determined, and strong-willed. Logan certainly would admire those characteristics in a woman. My butter knife slid through the sole biscuit remaining on my plate, cleaving it in two.

James eyed me from over his coffee cup. *"The healers are very skilled, Harper. They can heal the most complex wounds."*

Even wounds inflicted by a demon? Clearly, some wounds never healed.

I needed to figure out what was going on beyond the wall. Why were demons converging, and what did it have to do with everything that happened the day I was born? Why was the Alister willing to speak to me? Why had he befriended my mother? Perhaps speaking of her death had cursed me after all. The more I mulled it over, the more responsible I felt for everything that had gone wrong.

The mist. The wall. My mother's death. The raids.

Logan's injury.

The walk to the manor was pleasant enough. James and Father stopped to converse with some neighbors while I ran my boot over the curb's lip. When I arrived, none of the lamps were lit in the library, so I took a match to the oil wicks near my study area.

I combed through a book about the founding of Galloway. One hundred years ago, my great-grandparents had settled in the area, bringing their twin daughters and eldest son. The book richly described the area.

The sun shines plentifully betwixt the thick pine boughs. Interestingly, the soil from which they grow is a mixture of sand and clay. The pines appear to be the only crop of possibility, but the citizens have turned to milling the wood. Sand within the soil has been ripe for glassmaking. The nearby borough of Burlington has proven a stalwart trade partner, willing to barter wood and glassware for crops.

A dim light shone through the window, and I wondered what the town had looked like in the days before the mist. Indeed, the mill and glassworks were still a vital part of the town's livelihood.

It has been guessed that our settlement here has angered the fire realm. Each summer in the first decade, we have suffered from his fire. Many speculate if anything short of God's grace would be enough to quell the flames for good.

A shiver ran over my skin. My father and his brother had protected the Barrens from the fires since the day they were born, which was precisely why the Devil had vowed to take their thirteenth child.

I wondered if my father and uncles might be secretly grateful for the mist, a respite from the rays that could burn it all down.

In this world and others, it is known that there are thin places—areas where one can walk between realms. In the Barrens, the area between the Fire Realm of Hell and Earth appears to be concerningly thin. Indeed, we must consider that the demons here also walk in other realms. His playthings and pets are scattered over many versions of this world.

The words on the pages began to swim, and my eyes grew bleary as I read through numerous historical anthologies. My notes for the day included some accounts of the first recorded attacks by the demons. Although none were named, the injuries inflicted were mentioned in detail. I wrote down every note of claws and horses I could find, hoping to have some educated questions for the Alister the next time he came near the wall.

There was not one mention of silver scars that never healed.

It was not quite ten, but I desperately needed a third cup of coffee. I stretched my legs and gathered my notes before descending the stairs to the kitchens. The cook almost fainted when I appeared at her side. The poor woman was likely not used to the ladies of the household venturing into the lower floors.

It was different than the relationship we had with Maggie. Sometimes she would let me help her cook, teaching me as she chopped and stirred.

After fussing over the press, I assured her I could make my coffee without her help. I made a generous cup, picturing Logan resting in the infirmary. I could not help but wonder how he had been faring. The healer's quarters in the annex could get cold and drafty. I poured hot water into a cup and dipped a tea bag into it.

I burned myself several times with sloshing hot liquid as I strode up the cellar stairs to the infirmary annex, balancing my coffee and Logan's tea in each hand. I opened the door with my hip, and this time, no flustered healer was there to stop me. I was unsure if he was resting inside, but my careful quiet proved unnecessary.

A curtain was set up next to the cot on the far side of the

room, but the other beds were empty. I froze when I heard a familiar female voice purring on the other side of the white linen sheet.

"Does it hurt much, Lieutenant?"

"No, my lady. The healer has cared for me," Logan's voice rasped. "I think I may have heard the door open. Perhaps she's here with my next dose of pain tonic."

A set of lacquered nails pulled the curtain to the side, and Mira's face peered from behind it. At the sight of me, her painted lips morphed from a puckered pout into a sneer.

The weight of worry I had been carrying lightened when I saw Logan, pale but healthy appearing. In the mirror behind his bed, my reflection was peppered by blotches of red creeping up my neck. I stood there like a moody barmaid, balancing two cups of steaming liquid.

"Cousin, what a surprise to see you," Mira said, propping her hand on the sultry curve of her hip. She wore a pink floral gown, and her corset pinched so tightly around her slim waist that she appeared to be made of only hips and breasts. Her ample bosom spilled over the delicate cream-colored trim.

Before her, a tray of neat cakes and sandwiches was arranged near Logan's cot. Although his face was somewhat more drawn than usual, his eyes sparked with relief. "Yes, Miss Ledes. It is a delight to see you." He gestured to the seat beside Mira's. "Please take a seat."

Mira shot me a look that suggested she might try to bite me if I obliged. "I was merely bringing you a cup of tea, Lieutenant. I'll place it on your tray and take my leave."

Logan's sparkling blue gaze darted to my cup. "You have two cups. Surely, you intended to stay if you brought your coffee."

Mira's hand floated to rest on Logan's forearm. "Too many visitors might tire you, Lieutenant."

The sight of her hand on him made me want to fling the boiling water at her rouged face, but I composed myself enough to agree. "My dear cousin is right," I said. "I'm glad you're on the mend, Mr. Greer. Mira, I will see you at family dinner, I presume?"

She ignored my question. "How do you know Lieutenant Greer, Harper?" My name came out of her mouth like something sour on her tongue.

Logan answered for me. "Surely, you've heard there's been a mural commissioned at the barracks. The generals assigned me as Harper's guard while she paints."

Mira's eyes slowly narrowed. A viper's grin curled on her lips. "I do hope my baby cousin has been kind to you, Lieutenant. She has a reputation for her sharp tongue."

Logan managed a weak smile as he pulled up the edge of his tunic, exposing his marred flesh. "Not the only sharp thing I've endured this week."

Scabbed blood rested over three curved scars, haloed by iridescent blue tissue. Mira gasped, covering her mouth with the tips of her painted fingers.

The air punched from my lungs. When I tore my gaze away from the wounds, I found Logan's eyes fixed on me.

"What was it?" I rasped.

His brow furrowed. "An aamon."

I knew of the aamon. Wolflike creatures with sharp beaks and talons that breathed flame. An unlikely creature to dwell near the walls of a village guarded by gifted fire wielders.

First, the cryptid, now the aamon. What other vile creatures had flocked to our woods? We exchanged a knowing glance.

I nodded, attempting to shake the image of the creature from my mind. "Indeed, you need your rest then. I'll take my leave."

"See you at family dinner, cousin," Mira said with a tone of finality.

I didn't look back when I opened the door.

CHAPTER

TWENTY-ONE

Jacob's head was bent over paperwork in the police quarters when I found him, his wavy black hair spilling over his eyes.

I cleared my throat, and he jumped, causing ink to splatter on his records.

"Harper, what are you doing here?" He dipped his quill back in the well and blotted the paper.

"Nobody came to escort me to the mural today." I crossed my arms.

His brow knotted, and he tidied the stack of parchment. "I assumed you wouldn't want to work on it after what happened to Logan yesterday."

I pulled in a breath. "I need you to come with me to the wall. I only have time to paint for an hour before lunch, but I have questions." My voice lowered. "For the Alister."

Jacob's gaze darted around the office, assuring nobody was within listening distance. "Of course. Give me a moment."

It was nearly noon when we ventured toward the wall,

but I assured Jacob I wouldn't linger long. I had told my father I would meet him for lunch at one.

"Did you check in on Logan this morning?" he asked.

"Yes, as a matter of fact, I did. But he already had a visitor." I pulled the hem of my cloak through my fingers. "I didn't stay long, but he seemed well."

"Who was visiting with him?"

I pursed my lips into a line. "My cousin, Mira."

Jacob choked on a laugh and cleared his throat as we reached the mural. He set my trunk down. "I see."

I didn't need to look at him to know he was trying to hold in his amusement. *"I don't appreciate your teasing,"* I spoke into his mind. I turned to open my supplies, and he bent to help steady the lid.

"I simply worry for my friend's livelihood," he returned. *"Your cousin is dreadful and exhausting."*

I gave him a grateful smile, my heart warming toward the police chief now that his walls were down. *"She's a complete bitch."*

Words I would have never spoken aloud. I bit my lip as a group of militiamen passed us.

He laughed aloud. *"I'm sure he would have much preferred your company,"* Jacob said.

"I don't care if he would have."

A snort. *"Yes, you do."* He pulled the tray of supplies out of the trunk for me and placed them beside the mural.

I gathered my paints and oils. *"You don't know what you're talking about."*

"You're easy to read, Harper." He crossed his arms as he leaned against the wall.

"So are you." My brush started to make broad, confident strokes, flames coming to life with vibrant orange and red.

"*Please elaborate,*" Jacob said.

I dunked my brush in the oil and turned toward him, speaking aloud. "You care greatly what people think of you, don't you?"

He arched a bemused brow. "What do you mean?"

"I see how you talk to people in town, the other police-men. You want them to like you. You got nervous when you spoke with my father yesterday, too." I shrugged. "He's the easiest of the lords. You needn't be so concerned."

He nodded. "I want the lords to like me. I'm the police chief, and I'm not from Galloway. Bain hired me because he knew of my mindspeaking, but you understand better than anyone. It's not a magical gift most people are comfortable with. I want them to know I'm trustworthy."

"Well, nothing says *trustworthy* quite like blackmailing one of their daughters."

I took up my brush again as he laughed.

"You have feelings for Logan," he said. "Admit it."

My cheeks heated. "The only feeling I have toward him is aggravation."

"I think he has feelings for you, too, you know." Jacob cocked his head as my gaze darted toward him.

I went back to painting, holding in the questions that bubbled to the surface of my mind. "You're too bold, Captain Miller."

At that, Jacob shrugged before taking out his notebook and slumping against the wall. I painted in silence for a while, allowing the bright colors of the flames to wash away the nervous energy in my fingertips. I had been lost in the colors for some time before I heard the Alister.

"*Harper Ledes, you have returned to me. I have missed our talks.*"

I stilled, and Jacob looked up at me. He pointed at the wall. I nodded, aware Jacob could hear everything I said to the demon but not anything it said to me.

"Alister, is that you?"

"Indeed, Miss Ledes. Tell me, how does the injured militiaman fare?"

He had heard of the attack then. *"He recovered well, thank you. I called upon him this morning. He claims an aamon attacked him."*

A huff of dismay. *"Aamon have no business here, near a village of fire wielders."*

"What business do they seek?" My heart began to hammer. The demon was more forthcoming than usual.

"The lesser and greater demons become restless," he said. *"They sense now what I have long known."*

"And what is that?"

"That the time may be coming. To open the thin space again. To ask our master for a passage back."

Adrenaline surged through me. *"You're trapped here."* It wasn't a question.

His sigh rolled through me like thunder. *"My master is temperamental. We have not been given free passage between realms in decades. We grow weary of this place. It is not where we belong."*

"I thought you belonged here. The mist."

"My mist grew when your mother died. She was my only friend in this realm. The only one to speak to. That is, until you. It has grown with my mourning."

I sucked in a breath, trying to calm my racing heart. *"What do you know of my mother's death?"*

Another sigh rumbled from him, this one dripping in sorrow. *"She was terrified of the coming of the thirteenth child.*

When she learned she was expecting, along with Lady Patrice, she came to me, seeking answers. She was relieved when Raina felt one babe in her womb."

"Did Raina kill her?"

With my question, Jacob's eyes widened.

"I do not know." The Alister's words were drenched in despair.

I believed him.

"It was always curious that Sarah died by the element her husband controlled. Did you know she kept a locket of his power around her neck? Just in case,' she always said."

"Just in case what?" Did the Alister believe my father had killed his spouse? Or one of his brothers? Bile churned in my stomach.

"In case she needed him, and he was not there. In case she needed to quell or summon flames."

I squeezed my eyes shut. *"My father can't give his magic to others."*

"All fire wielders can. A small nugget of fire energy can be embedded into any metal, except for iron, of course. She told me of it the day he gave her the locket. You could do the same with your own fire magic."

My mouth was as dry as ash. *"I have no fire magic."*

A raspy chuckle.

I started to doubt the demon's sanity as I shook my head. *"I've never had fire magic."*

"Oh, Harper, I'm surprised. I thought you knew. How do you think you survived that fire, my dear?"

CHAPTER

TWENTY-TWO

Jacob escorted me back to the manor. I had missed lunch, but I knew my father would still be present for tea.

When I entered the drawing room, Father and Aaron sat with Beatrice, James, and Mira.

"I thought you were coming for lunch, traitor," James spoke into my mind.

"Was it that bad?"

Aunt Bea clapped her hands over her chest. "Oh, Harper. You're just in time. Mira has agreed to start courting, and we were discussing the possibilities."

Yes, it was that bad.

James opened his hands, gesturing for me to sit beside him.

Mira puffed out her chest. "Lieutenant Greer and I had such a nice visit today. It made me realize how fleeting our lives can be. Uncle Cade suggested Sergeant Brown. He's the second in command in the armory and son of one of the wealthiest smiths in Galloway."

164

Aunt Bea nodded in agreement. "It would be a fine match. He's handsome, too."

I wasn't surprised that the first word out of Mira's mouth was Logan's name. It was just like her to rub something in my face when she thought she had bested me. When we were children, and the music tutor had allowed her to have a solo in our small ensemble recital, she had gloated about it for over a year.

I had no doubt it would be even worse concerning her conquests with men.

"What a nice suggestion," I said, sending her a pert smile.

It was too bad for Mira that I had no intention of competing with her this time. She could have him—with her perfect, curly brown hair and green eyes, she was the prettiest of her sisters. She no doubt considered herself worthy of the highest-ranking husband in society.

Of course, she had set her sights on a lieutenant and a sergeant. Mira probably thought I deserved one of the dishwashers at the tavern. Perhaps the undertaker's son was on the marriage market. Surely, she would find out.

James and I listened, nodding while exchanging snide commentary mind to mind—the only way to get through tea with Aunt Bea and Mira.

It was my father who changed the trajectory of the conversation. "I just hope all four of the Ledes daughters find a love match, like all three of us did." His eyes darkened.

My uncle paled from across the table. It was so unlike my father to even allude to his late wife in conversation.

Uncle Aaron straightened his shoulders. "I agree, Cade. I'm so grateful James has found just that with Miss Hern."

Beside me, James stiffened a bit before pulling his lips into a tight smile.

Aunt Bea sipped her tea. She raised her brows at my father and said, "And what a bonus that her mother, Bess, is such a dear. They'll fit right into our family."

"Bess is a gem," my father said, and I could have sworn I saw his cheeks flush slightly as he sipped from his cup. "She's made the wedding planning an absolute delight. All the party vendors have been quite taken with her."

Bea hummed to herself in agreement before exchanging a meaningful look with Uncle Aaron.

Was my father *embarrassed?*

"Is there something going on here that I should know about?" I asked James, mind to mind.

He sighed. *"I'll tell you later."*

Uncle Aaron broke the tension by asking when the next party should be and who we should invite to family dinner this week. My father seemed more than happy to change the subject. Aunt Bea and Mira began making suggestions for guests.

Logan was first on the list to be the guest of honor this week. Recovering demon slayer. Mira's love interest. It was an obvious choice.

"Perhaps we should invite Captain Miller as well," Uncle Aaron suggested. "I hear he has done a fine job guarding my niece at the wall these past few days."

I shrugged. "He has done an acceptable job," I admitted. He was more laid back than Logan and easy to talk to. I might have even considered him a friend if the man hadn't coerced me into helping him solve a crime.

Teatime lasted much longer than I had hoped, but at least my belly was full, and I had been served my fourth caffeinated beverage of the day. I had much more important tasks if I wanted to find the locket the Alister had alluded to, and my plan didn't involve anyone in that room.

"Have you seen Aunt Pat?" I asked Beatrice as we stood to leave.

"She might be tending to the garden," she said, smoothing her dress. "I've never understood her desire to get muddy, but she finds some peculiar pleasure in digging that I will never comprehend."

"Ah, yes. If I find her, I'll remind her to wash her hands," I replied.

Aunt Bea sniffed at me in approval before I left, walking the long way along the conservatory toward the back gardens.

Aunt Pat was indeed in the gardens, kneeling next to some shriveled shrubs, pruning scissors in hand. Evergreens were the only things that readily grew under the blanket of the mist, but Aunt Pat enjoyed trimming them into elaborate shapes.

I approached her with care so as not to startle her while she was focused. "May I help, Auntie?"

Aunt Pat was startled, nonetheless. "Harper! What a pleasant surprise. Yes, I was pruning the last of these boxwoods before the first frost. I expect winter to come early this year. Grab a pair of shears."

Patrice showed me how to find the correct knob of branch to prune, and we set to work, falling into an easy rhythm of small talk and trimming before I gained the courage to ask, "Aunt Pat, did my mother own a locket?"

Her eyes darted back and forth, checking to make sure we were well and truly alone. She reached her hand into the top hem of her dress and loosened a long chain around her neck. A glimmering golden oval, fashioned with a charred clasp, was on the end.

"This locket?" She shot me a mischievous smile. Apparently, the portrait in the dining room was not the only piece of Sarah Ledes that my aunt had salvaged after her death.

I held out my hand, and Pat slipped the chain from around her neck and folded it into my palm. "How did you find out about it?"

My mouth dried out. I couldn't tell her about the Alister. It would cause her too much distress. "James said he remembered her wearing one. I was curious."

Pat raised her brows. "I didn't realize James had become comfortable speaking about his mother."

I shook my head. James was not comfortable speaking of her. "He had too much to drink last night, and it slipped out."

Guilt washed through me with the weight of the lie, but Patrice nodded. "It can happen to the best of us."

I nodded, swallowing down the lump in my throat. "Thank you, Auntie."

She smiled, and I could have sworn the air around us was lighter when she took her next breath.

"Why don't you wear it from now on, dear?" Patrice said.

I nodded and opened my palm to inspect the locket. It was deformed, half melted, but shaped like an oval. Despite the cold air, it warmed in my hand with an unnatural heat.

Perhaps there was a bit of my father's fire left within the metal. I slid the chain over my neck, and the locket rested over my heart. I closed my eyes, and I heard it once more. The frantic gallop of hooves on the forest floor.

A scream built in my chest, and pain seared across my

spine, but I pushed it down. Within my mind, the gallop continued before a baby's wail drowned out the hammering.

Terror gripped me as the baby's wails overtook my senses.

My eyes snapped open, and I found Aunt Patrice watching me, her brow scrunched in concern.

"Are you well, Harper?" She hadn't heard it. Of this, I was certain.

I gripped the table to steady my trembling hands. "Yes, Auntie. I must have had too much coffee." It wasn't a lie. I shuffled to my feet. "Thank you for the locket."

Your own fire magic. The voice of the Alister replayed in my mind.

She nodded. "Of course. Wear it well, Harper."

I nodded back before I left her. The locket heated my skin on the walk home, but I welcomed the burn.

CHAPTER
TWENTY-THREE

I ate dinner alone in my room, staring at the candle's flickering light.

How do you think you survived that fire, my dear?

I had never asked that question before now, at least not aloud. In truth, I didn't want to consider how my mother had died. How had she not survived an inferno with my father's locket of protection around her neck? Surely, Cade's magic would have protected the woman he loved. I hadn't asked Aunt Patrice how she had recovered the locket.

So many images of what could've happened that day flooded my mind. How had I made it out when my mother had died?

I recalled the early days of realizing my magic, of learning to mindspeak. James and I had been young, and for a long time, I hadn't even realized I was doing it. There were always special conversations and words between the two of us.

What if there was some connection between me and the flame? I focused on the candle, letting the fire into my heart.

I turned it over in my mind, to be with the flame. To be the flame.

Nothing.

I stared at it for so long that the fire began to burn a hole in my eye, so much so that when I closed my lids, the light remained as a phantom glow behind my eyelids.

I could ask Father.

No. It didn't seem right, especially when a large part of me suspected the Alister didn't know the whole truth. Was my father responsible for his own wife's death? Was that why he had become so consumed by his grief? Maybe my mother had used that kernel of my father's magic to protect me. Only me.

I shivered, reflecting on all the times my father had lost control of his magic over the years. It was always a mild slip when it happened. When I was young, I broke a platter that belonged to his mother while playing catch with Perry. When he found the broken porcelain on the floor, the flames in the fireplace had surged for a moment before he took a deep breath. Perhaps the fire magic responded to strong emotion.

Strong emotion. I had no shortage of that.

I couldn't help my mind from straying to that moment in the passageway to the barracks. The night I had pushed Logan against the wall. The first time I had inhaled the notes of his cologne. The way the musky scent mingled with the leather of his uniform. The way his eyes flared.

The candle's flame surged, and I jumped, nearly knocking the candleholder over. I bit my lip and closed my eyes, focusing my emotions on the flicker of light.

Logan whispering in my ear on the roof of the barracks. His arms caging me beside the fence in the park. The thoughts eddied through me, my pulse hammering more with each detail. When I opened my eyes, the candle had been burned to the end of the wick, the flame so high it was as tall as my hand.

I gasped, and the flame died out with my intake of breath. There was no smoke, just a heap of melted wax that had cascaded preternaturally over the side of the brass candle holder. What was left of the wick glowed as a mere ember of light. I blinked in the dark, trying to figure out what I had just summoned until realization threatened to choke me.

Had it been me? Had I started the fire that killed my mother?

Through the years, I had always blamed myself. But my guilt had always been tied to my simple existence. If I had never been born, she would be here, after all. James would have his mother, and Father wouldn't be living a half-life, trapped in the walls of this cursed village.

But now? Now there was a possibility that something about my birth had sparked the flames.

I couldn't go to my father or ask one of my fire-wielding cousins. They would ask too many questions. Besides, they likely didn't have the answers I sought.

This was not natural. Those who were gifted with magic did not possess different kinds of magic. It simply didn't happen that way. Unless they were witches or mystics, and there were no such powers that I knew of in our family. Unless my mother...

It was too much.

I needed to get out—to take a walk, to be anywhere but here. I was utterly alone. Suddenly, the stone walls around Galloway felt restrictive, like the stays of a corset pulled tight.

There was no limit to how far I would have to walk to process this information. Into the sea itself.

The clock in the front hall chimed midnight as I set out into the darkness. My father and James were surely in a deep sleep in their rooms down the hall, and I was glad for it. I pulled my cloak tight around my shoulders, shivering in the chill of the late autumn night. There was no moonlight, but I allowed the streetlamps to be my beacon.

My hand reached for the gate latch, but I gasped and froze as a tall, broad figure materialized beyond the spires.

"What are you doing here?" I whispered.

Logan was dressed in uniform, but his torso was wrapped with a thick swath of gauze from the outside.

His voice was raspy when he answered, "You're still awake."

"What?" For a moment, I questioned if he was real or some trick of the light—something from the pines that had made it over the wall.

"Your candle was lit," he repeated, gazing at the second story. "In your window. Until a moment ago."

"When were you released from the infirmary?"

A muscle in his jaw ticked. "Earlier this evening."

"It's past midnight."

He furrowed his brow. "Your light. The candle was still burning, so I knew you were awake."

I counted my breaths, expectant, but no explanation came. Logan stood before me, meeting my stare like his presence was as natural as the mist.

I blinked at him, convinced he must be some trick of my weary mind. "Have you been standing out here...waiting for me to extinguish my candle?"

He swallowed. "I'm your guard."

The air thickened around me, and despite the cold chill, my skin was burning. "Do you make it a habit to stand under my window?"

"Yes. Except for last night. I asked, but they wouldn't let me leave."

The heat bloomed under my skin, becoming an ember in my chest. I was terrified I would set the whole town on fire after what happened a moment ago. What had flared to life with the mere thought of him.

I blinked in the haze. "You were injured. You needn't be here. I don't require this kind of guard, Logan. I'm nowhere near the wall."

He said nothing, but his chest heaved. This man had tried to leave the infirmary to stand outside my room last night despite his still-open wounds. Despite the demon venom that was coursing through his blood, even now.

"Where are you going?" he asked, crossing his arms.

My eyes widened. "I don't know…"

"This proves it. You do need a guard," he said, seething. "Where were you going at midnight? Taking a walk?"

"I don't know. I just needed to clear my head." It wasn't a lie.

I opened the gate and closed it behind me. He was less than a foot away from me, and in the muted light of the lamps, his face was no longer pale as it had been earlier that day. His cheeks were flushed as he blinked down at me.

"You're one of the most reckless people I've ever met," he said in a hushed voice. "You were going to the Barrens. If I hadn't stopped you, you would have walked out into the woods, looking for a demon to have a chat."

Lamplight flickered in his blue eyes, challenging me to prove him wrong.

But he was wrong.

I stared into his eyes, realizing where I would have gone. In that moment, I had wielded fire magic, and there was only one person I wanted to tell. Only one person I wanted to help me.

"I was going to find you."

His eyes widened, anger melting into shock.

My heart was a drum. "I needed to speak to someone. I didn't know where I was going when I left, but I think—I would have found you."

"You were coming to find me," he rasped.

It wasn't a question, but I nodded, tipping my chin up. The fire in his icy eyes was so bright it threatened to burn a hole in my mind, just as the candle had. I wanted it to, so I didn't look away.

With the next intake of breath, his lips were on mine.

Logan kissed me, and I let him. And his mouth pressed against mine made me fear the entire realm would burn into nothing but ash. Heat snaked through me, threatening to take me over. I was flame and mist and smoke. Despite the chill, the air around us was a blanket of heat, and I pulled him closer, allowing my hands to roam.

I wanted to know the map of him. I traced the slope of his neck. Over the angle of his jaw. Dipping over the infuriating dimple on his cheek with my thumb. My other hand swept over his heaving chest, stopping short at the thick bandages wrapped around his ribs.

He tangled his fingers in my unruly hair, and as he drew me closer by the small of my back, a desperate moan climbed up my throat.

He bit down on my lip, and it was my undoing. There was nothing I wouldn't give him at that moment if he had asked for it. I knew it was true. If I had started walking in the dark, I would have walked right to that infirmary. There was no telling if I would have gone in. Despite it all, I would have found him. I had discovered this new thing about me with the mere thought of him.

He broke away first.

"Harper." The way he said my name. "It's late. You should go to sleep."

I could only nod.

He tucked a strand of hair behind my ear. "Good night." A smile ghosted over his lips. "My lady."

I turned and opened the gate as though I was possessed. My feet carried me up the stairs. I knew he wouldn't leave until my window was dark. I stepped back and turned away despite every particle of my body screaming to return to him.

When I returned to my room, I extinguished my lamps. I didn't need to touch the burner.

TWENTY-FOUR

The following morning, I woke to the patter of rain on the windowpane. There was no reason to rise early on a Saturday, so I lingered in bed, watching the shadows the raindrops left over the wavy glass.

What had happened the night before might have been a dream. I let my fingers graze over each spot Logan had touched me and wander to places I wished he had.

My entire life felt like a hallucination, and I was beginning to wonder how much of it was fabricated by my loneliness. Had Logan really kissed me? Had I been speaking to a demon only I could hear at the wall, or was his voice an illusion? Aunt Patrice had alluded to the fact that my mother was in an altered mental state before she died.

Perhaps I had met the same fate.

I was just as convinced that the kiss with Logan was a cruel trick of my mind. Logan had threatened me, prevented me from escaping to Delphi with James, and in doing so, had tied my father to this village without any chance of a new life. There was no reason to allow Logan to get close to me.

No reason I should be thinking about him like this. Warmth flooded my skin with the memory of his lips on mine, and I allowed it to crackle, even if it did mean I set something on fire.

Fire. Another thing that couldn't be real.

I remained in bed for a long while, until my thoughts melted away from lust and into anxiety.

The locket Patrice gave me was tucked under my nightgown on the long chain. I pulled it out and inspected it again, turning it over in my pale fingers. The ornate gold oval was about the size of a large coin, but the hinges had melted. I attempted to open the clasp, only to find the metal had been welded together on either side.

The locket was permanently closed—like my own fate was sealed within the walls of this damned village.

Delphi would never come to be. I would never practice at the art conservatory. I would never know what it was like to gaze up at a clear blue sky and mix the cerulean and cobalt into the perfect hue.

James would never enroll in a university to study literature. He would be married to a woman he didn't love, in forced proximity to a man he could only pine for. My father would forever be tied to a cursed nobility.

I had blamed Logan and Jacob for this all week, but under it all, it was my fault. All this time, I had been sure Father would have followed us to Delphi, but what if he had stayed? It had never been a good plan, but it was my only plan.

A knock on the door interrupted my brooding, and Maggie offered me a breakfast tray. I ate in my room, and the only sounds beyond my silverware's clinks were the clock's tick from my mantel and the rain on my window. I watched the drops slide down the glass through the holes in the lace curtains.

When I finally dressed, James and I spent the day in near silence, not even bothering to mindspeak as we sat on opposite ends of the parlor, reading. Father had remained at the desk in his study.

It took me a long time to fall asleep that night, and on Sunday morning, I woke with a groan, realizing I would need to endure another Ledes family dinner.

When Maggie helped me dress, she pulled out various options from my dresser, and I chose a midnight-blue silk.

"No black today, Miss?" Maggie asked, gently tugging the stays of my undergarments.

"I plan to wear my black gloves," I said.

Maggie tutted, but her lips pursed to hide a smile. "I would expect nothing less."

She fashioned my hair in a neat updo, leaving a few ebony curls loose, accentuating the slight plunge of the garment's neckline. To her delight, I allowed her to rouge my cheeks and apply kohl to my eyelids in the fashionable way, angled at the edges.

I didn't agree to the lip stain at first, but Maggie allowed me to put some on myself. The locket was tucked safely in my secret drawer, and I chose a set of gray pearls to replace it. The skin around my chest was already cold without the heat of the golden oval.

Maggie bit her lip as she studied her handiwork. "You look beautiful, my dear. But then again, you always do."

I held on to James's arm all the way to the manor. He trembled as we approached the entryway, gaze scanning the hallway, no doubt scouring the scene for any glimpse of Benjamin. My grip tightened, and he sent me a grateful smile. These dinners had never been easy for us.

In the shimmering glow of the chandelier, I found Logan, who was engrossed in a heated conversation with Uncle Bain. He wore a formal uniform that hugged his broad shoulders, and my gaze ran over the lines of his dark gray jacket. His sandy hair was meticulously swept away from his forehead, yet there remained an untamed quality as if those wild strands longed to tumble down into his eyes.

From across the room, a flash of blue struck me when he turned. His stare was like lightning, electrifying and paralyzing. My knees nearly buckled, and I was thankful to have a firm grip on James's arm.

"Are you well, sister?" James spoke into my mind.

I pinched him.

The bastard laughed, and I took the opportunity to find one of my more affable cousins to entertain me. To my relief, Axel was already present with a drink in hand, and he approached me with the offer of a full wine glass of my own.

"Harper, are you wearing *blue?*" Axel asked.

Perry was by his side a moment later. "Always the most beautiful woman in the room, even when she's not dressed for a funeral."

James snickered, and I gave him a warning glare. My heart skipped when a nearby oil lamp flared in response, but nobody seemed to notice.

"Thank you, Perry," I said before taking a large swig from the glass.

Mira floated down the stairs. She was dressed to kill, breathtaking in a tight red dress that hugged her curves and flared at the bottom, lined in lace. No gloves adorned her forearms, so the ornate swirls of her branded number *6* were on full display.

Aunt Beatrice was primed to burst with glee as her daughter arrived at the bottom of the stairs. She wasted no time ushering Mira over to where Bain and Logan were engaged in deep conversation.

The second swig I took from the glass slid down with a satisfying burn. I tried not to watch Logan's response, so I stared at the door instead. My shoulders sagged in relief when Jacob strode in, also dressed in finery.

Jacob approached us and bowed. James, Axel, and Perry didn't notice the captain's arrival as they debated an upcoming hunt.

"How is your evening, Lady Harper?" Jacob asked. A question he knew the answer to.

"Just grand," I said aloud before mindspeaking. *"Family dinners are not my favorite."*

He stood beside me, pretending to listen politely to the men's conversation. *"Is there something about this dinner that's distressing you?"*

The captain glanced at Logan.

"No." It didn't sound convincing, even in my own mind.

Mira laughed at something Logan said, and I visibly cringed when her hand floated to his arm.

"He doesn't care for your cousin, Harper." Jacob's voice was gentle in my mind.

"I wouldn't mind if he did."

Jacob raised his brows. *"You're a terrible liar. You can read him just as well as I can. He's uncomfortable. He's not enjoying the conversation."*

"I will not allow my magic to slither over there right now," I retorted.

"Unlike you, I'm giving my magic free rein in this ball-room, and I can tell you what I'm sensing from my lieutenant friend. Distaste, discomfort, distrust..."

I smiled despite myself at Logan's multiple emotions starting in 'dis,' nodded at the police captain, and took his arm. "Will you escort me into the dining room, Captain Miller?"

He glanced at James, waiting for permission, and my brother shrugged. Jacob rested a steadying hand on mine as we walked through the crowd of chattering Ledes.

"Have you always disliked family dinners?" he asked. "Or is tonight a particularly off night for you?"

"Don't events like this overwhelm your senses, Captain? Crowds have always exhausted me. Besides, I've always been the odd one in this family," I explained.

The youngest. Motherless. The only cousin without the brand. One of only four girls among twelve cousins, but Mira, Ana, and Grace had never let me in their circle.

He nodded. "I felt that way growing up as well," he said. "It made it easier to leave York when the opportunity arose."

"Did you also grow up in a large family?" I asked.

As he scanned the long dining table, a glimmer of melancholy danced in his eyes. "Quite the opposite. It was just my aunt and me. She's my only family."

I nodded. Jacob understood what it was like. Any mindspeaker would. I was certain he could sympathize with me, even though our circumstances were different.

Being a mindspeaker taught me a deep kind of empathy, and despite my sarcastic shell, I felt deeply for the people around me. I knew Jacob could relate to that. My coping mechanism had always been humor, but Jacob was kind and open. I remembered how the officers on the street responded to him, and a pang of jealousy echoed through me.

I let go of his arm to check where my name card had been placed and breathed a sigh of relief to see Perry on one side of me and Emelia on the other. I traveled around the table. Father was to be seated across from Emelia with Bess on his left.

I huffed a sigh when I realized Logan had been seated directly across from me.

Beside Father. Next to Mira.

I could picture Aunt Bea and Aunt Pat mulling over these placards all day, and I wondered how many times Logan's name had rotated around the table before they settled on the spot.

Jacob poured me another drink as family and guests began to file into the dining room. I found myself staring at the same place I always did when I felt lost or disconnected.

Pity washed over Jacob's face when he caught me studying the portrait of my mother. I sighed and plopped down in the settee under the painting. Jacob nodded at me with a compassionate smile as Uncle Bain cornered him, no doubt to discuss the mystery of the stolen arms. I held up my glass to the police captain, saluting him for escorting me into the dining room.

The cushion sagged on my other side as James found a seat.

"Is Emelia here? I was very relieved to see her name card beside mine." I said, scanning the group. Bess was in an animated conversation with Father and Uncle Aaron on the far side of the room, but her daughter was nowhere to be seen.

He shook his head. "Emelia won't make it tonight. She's

at the bedside of a friend, who is due to deliver her first child any moment. She's acting as midwife."

"I didn't know Emelia was a midwife," I said. The word tasted sour on my tongue, even when it didn't reference Raina.

"She's been learning," James explained, a note of admiration in his voice. "It's a noble profession, and Emelia is quite brilliant. She's been helping as an apprentice for months, but this will be her first time acting alone."

I nodded. Ladies betrothed to wealthy lords didn't need a profession, but it made me like Emelia even more to know she wasn't giving up her studies and her dreams despite her engagement.

The bell rang, and we were summoned to our seats. Bess slid into the chair beside me and rested her dainty hand on my forearm.

"Emelia can't make it, so I get to sit next to Harper," she said, smiling. "Your father thinks you and I are well-matched dinner partners. According to Cade, your humor is complementary to mine."

I chuckled as I unfolded my napkin. "Mrs. Hern, that may have been my father's way of subtly insulting you."

From across the table, my father laughed, and his smile lingered as he unfolded his napkin. I shot James a surprised look, and he shrugged.

"I assure you it was meant as nothing but a compliment, Bess," Father said. *Bess*. Not Mrs. Hern. A flush rose to the woman's warm, brown skin at my father's words. "Harper drives me up a wall much of the time, but it was always her wit that allowed me to forgive her sharp tongue."

Bess nudged me on the shoulder. "A woman well matched indeed, my lady."

I snorted. "Please, call me Harper."

It began to sink in just how much time my father and Bess had spent together over the past weeks. No surprise they had gotten past the formalities of lord and lady.

Logan pulled out his chair, his shoulders tense. Mira was close behind. I wanted to slap the smug grin off her face when he pulled out her chair. Instead, I gave her one of my most sanguine smiles.

"Ah," Father said. "My daughter's dutiful guard has arrived. Do you ever get a night off, Lieutenant Greer? Even after an injury?"

Logan smiled and unfolded his napkin. "Lord Cade, I'm off the clock tonight, but I assure you I will step up if need be."

I rolled my eyes and turned to Bess. "Don't try to stab me with that butter knife, Mrs. Hern. The lieutenant has sworn an oath, you see."

Bess let out a belly laugh and raised her brows at Father, and he nodded back. He had proved his point.

The woman beside me radiated cordiality. I reached out with my magic, and all I could feel was an easy contentment, a feeling that deepened as her gaze shot back toward my father. Bess and Father exchanged a glance, and the warmth that radiated from him sent a chill down my spine.

He had never looked so happy in the company of someone before.

Uncle Aaron chimed in from beside James, asking detailed questions about the wedding. Whenever James faltered or stumbled, Bess came to his rescue with a funny story or a joke. I was relieved to have her by my side, and I could tell James felt the same way.

We were halfway through the salad course when Mira finally chimed in.

"Harper," she said, stabbing her tomato, "I so wish to hear about your little art project on the wall. Logan has already told me so much about it, but his accounts are mostly dull. Surely, there must be something more exciting about it than he lets on."

Logan. Not Lieutenant Greer. She patted his arm again, and my hand reflexively tightened around my napkin. I prayed I would get through this evening without setting something on fire.

I grinned at the lieutenant before I replied, "Ah, Lieutenant Greer only tells dull stories because I don't allow him to look at me when I work. He stands some ways away. I could be painting in the nude for all he knows."

My father choked on his wine. "Harper, please."

Bess released another chortle, and James put his head in his hands. Uncle Aaron cleared his throat, but I could tell he was trying not to laugh.

Logan, on the other hand, flushed a bit. "I assure you, my lord, I'm watching her closely enough."

I shrugged. "Maybe the militia could benefit from some nude painting. You know, to boost morale. That's why I'm there in the first place. Right, Lieutenant?"

Logan's flush turned into a boil.

Mira merely scoffed. "I'm not sure what kind of morale boost that would be."

I was about to tell her about all the things I was capable of boosting when I was interrupted by a commotion. Shouts and hurried footsteps in the corridor sounded before the door flew open. At the sight of a frenzied militia sentry, my father and his brothers were on their feet before anyone else.

"My lords, there is a fire. In the pines."

PART TWO

CHAPTER
TWENTY-FIVE

There hadn't been a fire in the Barrens in over fifty years. Not since my father and his brothers had taken their first breaths in this realm.

Now, the triplet Lords of Galloway rushed to the door, running straight to the fire like there was nothing more natural.

Perhaps they were drawn somehow to the flame. The magic was possibly running within their blood, ready to flow toward its source at the first sign of heat. I wondered for a moment if my father had known the fires might return someday. Had he dreamed about it? Had he and his brothers spoken of it in hushed tones?

Axel, Bain's only son who wielded fire, didn't hesitate to join his father, and a rare flash of pride appeared in Bain's eyes. Behind them, the fire-wielding twin generals, Paxton and Brannon, started barking orders to the sentries who had filed in.

My breaths were already laced with ash, and something sinister tingled under my skin, beckoning me. Was the fire also calling to me? Was this what the other fire wielders in the room were feeling? I was frozen in my chair as my skin erupted with a heat so raw it was cold. Chills raked over my skin.

Surely this fire didn't have something to do with my own fire magic coming to the surface. Could it be? Maybe there was something sinister about the magic that had sparked within me.

I was going to burst into flame. If I didn't run to that fire, if I didn't let it soak into my skin, something within me would snuff out.

James sprang to his feet, unaware of my distress.

"Mrs. Hern, please let me escort you home," he said. "We can watch over Emilia."

Bess nodded, fixing her eyes on Father. She rose, giving me a nervous squeeze before she followed James out. Aunt Bea ushered Mira toward the stairs and the safety of their quarters. The manor had been standing since well before my father and his brothers were born. It was designed to withstand the threat of fire that had once plagued the Barrens.

The members of the dinner party began to scatter, pushing back their chairs in a shuffle as they fled. But I couldn't move. The burning on my skin was painful now, and I held out my hand, turning it to scan for scars and blisters.

There was nothing but pale, unbranded skin.

When I pulled my attention away, the dining room had nearly cleared out, but two men remained, and they were as unmoving as I was.

Jacob braced his hands on the table, considering me with a look of nauseated alarm. Beside him, Logan's eyes were wide, and his jaw was clenched as he stared at me.

Paxton approached Logan and Jacob with a furrowed brow. "Logan, come with me. This could be a diversion. I need you to take an urgent account of arms and guard the armory in case this is an attack."

A muscle in Logan's jaw flexed. He glanced in my direction, and for a moment, I thought he was going to say no. Instead, he said, "Of course, General." His voice cracked a bit when he added. "But first, I want to ensure Lady Harper gets home safe in the absence of my guard."

Paxton nodded, appraising Logan.

Perry and Rand appeared at my side. "We'll take her home," Rand said, taking my arm.

I blinked up at my cousins, dumbfounded, so transfixed by the fire that had crept through my skin that I was numb to his touch.

Paxton shook his head. "Axel is busy fighting the fire. You two need to watch over the tavern. Ensure plenty of water is on hand in case of a spread." He turned to Jacob. "Captain Miller, I charge you with escorting Harper back to the townhouse. Make sure Maggie is safe and that the town-home is equipped to handle an emergency."

"Would it not be safer for me to wait here?" I asked, my heart hammering at the thought of leaving the manor.

"The townhouse is in the center of town. It's just as safe as the manor, Harper. I can help you make sure the struc-ture is secure if the fire spreads within the wall," Jacob replied.

He must have been reading my thoughts. My cousins nodded in agreement.

The wall. I pictured my mural, the delicate gradations of red and yellow, being engulfed by real flames, and my heart sank into a black hole of dread. If the wall burned—if it fell, what would happen to Galloway without the physical barrier between the village and the pines?

Jacob and Logan exchanged words before Jacob took my hand and led me to the door.

We rushed down the stairs, past scurrying maids and butlers. Servants closed doors, covered furniture, and threw fabric tarps over portraits. Benjamin and a few other young men on the house staff carried buckets of water to the door.

As we ran out of the manor, the courtyard was already covered with ash-laden fog. Bells chimed through the village, alerting the citizens to the threat.

"How could a fire break out under the protection of the fire wielders?" I asked, breathless.

Jacob tightened his hand around my own, but I barely felt the pressure of his grip. "It's not natural."

Not natural at all. It was nearly winter. It was dark outside.

In the distance, a glow danced through the mist, and my heart swelled at the sight of it. My chest ached. I needed to go to it. I squeezed Jacob's hand, and his return grip was firm enough to sting through the flames that crackled through me.

"Do you think someone set the fire? Do you think it's the same person stealing the arms?" I asked. Ash burned in my throat, making my voice rasp.

"No, I don't think a person is responsible at all," Jacob said, his strides quickening.

We passed the tavern, where Perry and Rand were already stabilizing the structure, filling buckets from a nearby well. At the end of the street, my steps veered toward the alley.

The same alley that Logan and Jacob had cornered me

in. It had only been a week, but I was a wholly different person than I had been that night. Something strange and wild was stirring in me.

My arm snagged as Jacob directed me, not toward the alley or home, but to the park. The exact path Logan had followed me down on the way to the wall. Willows and oaks swayed like ghosts in the ash.

"The townhouse is that way," I said, my voice straining with the steady burn in my throat.

"We're not going to the townhouse," Jacob returned, tightening his grip on my hand so hard my bones threatened to crack.

As we veered toward the park, heat flared in my blood. "The gates to the Barrens are in the park," I shouted at him. "We're running toward the fire."

A wild, primal voice within me told me to run faster. I blinked, and I heard the frantic sound of a horse's whinny, desperate terror in the darkness of my mind. Unbridled fire roiled through me and settled over the spot on my spine that held my scar.

Jacob quickened his pace. "Yes, we are."

We were several steps into the park when I pulled against his arm, under the cover of the same tree where Logan had intercepted me.

"Jacob, stop!"

He halted and reeled toward me. "Harper, please. Listen to me. You're the only person who can stop this. You need to speak to the demon who's lighting the fire."

I pulled in an ashy gasp. "You think this is a demon?"

"I know it's a demon," he said, his voice a ragged whisper. "Only a pit demon can summon a flame against the power of a fire wielder."

My head spun as I remembered the notes I had taken in the library. A pit demon was *made* of fire. The text described them as the Devil's pets, only released into the mortal realm to deliver a message.

But how could such a creature be in the pines? It would have had to travel from the fire realm.

I had never communicated with any demon but the Alister before. Suddenly, a mist demon that spoke in riddles seemed like the least of my worries. The smell of sulfur hit me, wafting on the wind from the direction of the gates.

Jacob was right.

"I've never handled a pit demon, Jacob. I barely figured out the Alister. What makes you think I can communicate with this thing? What if it burns us to death?"

Jacob dropped my hand, pulling in frantic breaths despite the tainted air. His eyes darkened, the cloudy blue taking on an ashen hue in the low light of the lamps. He said nothing for a moment before looking past me toward the gates, where an amber glow flared.

"You will be able to communicate with it, Harper. There's a reason only you can speak to them." Jacob's face paled. "I can't. James can't."

I was going to vomit. "It's mindspeaking."

He squeezed his eyes shut, like he was searching for an answer in the darkness.

"It's not mindspeaking, Harper. It's what you were born to do," he said.

I shook my head. "I don't understand." Tears welled in my eyes with the weight of his words. "Make me understand."

Then, Jacob Miller began to cry—not tears summoned by the ash in the air. No, there was something deeper in these tears, and as the first drop fell over his cheek, I realized they were rooted in something much more dangerous than the flame that crept toward the wall.

Jacob wiped his eyes with his sleeve before he pulled back the thick fabric of his uniform. The wool peeled away, revealing pale skin, pale like my own. Branded upon the skin of his forearm, lines sung out in the delicate, familiar script that had been written on my heart.

The number *12*.

CHAPTER

TWENTY-SIX

I couldn't speak. All I could do was stare at the branded numerals on Jacob's arm. The same script that adorned the skin of all the Ledes cousins.

Except me. I peered up into his face, and my heart sank at the devastation etched upon his features.

My features. He fell to his knees before me, and I followed his lead, sinking into the tall grass under the willow tree. My hand drifted up, and I traced the arch of his eyebrow with my thumb, assuring myself that he wasn't a mirage.

Regret and unspeakable sadness were written into his eyes, blue like James's and gray like mine.

His dark hair resembled Father's, but the waves were similar to mine. I had never examined him closely before, so I had never noticed the mole in front of his left ear—a perfect reflection of my own. Tears streamed down his cheeks, and light caught in his eyes, reminiscent of my mother's likeness. The same features I had studied in the portrait my entire life.

Our mother.

My tears evolved into gulping cries, and Jacob embraced me and sobbed into my hair.

"I wanted to tell you from the moment I met you." His words rang through my mind like they had been stuck within him forever.

"This can't be possible," I said. But the longer he held me there, the more certain I was. This man was the other half of me.

My brother.

My twin.

Despite the fire raging from beyond the wall, I allowed myself to sit there, kneeling with Jacob.

And we cried. And he squeezed me so tight I thought he would never let go.

All of it made sense now. His nerves at family dinners. The way he stumbled when he spoke to Father and James was so opposed to his easy, casual mannerisms.

Flares of anxiety that I sensed from him in the townhouse. What it must have been like for him to sit down and eat breakfast with his family, unable to tell them that he belonged to them—and them to him.

The number twelve on his arm flashed in the lamp's light, and realization struck me.

"I'm the thirteenth child," I whispered into his mind. I was too terrified to speak it aloud.

His sobs deepened, and all he could do was nod.

"I'm the reason this is all happening. I'm the reason the Alister is here. The pit demon is here for me, too, isn't it?"

Jacob finally pulled away, holding my shoulders at arm's length. "I don't know. All I know is you're the only one who can stop it."

Because I belonged to the Devil.

The mystic had said it was so. The thirteenth child would belong to him. Bile rose in my throat, but I choked it down. A thousand questions swam in my mind, but they needed to wait. Galloway would burn if I didn't send this demon back to where it came from.

Maybe this was what was drawing me to the flames. Perhaps it had nothing to do with my fire magic. Was it my fire magic after all, or was it some part of the Devil's claim to me?

"I'll go through the gate," I said, standing. "Wait for me here."

He shook his head. "I promised to stay with you until the fire was out. I promised I would keep you safe."

He had promised Logan.

My knees threatened to buckle. "Does Logan know?"

Jacob shook his head. "He doesn't know. Nobody in your family knows, either." A muscle in his jaw ticked.

Our family. I shook off my shock as we ran toward the gate.

The iron gate was nearly as thick as the wall itself, and it took both our strength to swing it open. I was surprised there were no guards sentried there, but it made our passage easier.

The forest floor of the Barrens was heavily laden with pine needles, a perfect blanket of kindling, and they crunched under our feet as we ran toward the source of the flame. I prayed to a god who probably wouldn't answer someone so cursed as we ran as hard as we could, imploring that we wouldn't run into any of the guards.

Perhaps somebody listened to my prayer because we only

encountered a thickening flame. I didn't dare summon my new fire magic and didn't begin to comprehend how anyone could extinguish such a flame.

My heart hammered as we ran through the smoke, our vision becoming increasingly murky as we barreled toward the source. What would I do when I got to the demon? What does someone say to a messenger from hell?

I stopped in my tracks, an idea forming, and Jacob stopped along with me. I was beginning to feel lightheaded from the lack of clean air.

I screamed into my mind, "*I summon you here, pit demon! I summon you as a messenger of the Triplet Lords of Galloway.*"

Jacob nodded at me as he pulled an iron blade from the sheath on his back, angling it toward the fire.

The voice that returned was pure silk and smoke. Despite the heat of the flames and the thickness of the air, a hollow chill raked through me at the sound of it.

"*Tell your brother to put down his sword, Harper Ledes, and I will come.*"

My jaw tightened. The audacity of this thing. "*Tell me why you're here, and my brother*"—Jacob's eyes flared—"*my twin will put down his sword.*"

His laugh was a hiss that vibrated against my skin. "*Such daring. Such cunning. You are everything our master hoped for.*"

I was moments away from either passing out or vomiting on the forest floor.

"*I have no master.*" I attempted to make my voice sound strong, but even in my mind, it wavered.

The thing tutted at me. "*Oh, but you do. Now, tell your*

twin to put down his sword, and I will put out my flame. Then we can speak. Then I can give you my message."

"He wants you to put down the sword," I said aloud.

Jacob obeyed.

"*Good boy,*" the demon crooned. True to his promise, the flames began to wither, shrinking back into an otherworldly crack. Branches popped and snapped as the temperature adjusted. Soot cleared from the air, and ash began to recede from the atmosphere.

I took in a considerably lighter breath before I said, "*Thank you.*"

"*I'm true to my word, Harper Ledes. Will you be when I tell you what I was sent here to tell you?*"

My stomach clenched. "*That depends on what you tell me.*"

"*My master has grown restless. And with his restlessness, we grow anxious.*"

We. The collective *we* of the demons who had flocked to this part of the Barrens.

I blinked as a figure materialized before me, the shape of a man cloaked in nothing but flames. Jacob's hand clutched my forearm, and I gasped. A wicked grin, an empty void of blackness within the flames, erupted on the creature's face.

"*The Alister told me,*" the pit demon said, "*despite his reluctance to do so, you were unaware of who you were, Harper Ledes. Are you fully aware of who you are now? Is that why you came here to put out this fire?*"

"*Why don't you start by telling me why you're here? How did you get here?*" I was beginning to hate this demon more than I was afraid of it. Despite myself, I found myself worried for the Alister. I hoped this pit demon hadn't tortured him in pursuit of some information about me.

"*Very well.*" His voice was oily and crackled like fat cooking in a pan. "*My master knew of your ignorance. He hoped my presence would prompt your brother to tell the truth. He was right. You belong to him, you know. Power like yours is owed to him after everything he lost when the triplet lords were born.*"

I shook my head. "*I belong to no one. And my father and my uncles took nothing from him. They were born with this power. They didn't seek it out. The lords use their magic to protect this village from flames.*"

Jacob's hand tightened on my wrist, and one glance at him told me he was considering fleeing back to the gate. I dared not mindspeak with him in case the demon could hear the conversation. Instead, I met his stare and nodded slightly. His grip loosened.

The demon waved his hand. "*Indeed, they didn't steal it. Magic is born, not taken. But their birth, magic fueled by the power of three, sealed the Barrens. Before, the Barrens were my master's domain. He would come through the thin space and let some of his fire leak into this realm. He only wishes to return here to liberate flames. My fire, on the other hand, isn't real.*"

Indeed, the fire seeping from the pit demon seemed to reflect off the pine boughs. I watched them dance for a moment with wide eyes. None of the trees had ignited despite the bed of kindling at our feet.

The pit demon spread his hands before he continued. "*My fire could never take root here. It's only an illusion. Even the ash in the air is not true, a shadow of what it would be like. The thin space is cracking, and I was able to slip through those cracks. It needs to fully open before he can return.*"

The Devil wanted free rein to release his flames. It could be catastrophic for the village.

My head spun. *"My father and his brothers have kept our village safe from fire. How can your master return without risking everything we've built here?"*

The thing laughed, widening the blackness of his hideous mouth. *"Do you not realize what you have lost without his flames?"*

My brows knitted together. Was the demon suggesting the fires had been beneficial to Galloway somehow? My gaze swept over the landscape of pines, a tinderbox of dry needles covered by a canopy so thick the sky would be hidden even if there was no mist.

But there were paintings in the manor, older than my father. Older than this promise the Devil had made. Those paintings were the only depictions of the sky I had ever seen. Within them, my ancestors stood in lush gardens with actual flowers.

What had we lost when the thin place was sealed?

I met the demon's stare, inclining my chin toward him. *"Tell your master I'm willing to speak to him. But I will only communicate through the Alister."*

The laugh was low and sinister. *"The Alister and my master are not on good terms."*

I considered asking why, but I already knew it had something to do with me. *"I will only communicate with a demon who won't cause a panic in this village to get his point across."*

The pit demon shrugged his fiery shoulders. *"There is another to whom you may ask questions—the one who was made for you. Your counterpart. But right now, he is warded, trapped in a ruined house surrounded by an armory of iron.*

Free the horse, Harper Ledes." The gaping hole in his face was feral now.

And with that, the demon disappeared like he was merely a wick being snuffed by a damper.

Jacob and I found ourselves alone in the pitch-blackness of the Barrens.

CHAPTER

TWENTY-SEVEN

In the darkness, the only sound was our breathing. Jacob and I drank in the clean air, now free of ash and sulfur with the absence of the pit demon.

His voice was a whisper in my mind. "*What do we do now?*"

I reached for his hand in the darkness and found it like a magnet. "*Free the horse. I don't know what that means.*"

Jacob let out a ragged sigh. "*I do,*" he said.

He must have sensed my ripple of shock.

"*There's so much I want to tell you. So much I need to tell you, but we need to get you home right now. And get out of the Barrens before something else comes for us.*"

I nodded and let him follow, gripping his hand as we trudged through the wall. I shivered at how his palm fit over mine—like I had held it in some dream before either of us existed.

My twin.

There was so much I wanted to ask him. How had we

206

been separated? Who had raised him? I had a feeling I knew. They had never found Raina after our mother had died. Was she the one who'd taken him? I had so many questions, but the last thing I wanted was to ask them.

Not right now.

It was all too much to process. We walked through the trees, and as we trudged along, I didn't smell the char of burnt wood despite the extinguished fire. Only the unnatural taint of sulfur and dust. I wondered where Father was and what he and his brothers thought of the sudden inferno that had snuffed out like a candle, leaving no damage.

When we reached the stone wall, we followed it to the gate. The gate was never locked from the inside. It didn't need to be. Nobody in their right mind would attempt to leave the confines of the wall unless they were part of the militia and armed. A latch had clicked outside, arming the door with a heavy iron lock.

Jacob produced a skeleton key bigger than his hand from his pocket and worked the contraption. Before we slunk back into the village, he ensured nobody was posted around the gates.

It was eerily quiet, but tension was in the air as we walked through the park on our way to the townhouse. I opened my mouth to ask a question several times before shutting it again. I glanced at him as we walked. *How could I not have known this man was my twin?*

His long strides hit the pavement, and I marveled at how his gait was much like James's. He bit his lip and ran a hand down his jaw, a manner identical to Father's when he was nervous. I should have been angry at Jacob for keeping this from me. I should hate him for agreeing to blackmail me and making me help them solve these crimes despite what he knew all along.

I didn't know what to feel.

I knew now that a piece of my heart had been missing my entire life. I had just found something I'd had no idea was missing. There was no room for anger.

We turned onto our street, and he must have caught a glimmer of my thoughts because he turned to me, his brow furrowed. Before we could speak, a figure in the haze stalked toward us.

Logan's eyes were wide as he approached. "When I got to the house, your candle was out, and Maggie said you had never returned." His hand rose to brace the wound on his flank.

Jacob's jaw tightened as Logan glared at him.

"Jacob accompanied me home, but I left as soon as he turned away," I said. The lie came out easily. Sneaking out was something I would do, after all.

"*You don't have to lie, Harper,*" Jacob said into my mind.

I ignored him, sliding away from our secret conversation as effortlessly as I did with James.

"I wanted to see if the Alister knew how to stop the fire. I had been researching demons and suspected a pit demon. Jacob followed me and stopped me before I could get to the gate."

The muscles in Logan's jaw tightened. "I told him you would try to do that," he said, crossing his arms.

Jacob winced, confirming it was true.

I braced my hands on my hips and turned to Logan. "You couldn't spy on me yourself, so you sent one of your dogs to do it for you."

Logan let out a curse under his breath.

"*Sorry, no offense,*" I said into Jacob's mind.

"*None taken.*" Then Jacob spoke aloud. "I need to go. Extra patrols will be needed tonight."

Logan nodded to his friend, and Jacob nodded back. "*Good luck,*" he said into my mind. "*I promise I'll tell you everything. Tomorrow.*"

Jacob walked away, and Logan started to pace in front of the gate, only steps away from where he had kissed me.

"Is Maggie okay?" I asked.

He ran his fingers through his hair, loosening the strands that had been so neatly combed back during dinner. "Shaken up a bit. She went with James to the Herns' to help Emelia."

I nodded. "Has my father returned?"

"He hasn't, and he won't," Logan said, his eyes diverting to the sky as though he could see through the blanket of mist above us. "All the fire wielders remain at the barracks to ensure the fire is out."

I was sure Logan believed what the rest of Galloway believed. The triplet lords had saved them from fire and whatever demon summoned it. There was no possibility that he—or anyone else—could have guessed the truth of what happened in the Barrens. I glanced down at my arms, now bare without my ornate gloves. My skin had never been more naked.

"I'm surprised you haven't stationed yourself outside the manor," I said. The words left my lips before I could stop them, and I hated myself for it.

Jealous. That's how I sounded.

Anger flared in Logan's eyes. "After everything, that's what you think?"

"Did you come here to scold me?"

"It's not my job to scold you," Logan said, stepping closer. "I knew you would do something reckless tonight. I just knew it. That's why I asked Jacob to walk you home. I warned him you would go to the wall."

My hands clenched, tightening into fists. "You know me so well. Congratulations."

It took every ounce of strength to bite back my stubborn pride and not tell him what happened. How I found the pit demon. The books we had found in the library helped me after all. That I was the cursed thirteenth Ledes child, and he should walk away.

Each detail swam through me, dizzying and unreal.

I turned to the front gate, reaching for the latch, but he caught my wrist in his palm. He pulled me toward him, and I reeled, colliding with him.

He winced, but he drew me closer despite the pain from his healing wound. "You thought a pit demon was out there and wanted to chat with it, Harper."

I shivered when he said my name, like the word on his lips put some spell on me.

"I needed to try. You would have done the same thing if you thought you could save this village." My hands began to shake. I wanted to tell him what Jacob and I had done— what we were—so badly. I wasn't the kind of woman Logan wanted to protect.

No. I was no better than the creatures outside this wall.

Cursed.

Perhaps a part of me had always known.

His eyes darkened. "It's like you're trying to get hurt."

"You would be far better off if I were out of your life." My words hit him.

He let go of my arm, pure desperation wrought on his face. "I've been standing outside your window every night. They wouldn't let me come when I was in the infirmary, and it killed me. I worried about you. The whole time I was there, I was sick."

My lips parted. "The demon venom—"

"Had nothing to do with it," he interrupted. "The thought of you doing something reckless made me sick. Because you're the most reckless person I've ever met."

I *was* reckless. More than he even knew.

Because at that moment, I wanted to prove it to him. I wanted to pull him closer to me and sink into that feeling again. I knew how he would react. He would wrap his arms around my waist and kiss me, his lips parting around mine. His hand would have swept over my hip, over the buttons of my gown, while his other hand swept higher, over the bones of my corset.

It was late. I could have taken him by the hand and led him to my bed. I pictured how quickly his fingers would move, unbuttoning my dress—to feel his skin against mine —and I knew he was thinking about the same thing as he stood before me, his stare trailing over my lips.

I sensed it—all of it—wafting through his mind as he stood in silence, his chest heaving. And I let my magic slink through the heat and into his thoughts until it overcame my senses.

Lust. An unnerving desire to touch me, to taste me. To protect me. Logan had no walls up, and in his mind, his lips were on me, and his teeth were grazing over my skin. He was undressing me and releasing the weight of his fear as he held me closer, skin to skin. It almost felt real, so much so that I began to throb for him. He fantasized about what it would be like to slide inside me, and I lived through it with my magic.

I closed my eyes, drunk on his thoughts.

I wanted it to be real, not just a daydream I saw in his mind.

But I didn't allow my magic to dwell inside of Logan. Instead, I stepped through the gate and closed it between us. His blue eyes flared in the golden light of the lamps, their eerie sheen highlighting his scar.

Logan didn't deserve this. He didn't deserve a daughter of hell in his bed. That's exactly what I was.

My entire life, I had been the strange one.

The unbranded. Sharp-tongued, and now I knew the reason why.

Because my tongue was forked all along.

"I'm not going to paint tomorrow," I said. "You should have plenty of time to call on Mira in my absence."

His lust gave way to anger, sharp and raw.

"They've invited me twice, and I haven't gone," he said through gritted teeth.

"Well, you should," I replied.

My words cut through him like I had poured salt into the wound that still gaped on his flank.

Logan's eyes darkened before he spoke aloud. "You've asked for a new guard repeatedly. Tomorrow, I will honor your request." He swallowed. "I will grant your wish. You're free. From all of it. You've provided me with enough information. Nobody will blame you for abandoning an unfinished mural after what happened tonight. If you don't want to be a part of this anymore, I won't force you."

A part of this.

He wasn't referring to the wall, to the painting, or to the

raids. No, he was referring to this thing that had grown between us, despite the blackmail, all the secrets. Despite the demons. I blinked, not knowing what to say. Words were stuck in my throat. I was about to call his name before he turned and walked away into a mist so thick it swallowed him whole.

CHAPTER

TWENTY-EIGHT

I scrubbed my skin until it bled, but the scent of burnt wood and sulfur seemed to be a part of me now.

The words of the pit demon haunted my dreams.

Free the one who was made for you.

When I drifted into sleep, I saw Jacob's face etched with a bloody **12**. Someone had cut it into his skin, and my hands had gripped a knife.

Between the images of my twin, the hoofbeats pounded on the forest floor. There was not one baby crying now. Two wails echoed through my nightmares, one weak and one loud.

I had two pairs, kings and queens. A laugh echoed as I put the cards down on the table. Across the table, crimson fingernails rapped on the table.

"You think you can beat me?" Mira placed her cards down.

A royal flush.

I woke before dawn, inspecting the skin on my forearm as

though the knowledge I'd gained would have afforded me a branded *13*. After a rush to the chamber pot, I vomited, and everything that came up tasted like fire. I returned to bed and fell asleep before eventually waking to Maggie's concerned voice.

She fussed over me, brought me coffee, and was disappointed when I finally admitted I was abandoning my work on the mural.

I read her thoughts as I explained myself, and they all seemed centered on Logan's absence in my life. Perhaps she thought the lieutenant was a positive influence on me. More likely, she had noticed the tension between us for what it was.

I dressed and went downstairs. Father and James hadn't yet returned as I ate, and the bland bread did little to settle my stomach.

The rays of light through the window were at the height of midday when the back door opened, and Father entered the kitchen. His face was drawn, and his eyelids were circled in shadows.

He did a double-take when he found me sitting at the table. "Are you okay, Harp? You appear unwell." His voice was raspy.

"I was worried about you," I said. It wasn't a lie. Over and over, I had questioned how I would even begin to tell him everything I'd learned last night. Ultimately, I had decided I wouldn't tell him anything.

Not yet.

I needed to figure everything out first. James, too, would need to be in the dark for just a while longer.

He pulled off a chunk of bread and sank into the chair next to me, a man utterly unaware he had another son.

Unaware his lost child had shaken his hand. Had been invited into our home.

"James sent word to the manor this morning," he said between swallows. "The babe was born last night. Healthy and hearty."

Emelia had pulled it off. I wondered if the baby born at the height of a demonic fire would inherit any fire magic. I surmised Father was thinking the same as he stared into the hearth, and the embers there surged to life.

Something swelled in my chest as I realized there may be one thing I could share with my father after everything that had happened last night.

I stared at the light dancing in his eyes. "May I ask you something?"

He nodded, allowing his attention to pull away from the flames. "Of course, Pumpkin."

"Please promise not to overreact."

He raised his brow.

"And also, don't tell James. Or anyone for that matter."

A bemused smile broke through on his weary face. "A secret between just you and me? I promise."

"Would it be possible, if someone had a very small amount of fire magic, for it to manifest late?"

His smile melted away. "Why do you ask me this?"

I gestured to the fire, concentrating on pouring out every emotion I had experienced in the past few days. A single flame licked out, taller and brighter than the rest, before it swept into a circle.

My father's eyes widened. "That was you."

I nodded. "I only recently discovered I had it in me, but looking back, I wonder if it's been there all along."

He flinched, and I knew he was thinking of my birth—

how I had survived the fire that claimed his wife's life. I had begun to regret telling him when he stood. He put his hands on my shoulders and squeezed before he drew me up into a hug.

"Oh, Harper, I'm so honored you shared this with me." His words came out as a sob. "It will be hard for me to keep this secret. I want to shout it from the rooftops."

I squeezed him back. "But you won't, right?"

He pulled away and brushed a happy tear from his cheek. "A promise is a promise," he said. "Your magic is my magic, Harper. It makes me so proud to share that with you. I wish I could at least tell Aaron and Bain. They would understand."

Tears threatened to claim me when I remembered how proud Bain had been when Axel ran to help with the fire.

If my father only knew I had inherited something much more powerful from my mother. What would he think then? There was such a strong balance of them within me. I felt it, even though I never knew her.

A part of Sarah Ledes—her magic—was always there.

"Will you show me how to control it?" I asked.

He agreed. After shooing Maggie away to the market, we worked on basic techniques for the rest of the morning.

By the time we were finished, I could summon a flame to a wick and put it out again. I had been correct in assuming that deep emotions heightened the magic. Father showed me how to pull up a strong feeling and tie it to the flame. When the emotion retreated to the depths of my chest, I learned to use the same tether to extinguish it.

When we finished our lesson, his face was less drawn than I had ever seen it, and as I watched him relax, a part of me did, too. Because my father only showed happiness in this news. Not wariness over the possibility I could have been the one who started the fire that killed my mother.

If he believed my fire magic was a positive thing, then perhaps I should, too. It had always been this way between us. Even though I never let my magic intrude upon his thoughts, I knew how my father's mind worked. I knew he and I processed stress similarly. Knew he worried more than he should.

He always knew the right thing to say to James and me. As a child, when I was bullied, he always knew how to turn those feelings around. Even in this moment, when he wasn't saying anything at all, he was telling me all I needed to know.

"You seem happy," I said. Perhaps it was the closeness we had just shared, but he didn't recoil at my words.

Instead, he closed his eyes and let his head rest on the back of the chair. "I feel lighter than I have for some time," he admitted. "I think something is sparking within me that has long been extinguished."

I took his hand and squeezed, recalling how his face had illuminated with a genuine smile whenever he was around Bess. I reached out with my magic, and something I had never detected from my father washed through my mind.

It wasn't the wedding planning that ignited this fire. Bess had sparked this new feeling inside him. For the first time in my life, the heaviness of his grief was eased by something lighter.

Contentment.

"I'm happy for you," I said.

He squeezed my hand back, and I wondered if he knew what I was alluding to. Perhaps leaving Galloway was not the answer I had been searching for, after all. The answer may have been here within these walls all along.

All he needed was time and the right circumstances—the right person—to return to the man he once was.

When James returned home, Father retired to his room to rest after a long night watching the pines for rogue flames. I hadn't dared to ask him for his account of what had happened. I assumed he had expected the pit demon.

When James retreated to his room for an afternoon nap, I perched myself on the settee by the front window, searching for unsearchable shapes. My heart leaped when a tall, broad figure appeared at the gate, but as the mass of dark hair came into focus, I realized it was Jacob, not Logan.

He saw me at the window before approaching the door and slid into my mind, a gentle tap of his magic knocking on a door.

I let him in.

"*You're sitting in the window,*" he said.

"*You're standing at the gate,*" I replied.

He laughed. "*Can you come out?*"

I nodded and grabbed my cloak from the hook, trying to make as little noise as possible so I wouldn't wake the men upstairs. Jacob was leaning on the gate when I walked down the front steps, and for the first time, I took in my brother in daylight.

The slope of his cheekbones. The wave of his hair.

It was a marvel I hadn't realized the likeness before. Looking at him was like peering into a mirrored glass.

"If you're up for it," he said, glancing up and down the street, "there's someone I'd like you to meet."

I swallowed down my fear and nodded.

He started down the street, away from the manor and toward the edge of town. As we approached the dwellings adjacent to the wall, the homes became less grand and a bit dingier. I followed him, my heart thundering along with the clop of my boots.

"My flat is on the far side of town, near the east gate," he said.

Jacob exchanged friendly nods and greetings with some of his officers as we passed. Their presence on the streets was palpable as the militia police patrolled for signs of unrest. The houses got smaller and closer together before we reached larger buildings carved into flats.

We turned down a side street, and I was grateful for the lack of pedestrians as we slunk into a small but tidy brick building. Each step up the stairs to the third story was like walking through quicksand, and when Jacob opened the door, a woman sprang to her feet.

She was older, likely Maggie's age, and very petite. I was slightly below average height, but even I towered over the woman. Her wavy hair was the most beautiful shade of silver, and the waves were unbound and wild, framing a face creased in all the places where a person usually smiles. Her blue-green eyes shone like aquamarines, and it was clear magic sparked behind them.

She clutched a leather-bound book to her chest but placed it down before taking two measured steps toward me.

Jacob broke the silence before closing the door. "Harper, this is—"

"I know who she is."

The midwife. The mystic who had given each of my cousins and siblings their brands.

Raina's voice was a whisper. "Harper."

Simply my name. It was a question—a plea.

I nodded, and relief broke through her walls. Her shoulders relaxed a bit as she looked toward my twin.

Jacob spoke into my mind. *"We have so much we need to tell you."*

I had so much I wanted to ask.

"I know," I said aloud.

Jacob gestured to a chair before the small hearth, beside the one Raina had been sitting in.

"Can I get you something to drink? Tea?" Raina asked. Her voice was sprite-like and soothing, but there was a hint of anxiety.

"She prefers coffee," Jacob said. He pulled a wooden chair from the small dining set to sit beside her.

Raina chuckled and pulled the kettle from the hearth. "Just like you, Jakey. Let me guess, she'll skip the cream and sugar, too."

I wondered how many other quirks I shared with my twin. I swallowed as Jacob studied me, imagining what it must have been like for him—to eat so casually with his secret family that day at breakfast.

I politely took the cup from Raina, who sank into the big, soft cushion across from me.

"I never got a chance to examine you after you were born," she said. "I've assessed every baby I delivered from head to foot. I've counted fingers and toes and traced every line. You were the only one I never got to check."

"You never got to brand me either."

She paled. "No, I didn't."

Jacob cleared his throat. "I know it makes you uncomfortable to speak of your...our mother. But we need to start from the beginning."

I squared my shoulders. "Before you start, I need to know one thing." I pinned Raina with my glare. "Did you kill her?"

My magic slunk into her mind. Tears welled in her eyes, and sorrow cracked through her as she said, "I didn't kill her, Harper."

I fought back my own tears. "If you didn't kill her, then who did?"

Wet streaks fell over the midwife's cheeks, flowing like they had been held back for a long time. "She did, but it was an accident."

I shook my head, my heart hammering. "I don't understand."

Pure sorrow pulsed from her. "She was trying to save you."

TWENTY-NINE

Jacob squeezed Raina's trembling hand, and she nodded to him.

"This is too hard for her. She's not a mindspeaker, but being a mystic has its own emotional toll," he said. "It's best if I tell the story."

I nodded, biting my lip. I didn't know what to do with my hands, so I picked up the coffee cup and cradled it to my chest, bracing it against my ribs so my anxiety didn't vibrate through the hot liquid.

"When Sarah—Mother—was with child, Raina felt only one baby in her womb," he said. "Midwives can tell based on feel, but this pregnancy was more complicated. One of us was positioned behind the other. It made it impossible to determine. There was also something called discordance. I was much smaller than you when I was born. When I came out first, Raina was sure I would die."

The midwife nodded, finding her voice. "Jacob was so frail, so tiny. I'll never forget my relief when he took his first breaths and wailed, loud and strong as I painted the brand on his arm."

Jacob patted the woman's hand like he had done so a thousand times. Like he knew how to steady her. This woman was the only family my twin brother had ever known. All this time, I had pictured her as a villain who had stolen my mother.

In truth, she had saved my lost brother.

Jacob went on. "When you were born, it was a shock. The mist thickened all around the cabin in the Barrens as soon as you took your first breath. Sarah realized what was coming. That she had given birth to the thirteenth child, beholden to a promise made by the Devil. Our mother panicked and pleaded with Raina to take me and run to safety. She was convinced the Devil would come for you. She wore a locket Cade had given her, with a small kernel of his magic imbued within."

I put down my coffee cup and pulled the chain from around my neck, liberating the locket from its hidden place in the bodice of my dress. The metal was unnaturally warm as I cradled it in my palm.

Raina's eyes widened. "I thought it was lost to the fire," she rasped, her eyes fixed on the glinting gold.

I shook my head. "Aunt Patrice recovered it. She must have found it on the scene and held on to it. Last week, I asked about Mother's death, and she gave it to me."

Raina pursed her lips into a thin line. "Sarah knew Cade's magic was the only thing that would keep the Devil away. She yelled at me to grab Jacob and run. I tried to stop her."

She held out her trembling hand, and I placed the locket in her grasp.

She flinched a bit at the heat before she folded her fingers around it. "It all happened too quickly," she said. "The house was engulfed in flames within seconds, and the only thing I could do was grab Jacob. She clutched you in her arms so tightly, Harper. The last thing I saw her do was hold you."

Grief rose in my chest, choking me. "The mist was from the Alister," I said. I realized why the Alister was there and had appeared after my mother's death, covering the village, why he was not in his master's good graces. "He was hiding us."

My mother's friend. All this time, the mist hadn't been a curse for my mother's death.

It was a gift.

All this time, he was shielding me from his master. I put down my coffee cup and put my head in my hands.

"Cade's fire was stronger than Sarah anticipated," Jacob said.

"I ran through the trees," Raina said. "Jacob's little lungs were so delicate. I knew he wouldn't survive if he inhaled the smoke. I was certain he would die. I was still running when I heard the hoofbeats, and there it was. A beautiful, winged horse."

I recalled the description—a black horse with wings like a bat. That very beast had inflicted Logan's scar.

Jacob spoke. "The horse jumped into the flames and retrieved you. When Raina first saw your tiny body in the creature's mouth, she knew he had claimed you. Retrieved you for his master."

Horror danced in the woman's eyes, and my heart cracked at how devastating this must have been for her to witness.

"All those years, I didn't know what had happened to you," she said. "As the guards advanced on the house, the horse ran away with you in its jaws—one called to search for me. I knew Sarah had to be dead, and I imagined you were lost to the demons. How could I explain such sorrow to Cade? Nobody knew there were two babies." Raina choked back a sob. "One of the guards called out my name, giving a command to capture me."

Searing heat flared through me and settled into my back. If the horse had picked me up in its jaws, then its venom had been within my scar all along. I almost laughed at the absurdity of it. I had always believed I had been unbranded, but the horse had branded me, nonetheless.

Marked me as the property of the Devil.

The thirteenth child had been born, and only two souls in this realm had known it. One lost to the fire. One damned to a lifetime of blame. The midwife stared at the fire crackling in the hearth.

"I made the hardest decision I've ever made. I fled," Raina said, her voice small. "I panicked and knew they would accuse me of the whole thing if I ran, but anything was better than telling the lords the truth. I was there when the mystic in the woods told the village about the Devil's promise to take the thirteenth child. I knew what the villagers had whispered when Lady Sarah was with child. They were already in a panic, and some had speculated the village would burn to the ground when the Devil returned." She locked eyes with me. "I thought you were dead, Harper. I thought Jacob would die in my arms..."

It all made sense now. Raina fled to protect the village from the reality of my birth. She fled to protect the villagers from panic, from the truth.

A secret baby and a promise that would never come true. But the Devil had known all along.

Jacob furrowed his brow. "Raina ran through the woods for two days, using her magic to fend off the demons lurking in the Barrens. When she arrived in Hamilton, she boarded a wagon to York. She raised me there, posing as an aunt who took me in when my mother died in childbirth. I was a teenager when she revealed the full story of my birth."

Raina nodded. "We had a quiet life. Jacob's mind-speaking—it was not a rare gift in York, but we didn't tell anyone of it. It isn't a favorable kind of magic."

He nodded. "Two years ago, a traveler from Galloway came to our village. I heard his tale of the three triplet lords and their twelve children. He spoke freely of the mist that shrouded the town. I knew the story of my brand, that I was the true twelfth child, and I knew you were alive, Harper. My family had never known about me. I had never known my twin. It tore me apart to realize you had lived a life in which I didn't exist, but you always existed for me."

My brother turned toward the hearth, overcome with grief.

"Jacob told me he wanted to return when he learned of the wall," Raina said. "But I also knew I was not welcome here. I would have been arrested. Killed, even. I agreed to come under the guise of my magic, cloaking myself and giving a false name on the journey. When we arrived, I was not shocked to learn I was considered a murderer. The mist was thicker than I could have imagined. To this day, I still don't understand how you survived the fire, even if that beast had pulled you from the flames."

Pressure built behind my eyes, and my head swam, over-

flowing with my own secrets. "I survived the fire because...."
I gestured to the hearth, and the flames surged.

Raina gasped. "Mindspeaking isn't your only magical
gift, then."

Gift.

That was an ironic way to describe it. Perhaps some of it
came from my father, but in my heart, I knew. My fire
belonged to another realm, just like I did.

The color drained from Jacob's face when he spoke
again. "When I got to Galloway, I searched the pines for
months, looking for the horse. I knew I had to eliminate any
threat that would reveal the truth of our birth. I guessed
mindspeaking would allow me to communicate with it," he
said.

"Did you intend to keep your identity a secret?" I
asked him.

He nodded. "It would have been enough to be near you.
It would have been enough to keep your secret safe. When
Logan approached me about the stolen arms, I proposed we
involve you in the investigation. I had been watching you, of
course."

I swallowed. "You were watching me."

"Yes," he said. "I had a feeling the demons would try to
communicate with you. I knew of the horse and how it had
circled the village wall. I thought, perhaps, I could speak to
it. Now, I know you're the only one who can speak to the
demons. I don't know why our mother could speak to them.
I did find the horse eventually. Raina and I tricked him, and
she used her magic to corral him back to the very house
where he found you. I knew I had to start warding off the
demons, and that horse has been searching for you since the

moment we were born. It was the only way I could keep you safe."

Raina nodded. "I used magic to conjure the sound of a crying baby, and the beast came. When I saw the concern in its eyes, I immediately regretted it. Part of me wondered why the beast had sought you out. It made me question if it had saved you that day. The villagers say you were found near the gate after the fire. The beast must have brought you there. I believe you may be tied to it somehow."

The voice of the pit demon played in my mind. "*There is another who you may speak with—the one who was made for you. Your counterpart. But right now, he is warded, trapped in that burnt house surrounded by an armory of iron. Free the horse, Harper Ledes.*"

Fire flared in the hearth again. I winced at it. "The pit demon said the horse is warded with iron."

"Yes, he's warded." Jacob exchanged a wince with Raina. "With the iron I stole from the armory."

THIRTY

I stood, and the flames surged in the hearth with me, permeating the room with the smell of cracked wood and something unnatural. I pulled air into my lungs for several breaths before I could identify the subtle tang. Salt and sulfur clung to my magic.

A chill swept through me.

Jacob stepped in front of Raina and put up his hands. "I told you I had more secrets," he said. "I'm sorry."

"You were the one who stole the irons?" My head whirled. All this time, I was solving a crime with the man who'd committed it. Jacob was the reason Logan had been attacked. It was because of him Paxton and Brannon risked themselves. Because of him, so many militiamen were called to extra patrols.

Nausea bubbled through my abdomen, and blood rushed to my head. I was going to be sick again.

Jacob's expression was desperate. "Harper, I'm sorry. When I arrived here, my only goal was to control the demons. I needed to ward the horse. I didn't know if it would take you. When I learned I could ward the demons with the irons, I had to try."

"For me?" The words came out higher and faster than I intended.

His nostrils flared. "You had no idea you were the thirteenth Ledes. They're waiting for you. They've been swarming this village. The Alister has been shrouding the town since your first breath. The beast—that horse—jumped into a fire to retrieve you. What if it came for you again? You're the link, but until yesterday, you didn't know. The Alister is thickening. Demons from deep in the Barrens have been flocking here."

I braced my arm on the hearth. "You stole the irons, but still sought me out to solve the crime. You still agreed to blackmail me. Did you plan to trick me forever? What if Logan found out?"

Jacob's brow knotted. "What else could I have done? Saunter up to you out of the blue and tell you everything? You would have had me arrested. I came to this town selfishly. I needed to know the place I came from. I needed to know my twin. As soon as I arrived, it became clear the wall and mist had been shrouding you from the truth. I planned to ward as many demons as I could. Raina would have been captured and executed. Damn it, Harper, it's forbidden to *speak* of our mother in Galloway. How was I supposed to explain this to you?"

My fingertips rose to my temples, and my magic instinctively reached out to Jacob. He had no walls up, and I was smacked in the face by his remorse. He'd thought he was somehow keeping me safe by stealing the irons and using them to ward the beast, but nausea roiled through me at the thought of the thing trapped behind wards.

"Do you regret it?" I spoke into his mind. *"Returning to me?"*

The question was too hard to speak aloud.

"Yes."

His response gutted me.

The horse had saved me. The Alister had cloaked me. Now, my twin had returned with a singular mission to shield me. The pines tugged on me. I needed to find the horse. Suddenly, I was desperate to free the creature. Or to free myself. The presence of the wall had never felt so suffocating, and even though I was nowhere near it, the hum of it overtook my senses, vibrating through my bones and settling into the scar tissue over my spine.

"This is all wrong. The beast is trapped." I was trapped. I walked to the door and gathered my cloak. "I need to go."

Far away from this place. From this truth. A brother, a twin who didn't know me at all but was willing to return to me. I wasn't sure how else he could have told me or how else he could have gotten close to me. Certainly, there had to be a better way than this. Jacob had stolen the irons, put the militia at risk, and lied to my family.

He did it all to protect me.

I thought of all the men out in the Barrens, of Logan's brother defending the shore with limited supplies, of Paxton and Brannon patrolling without full defenses.

Of Logan getting shredded by a demon in pursuit of the irons.

I didn't care if the Devil himself marched into Galloway and asked for my hand. I would have gladly traded the truth for the safety of this village.

"Harper, please. I'm so sorry."

Jacob's words slipped past my walls as I reached for the doorknob.

I spoke back into his mind. *"Maybe I was better off not knowing the truth."*

His face fell, and he opened his mouth to speak, but I heard Raina's voice next.

"This doesn't change who you are, Harper. We need to fix this. What should we do now?" Her eyes were locked on me, clear pools of pleading blue.

I couldn't meet her stare. I opened the door and left.

Because I didn't know the answer.

Everything was broken. Jacob had come here in pursuit of his truth, but everything had begun to shatter as soon as he spoke. I had always carried this curse with me, but the weight of it threatened to crush me.

The wall held on. The Alister covered me.

But yet, the demons grew restless. The scales of fate had always been disrupted when it came to my birth, but with every kernel of truth, they threatened to spill over.

Walking through town was a blur of light and noise, and despite my unfamiliarity with the streets on the west side, I weaved through the avenues quickly and easily. There was no point in Galloway from which the manor could not be seen. I let the imposing turrets be my beacon as I ran away from my twin, toward the wall and the barracks.

I was terrified for Jacob and Raina and so furious that they were willing to put themselves at risk for my sake. Horrified they had been willing to put so many others at risk. I believed what they had told me, every breath of it, but it didn't stop me from feeling utterly betrayed.

He had known.

The whole time we had scribbled names in notebooks

and speculated on the thief's identity. It was Jacob. He'd organized the entire investigation, and the town was none the wiser. Rain began to fall as I trudged through the streets, but I welcomed the drops upon my face.

Nobody noticed me as I walked through the barracks quadrangle, and I was grateful for it. My trunk of paints and brushes was tucked into an alcove next to the armory, and I used all my strength to hoist the heavy thing over my hip before I stalked toward the mural.

I wasn't sure what kind of damage I would find after the fire. When I realized the pit demon's flames had left the mural unscathed, my knees buckled with relief.

Perhaps art made by a demon herself could not be touched by another demon's wrath. That's what I was, wasn't I? A child of hell.

I pulled out the paints and mixed the vibrant red and orange hues. Every ounce of my soul, every scrap of my energy, poured from me into the rendering of fire. I worked with a vigor not of this realm, allowing the buzz to drown out my thoughts. I smoothed the skin tones of the hands holding the flame, exaggerating the textures.

Plumes of smoke erupted from my brush, accentuating the mural's edges with clouds of ash so realistic I wondered whether the village would fear this mural.

The triplet lords wouldn't shy away from it, though, nor would Paxton, Brannon, and Axel because this fire—this magic—was part of them. It was part of me now.

This village was perched on the brink of an inferno. It was part of all of us, in truth.

It was almost dark when I stepped back and surveyed the mural. I stared, unthinking, until the light of day was spent. When darkness fell, I washed my brushes in the oil and closed the lid on the trunk. The mural was complete. So was the mystery of the thefts I had been brought here to help solve.

Fire in the Hands of the Beholder.

A completely different person had started this mural. I wondered when it would feel right to show the lords, but a part of me knew it wouldn't matter.

Not when they discovered who I was.

What was all of this for? Jacob had captured and warded the horse. *For me?* We could use all the iron in this realm, and they would never keep the demons at bay. What did this horse even have to do with me?

I placed my paint-speckled hand on the cool stone, allowing the buzzing to vibrate through me, a welcome charge that dulled the sting.

"*Alister?*" I called through the stone. "*Are you there?*"

His voice was a comforting whisper through my mind. "*I'm always here, Harper.*"

My legs failed to hold me, and I sank to the ground. Heavy sobs escaped my chest like they had been trapped and ready to boil over. The mural was enveloped in a thick haze. Nobody at the barracks could have seen me, and I was thankful for it. As well as the demon who embodied it.

The Alister said nothing for a few moments, allowing me to cry. The heavy pillows of air thickened, covering me in a protective blanket. "*I'm always here,*" he repeated. "*Just as I have been from the beginning.*"

"*How was my mother able to communicate with you? James and Jacob cannot. How can your mist come through the wards?*"

A sigh reverberated through my mind. "*Your mother could only speak to me once she was carrying you in her womb.*"

It was always you. Your blood is promised to us. Our master assured it would be so. The mist is not me. It is an extension of me, but it allows me to watch over you within the wards."

I held my head in my hands and slumped against the stone. *"Why do you protect me? The pit demon told me you're out of favor with the Devil."*

"I may be a demon, but I know what is right. You were a baby, too young and small to appease the master. It wasn't right then, and it isn't right now. I think even he understands that. He gave you the horse as a gift. I know it now. He wasn't sent to retrieve you. He was sent to protect you. Now that you are old enough and strong enough to let him."

"The master of the fire realm gave me a gift?" I knew the words were true before they escaped my thoughts.

"Even he's not purely evil, Harper. He will cherish you to the ends of this realm if you give him the chance to return here."

"Do I have a choice?"

Sadness wafted to me from across the stone. *"I'm afraid you don't. But you can do this. You can open the thin place between the realms. Galloway will be safe as long as you are here."*

There was a promise within his words, and I knew he didn't intend to let me fail. I stood. *"I need to free the horse, don't I?"*

The mist thinned before me, clearing a path into the center of town. *"You need to free them all. You have allies on both sides of the wall, my lady."*

When I walked home, it was nearly dark. I was acutely aware of the absence of the heavy, booted footsteps that had slowly become a mirror to my own.

CHAPTER

THIRTY-ONE

The following day, I woke in the late morning after fitful dreams of a horse's hooves clattering on the cobblestones. Maggie didn't chastise me for sleeping in and gave me an extra biscuit on my tray.

Maybe the dark circles under my eyes stirred some sympathy in her. She knew me well enough to recognize I wasn't myself.

I didn't realize I was walking to the manor until my boots fell on the path to the gate. Surely, the library would have some record of the horse. A part of me started to ache for the creature that was bound to the ruins of the cursed house.

You need to free them all.

I needed to go to it, to free it and return the irons, but I couldn't go alone, and I was running out of people I trusted enough to come with me. I still didn't understand what the horse was, but something in my bones called to it.

Jacob would accompany me, of course, but I didn't have

237

the courage to face him just yet. I felt horrible for running away from him.

But my twin had lied to me.

He had made a mistake, perhaps by coming back to Galloway at all, but certainly by thinking he alone could ward me from the demons beyond the wall. As if by caging the beast, it would free Galloway and keep me from my true fate.

I almost laughed at the thought.

Perhaps it was a noble attempt at protecting me, but Jacob and Raina could not be so delusional as to believe I could hide from this forever.

The steps to the manor were slick with rain when I reached them, so I gathered my skirts as I sailed up the flight of stairs to the front door. Not one maid or butler was present on the path between me and the library shelves. The rain had turned into a deluge as I opened the heavy oak door, and it beat like a war drum on the stained-glass panes.

The familiar smell of parchment, oak, and leather settled into my bones, and I took a deep breath of it. This library had always been my sanctuary, and I needed it more than ever.

A lamp flickered in the back corridor, an unusual sight at any time of day in this part of the manor. I moved toward the light, willing the flame to remain steady despite the pounding of my heart. In all the years I had retreated into these rooms, I had rarely found them occupied. I peered around the tall bookcase that enclosed the back reading area.

Logan sat at the desk, his golden hair shining in the lamplight. Longer strands fell over his brow as he craned his neck over a large, worn tome. He scribbled frantically in a notebook, his focus darting between the book and pen.

I could have watched him for a long time, silently from the shadow of the shelves—the slope of his shoulder, the way the muscles in his forearm twitched as he wrote, the swell of the leather straps on his chest as he took deep, steady breaths.

Instead, I stepped forward, allowing my boots to announce my presence by scuffing the floor. He sprang to his feet. The chair's scrape echoed through the desolate stacks of books.

"What are you doing here?" he rasped.

I was suddenly hyperaware of my rain-soaked hair and wrinkled frock. "I should ask you the same question."

"You finished the mural," he said.

"Yesterday."

His eyes raked over me. "I wish I could have been there."

A pang of guilt echoed through me. I wished he had been there, too.

A book was spread open on the table, and as I drew closer, I noticed illustrations of demons on one side of the page, accompanied by descriptive text on the other.

I gasped. "You found a book about demons?"

He nodded. Until now, we had pieced information together from texts that mentioned the demons, but nothing that described them outright. We had scraped the knowledge together, always wishing for something better. I ran my hand over the page and turned it. Page after page outlined the demon species.

It was the lexicon I had been searching for.

I could tell he was studying me as I flipped through the book. My face softened. Despite all the times I had dismissed him, Logan kept coming back. He hadn't abandoned our research.

He hadn't abandoned me.
I peered at his notes.

Demon venom. Ties the victim to the demon and to all other humans claimed by the demon that inflicted the wound.

Light shone from Logan's scarred brow, an iridescent silver the same color as the mark on my back. This was why Logan was so drawn to guard me. If the venom worked by binding us, it made sense that he stood under my window at night.

I cursed at my traitorous heart for the disappointment that struck me. Logan and I had been drawn together by something external to us, something much bigger than whispers in corridors and stolen looks.

"Did you know there's a locked room in the back of the library?" he asked.

I numbly shook my head. If I had known, I would have started there.

He got up from the table and nodded. "Follow me."

Logan took my hand and led me past the stacks, where he turned behind a shelf. His skin against mine sparked a current that ran straight to my spine, and I wondered if the scar on his brow tingled the same way. I dared not ask.

The wood paneling was uneven at the end of the stack, and at the far end, a keyhole stood out like a puncture wound.

I walked past the stained-glass window, where streaks of rain slid down the colorful panes like fat tears, then I ran my fingers over the keyhole.

When I turned to Logan, he was watching me. "I never noticed this before," I admitted. Granted, I had never gone hunting for secret rooms before. Until recently, I hadn't sought anything so drastic or controversial.

Logan pulled a pin from his pocket and ran his thumb over the keyhole. "Allow me," he said.

He slid the pin through the lock and turned it. After a few moments of tinkering, the wall swung open, revealing a dimly lit room with two small shelves and a dusty desk.

My brow arched. "You know how to pick locks?"

He shrugged. "My father's a locksmith," he said. "Working with him as an apprentice allowed me to get the job in the armory, and it's what makes my brother, Michael, such a good choice to take the role as lieutenant when I get promoted." He smirked. "My brother can pick a lock with his eyes closed."

He gestured to the secret room, ushering me inside. The room was small and dim, illuminated by a small window on the far side. Musty air infiltrated my lungs, making me wonder if my father and his brothers even knew of this place or if it had been locked since well before they were born. There was a heavy layer of dust, but one glance at the gilded letters was proof that these were valuable texts.

Highly guarded in the way something dangerous should be.

Logan closed the secret door, sealing us inside, and my eyes adjusted to the dusty light.

I could feel the quickening of my pulse through my gloved wrist. Since encountering the pit demon, the world was spinning off its axis, and I had been trapped at the core in a tunnel of mist. I was dizzy. Sick. But when that door closed behind Logan, a strange sense of calm gripped me.

"Why are you here?" I asked, taking in the curves of his frustratingly perfect face in the muted light.

"I'm researching."

"Why are you here, at the manor?" I clarified. He should have been at his station in the armory.

"I was invited to tea," he said. "By Lord Aaron and Lady Beatrice."

My skin prickled. I was sure they had invited him on Mira's behalf. I cocked my head and gestured around us. "This doesn't look like teatime."

He took a step, closing the distance between us. "Tea is over. I barely remember what they said to me because the entire time I sat in their chambers, I hoped you would be down here."

The scent of leather and musk surrounded me as he neared, drowning out the smell of the moldy books. He was close enough that I could have touched him. Close enough that I could have grasped the back of his neck if I had reached out my hand.

The skin on my fingers itched. Begging me.

I blinked, pushing aside my urge to reach for him. "I've been hearing a horse, the sound of hooves on the forest floor, in my dreams. Have you seen anything in the books about a horse?"

He held an ancient-looking tome clutched to his chest. "No, but I did find some information about demons associated with changes in the air."

"Why?" It was the only thing I could say. "Why did you come here? Why do you want to help me with this?"

His eyes darkened. "You keep dismissing me, but I refuse to let this go. There's something about you and the Barrens, Harper. Something connects them to you. I needed to know more. I think you feel the same way, or you wouldn't have come here today, either."

"That doesn't answer my question," I said, squaring my shoulders. "I asked you why. Why do you care so much? This has nothing to do with the missing irons."

"Fuck the irons, Harper." He let out a ragged breath. "Fuck them. It doesn't matter anymore. It's bigger than that. I started this whole thing invested in finding the irons, but now I can only think about this." He gestured to the stacks of books. "It's all connected. I know it. We need to figure it out."

Figure *me* out.

My lip trembled. There was so much I wanted to tell him. I wanted to bare myself to him, open the core of the Earth, and let him spin with me until I was sick and scrambled. The rain hammered against the small window harder in the storm's wake.

There was so much I needed to understand. Jacob had opened the door to the truth, but I was stuck on the other side, too terrified to cross the threshold. I couldn't do it alone, and I had a feeling Logan wouldn't let me.

My voice was a whisper. "I want to figure it out, too. But first, I need to show you something."

Light danced in his eyes as they widened.

I stepped toward him, so close that if he had taken a deep breath, his chest would have brushed against mine.

His brow furrowed in confusion as I turned, and I could hear his breath quicken as my fingers worked to untie the stays of my dress. I pulled the fabric down just enough to reveal the silver flesh that I could only see with a properly placed mirror.

I shivered as his thumb swept over my skin, tracing the scar like he was memorizing it.

"A scar. Demon venom. It's just like mine," he whispered, touching me with such reverence I thought I would set aflame.

I turned and examined his scar. "The beast that marked you marked me when I was born. It pulled me from the fire. It all makes sense, now. I saw your notes. The venom binds us."

He blinked at me, and his lips parted. "We may be bonded somehow. But it's more than that. You can't think that's all this is, Harper."

"The venom..."

"Venom? Do you think I stand under your window because of a demon?"

My eyes widened. "Don't you?"

His kiss was the answer to my question. A yielding. His lips pressed to mine in a promise, swallowing my words whole. Right now, all that mattered was that we had aligned, and the moment we did, I didn't feel so ruined anymore.

My heart hammered. Logan and I were so utterly alone, locked in a forgotten room in the depths of the manor, my dress untied. We might as well have been in a different realm, and I wished it to be so. I wished that on the other side of that little window there was no mist.

No voices. No magic.

His hands on me were the only thing I needed as he drew me closer, allowing his fingers to sweep over the swell of my hip. A gasp escaped my throat when he withdrew his kiss. I sucked in air laced with the smell of him, and it was like the sweetest wine, pulling me into the depths of drunk neediness.

My hands tangled through his hair, and I pulled back to watch the golden strands run through my fingers. I kissed the stupid dimple on his cheek and traced the angle of his jaw before my lips strayed down the column of his neck, where I allowed my tongue to taste his skin.

I tugged at the leather strap of his uniform, and a sigh escaped him.

"I know what you are," he said, breathless.

My lips froze against his skin. "What am I?"

I barely knew the answer to that question myself. I knew who I belonged to, but I dared not say it, not with the thick heat that built between us.

"They yield to you," he said. "You can speak to them. I want you to know I don't care. Even if you were one of them, it wouldn't stop me from wanting you."

I stilled. He couldn't mean it. There was no possibility Logan would want someone so cursed.

He pulled back, staring at me as though he were the one who could mindspeak. He projected his thoughts so strongly that they echoed through my head. *They're tied to you. I'm tied to you, too.*

I blinked up at him. Not strong enough to speak aloud, I spoke into his mind. *You don't know what you're saying.*

He pulled away, but his lips moved against my cheek. "Since the moment I met you, you've infuriated me. You've occupied my thoughts every moment since, and at first, I thought you had placed a spell on me."

Maybe I had. I could only kiss him back.

He tugged me closer, pulling me up onto the desk table. My hips were the same height as his, and he trailed his hands over my back, letting his fingers dance along the loosened ties of my corset.

"It wasn't a spell at all," he said. "You're special. Different. You consume every thought I have, and all I've wanted to do since I kissed you the first time was kiss you again. Because being apart from you is torture."

I was too breathless to speak aloud, so I entered his mind as his teeth grazed my lower lip. *"I don't want to hurt you."*

This was the venom. It had to be.

My breaths were ragged whispers even though we were hidden from everyone and everything. We were locked within a secret room that seemed meant for us—a place where there was no wall and no secrets.

He kissed me like he would never let me dismiss him again, and with every press of his lips, he kindled a fire so complete I feared I would burn the whole manor down.

My body arched into him, every muscle coiling as my mind remained open and connected to him with my magic. Every breath of his need, every beat of his lust. The Earth slowed, but I was still trapped in the core.

I couldn't let this happen. It wasn't fair to him, but I couldn't wrench away. I allowed him to feel everything I felt through that bridge between our minds where my magic bound us. Want, fear, desperation, terror.

He slid his lips over my neck, and I shivered. "Tell me what you know, Harper."

I pulled away, unable to form words. How would I even begin? I stared at him for a long time.

Logan was everything I wanted and everything I couldn't have. I could've done the brave thing and answered his question. Then, at least, he would have had a reason to run.

Instead, I spoke the words of a coward. "I know where the irons are."

CHAPTER

THIRTY-TWO

I told Logan I knew without question that the irons were in the burned ruins of Raina's house. I told him the reason they were there.

Well, I told him part of the reason.

The locket Aunt Patrice had given me. My fire magic. How the horse had been bound to me and saved me from the fire that killed my mother.

When I told him the irons were at the midwife's house, his jaw tightened. I didn't mention Jacob or Raina. When he asked me how I knew they were there, I explained that the Alister had told me.

It wasn't a lie.

"I've been hearing the horse in my dreams," I said, holding my head in my hands.

He cocked his head. "You're certain the irons are warding this horse?"

I nodded. "Yes. He needs to be free."

I needed him to be free.

Logan's brow furrowed. "Why does the horse need to be free?"

"I can't explain it. I just...know."

Keeping secrets from Logan felt wrong, and the ghost of his touch was still swirling through me, dizzying me. *That kiss.*

But it was only a partial lie. I still had no idea how I innately knew the horse needed to be free, only that I held the injustice of his captivity in my bones.

Logan's hand rose to his scar.

My instinctual pull to this horse was inexplicable. Since the moment I'd learned it was warded, trapped in the shell of the building it saved me from, something felt wrong. My skin crawled. I could sense the horse—tight dread coursing through me.

The silvery scar on Logan's brow caught the light. He shivered, and I knew he felt the same way, an inherent wrongness that needed to be rectified.

Logan nodded. "Then we free the horse. We recover the irons, and we break the wards."

I hastily tied and fastened the stays of my dress before Logan grabbed my hand and led me back into the library. We didn't pass a soul as we navigated through the halls of the manor, and when the door clicked soundlessly behind me, I pulled my cloak around my shoulders and drew the hood over my head.

It was nearly dusk now. The day had melted into a heavy mixture of betrayal and shock and lust, and all I could do was ride on the high of feeling Logan's hand in mine as he escorted me to the west gate.

We took the same path I had taken the night Logan had

tracked me to the gate, under massive willows and oaks, sleeping monsters from some other realm.

Logan's gaze darted up and down the path, assuring we weren't being watched.

"When we venture into the Barrens, don't leave my side," he said, clutching the iron blade strapped to his thigh. "I promise I won't leave yours."

I sucked in air heavy with vapor, and my exhales were frosted with cold. "Do you know where the house is?"

He nodded. "It's not far from the wall, but the trees have grown around it in a dense thicket."

The gate didn't creak as it swung open, as though it were a willing participant in our plan. I hadn't walked ten steps into the pines when I heard it.

"*Harper Ledes,*" the Alister slunk into my mind. "*I see you took my advice to heart.*"

I stilled, and Logan froze. I knew exactly what he meant—I had found my ally inside the wall. Logan nodded at me and drew his sword.

The Alister tutted. "*Tell the lieutenant to put away that iron before he gets himself in trouble.*"

I put a hand on Logan's wrist, and he withdrew his sword. "*I need to free the horse,*" I said to the Alister. "*My horse.*"

"*Have you realized now, Harper, what is at stake? When I saw the horse—my master's beast—fetch you from the fire, I knew he was aware of your birth. But it wasn't fair. This is your realm. He may have gifted you the beast, but the horse will only answer to those he has marked.*"

I spoke aloud. "I plan to free him."

Logan paled, and his knuckles tightened on the sword in his grip.

The Alister sighed, and it was deathly cold as his vapor rumbled through me. "*I spoke the truth.*" He paused, and the mist grew so thick around me that I could see nothing but haze. "*Did you speak the truth to the lieutenant?*"

The skin on the back of my neck prickled. "*I told him I knew where the irons were.*"

Another tut. "*But your lover does not know you are the thirteenth child?*"

"*He's not my lover.*"

I didn't want to continue this conversation. Would I have any friends left, on either side of the wall, when the truth of my identity became common knowledge?

I gripped Logan's arm. "Which way to the cottage?"

The lieutenant's goal had always been to find these irons, and we were about to accomplish that. If we had grown together during that time, I was sure the venom influenced the attraction.

Because Logan would eventually learn who I was. He would learn that Jacob was lying to him. What choice would he have?

Logan's hand around mine was the only thing I could see clearly as he led the way, ducking under bushy pine boughs. Our feet sank into the sandy soil, and I tried to ignore the whispers around me as demons flocked.

Some hissed at Logan, and the sound deepened when he raised his iron, angling through the boughs with the expert strides of a trained militia lieutenant. We slunk between the trees like ghosts, and his grip tightened as a glow permeated the air ahead of us.

I dared not speak aloud. "*Is there a fire?*"

Shaking his head, Logan pulled me into a thicket of trees where three golden torches illuminated a ruined stone structure. I gasped when I saw who wielded the torches. Paxton, Brannon, and Uncle Bain held the flames, buoyed in the air with their magic.

The atmosphere parted before us as if the Alister had opened a window. In front of the charred, skeletal house, Jacob knelt on the ground, his hands bound and his lip bloodied, while my cousins aimed their irons at his neck.

I lurched forward, but Logan clasped a hand over my mouth and ducked lower. "Don't," he whispered.

Uncle Bain crossed his arms. "All this time," he said, his voice gruff and powerful. "It was you. Brannon suspected you were the one who was stealing, but I dismissed him."

Brannon knew? Beside me, Logan froze, and I slid into his mind. Horror eddied through him.

In the clearing, my cousins stood like stone sentries on either side of our uncle, arms crossed.

Bain spread his hands, and the torchlight shone on hundreds of irons staked into the ground, crossed like they were forming a fence. Beyond it, I heard a whine and stomping hooves, and my heart cracked open.

"My lord, I'm sorry," Jacob said, his voice cracking. "I stole the irons and placed them around this house to trap the beast. The horse was becoming aggressive, and—"

"And you saw fit to take matters into your own hands? And keep it from your commanders?" Paxton cut him off, his words filled with ire. "This is where you chose to ward the beast? In the very place where the lords of this village were born? Where one of the kindest, gentlest people in the realm was taken from us? What was your plan, Captain? Did you intend to use the beast to bring down our family?"

My heart pounded. I wanted to scream. If they only knew.

Jacob was one of us. A Ledes.

Would they accuse him like this if they knew? After everything Jacob had done, he didn't deserve to be charged with treason. He had done all of this for *me*. For Galloway. I had to do something.

I shouted into my twin's mind. "*Show them your arm.*"

Jacob's eyes widened at my voice, but he dared not look for me.

"*Show them your brand.*"

He ducked his head. "*It's over, Harper. If I show them, they'll know you're the thirteenth child. The demons will come for you. They'll come for the village.*" My twin got to his feet, hoisting his weight against his bound wrists. He spoke aloud, directly to Bain. "I deserve your punishment, my lord. But I worry what will happen if the irons are removed and the beast is freed."

"*Show them!*" I shouted a desperate plea into his mind, wishing I could force him to do it against his will.

Brannon shook his head. "Uncle, we should take him to the holding cell tonight and investigate the beast. I don't trust his word, but I think it would be unwise to recover the irons with so little information."

Paxton nodded at Bain in agreement.

My uncle huffed at them, agreeing before he addressed Jacob—his secret nephew. "Jacob Miller, I charge you with theft and treason. Your sentencing will be tomorrow after the irons are safely recovered and the area is deemed secure."

Every muscle in my body stiffened, and Logan's grip on me tightened in our hiding place. Treason was an offense punishable by death. Beyond the charred remains of the cottage, the mist was thicker than ever. I sensed the Alister there, breathing with every swirl.

A grunt broke through the edge of the wards, and my stomach hollowed. The horse was there, just beyond those walls.

"*Show them, Jacob,*" I screamed into his mind. "*Do it for me.*"

Jacob shook his head before he tipped his head back to the sky, and I mirrored him. I nearly fainted at the sight of it.

The air cleared above him, revealing a sky illuminated by the first stars of dusk. I had never seen stars before, but I had read about them. Painted what I wished them to be from my mind's eye. Seeing them for the first time didn't do justice to what I had imagined. Beams of light shone above us, and my brother smiled at them.

He turned directly toward our hidden spot before his gaze returned to the ground. "*Harper,*" he spoke into my mind. "*Do me one favor.*"

"*Anything.*"

"*Don't let them hurt Raina.*"

My brother's head tipped up once more before he was chained behind Uncle Bain's horse and disappeared into the mist.

CHAPTER

THIRTY-THREE

Logan and I crouched in our hiding spot until the party of men had gone, and I waited until the clopping of their horses had faded away before I let out a full breath.

I almost told him then. My limbs wanted to take flight and run after my twin. I was at risk of being pulled apart, torn in two.

But Jacob was right. I couldn't tell Logan here, in the middle of the Barrens, without the protection of the wall to guard us from the demons that would come to claim me.

I stood between the pine boughs, staring up at the canopy of stars. Smog blanketed the air just outside the perimeter of the cottage.

Each step toward the irons was heavy, but my footfalls were nearly silent in the sandy soil. I reached the irons and ran my hand across the sword's hilt before me. Jacob and Raina had arranged them like a trellis. Each sword speared into the earth like a spike crossing with the one beside it.

254

Humming, akin to the sound that vibrated off the wall, overcame me as I neared them.

Logan was a step behind, and when I looked back at him, he nodded. Only I could pass through that perimeter of iron. Even though the beast had marked Logan, there was no way for Logan to speak to it. Only I would be safe with the beast trapped within. I took a stabilizing breath and stepped between the irons into the charred remains of the property where the cottage once stood.

Humming melted into a concentrated, flat silence. The ward's magic was strong, much more imposing than the wall.

A stone half-wall that had survived the flames still stood. Above it, only a few charred pieces of wood remained. The stone foundation resembled an animal pen. No wonder Jacob and Raina had chosen to ward the beast here.

I passed through what used to be the threshold, and my blood began to vibrate. Fire magic had touched this place, and it sang to me, willing to whisper its tale. Rays of starlight beamed through what was left of the roof. Where had my mother taken her last breath? Was I standing in the very place she had left this realm?

"Hello?" I spoke aloud, but my voice sounded wrong. It was muffled by magic.

"*Harper.*" It was not a statement or a question. When the beast spoke, it was a claim—an admission of truth.

"*Are you the horse?*" I asked.

"*I am* your *horse,*" he replied. His voice was a deep baritone, but it had a melodic softness. If the pit demon's voice had snaked through me, the words of this beast were like a soft caress.

"*Please,*" I said. "*Who are you? What are you?*"

My heart stopped. As the source of the voice approached me, nothing had ever felt so right. I had never felt so *safe*. The scar on my back tingled, pulsing through me like an embrace.

A great figure emerged from the shadows, his black coat shining. I stepped back to take him in. He was much larger than a regular horse, but not so large that someone couldn't climb astride him. His coat was as black as the bottom of a well.

I gasped as he shifted to me, his beautiful head bowing in time with the reveal of his wings. Their span was almost too large to contain within the structure, and deep sorrow wafted over me, knowing that the creature had been trapped here for so long. Logan had described the wings as leathery, like a bat, but they were iridescent.

With a sheen identical to the way light reflected on scar tissue.

"*You do not know who you are?*" he asked.

"*I'm Harper Ledes, thirteenth child of the Ledes Lords of Galloway. Daughter of Sarah and Cade. I only just learned this.*"

He huffed aloud, his breath leaving wisps of steam around his nose. "*I took you from the fire. The moment you were born, so was I. He sent me through a crack between realms to save you. I'm a guardian. I heard your cries and ran to you.*"

A guardian. For me?

"*The master of your realm made you?*" I asked. "*To save me?*"

The Devil didn't want to save me. He wanted to take me as his own. Perhaps the beast didn't know about his promise.

He bowed his head, tucking in his wings. "*Yes, but this is my realm now. Master has many names. Some call him a devil.*"

"*And what is your name?*" I asked.

"*I have no name. You have yet to give me one.*" His solemn eyes swept over me, expectant.

I stepped toward him and extended my trembling hand. The beast bowed his head to me so gently, I almost forgot he was a demon. I swept my fingers over the feathery coat of his neck, realizing it was hard, scalelike. I gazed up into the black pits of his eyes and saw the light reflected there—flickering like a star. At that moment, I knew.

"*Starling,*" I said. The word rolled through my mind—sure and steadfast. "*You are the light in the darkness.*"

He nudged me with his muzzle. I took it as a sign of approval.

"*I'm sorry my brother trapped you here.*"

"*Your brother did not understand,*" he said. "*He cannot speak with me. If he could, he would have known I would have come willingly. He did not need to ward me in these stone walls. I would have found you the moment your own wards were gone.*"

Unease prickled through me—*my own wards.*

The wall had been built just after my birth. Magic and iron had been erected around Galloway to keep out the demons, but they had been just as effective at keeping me in. I had never left those walls, not until I knew the truth, and now that I did, there was no going back. Walls would never be able to hold me again.

Perhaps I belonged out here in the Barrens.

"*What will happen when I free you from the wards?*" I asked.

"*We will do what we were born to do,*" he said.

"I still don't understand what that is." I stroked his silky mane.

"The demons wish to have free passage between realms. It is why they flock here. You have the power to open the gate. Free Galloway and bring the demons home."

Tears welled in my eyes. *"If I open the gate between realms, the fire will return. The Barrens won't be safe."*

"It will be safe because we will keep it that way, Harper."

CHAPTER

THIRTY-FOUR

Starling didn't wear a bridle, but I led him to the irons with a soft hand on his muzzle. His coat was like hardened silk, and his mane reflected the soft light bouncing off the blanket of air. He shuffled on his hooves, and for a moment, I forgot this creature was a demon of hell. I reassured him with a gentle pat, the same way James had taught me to calm my mare at the manor.

I loosened enough of the irons from the ground to clear a path, and when the circle broke, the wards fell with them.

Without magic, the muffled silence was released, and I could once again hear the wind through the boughs and the hooting of owls. The mist had thickened again, obstructing the night sky. I didn't know if I had been within the ward for hours or mere minutes. Had the magic imbued in the irons warped time?

It was too thick to see into the clearing before me, so I held out my hand and allowed an ember of fire to glow above my palm.

This new magic felt so natural that I realized it was not

260

new at all. It had been dormant, waiting for the moment I needed it most. Starling nuzzled my cheek.

I scanned the pines, but Logan was nowhere in sight.

My mouth went dry. My guard—the man who had stood under my window every night like a sentinel—had surely not left me in the Barrens alone with an uncertain beast. My heart hammered as I ran from tree to tree, searching.

"*What's wrong?*" Starling asked, pawing at the ground with his hoof.

"*My guard was here, waiting. Now he's gone.*"

My guard. It was the wrong word. Incomplete. Logan was so much more than that.

"*Perhaps he left. Perhaps he was frightened of me.*" There was a trace of melancholy in his tone.

I shook my head. There was no possibility he left on his own volition, of that, I was sure. I started to pace, searching the floor for signs of a struggle, signs of blood. "*Perhaps another demon...*"

Starling huffed the air. "*I smell my venom in this clearing, and not just upon you.*"

I whirled toward the horse with wide eyes, churning over the link between Starling, Logan, and me. "*You had bitten him. Years ago. He was attacked by imps on patrol, and you swooped down on them.*"

Disgust wafted from the beast. "*Yes. I recall him. I grazed the face of a soldier that day.*"

"*You can still smell your venom on him?*" I made a mental note to return to the books we had discovered and learn more about demon venom.

"*Venom never goes away. It becomes a part of the human, and it pulls us to them. My venom is in his blood forever, as it*" *is in yours. I have sensed you moving beyond the wall since you were born. A human marked by venom is tethered to the demon that marked them."*

Dizziness overcame me. I really had been branded, all this time.

Logan had become so attached to me so quickly, so keen to fall into the role of my protector. This beast bound us. I blinked in the light of my flame. Was that why Logan had fallen so easily into the role? Was that why he had sought me out to help him solve the theft of the irons? Perhaps this thing between us was fabricated by magic. Maybe it wasn't what he claimed it was.

I pushed the words Logan had said to me in the library out of my mind.

"Can you track his scent?" I asked.

In answer to my question, the beast knelt, giving me access to his back. I pulled myself onto him with sweaty palms, grateful for all the riding lessons James had insisted on giving me as a child. He wore no saddle, but the scales of his coat were easy to grip, even if they had fine, pointy edges that cut into my thighs.

"Hang on to my mane," Starling said, and with that, my heart leapt into my throat as he broke into a gallop. He weaved through the trees like they were reeds of grass, easily and expertly, his trot barely audible in the sandy soil. I held on with all my might, praying Logan hadn't gone too far, that whatever had found him had not killed him.

Before long, Starling's pace slowed. *"Summon your flame,"* he said. The boughs were so dense I could barely see, but I heard water rushing nearby. I had no sense of direction but reasoned we must have galloped north. The Mullica River was not far from the wall.

An ember flared to life in my palm, brighter this time, confirming my suspicions. Logan walked ahead slowly, his footfalls dragging, like he was a puppet with invisible strings. Before him, a horned, hairless beast the size of a large man beckoned him with a crooked finger. It appeared humanoid, but its arms and legs were unnaturally long for its body.

When the creature spotted us, a hiss echoed through my mind, and I knew what I beheld. The cryptid stalked toward us, and Logan collapsed to the ground, unconscious but released from its thrall.

"I found it first, Devil's horse," the cryptid hissed. *"The wound from my aamon's talons has barely closed. He may have escaped the first time, but the human belongs to me. He's such a pretty man."*

The demon crooked a spindly finger along Logan's jaw, and the flame in my hand flared. The cryptid had set the aamon demon on Logan, inflicting the wound that almost killed him. Desire to kill this thing swelled within me.

Starling's wings spread behind my thighs, stretching out to their full, terrible length. *"You're wrong, Cryptid. Perhaps you did not use your senses, or you would have smelled the truth on him. The human is mine. I claimed him years ago. My venom still runs through him. Your pet's attempt to mark him was futile."*

A growl rumbled from the cryptid, and it stood at its full height. *"I see you brought your own pet with you,"* it said. Its voice snaked through my mind like a centipede, hundreds of legs writhing and twisting.

Within moments, my sense of repulsion for the demon gave way, and I was overcome with a deep desire to go it. Like it knew, the beast smiled with a curled, crooked, too-wide grin.

My gaze connected with the beady pits in its face, and I was in its thrall.

Starling let out a growl as I slid from his back, but I had no doubt he would stay by my side. Mist thickened around us in a swirling vortex of churning air, and I knew my horse was not the only demon with me.

The Alister didn't speak, but he was there, wrapping me in darkness.

Blood drained from my face as the creature unfurled his claws, sharp talons extending from oddly long fingers. My legs began to take me to it. The creature was a walking nightmare, but my terror deepened in a flash of light as the thing transformed.

Before me stood James, smiling broadly. *"I found a way out of here, Harp. Follow me."* He extended his hand, and an eerie calm gripped me. I knew the demon was a shapeshifter, but my rational brain melted away.

James.

He needed me. He'd found a way out of here. I took a step toward my brother, propelled by muscles that were not my own.

A way to Delphi where he could study and write. Where I could paint and see the sky. Where he could love Benjamin and be free. Father would follow us. We would make a better life there.

Another flash of light, and Maggie was there. *"Come, my lady. Lord Cade has called for 'ya."*

Father needed me. Yes, in so many ways. But I couldn't save him. I couldn't save any of us.

Starling's voice was a thousand miles away as he called to me. *"Do not yield to him, Harper!"*

Light flashed again, and this time, Jacob was before me.

Chains bound his wrists, but his sleeves were pulled up, revealing the brand, the number *12* that used to be mine. *"I've been sentenced to death. Help me, sister."*

Fear washed over me. Desperation overcame me. I would never know him, and he would never get to be who he was meant to be.

Twelve. Thirteen.

Twins torn apart by a devil's promise.

Light panged over the form, and Logan stood before me, his arms crossed. *"You lied to me. I would have loved you, but I cannot love what you are."*

Behind him, Mira appeared. She stood beside my guard, her lieutenant, proud and disgusted. When Logan put his arm around her shoulders, her scowl curled into a satisfied smile.

"I always knew," she said.

Another flash of light, and my father stood there.

His face was long, shadowed. *"Galloway is my prison, and there is nothing you can do to free me from it. You never knew Sarah. She would be ashamed of me. I wasn't strong enough to heal."*

I began to cry. Hot tears left lines of scorched skin on my face, the fire within me boiling over. I was a kettle of water in a roaring hearth. The fire rose as I walked toward my father, the two of us sobbing in the darkness, utterly alone. We shared the magic that left my skin blistered and raw. I let the heat come, and I reveled in it.

Everything was ruined. My father would die in Galloway, consumed by a life of sadness and grief. James would be committed to a life of lies, bound to a woman he would never love or desire. I would never know the twin who had risked everything to tell me the truth, and I would never get a chance to tell him I forgave him.

Logan would never love me. Love wasn't something I deserved.

I understood now. This was bigger than me.

Flames burst from pine needles under my feet, but my skin didn't burn this time. The flames were a part of me, a hot, scalding magic that could never hurt me. I allowed them to lick at my skin before they bloomed in the sandy soil. Before me, another burst of light, and the image of my father was gone. I stood face to face with the horrible creature who had compelled me.

The cryptid's beady eyes were wide as it beheld me. Flames reflected in its black irises.

"What are you going to do, thirteenth child?" Its lips curled into a sneer as it spoke, revealing sharp, gray teeth.

I let the fire swell around me before I spoke into its mind. *"I'm going to send you back where you belong."*

Something primal loosened within me, like the master of the fire realm himself had a hand on my back. Maybe he did.

The creature screamed as I allowed the flames to swallow it whole, bathing the fog in a swirling, amber glow. Its long, spindly fingers covered its face, clawing at its eyes and leathery skin. The flames grew and morphed into a deep indigo. Inky, hot smoke blanketed it in darkness.

With another flash of light, the flames were gone. The air was bursting with dust, peppering the mist. When I focused through the dark, the cryptid was gone.

I had sent it back to its realm.

THIRTY-FIVE

ithout the influence of the cryptid's thrall, it took several moments for Logan to regain consciousness. I knelt beside him, counting his breath and cursing myself.

He could have been killed.

It took several more moments for him to get used to the enormous, winged beast at my side. If Logan was shaking, I was as still as stone. He had almost died, and it had been because of me. I shouldn't have asked him to accompany me on this mission, especially without telling him the truth about who I was.

"Are you okay?" I asked, helping him to his feet.

"I'm fine," he said through gritted teeth. "Furious with myself, but fine."

"Do you think your guard will ride on my back?" Starling asked, nuzzling my shoulder.

I managed a weak laugh before I answered. *"I strongly doubt it, but it would humor me greatly to suggest it."*

The beast huffed into the air.

"Did you just tell it a joke?" Logan asked with narrow eyes.

I shrugged. "Perhaps. His name is Starling, by the way."

Logan inspected the beast. "Starling. It suits him."

The horse huffed in agreement.

"What happened to the cryptid?"

I recounted the story to Logan, and he soaked in every detail, from when we found him to when I banished the creature from our realm.

He nodded, his jaw working in a firm line. "You have the power to banish them."

Ice flooded my veins as he spoke the words aloud. I had no idea what this meant or what I would do with this power, but there was one thing I was sure of.

This was no gift of magic. No.

This was a curse.

I glanced down at the skin of my forearm, blank skin where the number *13* should be.

Over the past week, I had befriended two demons, and I was beginning to trust them just as much as my allies within the wall.

Logan's gaze trailed over the same spot on my forearm, his brow furrowing. Was he starting to see the truth? My mindspeaking magic never worked when my own emotions were high, and it certainly would have failed me then if I had tried to slink into his mind.

My desire to read him was palpable, but all I could do was study the set of his jaw and the hard line of his lip.

"We need to speak to Jacob," he said.

Logan's mind roiled with a deep wave of anger, an emotion so strong it overcame my own anxiety. If Logan had been able to read my feelings, he would have been struck by my guilt. Logan deserved to know the truth about who I was. After tonight, would he even be surprised?

I had ripped a hole in this realm with my fire magic and sent a cryptid demon back to hell. Bile rose in my throat. Would this become my role? Is this what Starling meant when he said Galloway would be safe because of me?

Was I strong enough to do this?

This time last week, I had been worried about family dinners and unwanted weddings. I had been thoroughly preoccupied with running away from this place and starting over. I'd had no idea how strong my tether was to Galloway.

Jacob's sentencing was in the morning. I needed to convince my twin to tell the truth before his trial. I needed to tell Father and James.

We had to tell the truth. Only his real identity would set my twin free, but what would become of me? Would they put me in a jail cell instead? Would Logan ever speak to me again? Perhaps it would be a fitting punishment.

It was harder than I anticipated to say goodbye to Starling at the gates, but something within me was lighter, knowing that he was free in the Barrens. The beast's words repeated in my mind as I entered the wards.

My wards.

This wall had been built after my birth, but those who built it hadn't realized who they were caging inside. How could I ever look at the wall the same way again?

Night had fallen, and the streets were eerily quiet as Logan escorted me home.

When we arrived at the townhouse, James stood at the front gate, wringing his hands. I had so much I wanted to tell him, but his nervous energy struck me as we neared.

"What's wrong?" I asked.

"Father is staying at the manor tonight, and Maggie has gone with him," he replied. "Maggie left you dinner in your room."

A thousand questions floated to the surface of my mind. "James, are you okay?"

Beside me, Logan shifted uncomfortably on his feet. James spoke into my mind. *"Benjamin will be here any moment,"* he said. *"I've decided to tell Father about us, to explain everything, and tonight, I need to convince Benjamin it's a good idea."*

My head swam. James had chosen the worst possible moment to do this, but I couldn't stand in his way. "I'll give you some privacy then," I said. "Logan can escort me to the manor, and I can also stay there tonight."

James's shoulders slumped in relief. "You're the best sister in the world, Harper," he said aloud. Another wave of guilt washed over me. Would he feel the same way knowing our brother was locked in the holding cell?

James was brave and true, and he deserved happiness more than anyone I knew.

I wrapped my brother in a hug, lingering in his arms just long enough to tell him how proud I was, before returning to the pathway and treading to the street. Logan, to his credit, didn't ask for details. My guard was uncharacteristically quiet as we walked under the glow of the lamps. No witty remarks. His usually confident boot clicks were slower, muted.

We walked silently for a moment, and I nearly returned to be with James. All this time, I had been trying to give James a solution—an escape. Perhaps the best solution all along had been to explain how he felt.

"I'll escort you to the manor," Logan said.

The thought of going to the manor nauseated me, especially with the prospect of running into my uncles before I could speak to Jacob. "The idea of seeing my family right now terrifies me," I said.

Logan's throat bobbed. "We can return to my quarters, then."

I nodded, barely registering what he suggested, letting him lead me along an alley near the barracks entrance. The stone building was tucked away from the light of the lamps. Logan's gaze darted to the road before we reached the doorway.

It would have been a scandal if anyone had seen me enter the lieutenant's private quarters, not quite so different from the scandal James was about to reveal to our father. The reality of our destination struck me.

Logan was leading me to his private quarters.

He had suggested I stay there with him all night. I nearly stopped and turned, an excuse ready on my lips. He bounded up the steps so swiftly I didn't have time to speak, and the fear of getting caught with him propelled my feet to follow.

We entered a small, neat apartment that was sparsely furnished, and he hung his weapons on a few hooks next to the door.

As soon as the latch clicked shut, my skin tingled. Logan's mind was not projecting any thoughts of heightened emotions, but his hand trembled slightly as he lit the fire in his lamp.

He moved immediately to a shelf and pulled down a small glass decanter. He poured himself a hefty dram and downed it in one gulp.

"Whiskey?" he asked, pulling a second glass from the shelf.

I nodded. "What a great idea."

He started to pour. "Would you like a little water or sugar?"

"I'll drink it neat," I said.

He raised a brow as he poured. "Of course you will."

I examined the room, stealing a glimpse of Logan Greer's private life, and I wasn't surprised to find the man was somewhat minimalistic. I let my hand glide along the mantel, where several small wooden animal carvings were the only ornamentations I observed.

"Did you carve these?" I asked.

He nodded, and I inspected them, realizing they weren't animals at all. A bear with unnaturally large claws perched beside a tall, spindly-legged creature. A winged horse.

My winged horse. The same one who had branded us with his venom.

"They're beautiful, Logan."

They were demons. He had carved demons from wood, painstakingly haunting forms.

He was an artist as well, and he had never mentioned it to me as he watched me paint. I winced. It would have been hard for Logan to tell me something like that between my protests and insults.

"Thank you for helping me free Starling," I said, running a hand over the carved wing of his likeness.

He swallowed, and his hand drifted up to the silvery scar on his brow. "Thank you for saving me from the cryptid. And for leading me to the stolen irons."

Panic gripped me.

Logan didn't deserve lies and secrets. He and I were not

so different, after all. Only his brand from Starling had been earned, a battle wound he had gained defending Galloway.

The skin on my forearm prickled with the implications of the number *13* hidden beneath the surface. My brand hadn't been earned. I was cursed. And what protection would I offer Galloway by opening the thin space between realms?

I was pinned against the stone wall surrounding me, somewhere between damnation and villainy.

Logan had helped me today against his better judgment. Would he have if he knew I was the thirteenth child? If he knew, he certainly wouldn't have kissed me. He wouldn't have said the things he said.

"It was foolish of me to ask you to accompany me today. It was even more foolish of you to agree," I said.

Logan's eyes darkened. "I'm not a fool, Harper."

My throat went dry. "You are."

He was a fool for trusting me. He was a fool for trusting Jacob.

He braced his hands on the table. "Did you think I wouldn't have figured out who stole the irons?"

I took a step back. "What?"

He pushed off the table and walked to me. Slowly, like he was a cat cornering a bird. "Brannon and I figured out Jacob stole the irons days ago."

I sucked in a breath. Had Logan been the one to turn Jacob in? Disbelief gripped me, but only for a moment. Within two heartbeats, it was replaced with anger.

"Well, congratulations," I said. "You figured it out before I did. Because I only learned yesterday."

Logan downed his whiskey in one gulp. "When were you going to tell me? I know you weren't helping him. You must have been just as shocked as I was. I thought we were in this together. I've worried over my brother every day, out there unprotected at the shore. You confided in me today about your mother's death. About the horse. Your fire magic."

Fire surged in the hearth, but Logan didn't notice. The flames reflected within the depths of his eyes, dangerous red streaks in icy blue. My heart drummed, threatening to rip the realm open beneath my feet.

"I didn't tell you everything," I whispered.

Logan cleared the distance between us. His hand swept behind me, pulling me in by the small of my back. His cheek brushed against mine as he whispered in my ear. "Why do you hold back from me?"

The Alister's words replayed in my head. *Find your allies within the wall.*

I melted into Logan's touch, wondering if he possessed some magic after all.

He grazed his lips along my jaw. "I'm on your side, Harper."

Some things cannot be spoken aloud, so I spoke the only way I knew how. Directly into his mind. *"I am the thirteenth child."*

THIRTY-SIX

Logan's lips lingered on my cheek. "I know."

I pulled away. "What?"

He cocked his head. "I know you're the thirteenth child. Jacob is your brother. I figured that out, too."

He knew. And he had still held me in his arms. He had still helped me.

"How did you—" It was getting harder to breathe. "Does Brannon know?"

Logan shook his head. "When I saw what Jacob had done with the horse today, I figured it out. And then you banished that demon in the Barrens. Jacob looks just like you, Harper. You can both mindspeak. You told me your mother died tragically by your father's magic when you were born."

"Raina fled with Jacob," I said. "He's the twelfth child. You can go to the prison right now and have him show you his brand."

Logan shook his head. "I don't need to make him show me. I believe you."

I couldn't feel my limbs, so I braced myself on the mantel. "I'll go to the manor." But my traitorous feet didn't move. Instead, I was rooted to the spot. I couldn't look at him.

He knew. He knew, and he'd stayed with me.

He knew, and he'd invited me to his home.

Logan's voice was low and rough when he said, "Don't go to the manor."

I squeezed my eyes shut. "It's dangerous to be this involved with me. When you were assigned to be my guard, you were merely standing with me when I painted. You can't continue to be my guard now, Logan. Your job is done."

He grabbed my hand, forcing me to face him. "It will never be done. You can't do this alone. I will never stop guarding you, Harper. The only thing I can think about is guarding you. I don't care what you are or what it means."

My lips parted, and my magic swirled toward him, sliding into his mind. There was no lie. Logan's eyes fluttered closed as I entered his mind. My heart surged when I realized he wanted me there—wanted me to read his mind.

"Starling saved me when I was born. That's how I got my scar. His venom will be in our blood until we die," I said. "Perhaps that's why you feel so compelled to guard me."

He released a breath. "That's not why I've been compelled to guard you." His words were sure, almost angry.

"It makes sense, though," I returned. "You've always taken your guard duty so seriously. Starling is tied to us. His venom was in your veins before you knew me. There's a link."

There was magic at play as ancient as this realm. Starling was my guardian. Did that make Logan my guardian through association?

Logan shook his head. "That's not why I took my guard duty seriously. The idea of something happening to you is a sick torture, and I knew you would do something reckless if I didn't intervene."

My heart pounded so hard my chest threatened to explode as he tightened his grip on my wrist. *Reckless.* That's exactly how I felt when Logan Greer was touching me. "The venom..."

The muscle in his jaw tightened. "You think you can explain how I feel about you with demon venom?"

I nodded. "Yes," I stammered. "I mean, no."

He hooked my chin with his thumb, forcing me to look him in the eye. "Is that really what you think?"

My lips parted, but no words came out.

He held my stare. "I've never seen you speechless before, my lady. I think I quite like it."

"I'm not speechless." Desire flooded me, and my cheeks heated. "And I'm not your lady."

The words cut through me like I was telling myself the foulest lie. I was his lady, and the thought of belonging to this man—the idea of him belonging to me—set fire to my blood.

The leather of his uniform creaked as he pulled in a breath, his gaze lingering on my lips. Before he could argue with me, before he could try to justify his actions with any other explanation, he kissed me.

I kissed him back, insistent and pleading. His tongue traced over mine, evoking a gasp from me that made him grin against my lips. He had won, and he knew it. I could not argue my way through this thing that had developed between the two of us.

I was dizzy, surrounded by air that smelled like him.

That musky scent had woken me from sleep every morning since I met him. Teasing me. Torturing me. Now, it was real. It was here, and I was drowning in it.

I wrapped my fingers into his hair, and he broke free, trailing kisses down my neck, scraping my throat with his teeth. Every push and pull of his mouth sparked over my skin, threatening to ignite me.

His bed was in the far corner of the room. We were utterly alone, and I wanted to be reckless with him. I wanted to surrender my body, my control. To feel weightless and consumed by something that was pure pleasure. He caught the direction of my stare, and his icy blue eyes widened.

He opened his mouth to speak, but I interrupted his words with a kiss, this time soft, pleading. My desire for him won, pushing back any fear, any doubt.

"Have you been with a man before?"

His thoughts softly brushed against my mind, and I wondered if he had accidentally projected them to me. A shiver slinked down my body as I nodded. There had been flings, forbidden moments stolen in the halls of the manor, but nothing like this—nothing this intimate, this tucked away.

I wanted to savor Logan Greer—to trace every line of him in the dark. I needed to appreciate every moment with him.

We both shuddered a breath as he hitched a hand under my thigh, bracing my leg against his hip. He slid his hand under my skirts, the other untucking my tunic, and the feel of his rough skin on my back was pure torture.

His fingers trailed over my spine, over the scar tissue there, and a bolt of lightning flashed through me.

I craved more—wanted his hands everywhere, wanted to

know what his skin would feel like bare against mine. I reached behind me and pulled on the ties of my tunic, loosening the lacing.

The neckline fell away, revealing my breasts to him. I had never felt so exposed, but I reveled in it. I reveled in how the candlelight danced over his face as he took me in.

His lips on my skin were my undoing, and I let out a pleading moan as his kisses closed over the sensitive peaks of my breasts. I was still half-dressed when he dragged his hand up my thigh and over the smooth satin of my undergarments. I gasped when he slipped under the silky cloth.

I gripped his shoulder, arching toward him as he teased me, tracing his thumb over the sensitive spot where I throbbed for him. Logan Greer had crept into my mind and grown there like a vine, setting roots through me since I had first seen him in the alley.

Since that day, I had dreamed about him, about the lines of his face and his ridiculous dimple. Dreams of pressing him against that wall near the secret passageway and staying there, letting him have everything I knew he wanted.

I tugged at his belt as he touched me. I wanted much more than he was offering with his gentle strokes. The thick fabric of his uniform was not enough to hide the hard length of him. I gasped as I traced it through the material, enjoying how his arms contracted around me in response to my touch.

I unfastened his belt, and he freed the fabric. I had been with other lovers before, but not with someone so sure. His hands roamed over me like he knew what he was doing. Like he knew where he wanted to go. I encircled him within my grip, stroking him slowly.

His head tipped back as I ran my palm over every impossibly hard inch of him, and he cursed under his breath.

"*Bring me to your bed.*" A command. I managed to say it, but I was not strong enough to speak it aloud.

He locked his gaze with mine. "Are you sure?"

I had never been more sure about anything.

My clothes fell to the floor as I nodded and claimed his lips. He unstrapped the buckles of his uniform with steady fingers, and I greedily slid my hand up the hard ripples of his abdomen. His chest was smooth skin over hard planes. I ran my hands over his scars, taking in the full extent of the newly healed flesh.

I traced my fingers over the silvery blue mark on his forehead, and he shivered. Had he experienced the same jolt of energy fueled by the marks that bound us? There were scars on his body I had never seen before. A jagged mark under his collarbone, a patch of irregular tissue over his chest.

None of them was as beautiful as the mark that Starling had given him. I wanted to memorize every line, every divot in his flesh. I ran my lips over his collarbone, and he took in a gasping breath.

By the time we made it to his bed, his clothes were entirely abandoned. Logan was even more beautiful to behold without the leathers and the weapons strapped to him. His body was thick and muscled, like the finely-honed swords surrounding him in the armory.

If Logan Greer were forged from iron, I wanted him to surround me and drown out my senses like the wards in the wall.

Because this man had become my ward. There was some untold magic in him that grounded me to this realm and made me feel safe.

My legs wrapped around him, and his body pressed against mine, making me breathless.

He delicately set me down on the bed as if I were something breakable, and perhaps I was, in a way. His hand roamed back to my thighs, and he parted my legs.

"Harper, I want you to know something," he said. "No matter where you are, I will never stop protecting you. I will follow you into the fire."

My eyes widened, and I pulled away from him. "You don't mean that."

"I mean it," he said. "I won't be able to stop, even if you tell me to, even if you forbid me to follow you." He stared at me with glistening eyes. "I promise."

I opened my mouth to object, but he claimed me with a kiss that made my body arch into his. I begged for him, and he obliged me, sliding in until I was so full I could barely breathe.

He moved within me, taking me apart, unraveling me bit by bit.

Slow at first. But he built into a steady rhythm that was so good it almost hurt.

I was burning from within, and the friction between our bodies kindled the flame. My skin seared at his touch, and it was the most delicious kind of pleasure and pain.

My fingernails dug into his back, urging him to give me more, and as my body tightened, we found our release together.

I pulled air into my lungs, trying with all my might to breathe him in. He caught his breath as he whispered into my ear.

"I promise." He said it until it was the last thing I heard before falling asleep in his arms. "I promise, I promise."

CHAPTER
THIRTY-SEVEN

Logan was already gone when I awoke. Sneaking back to the townhouse would have been too risky, so I slunk from his apartment, keeping to the shadows and hoping nobody would notice I was dressed hastily in a wrinkled tunic and rumpled skirts.

When I arrived at the barracks, most of the activity was concentrated near the armory. The men were focused on taking stock of the recovered irons before Jacob's sentencing. I went into the police station under the guise of inquiring about Paxton and Brannon.

The men must have become accustomed to my occasional presence, and one of them even congratulated me on such a fine, finished work at the mural.

Perhaps they had been watching me more than I realized.

Or perhaps the mural had brought the morale boost that Jacob and Logan had initially speculated. It almost seemed insignificant to me now—an afterthought. A miniature portrait compared to the bigger canvas crumbling before me.

I waited politely for the men to disperse before sneaking through the back hallway to the cellar's holding cell. As I descended the stairs, the flames in the sconces flickered in time with my footfalls.

Jacob was crouched in the corner of the cell, his head slumped in his hands as if trying to sleep sitting up. There was a shabby, naked cot in the corner and a small, barred window. I was grateful he was the only prisoner housed in the cold stone walls and rusty bars.

I cleared my throat. "Good morning, brother."

My twin jolted out of sleep, his eyes dragging up to me with exhaustion. "Harper? What are you doing here?" he asked, his voice raspy and dry.

Jacob's face was wan, pulled tight over an exhausted frown. I extended a tendril of my magic to him, but I met the same solid walls I had grown so accustomed to.

I cocked my head. "I would have thought that would be obvious."

A raised eyebrow.

I bit my lip, gaining frustration. "Jacob, if you don't tell the lords the truth, then I will."

He shook his head heavily. "If we tell them my truth, we tell them yours. I would never put you in that position. I came here to help you, Harper. Not to damn you. You aren't ready."

His words hit me, bouncing off the walls I had put up in my own mind.

Ready.

The idea was laughable. Did it matter if I was ready? The Alister had bought me twenty-one years of borrowed time from a fate I couldn't escape. I had run out of time.

I scoffed despite myself. "Ready for what?"

"Ready to accept your fate. If I tell them who I am, you'll be revealed as the thirteenth child."

The suggestion that I had a choice in the matter bit me.

I pushed down a bubble of fear. "I know."

"You know the family better than I do," he said, staring at the floor. "How do you think they'll react?"

Despite the stone and brick around his mind, I was beginning to understand my brother. The sadness in what he suggested gutted me. Of course, I knew our family better, but he'd never had the chance to. The chance had been ripped away from him.

I waited until he returned my stare before I answered, "I can speculate, but I honestly don't know."

"You haven't even processed it yourself," he said.

I realized then that Jacob had come to know me as well as anyone could. Those months before our birth had bound us irrevocably in a way that could never be dissolved. It took only several days to reconcile the years apart.

Shadows eclipsed the barred window. We had run out of time.

"I'm asking you to tell them the truth, Jacob," I pleaded, pulling my cloak around my shoulders. "If you don't tell them before the sentencing, I will."

"And I'm promising you, Harper. I will protect you to whatever end. Even if it means my own."

Fear gripped me when voices echoed from the stairwell, and that fear choked the words that bubbled up my throat. I should have stayed, let the lords find me, and told them the truth. But something desperate in my brother's blue-gray eyes made me turn back to the stairs.

"*Go,*" he pleaded into my mind. "*Promise me you won't tell them yet. Come back tomorrow morning.*"

There was no time to reply.

I hurried up the steps, and the torches died a bit, like they were pushing me along, the fire hushing my steps.

Bain, Aaron, and Father were in the station when I reached the lobby, accompanied by Logan. His eyes flared when he saw me emerge from the cellar, but the lords had their backs to me.

"Lieutenant, your work collecting the stolen irons has been invaluable," Uncle Bain said. "Without your testimony, we would have never had enough evidence to bring Mr. Miller to trial. Unfortunately, the beast he was warding has escaped."

I staggered back, bracing myself on the cool stone. Would they hunt Starling? I had no doubt my horse could handle himself out there, but a threat to him felt like a threat to me.

"I'm relieved to know my brother's battalion will receive the recovered arms first," Logan said.

Cade put his hand on Logan's forearm. "Your brother's bravery leading that battalion will be rewarded. I want to thank you for guarding Harper, especially after learning that Captain Miller had coerced us all," Father said. "It pains me to think I let that man into our home—let him guard my daughter in your absence."

I wanted to scream. I wanted to lead Father by the hand to Jacob's cell and pull up my brother's shirt sleeve, exposing his brand. Promises were pointless when Jacob's life was on the line, but my twin had been so insistent.

There was never going to be a good time to tell them, so I stepped forward, filled with resolve, when a large group of men pushed into the room. From the far end of the station, a team strode in, their arms heavy with iron, and began unloading weapons onto the wooden tables.

Logan cleared his throat over the clanking of metal on wood as he glanced toward my shadow in the doorframe. "Yes, it was quite a shock to learn who had been stealing from my armory." A truth wrapped in a secret. "Lords, I ask that you review my inventory," Logan said, gesturing to the desk. "I'm quite sure every weapon is now accounted for."

I seized my opportunity as the triplet lords' attention shifted to the accumulating pile of weapons. I slipped through the open door unnoticed into the cloudy quadrangle and leaned back against the stone, my palm pressed against the cool surface. The same kind of stone had been used to build the wall.

I willed heavy breaths into my lungs as steam swirled around me.

Every moment that passed put Jacob at risk. Nausea bubbled in my stomach as Father's words replayed in my head.

It pains me to think I let that man into our home.

That man was his son.

The damp air wrapped around my shoulders like a blanket on a winter night, steadying my racing heart. It was not the first time the mist had comforted me in a time of stress.

My eyes reflexively closed. The Alister's magic shrouded me in safety. If all the demons in the pines could be half as good as the Alister, I would not hesitate to take my place among them.

The Alister was not my only friend in the pines. Starling was free, likely prancing or soaring through the trees right now, and I fought back the urge to run to the gate and join him.

I could race through the pines on his back and take to the air. If I asked him, he would take me far from here. I could leave this village and everything that tied me to it. Starling and I could fly over York, north to the Hampshires. I wanted to get as far away from this place as I could.

Some things never changed.

My limbs were numb as I set out on the familiar path back home to the townhouse, my steps barely registering as my muscles carried me out of sheer memory.

I pushed open the front door, hung my cloak on the hook, and didn't hesitate to collapse onto the sofa in the drawing room. I nearly jumped out of my skin when I heard a man clear his throat.

James sat beside the fire, his elbows propped on his knees and his hair ruffled from resting his head in his hands. "You didn't go to the manor last night," he said aloud.

I bit my lip and blinked at him. "No, I didn't. Where's Maggie?"

He raised a brow. "At the manor, awaiting Father's return from his meeting at the prison."

It all flooded back to me. "You told him then? About you and Benjamin?"

He nodded.

"Well, how did it go?" I prodded, leaning forward in my seat.

"I started by telling him I wanted to cancel the wedding."

I winced. The wedding had brought Father so much joy these past few weeks.

"And?" I prodded.

"He wanted an explanation, so I told him I would never be a good husband to Emelia. She deserved a man who would love her—who *could* love her."

"Oh, James."

He dragged a hand through his dark brown hair. "I explained to him I could not grow to love Emelia—or any woman—because I was not drawn to women physically or emotionally."

"Did you tell him about Benjamin?"

James settled onto the cushion beside me. "I didn't want to, but Ben insisted we do this together."

Benjamin had just received a promotion at the manor and was willing to throw it all away for the truth. Sadly, the truth could not be taken for granted in matters of the heart. I had learned that the hard way.

"How did it go?"

James sat back in his seat. "Father offered me the townhouse."

"Excuse me?" I almost choked.

"He said he would never impose marriage on me, that Benjamin and I deserved happiness, and we could live here. We would have our privacy, and he would convince Uncle Bain to get a new valet so Ben could be 'employed' as mine."

I was so relieved I almost laughed. After all this time, all the scheming to get James out of this town, Father had devised a way to make it all work.

"Where will he and I go?" I asked. "Are you going to kick us out?" I couldn't imagine what it would be like to move into the manor with my father, but as long as I had Maggie and could stay away from Mira, I would have the comfort of James's happiness.

"Father simply asked for time to get his affairs in order before he makes his proposal."

My eyebrows rose. "What proposal?"

James smiled. "Yesterday, Emelia confessed to Bess that she also wanted to cancel the wedding. She was accepted into York's most prestigious midwifery program and couldn't dream of asking me to leave my family."

Emelia's logic was the same as mine when I'd fabricated the plan to move to Delphi. I shook my head. She couldn't ask James to leave this place.

"Emelia was going to propose this plan to Father?"

"No," James continued. "When Bess heard the news, she was overcome with emotion. She came straight to Father to discuss it, and apparently, he realized at that moment that the reason for his happiness during the wedding planning had nothing to do with our union. His happiness was because of Bess."

My heart leaped. "Father has feelings for Bess."

James nodded, a smirk tugging at his lips.

It all made sense. The waves of unexpected happiness and sheer brightness James and I had been picking up with our magic. It had nothing to do with the wedding at all. Father had been spending his days with Bess, and it had kindled something in him: his unexplained enjoyment in wedding planning, his joy at family dinners when she was by his side, the apparent care Bess had for James and me.

They had grown together.

James nodded, a broad smile spreading on his face. "He plans to propose to her tomorrow night. At the lords' presentation of the mural."

All this time, the one thing we were trying to escape from had become the catalyst for something I'd thought was impossible. Cade Ledes was finally at peace. Jacob and Logan would never have intercepted me if I had won that gambling money in time, and Father would have left with us for Delphi. He would have never had a chance to develop that bond with Bess.

James must have been reading my emotions. "It was a good thing, after all. When the police captain blackmailed you," he said. "Even if he does get sentenced to death, we owe the man some small gratitude before the gallows, I suppose."

My brother's amusement melted away when he saw my face fall.

"James," I said, my voice shaky, "I have something important to tell you."

CHAPTER

THIRTY-EIGHT

James paced before the fireplace as I told him everything. I explained how Jacob had led me into the Barrens to confront the pit demon after revealing who I was. I was the thirteenth Ledes child, and Jacob and I had been separated at birth. Raina was alive. The true story of our mother's death. Starling and the stolen irons. I told him how Logan and I had freed the horse and how I had banished the cryptid out of this realm.

James stopped to stare at my painting above the mantel. "Jacob Miller is our brother."

"Not just our brother," I said. "My *twin*. He has the branded *12*."

"And you spoke to..." He rolled his neck as though bracing himself for the name. "Raina."

"She's hiding in Jacob's quarters on the east side of town."

James began to pace again. "You can't accept this, Harper."

291

"I don't think I have much of a choice."

He stopped in his tracks, his jaw firm. "You'll be damned forever. Jacob will be sentenced to death," he said. "If he dies, this secret dies with him."

My back straightened. "What did you say?"

"Brother or no, this man has put you in danger—has put our family in danger—time and time again. If he reveals who he is, then everyone will know."

I could not believe what I was hearing. Was James suggesting we let him hang?

I stood, and he backed away. My heart cracked. James *cowered* from me, and I didn't blame him for it.

"Does it matter if the people in this village know? The demons in the Barrens already do. The secret is out. If the demons know, it's only a matter of time before their master returns. We can't let our flesh and blood hang over some false hope that I can be saved from this."

James paled, and his eyes widened before he closed the distance between us. He braced his hands on my shoulders, tears welling in his eyes. "Of course, we won't let him hang. And nobody will take you. We have the wall for a reason."

I inclined my chin. "The wall means nothing. They'll find a way in if the Devil knows I'm here. We need to save Jacob. We need to tell the lords the truth."

"You just told me even Jacob doesn't want that," James retorted. "Even he knows the value of taking the fall for you."

"I've come to know Jacob these weeks," I said, my voice cracking. "I see so much of you in him, so much of Father."

Devastation darkened James's eyes. "Then he likely made the same choice I would have made if I were in his position. If it were me, Harper, I would rather die than tie you to this fate."

He had made that choice—*to whatever end, even my own.* I broke away from James's grasp. "If you know me, you know I will never stand for that."

Because James did know me—better than anyone, and he always had—his legs gave out, and he sank onto the couch. "I could never stand for that, either." He scrubbed a hand through his hair. "I have a brother."

I fell into the cushion beside him. "I have a *twin.*"

"How are we going to tell Father?"

I sighed, unsure how we would even begin to tell Cade Ledes that he had a long-lost son. Although I was sure he would welcome Jacob once he got over the crimes of the last few weeks, the truth would crush him.

Father was finally happy. After years of grieving, he had found someone who had allowed him to live again.

Bess had ignited a spark that I had never seen in him. He had always been kind, fair, and nurturing. For the first time in my life, the flame within him was not muted to an ember. There was no underlying sadness shadowing his smiles.

The triplet lords had always lived in fear that the mystic's words would come true, and they would surrender one of their children to the fire realm. My truth would devastate him. It would pull him apart just as he found himself again. It would undo everything.

I leaned my head back on the cushion and watched the second hand of the mantel clock. Every tick moved me toward the moment when I would crush my father back to the wick.

Cade Ledes was the father of the thirteenth child, the

bearer of the curse, and the bringer of the promise made when we were born.

A knock sounded on the door, clipped and quick. James sprang to his feet, and I followed.

Logan's face was drawn, and his eyes were wide on the other side of the door.

"Jacob has been sentenced to death."

THIRTY-NINE

I pulled Logan into the house by the arm. The mist was thick, but not thick enough for this kind of news.

"Did you speak with him?" I asked, my voice shaking.

Logan shook his head and exchanged a meaningful glance with James.

I turned away from them and stomped down the hallway to the kitchen, the sizzle of heat crackling on my fingertips. When I entered the room, the hearth flared to life, thick flames licking around the brick in angry tendrils.

When James turned the corner after me, his eyes widened, catching the reflection of the flames. He studied me, realizing my new, unruly magic was the source. "Calm down, Harper."

"James, I know this is technically your house now, but I swear to you. I'll burn it down if you don't help me figure this out."

Horror gripped me, and my magic squeezed with it. The fire was too new, and I doubted I would ever learn to control it. How was I supposed to protect Galloway from the Devil's flames? I could hardly control my own emotions. How was I supposed to reel in the wrath of the Devil?

I turned my back to Logan as he lurked in the doorway. "Too scared to come in?"

His boots clicked as he stalked into the room, coming as close to the fire as he could without being burned. "I'm not scared of you," he said, his voice thick and deep.

"You should be," I said. "Scared of me."

"I told you I would help you get Jacob out," he said. "We won't be able to do that until we begin unraveling this tangle of lies, or he'll die. His public execution is in two days. We don't have much time."

My spine straightened. He was right. "And how do you propose we approach this? If we tell the lords the truth right now, there's no telling what will happen to the demons beyond the wall."

I had no idea what would happen when my identity was revealed to the village. Would the demons become more aggressive? Would they attack the soldiers stationed in the Barrens? Dread eddied through me when I thought of Logan's brother, all those like him, vulnerable and exposed without the protection of the wall.

How many demons could the wall even hold? Would the wall withstand an onslaught of them?

No matter what, telling the truth would put everyone in the Barrens at risk—even if it did save my brother.

Logan nodded at James, and my brother left the room. "The lords need to know the truth, or Jacob will hang."

What if Bess didn't accept Father's proposal when she learned the truth tomorrow night? What if Father decided he wouldn't bring her into it? There were so many uncertainties. It was dizzying. "I wish we had more time."

Logan stepped toward me, and I shivered, cursing the need for him that ran like a current under my skin. He studied my face for a moment before running a thumb over the swell of my lower lip, and I didn't realize it had been trembling until his touch softened me.

"You cannot continue to live like this," he whispered. "You're so concerned about everyone else's well-being. What about your own? We don't know what will happen. We don't even know what the Devil will want from you."

I stepped back. My well-being was the last thing on my mind, but I had begun to feel vulnerable in a way I never had before. I had let this man in—had decided to trust him—and it terrified me. My heart was lying raw on the floor, mere inches away from the sharp edge of the truth, Logan Greer's boot, and the Devil's fire.

I would be burned, lacerated, or stomped on, no matter what happened.

"You promised me you would protect me," I said. "But who will protect me from you?"

Shadows darkened his eyes as the fire in the hearth sucked into the void of my fear, snuffing out. The room was cold in the absence of its glow.

"You have nothing to fear when you're with me," he said.

I laughed. "I'm terrified, Logan. Everything is about to change."

He closed the distance between us and wrapped his hand around the nape of my neck. "I'm sorry. I was wrong to force you to help us with the investigation," he said. "I was desperate, but along the way, everything shifted. Your safety is the only thing I'm desperate for now."

I cursed myself for bending to his touch, but no words came.

"I'm sorry Jacob was captured," he continued. "And I'm sorry I helped the lords discover him. I'm sorry I was assigned to be your guard. But I refuse to have any more secrets. What I said last night was true, Harper. I promise to protect you because I love you. Nothing about you scares me."

Magic roiled through me, begging to slide into his mind, but I held it tight like the reins of a wild horse. Because I knew he was telling the truth, even without magic, and that truth was enough to send me tumbling over the edge of what this was becoming.

What I was becoming.

He stared at me for a moment before he took the stance of a soldier and said, "Tell me what you need."

I needed my brother to live. I needed to escape my fate as the thirteenth child. I needed to understand what the Devil wanted from me. I needed my Father to be happy. I needed Logan. All of him and everything he promised.

There was no way to connect everything I needed without hurting someone.

"I need to think."

CHAPTER

FORTY

I waited until Logan had disappeared into the mist before I took my cloak from the hook, pulled the wool around my neck, and drew the hood around my face.

This time, nobody stopped me in the dark as I walked under the willows on the path to the stone wall. I pushed open the heavy iron latch of the same gate Jacob and I had run through to confront the pit demon.

The gate did not creak, and my feet fell silently on a bed of pine needles.

But I had no fear in my heart as the ground crunched beneath my boots. I had taken less than ten steps before I heard the soft approach of hooves in the thicket of trees.

My muscles relaxed as Starling approached, and I blinked when his form appeared through the haze. It was hard to believe I had been afraid of demons only days ago. The presence of the demon horse brought me more comfort than almost anything else in this realm could right now.

Starling huffed a breath and spread his batlike wings. *"Something troubles you."* It was not a question.

299

I nodded. "*I would like to take a ride,*" I said, stroking his nose. "*Things have started to fall apart on that side of the wall.*"

The horse bowed on one knee, giving me access to his back, and I climbed on, gripping the feathery scales of his neck. Starling broke out into a canter as the mist cleared through the top boughs of the trees. I tipped my head back and smiled, grateful to the Alister for allowing the sky to break through.

Sensing my sentiment toward the clouds, Starling broke into a gallop, weaving through the trees like a phantom breeze. The wind whipped over my face, and I was lighter.

We rode swiftly, and there were no family secrets. There was no responsibility to anyone's heart but my own. We reached a clearing, and I heard the waters of the Mullica bubbling just out of sight.

"*Would you like to take to the sky?*" Starling asked.

My heart leaped into my throat. "*Very much, but I'm afraid of falling,*" I admitted.

"*Then I shall not allow you to fall,*" he said, and before I could protest, his wings stretched to their full span.

He picked up speed and soared into the air at the exact moment his wings flapped against the breeze. My stomach dropped, and I tightened my grip on Starling's mane as we flew. Higher and higher until suddenly, we were above the canopy.

My weary eyes adjusted to the bright sunlight, more brilliant than anything I had ever seen, and the warm sun glowed like a beacon, heating my skin despite the autumnal chill in the air. I squinted at the village below me from our place in the sky.

"*It looks so small from up here,*" I told Starling.

"This realm is small compared to others," he replied.

"How do you know?" I asked, peering down at the landscape below me. I could see the long beach of the sea as we sailed to the east, and I hoped Logan's brother was on his way home to the safety of Galloway's walls.

"I am a creature that belongs to more than one realm," he said. His wings stretched, catching the wind in such a way that he hardly had to flap them. *"I was born in the realm of fire, but I was sent here to be yours. All the realms are layered upon each other. The fire realm is much bigger than this. It has many names. Just as my master has many names, some know him as the master of fire, some call him the Devil. Every world is interconnected, but there are hints of us in all of them."*

Awe gripped me, and I felt impossibly small as we turned course to the south. I could see the southern cape before me, bathed in brilliant light and surrounded by shimmering water. I had never seen the ocean before. I took in the deep blues and the way the sun reflected on the waves, and it was as though I had somehow known it.

"Are there hints of you in other realms?" I asked.

"Yes," he answered. *"I have been seen in other worlds, soaring between the trees. Some believe me to be a devil. We are ghosts, shadows, stories, whispers in the dark told around fires."*

"Why does your master wish to come back here?"

"He is fond of this realm. The Barrens are his grounds."

We began to bank toward the village again, soaring down to the tops of the trees. We swooped back into the clearing, and wind prickled my skin as we receded into the mist. With a pounding heart, I held on to Starling's mane as his feet found purchase on the mossy ground.

His canter slowed, and I allowed myself to lie forward, resting my head on his neck.

"When he returns, we will keep peace, you and I," Starling said. *"It will not be as hard or frightening as you imagine."*

"I'm beginning to realize that." I could picture myself riding through the pines with Starling, being safe no matter what met us.

"Things fall apart, Harper. They fall apart whether confined within stone walls or layered between realms. We must not fight the fabric from unraveling. Rather, we can become the threads themselves. When we tie the fibers together, we can weave something new, something stronger."

I dismounted, letting the creature's words ring through my mind. Demons tended to speak in riddles, but what Starling had just told me did not feel puzzling at all.

It felt like truth.

CHAPTER

FORTY-ONE

I needed to tell my cousins.

Just after dusk, James and I walked to the bustling tavern. Perry was waiting at the bar and nodded when he spotted us, throwing down his towel and ushering us to the cellar. We followed him, past the card games and smoldering cigars, past the women sitting on the laps of militiamen, whispering in their ears. Past the tables where I had once sat, swindling villagers.

When he opened the door, I steeled myself. Paxton and Brannon took up seats at the heads of the table. Axel and Rand turned in their chairs to nod a greeting at us. Across from them, Mira sat primly.

Mira inspected her brightly painted nails as though bored and thoroughly bothered to be called from the manor.

Logan stood alone in the corner, and his back straightened when he caught my eye. James had insisted we invite him. My brother had read the lieutenant's intentions and was comfortable trusting him with such a delicate family matter.

Logan waited until I was seated before he moved to a new position in the room.

To the seat beside me.

I turned my focus to the table, forcing my eyes away from Mira, but her stare was palpable. I needn't be a mind-speaker to sense the contempt wafting around my cousin.

The Galloway Ledes cousins had all come together. Samuel and Jackson were missing, but I had written to them in Delphi this afternoon. I was certain Mira would fully update her sisters at the conservatory. I had considered not inviting her to this meeting, but James had convinced me she would be easier to deal with if she was properly informed.

In several days, the entire town would know every truth spoken at this meeting. Every damning, inescapable truth. And there was no telling what kind of dangers awaited us when every demon in the Barrens descended upon the walls of Galloway.

It was Jacob's absence at the table that troubled me most.

I picked at my cuticles, trying to push the image of his jail cell out of my mind. It hadn't made it easier to see that the gallows had been pulled into the square. On our way to the tavern, little children had played and climbed on the crude wooden structure, unaware that one of their lords—one who was hidden but no less noble—was to be hanged there in less than a week.

Every eye at the table was fixed on James as we took our seats, and Perry served us drinks. I almost kissed him when he filled my wine glass to the brim. James had requested this meeting, and curiosity bubbled through the room as we settled in.

"Well, James," Brannon finally said, raising a stein of ale

to his mouth. "Have you called us here to decide who will be your best man, or are there more serious issues you want to discuss?"

James shifted in his seat beside me.

"*We do this together*," he said in a voice no one else could hear. "*I'll be on your side, no matter what.*"

Jacob's voice echoed through my mind. *To whatever end.*

I cleared my throat. "Actually, it was my idea to call this meeting," I said. "And the matter at hand is my own."

Mira crossed her arms and shot her brothers a withering glance. Paxton met her stare with an expression of warning, and Brannon released a heavy sigh.

"And yes, there is a very serious matter to discuss," James said.

Paxton spoke up. "I'm keen to hear it." He turned his attention to Perry and Rand, flanking him on either side of the table. "But first, I would like to assure the tavern owners that nobody at this table will speak of what we just saw in the cellar to Uncle Bain."

"Here, here," Brannon said, raising his glass.

The tavern owners laughed, breaking some of the tension. Even Mira nodded and smiled. Some things were bigger than the law, even for the twin militia generals, and I was grateful for that, especially now. I couldn't help but smile at the thought of Paxton and Brannon keeping the secret of the illegal gambling operations from surly Uncle Bain.

I took in a steadying breath. "The reason I've called you here is because of the prisoner Jacob Miller, who is being held in the cell below the barracks. We need to ask the lords to release him."

Paxton's back stiffened, and he crossed his arms, his

branded numeral *1* catching the lamp light. "Mr. Miller was sentenced to death this morning, Harper. He was charged with weapons theft, treason, and tampering with an investigation. Lieutenant Greer's own testimony helped convict him." Beside me, Logan stiffened. "You'd better have a damned good reason for that request."

James spoke up. "If you were to go to the prison right now and roll up Mr. Miller's sleeve, you would find a branded number *12* on his forearm."

Mira gasped.

I swallowed the knot that had been collecting in my throat. "Jacob is our brother," I said, my lip trembling.

James put his hand on my forearm and nodded gently.

"He's my twin. We were separated at birth. I only just learned this information, immediately before his arrest."

James squeezed my arm. "He's one of us—a Ledes by birth and brand," he said.

I nodded. "We must convince the lords to hear our case to free him. Jacob isn't willing to tell them. He's willing to take the fall...for me. So the only way for us to save him is to tell the truth ourselves."

Mira stood, bracing her polished fingertips on the table. Her green eyes darkened as she narrowed her gaze on me. "If Jacob is the true twelfth Ledes cousin, that makes Harper the thirteenth."

Paxton and Brannon stiffened. Perry, Axel, and Rand exchanged shocked glances before turning to me.

"All this time," Mira said, shaking her head. "There was something wrong with you, Harper. Since you were a little girl, you wanted nothing to do with us. You wanted to be apart, always content painting somewhere alone. Leaving lessons to hide in the library."

Perry stood now. "The reason Harper distanced herself, Mira, was your own doing. You made her life miserable. Do you know how many times she ran to our quarters in tears because of you? She was younger than you. She looked up to you."

Fire from the lamps danced defiantly in Mira's eyes. "I only said the things I knew to be true," she spat back. "It never sat well with me that she didn't have a brand. I knew something was...*wrong* with her. What you just admitted only proves it. She never enjoyed our company as a child, and now I know why. She's a devil. Why would a devil want to play nice?"

Her words were sharp enough to lacerate my heart, and I was content to let it bleed. I did not have a comeback this time. No curt reply or sarcastic dig. Mira was right. There was something wrong with me.

"Of course, she didn't enjoy your company," Brannon chided his sister. Even Mira paled at her brother's tone. "How often did Pax and I ask you, Ana, and Grace to play nice?"

Mira glared down at me and huffed a laugh. "We finally know the truth. The curse has already taken root. The mist has been getting thicker every day. We didn't need the wall until you were born. It all makes sense. The demons are coming for us. Fire is returning to the Barrens, the Devil will claim this land, and it's all because of you."

"Enough," Logan said, slamming his palm on the table. "It's not *because* of Harper. She's the only person in this realm who can finally free this town."

Mira's eyes widened, and I saw her realization. The moment when she understood Logan Greer had been more than my guard these weeks. A slight flush rose to her cheeks, and she sat down.

Logan continued, "Jacob had a clear motive for stealing the irons. A noble one. He captured the horse with the stolen weapons to keep Harper safe before he revealed his identity to her. But Jacob was wrong. The horse was sent to protect Harper, not deliver her to the fire realm. Harper and I went to the Barrens when we heard the horse had been warded with the stolen arms, and she freed the beast. When she was inside the cottage, I was taken by a cryptid. She and the horse followed me through the woods, and Harper banished the cryptid out of this realm. She sent it back to hell."

"You were the one who freed the horse?" Paxton asked.

I nodded.

Brannon paled. "You banished a cryptid?"

"The horse is my guardian. Not my abductor," I explained. "According to Raina, he saved me from the fire when I was born."

"Raina?" Brannon said, eyes widening. "She's here?"

James spoke next. "Our mother's death finally makes sense."

He told the tale of how Sarah Ledes had died, how she had used Father's fire magic to save me from being taken. Mira, Ana, and Grace had been too young to remember my mother. Perry, Axel, and Rand had been newborns when she died.

But Paxton and Brannon listened on, their jaws firm. When James had told them everything, Paxton spoke first. "That's something Aunt Sarah would have done," he said.

Brannon nodded. "I always wondered what happened that day. Uncle Cade was so devastated. We were forbidden to ask questions. Mother told us death by magic came with a curse." He glanced at James. "James never got to mourn her."

Fat tears welled in my brother's eyes, but he blinked them back.

"Our mother died to save me—and Jacob," I said. "And now Jacob is willing to die for me, to keep my true identity hidden. We can't let him die. I tried to convince him to tell the lords, but he refused. When we reveal his identity to the Lords, the entire village will learn the truth. Jacob doesn't want to put me in danger, but we need to tell the truth before he's taken to the gallows."

Axel locked eyes with me. "Aunt Sarah could mind-speak," he said. "It wasn't widely known, but she would speak to us through her mind at the dinner table."

Paxton smiled. "She loved to tell us jokes whenever the dinner conversation got too serious. I think our parents knew, but nobody mentioned it in conversation."

My heart cracked. They had known all this time.

"James and I can mindspeak, too," I said. "James can't communicate with the demons, but it's how I speak to them."

Paxton and Brannon exchanged a nod. "We always wondered if the two of you could. You would get that same glint in your eyes. So like Aunt Sarah—like you were sharing a secret."

I huffed a laugh despite myself.

"We knew Jacob could mindspeak when we hired him," Paxton said. "Thought it would be a good skill for a police captain. It never made sense to me that these raids were happening under his watch. I suspected him immediately."

Brannon nodded. "It's why we returned to town from

the Long Beach outpost," he said. "We had a feeling he was involved."

Logan scoffed. "I vouched for him at first."

Paxton gave him a satisfied grin. "Why do you think we assigned you to be Harper's guard? It forced the two of you apart. Don't worry. We never suspected you were involved, Lieutenant," he continued. "You're too much of a do-gooder."

Logan shook his head and leaned back in his chair.

James interrupted. "Mindspeaking isn't the only thing Harper inherited from our parents," he said. "She can also wield fire."

Logan spoke up. "She can banish the demons and keep the fires controlled." He made it a point to speak directly to Mira. He explained how I had spoken to the pit demon the night of the fire.

My cousin slumped in her chair a bit at his words. Paxton, Brannon, and Axel studied me, and I swore I could see the embers of their magic sparking in their eyes.

Brannon gazed at the lamp, alight with fire magic. "That's a lot of responsibility for one person to take on."

"If the space between realms has started to thin," Axel said. "If the master of the fire realm returns to the Barrens, the fires will return with him. When the villagers learn there's a thirteenth child, the demons will feed on their fear."

I nodded, mustering a shred of confidence into my words. "I'll have Starling—my horse—to help me. When the fire returns, I'll keep it away from Galloway. I'll banish any demon that breaches the wall."

Perry spoke this time. "What of the other settlements? The Saunnils? What of the people at the grist mills at

Chatsworth? How will tradesmen safely travel from Delphi to Long Beach?"

Nausea bubbled in my stomach. "I'll patrol with Starling and keep the fires contained," I said. "I did it the other night with the pit demon. I can do it again."

I could do it forever. My greatest fear.

Axel stood, his shoulders square. "You won't do it alone," he said, glancing at the twin fire wielders. "You can't."

I stood to face him, fear gripping me. "I will not ask that of you."

Tears welled in my eyes as Paxton and Brannon stood and put their hands over their hearts.

"You'll never be alone while we're here, Harper," Paxton said. "You're the thirteenth child of the triplet lords. The Devil promised a return by your hand, but he never said the other children could not have their roles. As the first child, I will be by your side."

"So will the second child." Brannon bowed his head. "You have our allegiance."

Another chair scraped across the floor as James stood beside me. "The fourth child will not let you do this alone. Even though I barely know him, I know the twelfth child won't let you down."

Axel and his brothers stood with him and nodded. Mira peeled herself out of her chair, crossing her arms.

Tears fell freely down my cheeks as my cousins circled me. There were thirteen of us, and we were stronger than the sum of our parts. I knew their support would help me free Jacob, but I also knew there were some things they would never be able to help me with.

"What if I'm exiled from the village?" I asked through

sobs. Would they visit me in the Barrens? I could build a small cottage. Perhaps Raina could help me ward myself within it, allowing me a chance of intermittent peace.

Perry laughed. "What nonsense, Harper. If you're forced to leave, we'll threaten to shut down the tavern."

Axel nodded. "The villagers would welcome you back in exchange for a well-poured drink. That's for certain."

Logan's jaw ticked. "I'll guard you—in the Barrens or within the walls of this town. Even if it means I must endure that horse and your secret conversations."

I rolled my eyes, fighting back a sob.

His gaze locked with mine, not letting go as the corner of his mouth ticked up.

I knew what he was doing. Logan was owning this thing that had developed between us, here in this room full of my family, in front of Mira. I didn't dare glance her way as I met Logan's stare.

Paxton's voice broke the tension. "I'm glad you seem so devoted to our cousin, Lieutenant Greer."

"Yes," Brannon said. "Because we have no intention of relieving you of your duties as her guard."

The dimple on Logan's cheek deepened. "I had no intention of giving up my post."

"Okay, so we know what we need to do," Rand said, clapping his hands. "What's next? How do we get our cousin out of prison?"

Brannon ran his hand through his hair. "Uncle Bain is livid with him. Ledes or no, he may still enact some punishment."

Perry nodded. "Father and Uncle Aaron came to the tavern last night for a drink," he said.

If my cousins were shocked to know that I was the thirteenth child, they were more shocked to hear Uncle Bain had set foot inside the tavern.

Rand sighed. "I've never seen them more worked up."

"Then there's the matter of breaking the news to Father that he has a long-lost son," James said. "And the truth about our mother's death."

Axel chewed his lip. "Maybe we can tell them tomorrow before the mural's unveiling," he suggested.

Perry nodded. "Yes, the mural dedication might soften them to Jacob's case."

James shook his head. "Father has his own plans for tomorrow night. He's proposing marriage to Mrs. Hern."

"What?" Perry, Axel, and Rand said in unison.

James stiffened. "Emelia and I have called off our engagement. We weren't the ones meant to be married, after all."

My cousins gaped as I spoke into James's mind. *"You don't need to tell them anything else."*

Perry clapped him on the shoulder. "Sorry to hear it, James. Tomorrow night, let Uncle Cade have his moment, and we'll approach them the next day as a unified front. We can meet at the manor and explain everything the next morning."

My stomach churned. Father would propose to Bess at the ceremony and learn of his son's true identity the following morning, the day before the scheduled execution. Everything was moving too fast, and I prayed Bess wouldn't call off her engagement when she learned her betrothed had sired a harbinger of fire.

My cousins exchanged nods of agreement, but I cast down my gaze. I was less than two days away from embracing my fate. I wasn't sure how to get through the mural presentation and wished there was a way to skip the whole thing. Perhaps I could feign illness or exhaustion and spend the entire night in my rooms.

Starling and I could ride away, hide in the Barrens in some cave by the river until the truth was out. My cousins knew the truth now. Paxton and Brannon wouldn't let Jacob hang, even if I were to disappear. I knew what it felt like to soar above the mist. Now that my cousins knew, I could fly away. I trusted them.

Most of them. Mira's damning words were still ringing in my ears, but a part of me agreed with her. I had always been the outsider. Mira had always picked up on that, and no matter how vile she was, it made sense for her to be wary of me. She had seen some truth in me that everyone else hadn't.

I could let James present the mural. Even Logan could do it. It was all his idea, after all.

I lifted my head, and Logan was staring at me as though he were the one who could edge into my mind and read my emotions. In a way, maybe he was.

"A toast, then," Axel said. "To everything to come."

My cousins raised their glasses.

FORTY-TWO

Paxton and Brannon flanked me as we walked to the prison—two fire-wielding generals at the service of a herald of hell.

We received a nod of approval from the officer at the front desk, but I could not ignore the sadness that wafted from him. Jacob had been a fair and beloved leader for the police, and the men who admired him were now in charge of his captivity.

"The officers appreciate your beautiful work on the wall, my lady," the officer said. He tipped his hat. "Many of us hope you may adorn the police station wall next."

I nodded and gave him a polite smile. What would I paint on the wall of the police headquarters? What kind of image would be fitting after the town discovered the truth about who I was?

Brannon cleared his throat. "We hope to see you at the presentation ceremony tomorrow, Officer." There was an authority in the way he spoke that made the officer close the conversation and return to his books.

Paxton extended a hand, leading me to the staircase for the holding cells. I swallowed down the knot of dread in my throat and led the way.

The prison was musty and dark, and the light emitting from the lamp was an eerie blue, as though the magic that kept it alive somehow sensed my brother's presence.

Jacob's ebony hair was mussed at the edges. He sat on the dusty floor. Only his top half was positioned against the bed. A plate of untouched bread was beside him, and as we neared, soft snores indicated that he had fallen asleep in that uncomfortable position.

Paxton cleared his throat, and Jacob jumped. My brother scrambled to his feet, and when he realized the generals had come to his cell, his eyes widened.

"Mr. Miller," Paxton said. "Our cousin has called upon us, requesting your release. She claims she has compelling evidence regarding your innocence."

Jacob paled. "My lady was not involved in the theft of the arms, General. I assure you. Her duties were only at the wall."

Brannon put up his hand. "Sit down, Mr. Miller."

Paxton reached into his pocket and produced a key. He fit it into the keyhole and jiggled it in the lock.

"*What did you do?*" Jacob asked into my mind. His shoulders slumped with defeat.

"*I did what was right,*" I replied.

"I beg the two of you to keep the mindspeaking conversations to a minimum," Paxton said, glaring at Jacob.

I diverted my eyes to the floor.

"You told them," Jacob said. He scrubbed a hand through his hair, desperation drawn on his face.

"I had to," I said, forcing myself to look my brother in the eye. "I won't let you hang for me."

His jaw worked as Paxton entered the cell. Brannon stood beside me on the other side of the bars.

"Pull up your sleeve," Paxton said. There was authority in his words and a subtle kindness to the command.

Jacob tugged at his shirt sleeve. As the fabric peeled away, the familiar curly script of his brand was exposed—the brand of the twelfth child.

Brannon left my side, joining the two men inside the cell. They stood beside Jacob and pulled up their sleeves, revealing their own numeral *1* and numeral *2*.

My breath caught as my eldest cousins raised their arms, angling them beside Jacob's so the numbers lined up. The brands were identical, from the way the top of the one curved into a gentle serif to the loop on the bottom of the two.

"Do you know why we wanted to see it?" Paxton asked. His voice was soft now, allowing the general's mask to slip away.

Jacob shook his head. "I suppose Harper told you my story, and you wanted to assure the brand matched your own."

Tears welled in my eyes. "They don't think you're lying if that's what you mean," I said.

Brannon shook his head. "We came here to show you we are the same. You bear the mark of the one and the two. Paxton and I do as well."

Jacob's brow furrowed, staring at the mark on his forearm. "I was a teenager when Raina told me the truth. When I learned about my birth, I wanted nothing more than to reunite with my sister. But I regret coming here. It was selfish of me. If I had stayed in York, Harper would have never had to meet her fate. But now I'm here, and the whole family is damned because of my failure."

"I'll tell you what your brand really means." Paxton stood and faced my brother, my twin. "It means we're with you. That's what the brand means to us. If you have that brand, you're one of us. We'll stand with you and defend you. We understand why you did what you did. You broke the law to protect your twin."

The tears spilled onto my cheeks, and I swallowed a sob. I entered the cell and folded my brother into an embrace.

Jacob hugged me back, and we fell to the ground. We cried together on the dusty floor of the prison.

For all the moments we missed, for the connection we always shared that had been ripped away from us. I don't know how long we cried, but Paxton and Brannon stood watch over us.

Tendrils of their thoughts wafted into my mind. They pitied us. They wondered what it would have been like if they had been the ones pulled apart at birth. My twin cousins had been raised in lockstep to be mirror images of each other.

The leaders of this village.

My twin and I had been raised a world apart, and we would be the ones who tore this place down. Jacob's lies held us together, but my truth would rip us to shreds. Together, Paxton and Brannon provided this town with the security of their protection. But the moment Jacob and I were reunited had solidified the Devil would, in fact, return. Through some providence I still didn't understand, he would crawl back through the thin space into this realm and unleash his fire in the Barrens once more.

"I broke the law," Jacob said into my shoulder. "I stole from the lords. I deserve my punishment. I welcome it if it keeps Harper safe. If I die, the truth dies with me. The Devil's promise won't be fully realized if the twelfth child doesn't exist."

Two twins forced apart, yet that connection could not be severed. Time could not splinter it, and distance could not thin it. I knew I would say the same thing if our positions had been reversed.

Paxton's voice seemed far away. "You're wrong. There's no guarantee your death would stop the Devil from fulfilling his promise. Everything you did, you did to protect Harper. The irons were recovered, and the lords will reverse the sentence. We plan to explain everything after Harper's mural presentation tomorrow."

Jacob didn't argue.

"James knows?" he asked.

"Yes. And now so do all our cousins. One more day, and we can tell Father," I said into his mind.

"What if learning about me saddens him?" he asked.

"If you need to ask that question, it tells me all I need to know," I replied. *"When you get to know him, you'll realize how alike you are."*

CHAPTER

FORTY-THREE

I tossed and turned in bed for hours before I abandoned the hope of falling asleep. Light flickered from Father's study, and I pushed open the door to find him sitting in his leather chair, spinning a pen between his fingers and tapping his foot in the way he did when his mind was working like a wheel.

He sat up smoothly, gathering the parchment before him into a neat pile. "Why are you up so late, Pumpkin?"

"I can't sleep," I replied, sinking into the chair near the door.

The way he grinned at me from behind his desk reminded me of all the times, as a child, when I would sneak down to his study at night. He would hear my slippered feet approach in the dark and suggest I return to bed. It would never take much prodding before he settled down next to me, content to read to me until my eyelids drooped.

I would fall asleep in his chair, tucked into the crook of his arm, and wake up the following day, warm under my quilt, with my father sleeping in the armchair beside my bed.

When he fell asleep in my room, the fire would never die. Father kept it alive by a magic chain as he slept.

"Is there something on your mind?" he asked, pulling off his glasses and tucking a bookmark into his page.

I bit my lip. There was so much on my mind, so much I couldn't yet share with him, that it didn't seem so daunting to say the words I said next.

"Why aren't we allowed to speak of Mother?"

His eyes dimmed, reflecting the gleam in the hearth. Wood popped in the flames. "Aaron and Bain decided it to be so, given she had died due to magic. Some legends say death by magic can be transferred to another if you speak of it. But they aren't legends I believe in. I guess I never had the energy to tell them it wasn't...necessary."

"Is it?" I pulled the hem of my sleeve through my fingers. "Unnecessary?"

"I've been ready to speak of her for a long time," he said, leaning back in his chair. "Would you like to know the thing that helps me the most? Whenever the thought of losing her becomes overwhelming?"

I blinked up at him, expectant.

"You remind me so much of her, Harper. James, too," he said, smiling sadly. "You have your mother's mind. She had the same dark sense of humor you do, the same sarcastic wit. James has always been so soft-spoken, kind yet strong, just like she was."

I swallowed a lump in my throat. Father had always said my sense of humor was a comfort to him. Now I knew why. Mother and I shared a likeness, but I had no idea I shared her mannerisms. I wondered how it could be so. How someone who had never had a chance to know me—couldn't tell me a story or sing me to sleep—could impress upon me in a way that was so formative.

"Aunt Pat ensured her portrait remained in the dining room," he said. "I think it was a contention between her and Uncle Bain, but I was glad for it. I often glance up at it while we're eating and like to think she's there with us. Sometimes I feel her. When the wind blows a certain way, or when I hear a bell chime in the distance."

I had seen his gaze wander to the portrait many times. "I would often stare at it and wonder how she and I could look so alike," I admitted.

He nodded. "You have the same eyes. James, too, only his are a touch bluer. It's funny. Sometimes the mist reminds me of your mother's eyes."

I swallowed and bobbed my head. Jacob shared the same blue-gray eyes. He and I both shared Sarah's wavy, black hair. Father would realize it soon enough, but what would he think of it? Would he accept it?

It was a silly question. Of course, he would. He had to.

I squared my shoulders. "Do you ever think about the mystic? From the story of your birth?"

He smirked, leaning back in his chair. "As children, my brothers and I often wondered if that story had been made up. Our father would bring it up so often. Any time we stepped out of line, he would threaten to summon the master of the fire realm to avenge his grudge."

"Surely, my uncles would never get into trouble," I said. A smile curled on my lips at the image of Uncle Bain misbehaving.

Father tipped his head back as though picturing the scene. "Oh, Bain was in trouble the most. Aaron and I were sure he would get dragged out of our realm, wrapped in angry flames."

I laughed. If only the tale had been false folklore meant to keep young children from mischief.

The Alister's words replayed in my mind. There were thin places all over this realm. How much of our folklore had bled into other worlds? If the elemental realms existed on top of ours, maybe one world's nightmares were realities of another.

I shivered, remembering what Starling had said. He was of more than one world, and I could imagine a place where he was merely a shadow, a story told to dissuade children from walking alone through the pines.

Father must have seen the wheels working in my mind. "What makes you so curious tonight, Harper?"

"I don't know." I did know. "There've been so many changes around here. James told me you're giving him the house."

He raised his brows.

"I know about Benjamin," I said, "I have for a long while. It's kind of you to give them the life they deserve together."

"I must admit, I'm ashamed of myself," he said, leaning back in his chair. "I never realized James might not be happy with the marriage to Emelia. A better father would have asked more questions. I shouldn't have presumed he'd be pleased."

"Emelia is wonderful," I said. "You chose a kind, smart woman for him, and when you realized it was not in the best interest of his heart, you respected that. I would say that makes you a good father, indeed."

He rubbed his chin for a few moments, mulling over my words. "What kind of father would I be to ask you to let someone new into your life? For my sake?"

My heart rose into my throat. I knew he was referring to Bess, but he was still supremely unaware I would ask him the same question in two days. A part of me wanted to leap from my seat and tell him everything, but a larger part—a more rational part—knew it wasn't the right time.

He needed to have this moment with Bess before he found out about Jacob.

"I'll always have room in my heart for someone who makes you happy," I said.

He let out a sigh and stared at the fire for a moment. The flames lit the curves of his face, aged with grief, weariness, and the weight of responsibility. But there was something light there. I glanced down at the bare skin of my forearm, pure and unmarred by a brand.

The number thirteen had been written there, just under my skin, from the moment I took my first breath. I tried not to think of my twin, sleeping in his cell, covered in a threadbare blanket. I let the flames dance in my weary eyes, and the weight of sleep finally overcame me. Heavy enough to wipe away my worries.

"Harper," Father said, and I startled. "Would you like me to read to you?"

I nodded and leaned against the winged back of the leather chair.

Father cleared his throat as he opened his book, and when I woke in the morning, I was still in the chair, a blanket draped over me. The fire was still crackling, but Father was nowhere to be found. I blinked in the gentle morning light, and the fire flared slightly.

This time, my own rope of magic had kept it burning through the night, and without knowing it, Cade Ledes had taught his daughter how to do it.

CHAPTER
FORTY-FOUR

Maggie began to fret over me the moment I trudged into the kitchen, seeking coffee. When I made my way to my room, piles of silk had exploded onto my bed like my wardrobe had projectile regurgitated its entrails. She barely glanced at me as she straightened the delicate fabrics.

"Lord Cade mentioned you fell asleep in his study last night," she said. "Glad for it, if I'm honest. I've had plenty of room to spread out our options without you lazing around in bed."

The idea of prancing around in one of those dresses while Jacob sat in prison made me almost as nauseous as my dresser drawers. I rubbed the knot in my neck that had bloomed while sleeping curled in the chair. Pain pulsed over the site of my scar.

"Which one have you chosen?" I asked, plopping down beside them.

Maggie's brow furrowed as she turned and took me in. "You want me to choose?"

I shrugged. "It doesn't matter."

"Okay," she said, narrowing her eyes. She rifled through the pile. "You should wear this one. The color will complement your complexion."

She held out a peach satin dress adorned with elegant, stitched floral blooms. It was not my taste at all, but I wondered if people might not notice me if I wore something so uncharacteristically cheerful. I twisted my mouth and shrugged my shoulders. "That one will be fine."

Maggie threw the dress onto the bed. "What's wrong with you?"

I raised my brows at her. Usually, Maggie would delight in parading me around in such a frilly display. She had been trying to convince me to wear that very dress for years. "What do you mean, what's wrong with me?"

Her arms slacked at her sides. "The last time I pulled that dress out, you told me the fabric was a *floral nightmare.*"

I winced. That sounded like something I would have said, and it was an unfortunately accurate description. "Maybe I've warmed to the color peach."

She shook her head. "Something's bothering you. I can tell." Of course, she could tell. She braced her hands on her hips expectantly.

My shoulders deflated, and I slumped to the bed, allowing my head to rest on the pillow. "I don't want to live in the manor," I said. It wasn't the biggest problem weighing on me, but it wasn't a lie. "I've lived here my entire life. That place doesn't feel like home."

"Ah," she said, sitting beside me. "It was only a matter of time before Master James inherited the townhouse. It was the least Lord Cade could do after Miss Hern called off the wedding. But I'll stay with you. Master James already told me he was interviewing valets. He hardly needs a maid and a valet, being a bachelor."

My heart warmed at her words. "Thank you, Maggie. That is a comfort."

"And who knows, my lady," she said, squeezing my hand. "Before long, you may find yourself in a house all your own."

I bit my lip as I pictured the house I would find myself in. Some dark, dank cottage in the pines, covered in brambles and cast in shadow and mist. The village children would likely tell tales about me, alone with my demon pets, riding through the pines on a winged beast in between my trips to the fire realm. Maybe some of them would even dare their friends to approach me if they saw me on the streets.

The cursed thirteenth child of the triplet lords. A devil living in the pines.

I glanced out the window. "Perhaps."

"That handsome lieutenant hasn't been to call on you in a few days," she said softly. "Don't think on it, my lady. He'll be back soon enough."

I sat up, blinking at her. "Why do you mention him?"

She wrung her hands. "You seem to fancy him. I didn't know if that was weighing on your heart."

Blood rushed to my cheeks. "Logan Greer does not weigh on my heart."

Maggie tutted. "I heard he'd been invited to tea with Lady Mira." She said Mira's name as if it left a sour taste in her mouth. "If you ask me, he'd be a fool to choose her company over yours."

I wanted to throw my arms around her, but I simultaneously wanted to crawl under the pile of dresses on my bed.

Because I wasn't going to have a normal life. I couldn't be a wife or a mother when the threat of fire forever plagued me. Voices of demons would always inhabit my mind. The danger of going mad from it all was real and crushing. What kind of life would it be, following me into that cursed, bramble-bound cottage in the woods?

"I haven't thought of it much," I said.

Maggie arched a brow before she stood. "Now, pick a dress you truly love. This night will celebrate your artwork. You should pick something that complements your talent."

I got to my feet and circled the silk pile. With the exception of the few Maggie had picked out with the hopes of coaxing me into something colorful, it was a hill of midnight black, murky gray, and blue as dark as night.

In the middle of the pile, a bold fabric caught my eye. "What about that one?"

Maggie quirked her head and cleared the other dresses from atop it, revealing fabric of the deepest red. The silk was soft, and the color was rich like a blood-soaked wine, but it had a subtle sheen when it caught the lamp's light. The bodice was covered in black lace, sheer over the rich fabric below.

Maggie smiled broadly. "That one suits you, my lady."

***

By the time Maggie had scrubbed, brushed, painted, and tied me into the dress, night had fallen. I didn't protest when she expertly painted the kohl onto my eyelids or slid the brush into the darkest lip stain I possessed.

James was waiting for me in the foyer when I arrived at the top of the staircase, lines of worry flickering on his face.

Father had gotten dressed at the manor with his brothers, but my brother had stayed behind to escort me to the barracks. He froze when I fully descended, his lips parting.

I offered him my arm, and he took it.

"*You're a living flame,*" he said, a hushed whisper in my mind.

My breath caught in my throat as my gaze trailed to the mirror by the door.

I was fire incarnate.

It felt natural and authentic, a part of myself that had been locked away and ready to spark into something more. I managed a nod before he led me to the gate on trembling legs.

The walk to the barracks was gratefully short, and the air was unusually light as we walked through the streets. Lamplight cast a shimmer over the gown's red silk, almost making it glow.

The quadrangle, usually gray and drab, was decorated with pine boughs and shimmering candles. A string quartet played a soft, romantic tune. The musicians were situated near the armory, and I wondered if Jacob could hear music from his cell. A squeeze of James's hand on my arm made me wonder if he, too, was thinking of our brother.

One more day, and he would be free—if we could convince Bain to take it easy on him. By this time tomorrow, the whole village would know I was the thirteenth child.

What would the truth bring? Would demons swarm the wall until the wards were overwhelmed? Would the pines ignite with the wrath of the Devil after being held from the Barrens for so long?

I could almost see the mural from the middle of the quadrangle. From this distance, I was struck by the size of what I had created. Flowers and candles had been set out around the mural, and a crowd stood around it, drinks in hand.

My stomach tightened in the familiar way it did when I caught someone appreciating my art, as if a raw part of me was on display for the sake of something pleasant to look at.

The floral arrangements around the mural reminded me of a vigil, and I couldn't help but feel the onlookers were mourning me without even knowing. Because the woman who had set out to paint it would never be the same. That woman had died beside that wall as soon as the truth was whispered into her ear.

A butler came by with a tray of champagne, but I smiled politely and waved him away. It felt odd to celebrate my own death.

James finished his glass in one gulp before he sighed and led me to Aunt Patrice and Aunt Bea.

"Get ready for a thousand condolences," James said in my mind.

"James, Harper," Aunt Bea said, extending her arms to hug us. "What a beautiful night. I haven't seen the mist this light in years."

"Yes, Aunt Bea," James said, after kissing her cheek. "It's almost like the Barrens want Harper's artwork to shine."

A lump rose in my throat. Galloway was lighter because the Alister wished it to be so. The demon that had shrouded me from the pines for twenty-one years was—he was showing off the mural. It was almost as though he was proud of me. I nodded politely.

"Aaron and I were heartbroken to hear Emelia had called off the wedding," Bea said, fixing her mouth into a pout. "How are you feeling, James? Is there anything I can do?"

"There are no hard feelings. I'm quite happy for Emelia," James said, straightening his shoulders. "I was overcome with pride when I heard she'd been accepted into the school. I would never get in the way of that."

"Besides," I said, tapping James's arm. "I would never forgive my brother if he had moved to the big city and left me alone."

My brother and I shared a hidden laugh as if we hadn't been secretly plotting to move to Delphi mere weeks ago.

"It was good of Cade to invite the Herns here tonight, despite it all," Patrice said, nodding toward my father, who was entertaining Bess and Emelia near the mural.

Bess said something that made him laugh loudly, throwing back his head while Emelia giggled beside him.

"It was certainly good of him," I agreed, and my heart swelled, knowing what my father planned to do tonight. He didn't appear at all nervous, only bright and happy. This was his night, much more so than it was mine.

"Harper, the mural is a masterpiece," Aunt Pat said. "Bain teared up when he saw it."

Aunt Bea guffawed into her champagne. "Now that's saying something," she said. "Aaron was so moved he could barely speak. He has a similar reaction, of course, when Mira writes him a song. The women in this family are surely talented."

I smiled tightly. "Yes, Aunt Bea."

I scanned the crowd. Locating my cousin didn't take much effort. Mira was outfitted in powder blue, the low-cut silk tight around her thin waist, but there was something off with her as she gently touched the arm of the officer she was standing with—a weariness combined with...

Disdain. My magic recoiled from her, and my heart skittered.

Mira's chin was high as she spoke with a handsome man I didn't recognize. My eyes locked with hers momentarily, and her smug smile immediately melted. Her lips curled into a sneer that made magic sizzle in my veins.

I tilted my head at her, speculating what in the realm could make her look at me that way, when a gentle tap landed on my right shoulder. I nearly jumped out of my skin as I turned and found Logan beside me.

In response to his arrival, Patrice and Beatrice painted broad smiles onto their faces, but James stiffened at my side.

"Would you like me to distract them?" James asked into my mind.

"No," I replied. I could do this. Logan was dressed in his finery, the most formal uniform reserved for the upper ranks of the militia. He nodded, locking eyes with me, and the way his throat bobbed made my skin prickle.

"I beg your pardon," Logan said, bowing his head. "I ask for Harper's attention for a moment, please. I guarded her when she painted. I would be honored to be beside her at the formal presentation."

My blood turned to ice as I faced the mural, where Father, Aaron, and Bain stood with a gathering crowd. My vision blurred, but James nodded encouragingly from my periphery. Aunt Patrice beamed as she nodded to Logan, but Aunt Bea's smile was pert, calculating.

Logan extended his arm to me, and my hand rose to it like a phantom. The crowd parted as he guided me to the mural, through a throng of smiling faces and high-ranking militia members watching me expectantly.

"If you notice me staring at you, my lady," Logan said,

"It's because I'm trying to burn the image of you into my mind. You. Are. Breathtaking, Harper."

I swayed.

"Just hold on to me," Logan whispered into my ear.

His voice shot through me. *Hold on to him.* Yes. That's exactly what I needed to do. I squeezed his elbow.

He steadied his hand over mine. "You don't need to say anything. Just smile and nod."

Father and his brothers stood before the mural. I allowed my gaze to trace the painted shapes—three clasped hands cradling a flame haloed with an ethereal glow. Blinking tears out of my eyes, I diverted my attention to Father.

"Tonight is a very special night," Aaron said to the crowd. "When we dedicate the mural on the wall, rendered in haunting beauty by my talented niece, Lady Harper Ledes."

He gestured to me, and the crowd broke into hearty applause. *Smile and nod. Smile and nod.* I managed my best appreciative grin.

"When I learned my niece would be standing this close to the wall," Uncle Bain said, "I was admittedly furious at the prospect." The crowd chuckled in appreciation. "But when I learned Harper planned to dedicate the mural to my brothers and me, my heart softened to the idea."

"Harper has been a talented artist since she was a young girl," Father said.

He smiled proudly at me, and I leaned into Logan.

He continued, "When she told me she was painting this mural, she explained her reasoning. She wanted to boost the morale of the militia by bringing something beautiful and inspiring to the wall that protects them." He swallowed thickly. "This wall has been standing since my beautiful daughter was born."

I was suspended by air. The mist was so thin. I nearly called for the Alister and begged him to cloak me in the familiar shroud of humidity.

Father inclined his head. "This wall has kept us safe in Galloway, but it has always held a darker meaning for me. For twenty-one years, I could not go near this wall without being reminded of the darkest time of my life."

Aaron and Bain stiffened as a hush fell on the crowd. Magic snaked through my mind, and with it, the sentiments of the crowd whirlpooled into my brain.

The lords have not spoken of the darkness beyond the wall.
Lady Sarah's death.
He's speaking of Lady Sarah.
Lord Cade has never spoken this way.
Does he mean to speak of Lady Sarah?
This will curse us all. Death by magic.
Death by magic tied to a curse.

A hush fell over the crowd as he paused, but my magic was awash with their thoughts. I wished to float away, sail high above the wall until Starling could find me, and I could slip onto his back and fly to the sea.

"Harper has changed how I think of this wall," Father continued, gesturing at the mural. "Now, when I see this mural, I look upon it with pride and love. The hands cradling the flame will remind me of the strength my brothers have brought to this village—have brought to me. This wall represents much more than loss. It represents strength. Galloway's strength. The militia's strength. Thank you, Harper, for capturing that strength so profoundly."

Aaron and Bain burst into applause. The crowd

followed them, and the sound of their hands clapping rang in my ears. I leaned into Logan, fully aware that, at this point, he was holding me up.

My gaze met my father's, and he smiled. A smile so genuine it made my heart crack. It didn't matter that I had painted that mural begrudgingly. All that mattered was Cade Ledes.

My birth had set the stones into the mortar. Mother's death had raised the wards.

The mural had redefined what this wall meant to Father. I had done something good, something meaningful, before everything was about to change. I still didn't know what the future held for me, but this image could give our people hope when they gazed upon it, even if the woman who'd painted it had set a promise from the Devil into motion. Perhaps they would find courage here despite it all.

Father held up his glass in a toast, and I heard glasses clinking as the group gave cheers. For one moment, I was relieved, and then that moment was shattered.

The crowd hushed, and Logan's grip on my arm tightened as a group of uniformed militiamen arrived in front of the mural.

Behind them, Jacob was pulled forward, his hands in chains.

My stomach dropped, and my legs almost gave way as my twin was dragged into the space between the mural and the quadrangle.

His face was bloodied, and his shoulders drooped like he had resisted this moment with every ounce of his soul. The militiamen who dragged him wore wary expressions as Mira edged her way to the front of the crowd.

FORTY-FIVE

Mira held up a gloved hand, silencing the villager's curious whispers. "I must insist on a moment of your attention."

Jacob ceased his fighting as she spoke, a trail of blood dripping down his nose. I wanted to call out to him with my magic, but I was utterly frozen as I took in the sight of my bloodied twin.

"Most of you in this crowd will recognize the man before you," Mira continued, gesturing to my brother's slumped frame.

Paxton edged his way to the front of the crowd and drew his sword. "Mira, what is the meaning of this?" He addressed the soldiers. "I command you to stand down," he bellowed at the guards.

Mira held out a hand to him, even as the soldiers loosened their stance, heeding their general. "This is bigger than you, Paxton. It's bigger than all of us." She turned back to the mass of villagers. Every eye was fixed on her, and a deep satisfaction burned in her eyes. "Many of you knew Captain Miller. Many of you risked your lives, daily, on his orders."

Some men on the edge of the throng, dressed in police militia uniforms, exchanged worried, confused looks.

"What your captain failed to tell you..." She paused dramatically. "It was an insult to everyone in this village. And it put us all in danger. He failed to tell you we face a far greater threat, one that comes from beyond this wall. You may have heard of his recent crimes, but I fear the truth is far worse."

My hand around Logan's arm tightened.

He leaned down and whispered into my ear, "If I tell you to run, you run."

I nodded, unable to even project a thought into his mind. My magic was swirling through me like a storm—a mixture of the crowd's trepidation and the flames' heat.

Bain stepped forward, his expression serious. Behind him, Father and Aaron gaped at the scene unfolding before them.

"Explain yourself, Mira," Bain demanded. "Or I will have you removed from this stage."

Mira smiled sweetly. "I'll let the captain speak for himself, Uncle."

She nodded at the guard restraining Jacob, and he lifted my brother's arm over his head.

"We are here tonight to celebrate the talents of my cousin, Harper," Mira said

Mira's hateful gaze connected with mine, and her thoughts bombarded me. "*Everyone thinks you're so special, but now they'll know what I've known all along. You've been living a lie. My smart-mouthed, pretty little cousin. So innocent. So worth protecting after the way you were born. My brothers always adored you. My father always thought you were so clever."*

I was going to vomit. All of a sudden, I was a little girl again, pushing back tears.

Her eyes narrowed. *"I see how the lieutenant looks at you, even if he does insult me by accepting my poor mother's invitations to tea."* She continued aloud. "But there's a dark secret behind this mural, and the people of this village deserve to know."

The guard pulled Jacob's sleeve to his elbow, exposing his forearm, the branded **12** gleaming in the firelight. Gasps echoed through the crowd.

The moment the brand caught the light, the mist began to thicken.

"Jacob Miller," Mira said. "Or should I say, Jacob Ledes —is the true twelfth child."

Jacob's eyes met mine, wrought with sorrow.

Mira continued, "Which makes the woman who painted this mural the thirteenth."

The last thing I saw before the air thickened beyond sight was my father. He stared at Jacob—at his son. Jacob strained against his guards, but the cloud of mist blocked my view of what happened next.

Panic gripped the crowd as a dark fog fell over the quadrangle, shrouding the party in thick, intangible air.

I wasn't sure who extinguished the fires in the lamps. It could have been Paxton or Brannon. It could have been Father's shock.

It could have been me.

But light was sucked from the flame, snuffing them wholly into nothing but smoke and charr.

Logan's grip on my arm tightened, and I heard the

scraping of iron against leather as he unsheathed his weapons. A metal hilt, cold and humming, was thrust into my hand.

"Take my knife," Logan said in the darkness. "And run."

I didn't have time to respond before Logan was gone.

My heart pounded as I glanced down at the milky white skin of my forearm. I couldn't see in the darkness, but I knew it was there. In my mind's eye, I watched the vapor swirl around my bare skin. The tiny droplets of air were nearly the same color as my flesh, blotting out my very existence.

Someone screamed. Boots fell heavily on the stones in frantic attempts to run away. I knew what they were running from. The mist. The demons beyond the wall that would no doubt swarm to the village now that my secret was out.

From *me*.

A commotion stirred in the distance as a thunderous *boom* came from beyond the wall. A deafening hum swelled in my ear.

The wards around Galloway were blistering as the demon onslaught crept in from every dark shadow within the Barrens.

On the other side of the wall, the demons that dwelled in the pines had heard Mira. They had heard her affirmation, felt delight in the panic, and now they fed on the fear and chaos that ensued.

I pushed my way through the crowd in the opposite direction. Everyone seemed to be headed to the manor, the haven within the massive stone, but I was pulled away.

My slippered feet fell silently on the ground as I ran in the darkness toward the path to the east side of town.

I had no choice, now. Hiding was not an option. Shame was not an option, and I certainly couldn't stand there and do nothing. If the demons were coming, they were coming for me, and I would be damned if the people of this town were endangered simply because I'd been born.

I wished I had never been. Wished I could somehow extinguish myself like fire in the lamps.

What could I do? There was only one option now, and it had nothing to do with hiding, or speaking secrets into someone's mind, or building a wall.

I realized what I had to do and where I had to go. I was running straight into the flames, and it was the only direction that I could go.

I could never be blotted out again. Even if I wanted to, it wouldn't be possible. Never again would the mist, or the wall, or Mira, or anyone else in this town tell me that I didn't exist. Never again would I shelter the secret that had haunted Galloway since I took my first breath.

Because I counted.

I always had.

Now, more than ever, I counted, and I had to do this the right way. The truth was out, and I had no choice but to embrace what it meant.

I retraced the steps Jacob and I had taken. I sailed from street to street, my dress billowing behind me like flames in the wind. I reached the throughway and ran to the simple, painted door when I recognized it.

I took the stairs two by two, and when my knuckles rapped on the door, it took all my restraint not to bang it down.

Raina's weary blue eye appeared in the peephole before

she unlatched the door. Her hand caught my wrist and pulled me into the room, her lips pursed.

"Harper. What are you doing here?" she rasped.

"I'm here for my brand."

CHAPTER

FORTY-SIX

The midwife closed her eyes, and a sound reminiscent of the wall's buzz hummed in my ears. I recognized it now for what it truly was.

The hum of magic.

Wards were undoubtedly in place at this apartment, but through the window, yelling echoed in the street as word spread about what had happened at the mural. Screams followed as the residents of Galloway took cover.

The wall was only as strong as its wards, and wards could fall.

The demons beyond it were closing in.

"Has no one come to investigate Jacob's quarters?" I asked. Not a single item was out of place from my last visit. If someone had recognized Raina while investigating my twin's crimes, she surely would've been sent to the gallows with him. I shivered at the thought and the promise I had made to Jacob to keep this woman safe.

Heat surged through me. Mira hadn't only endangered my twin tonight. She had put everyone in this village at risk.

343

Raina shook her head. "Jacob's other living quarters were listed on his militia paperwork. This is his secondary residence."

I nodded, grateful my brother had been so careful.

The skin on my arm began to prickle in anticipation. I held out a trembling hand for her.

"My cousin, Mira, spilled the truth to the whole militia. Tonight, at the dedication of the mural. She made Jacob reveal his brand. Please, brand me. I need to go out there and banish as many of them as I can. I need to tell my uncles that Jacob was trying to protect me."

Her skin paled. "If I brand you tonight, there is no going back."

I almost laughed at the thought, as though I could ever return to the person I was. As if I could stop this.

But I didn't laugh. "Do it."

Raina wrung her hands and hurried to the cupboard in the far corner of the room, where she retrieved a small ceramic jar.

"Salt," she said.

She pinched the grains between her fingers, her jeweled rings glinting in the lamplight, and sprinkled the salt in a wide circle on the wooden planks of the floor. She stepped within the confines of the circle and beckoned me to do the same.

The hum of magic intensified within the salt circle, and all the hair on my skin stood at attention as the weight of her magic washed over me.

She took my hands, and I realized she was shaking, just as I was.

"The salt will keep us hidden," she explained. "When I brand you, it will claim you as the fated thirteenth child, and the fire realm will respond. The Devil would feel it, just like he felt it when I branded each one of your cousins. The salt will keep the act a secret, at least for now." Her lip quivered. "There's no way to protect you forever, I'm afraid."

A pit of nausea opened in my stomach, and I sank to my knees. She told me nothing I could not surmise for myself, but the weight of her words pressed upon me. My lips parted, but no sounds came out.

Raina's blue eyes twinkled as they glazed over with tears. She sat before me. "You remind me so much of her, you know. Your mother was strong and determined, like you are."

"I wish I had known her," I said. "But in a way, I think I've known her all along."

Raina nodded. "The brands were my idea," she said, casting down her gaze. "Just before Paxton and Brannon were born, the lords had asked me if any magic could help with the curse. The only thing I could come up with was the brand. It was a promise meant to protect each child. To prove they were not the thirteenth. The only way to ensure the curse didn't come to be—was to ensure a thirteenth child was never born."

But I had been born.

That promise was never made because my mother had released the fury of my father's magic, and it had cost her everything.

Nausea gave way to numbness, and I closed my eyes, picturing the portrait that hung in the dining room at the manor. The determined gray eyes, the wild ebony hair, the slight quirk of her lip. Sarah Ledes's features were not unlike what I typically saw in the mirror.

The brands had been there to protect us, but over time,

they had become status symbols—pride in family and birth order. What would my brand say about me? Not that I was proud, not that I was a part of something big.

I was cursed, but I counted.

"She wanted children so badly," Raina continued. "When James was born, she doted over him as though he were the realm's grandest prize. He was always in her arms when I called to check on her. She loved to stand in the window at the manor with him, swaying her hips in a comforting circle until he fell asleep."

My lip trembled.

"Don't you dare cry, Harper," Raina said, choking back her own tears. "She died honorably. Her last act in this realm was protecting you and Jacob. I would've expected nothing less of her." A tear streaked over her cheek. "Just as I know you will do the same for your family. For this village."

I sucked in a breath. "For the Barrens."

Raina nodded, satisfied with my words, as though hearing them had given her magic a nudge. She held out her hands, and I gave her my arm.

So many times, I had caught myself staring at James's number 4, pondering what it would feel like to have a brand of my own. I had watched Paxton roll up his sleeves with satisfaction in his eyes, Perry flexing his forearms at the tavern. Mira's dainty gloves highlighting her brand in the softest lace.

What did Jacob feel when he ran his fingers over his brand? Was it loneliness or longing? Curiosity? Had he thought about it all those years before Raina told him the truth? Maybe he knew he was something special. Perhaps he'd covered the mark in shame.

Thick tears fell down my cheeks as buzzing filled my

ears. Safe within the confines of the salt circle, I was nobody. I was not a woman with a secret past. I wasn't fated or bound to be a devil within these pines. Here, I was nothing and everything all at once, as if I were standing on my own stone wall between fear and truth.

When Raina's finger pressed into the crease of my elbow, one foot swung forward over the edge of that wall. Her touch raked down my forearm, and a cool tingle of magic danced over my skin. I stepped forward, and I fell. I had walked off my wall into the crisp, clean air, thick with mist.

Her nail gently scratched over my wrist, and my body struck the ground. It was not hard or painful. No. My landing was soft. Here in the sanctity of the salt circle, I had stepped over that wall, and I had not fallen into a harsh, cold landscape.

Though my eyes were closed, I knew I had landed somewhere meant for me. Somewhere I truly belonged, where the thick boughs of the pines swayed in the wind, where the rhythm of hoofbeats on sand mirrored the beat of my heart.

Somewhere where fire raged and danced through the trees, warming my skin.

When I finally opened my eyes, I smelled the char of wood. Raina stood before me, staring down at my arm.

Scrolling over my skin, the familiar twirly script glowed, a stark contrast between the numerals and my pale flesh. I raised my forearm to the height of my face and stared for a moment before touching it.

My fingers ran over the brand slowly, tracing the numbers. I knew now that it had always been there, a phantom of truth below the layers of my skin. Raina's magic had allowed it to bubble to the surface.

"I am the thirteenth child," I rasped, my words cascading through the hum of magic in the air.

The words had barely fallen on Raina's ears when the midwife paled.

Bells rang in the distance, and shouts rose from the streets.

The Barrens were on fire, and I knew why.

The realm had come to claim me.

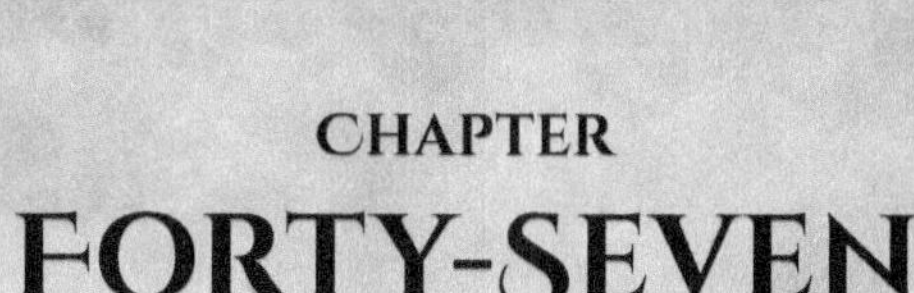

CHAPTER

FORTY-SEVEN

I said a hasty goodbye to Raina, noting the weariness written on her face after expending such magic.

Before I ran into the street, I took a deep breath, grateful to the Alister for the weight of the mist. The wall was near. I was only two blocks from the Western gate, where flames flickered in the distance.

The smell of charred wood wafted into my nose. Something else was in the air, something sulfuric that reminded me of the night the pit demon had set the Barrens aflame.

It smelled of chaos and mischief.

It smelled of demons.

I knew what the residents of Galloway would say about me.

The fire would be my fault this time. I tried to push back the image of Father falling to his knees before Jacob. Would he be strong enough to fight the flames after learning about his lost son that way?

Thanks to Mira, everything had been revealed at once.

Would Mrs. Hern accept Father's proposal now? Would he go through with it and ask her to move past this?

Every step toward the gate was heavier than the last, and my nerves were on fire with fear and anticipation of the unknown.

"*Thank you,*" I said to the Alister as I leaned against the heavy iron lock.

"*I am with you,*" he replied. Just like he had been from the moment I took my first breath.

The Alister's solemn tone confirmed what I already knew. The thin space was cracking. I would meet the master of the fire realm, the one who made a promise to the thirteenth child.

Clopping hooves rebounded past the hum of the wall. Starling had found me.

"*You did not intend for it to be tonight, did you?*" he asked.

I shook my head and clenched my jaw. "*No, I did not.*"

Starling's angry whinny was a compliment to my inner rage. If Mira had stuck with the plan, Paxton and Brannon would've had time to plead Jacob's case.

Mira wouldn't give me a second chance. In her eyes, I was vile and dark, and I deserved the fate that had been forced upon me. She had always known I didn't belong.

And now, she had won.

I mounted Starling as he bent on his foreleg. "*I've been asked to take you to him.*" His voice bled into my mind with sorrow and guilt.

"*Take me to him, then,*" I replied, and with that, we were riding through the trees, the Alister trailing us, so thick we almost appeared corporeal. Fire picked at the trees like drops of paint splattered from the sky.

Flames snapped through the boughs before me, and my pulse skittered as I noted six riders on horseback charging from the direction of the eastern gate.

I recognized Father and his brothers in the front, followed by Paxton and Brannon, Axel bringing up the rear.

The fire-wielding Lords of Galloway were charging directly toward the flames, and Father's eyes widened as I approached him on Starling. We leaped over a smoldering, felled tree and came up beside them.

My hair had come loose from the ride, and I knew how wild I must have appeared in my crimson dress, riding a winged horse. I could not help but picture it in paint—a shroud of mist surrounding a figure as red as blood.

This was not fire in the hands of the beholder.

I was fire incarnate.

"Harper, what are you doing?" Bain barked. "If what Mira claims is true, you aren't safe this close to the flames."

Starling halted, and my father gaped at me. I had become the thirteenth child, a stranger to him. Tears welled in his eyes as he took me in, and when he saw the newly branded skin on my arm, he swallowed.

"I'll present myself to the master of the fire realm," I said. "He's asked to speak with me."

Everything I ever was suddenly made sense. Mind-speaker, fire wielder. I was the only person in this realm who could communicate with the demons. Now, I would speak to their master.

Axel pulled his horse beside me. "You won't do it alone. We'll contain the flames for you."

Brannon's horse reared as embers flitted into the air around his hooves. "Don't enter the fire realm, Harper," he said. "Whatever you do, don't go with him."

The air was acidic in the back of my throat. I hadn't even considered the possibility of leaving this realm. All I could do was nod, and as I rode away, I made it a point not to look at Father. I wouldn't let terror be the last expression he saw on my face.

I didn't know what the Devil needed from me. My magic? My life?

Around us, embers fluttered to the ground. The tops of the pines glowed through the canopy of mist. Starling sailed through the trees like a ghost, ducking and weaving in all the right places. We rode north, and it was not long before I heard the river rush in the distance. The site was close to where I had banished the cryptid.

"How do you know where to go?" I asked Starling.

"I can sense him. Just as I can sense you," he replied.

Within a heartbeat, he stretched his wings, and we soared into the sky. I could feel the shocked stares of my father and his brothers on me as we sailed over the fire, over the plumes of smoke, and into the starlit sky.

From above, it was clear the fire had made a ring, the edge of which was a short distance from the wall.

"That's where the thin space is?" I asked.

"That circle is the space between realms, like a door or a rip in fabric. Throughout your realm and others, there are places like it. Doors over the ocean to realms of water where ships disappear forever, stony mountain tops where realms of air suck people in. There are realms at the bottom of canyons, where the earth is thin, places where plants cannot grow."

"Why do demons live in the fire realm?" I asked. *"Do they inhabit these other realms as well?"*

Starling huffed a plume of dewy air into the night sky. *"The demons inhabit all these realms. So does our master."*

"If he's present in other realms, why is he so insistent on returning here?"

"That is his tale to tell," Starling replied, and it made me question if he, perhaps, did not know the answer.

We banked near another cluster of flaming trees, toward a clearing within the flames. The air was surprisingly free of soot and debris as we sailed down to the forest floor, and I realized with horror that the pines had been singed down to the ground, as if they had melted. Above us, the sky was flawless, and starlight broke through the clearing.

A voice cut through my mind. *"At last, we meet, my daughter."* The words weaved through me like silk dragged between my fingers.

Cool, confident. Serene, despite the chaos it embodied.

In the clearing, I slid from Starling's back as fire materialized into a bodily outline of ember and smoke. A spindly form, taller than any man and infinitely imposing, appeared before me. Starling bowed his head, and I knew at that moment I was in the presence of the master of the fire realm.

The Devil himself.

I inclined my chin, refusing to bow to this being who had claimed me before I was ever born. "I am not your daughter," I shouted, as though somehow my words would drift over the wall and set me free. "My name is Harper Ledes. I'm the daughter of Sarah and Lord Cade. I am the thirteenth child of the Galloway Ledes, and I belong to no one."

The being tilted his head and laughed. The sound was so hot it was icy. *"I knew you wouldn't disappoint me."*

"Why do you wish to be here so badly, in our village? Why can't you leave Galloway alone?"

He crossed his arms. *"I have inhabited this realm for life-*

times before the village of Galloway stood. When your father and his brothers were born, their fire powers were born out of my realm, as is the birth of all fire wielders. But for magic to transfer to triplets—it was enough to seal the door, thicken the magic of this realm and my own."

"Why did you give them the power, then?" I asked. "If it ruined your connection to this place."

The Devil cocked his shadowy head. "*I did not give them power. Their power was born to them. Just because magic comes from my realm does not mean I gift it to humans. I rule the fire realm, but no one, not even I, can rule the magic there.*"

"You inhabit all realms," I said, my voice rising. "Why not leave this one?"

"*Humans are not strong enough to wield magic in other realms. I am called a devil, a harbinger of evil, a bringer of misfortune and atrocity.*"

"That's what we think of you as well," I said.

Within a blink, he was upon me, a rush of hot, spindly arms and legs. So close I could have touched him if he had been solid.

"*I have every right to be here, as you human creatures do. This is my birth realm. I started here.*"

I took a deep gasp of the hot, dry air. The master of the fire realm had been born in the Barrens? My knees threatened to buckle.

"Then what do you want from me?" I forced my voice not to shake.

"*If the triplet lords, their magic amplified by the power of three, were enough to seal the door, I knew their thirteenth child would be powerful enough to open it again. There is magic in numbers, Harper. Surely, you must have read about that in your trips to my library.*"

I gaped at him. That library had been my solace. The only place I could go to escape the doubt, a place where I could create art in peace.

Perhaps the only place in Galloway where I was entirely myself.

I inclined my chin. "The library belongs to the lords."

Another flash of hot air, too close to my face. "*It belonged to me. I gifted it to the lords before them, and they repay me by locking away the tomes, keeping the texts about my realm trapped in a secret room.*"

It was too much to bear. "I need to understand."

His arms came together, gangly flames forming fingers that clacked together. "*Then you must let me explain.*"

FORTY-EIGHT

The Devil was upon me now. He laced his fingers through mine, and I braced myself, readying for the pain. But the burn never came. No. His fingers were cool and soft despite their elemental nature.

"Harper!" a deep voice called from beyond the clearing. A figure materialized from between the trees. "Don't go with him."

My body turned to stone when Logan ran to me.

The Devil tightened his grip. "*Well, this is unexpected. Who is this man, daughter?*"

I knew I wouldn't be able to shake out of his clutches. "He is my guard," I said aloud. "He means no harm."

Fear seized me. If I were about to be dragged out of this realm, there was no telling what the Devil would do if Logan tried to stop him.

"*I see.*" The fiery lord cocked his head. With a snap of his fingers, Logan was beside us.

His eyes were wide, and the fire's reflection danced

within them. I watched with horror as the master of the fire realm gripped Logan's hand.

I screamed, but Logan did not flinch.

"If your guard is with us, Harper," the Devil said aloud, "I'll stop mindspeaking for his benefit. I want him to hear what I say when I pull the two of you out of this realm."

Brannon's words of warning rang in my head. *Whatever you do, don't go with him.*

"We will stay in this realm," I said.

The Devil cocked his head again. "You said you wanted to understand. This is how you will understand."

Logan and I were connected through the monster's grip, but he didn't seem afraid. "I told you I would follow you into the flames, Harper."

I gaped at him. This. This was everything I feared. I had been so selfish, giving in to my desire for Logan. Now, we were both damned. What if we never returned? What if we were stuck in the fire realm for eternity?

I reeled at the figure of fire. "You will not hurt him," I demanded.

The being laughed. "Killing him does not serve me."

Before I could plead with Logan to run, an invisible hook harpooned me, tugging behind my naval and sucking us out of thin air. I don't know how long it took us to travel away from the spot in the Barrens where we had been standing.

It might have been a year. It might have been a second, but when I opened my eyes, I felt like we had traveled through lifetimes. I was not holding onto the Devil's hand, and my first instinct was to reach out. I had to find Logan.

He must have had the same thought. We found each

other. I didn't walk or run—we floated toward a common point. Logan's arms were around me, and we were solid. Real, despite the unrealness of this place where we had been taken.

There was light here, but it was eerie, otherworldly. Nothingness was all around us. We were surrounded by a wispy, gray void where light and shadow did not seem to exist on the same plane.

Logan and I were the only solid things in this place.

"Where are we?" Logan asked, awestruck.

The figure beside us was no longer made of flame. He had morphed into a figure of shadow, empty of light and color. "We are in the place between worlds," the figure said. "The liminal realm."

He extended an arm and gestured above us, where shapes appeared and disappeared into the fabric of light. I watched in amazement as a figure appeared, the shadow of a bear. It moved into the light and padded along the sky before being absorbed into darkness.

"They are spirits," the Devil said. "Spirits of intent. Some of them, like your horse, are tied to an intention or a person. Others, like the angels of the sky realm, are tied to goodness and holiness. The spirits of the fire realm are the ones you're most acquainted with. They are tied to chaos, mayhem, and discontent. But they are all the same. They are spirits that walk between worlds."

"They walk in and out of these realms?" I asked.

The shadow being beside us nodded. "They do. You can see them above us, coming and going between thin places. This is broken in your realm. This is what I intended to fix."

I shook my head. "I still don't understand."

The Devil sighed, and some of the light sucked into his

chest. "Every realm must be open, daughter. That is how we achieve balance. Spirits come and go. In Galloway, demons have flocked to your village because the way out is blocked. There is no way for them to travel between realms. Spirits, like demons and angels, are not meant to be trapped in a place of the living. When your father and his brothers were born, it disrupted the thin place in the Barrens. There had always been demons there, but they became ensnared."

Logan's brow furrowed. "We are told stories of a mystic. When the triplet lords were born, it angered you."

A ripple of darkness rolled from him. "The number three. When triplet fire wielders were born, it disrupted the fabric of magic in the Barrens. A ring of fire magic sealed the thin place. All fire magic comes from here. It did not anger me. It sealed the door to my birth realm."

"Then why promise to take me?" I asked. "What is my role as the thirteenth child?"

The being swelled, becoming taller. "The number thirteen is a multiplier of magic. You were born a fire wielder who can also mindspeak. Your power is enough to restore balance. There was a time when the sun shone in Galloway. When fires cleared the pines, the soil was enriched. Crops and flowers could grow. Demons and angels lived in harmony, able to traverse between worlds as they were meant to. My fire could come and go. The sun could no longer reach the forest floor when the thin space closed. So, the pines became overgrown. Other plants could not thrive. When you were born, the demons came closer still, sensing you, waiting for you to free them. The lords saw it as a threat. They erected a wall to keep the demons out."

I closed my eyes. The paintings in the manor rose to the

surface of my memory. Rich gardens and brilliant sunshine in a depiction of the pines that felt imaginary.

Those gardens had been real. They hadn't been made up. Maybe that kind of life could return.

"If I open the thin space," I said. "Then what? Do I control an unending fire? Banish the onslaught of demons that are free to come and go?"

The devil shook his shadowy head. "When you open the thin space, you will guard the thin space. As long as you're living, the space cannot close. That is how I will claim you. You are a guardian of my birth realm. The fires will control themselves. They will come and go. The Barrens will control them. Balance will return."

Light crept through my chest, coupled with a great warmth. "If I open the thin space, that's what you need from me? I guard the thin space?"

Logan squeezed my hand. "You said you would take the thirteenth child as your own. If Harper's obligation is over to you after the space is open, then what is her link to you?"

The shadows wafted into the light, dissolving in the air like paint within the oil. "The thirteenth child belongs to all realms as a guardian. Open the thin space, my multiplier of magic. Galloway will be restored."

There was still a missing piece. "How do I open the thin space? What kind of magic do I use? I don't know how."

My gaze drifted to the wispy veils of light and dark that made up the fabric of this place. Forms of shadow and bright light appeared between them, sailing smoothly through.

But there was one shadow above us that appeared solid. The form was not made of something that moved and breathed like the rest of the canopy above me.

It was a ring. An impenetrable circle that appeared to be

made of iron. I studied it from afar, and a steady hum settled into my bones.

Humming of magic and wards and iron.

The master of the fire realm's voice was a whisper as his form faded into the light. "Bring down the wall, my daughter. The rest will follow."

CHAPTER

FORTY-NINE

Logan and I hit the ground, landing as if we had been catapulted back into our realm. The solid earth was shocking after being in a liminal realm of light and shadow.

I didn't know how long we had been there, but the realm appeared as we had left it.

Beside me, Logan gasped like he had been submerged in water. "Was it a dream?" he asked.

"I don't know." I was telling the truth. Maybe it was a dream we had shared. I shut my eyes tight and wished everything that had happened to me these past few weeks had been a hallucination.

Logan's hand closed over mine.

This man was not a dream—he was real. My twin was not a dream, either, and he was still in trouble. My father and James had found happiness. I hadn't been dreaming when I saw the way Father looked at Bess.

None of it would be real, though. None of it would hold together if the thin space remained closed.

"You heard what he said about the wall?" I asked Logan.

He nodded. All this time, the wall had been our solution. I had wanted nothing more than to be free from Galloway, but Galloway itself had been trapped. The power of the wards breaking would be enough to weaken the thin space. The rest would follow.

Whatever that meant.

I turned to him, allowing my cheek to rest on the cool moss of the forest floor. In the distance, the snapping and crackling of fire seemed far away. The air was calm and clear, devoid of ash.

When my father was born, the thin place had sealed, and the wall was a cork. We had to unbottle the demons before pouring them back through the rift between realms.

Logan ran his thumb over my jaw. "After you open the thin space, the fires will control themselves."

I had heard him, but a part of me wondered if it could be true. "But there will still be fires that threaten the village."

"Fire can be controlled," Logan said. "Can you imagine what it would be like to see the sun? If what the Devil said is true, balance will be restored."

Logan had once told me he would follow me into the fire. Tonight, he had proven it.

"What if he lied to us?" I couldn't stop the tears from falling. I had resigned myself to a lifetime of guarding this thin space, but the Devil had just promised me balance.

He had promised the Barrens freedom.

There would be fire, but with it, equilibrium. I didn't understand. It seemed too good to be true.

Logan sat up and swept me into his arms. The red fabric of my dress draped over him like a blanket of flame.

I sobbed into his neck. "What if we bring down the wall,

and he burns everything down? What if the demons swarm the village and break it into pieces?"

He slid his fingers into my hair. "Everything is already broken into pieces. We're trapped within the village, and the demons are trapped within the realm."

I pulled back, examining the lines and chiseled edges of his face. "Lieutenant Logan Greer, the man who blackmailed me to find his missing weapons, is now the man urging me to listen to the Devil and dismantle every defense we have?"

"Yes." He smiled, and the mischievous dimple resurfaced on his cheek. "Because that man fell in love with a woman who made him realize the solution to everything can be hidden within all his problems."

He took my head in his hands and kissed me. For a moment, I was back in that place between realms again. Everything between Logan and me, everything that connected us, was made of light and shadow.

Brightness brought out by darkness. The world was woven together by fabric, through which spirits could roam. He kissed me, and we were gone, moving within that fabric like I was nothing and everything.

I knew then that the place between realms hadn't been a lie. Neither had the promise that was made there.

The sound of hooves on the forest floor hooked me back to reality, and I broke the kiss. I allowed myself to linger in Logan's arms until Starling was there, stomping into the pine needles.

"Our guard has found you again," Starling said. *"Do you think he will allow me to bring you both back to the village?"*

I turned to Logan, but he had gone pale. He stared up at the horse, as if he beheld a ghost. I furrowed my brow in confusion.

Before I could ask what was wrong, Logan spoke. "I can hear you," he said.

Starling let out a sound that might have been a laugh. *"My master has brought you to the place between realms. I'm a creature of multiple realms. And now, Lieutenant, so are you."*

We didn't have time to ask questions. I barely had time to fathom what this meant. Would Logan only be able to hear Starling through the connection of the venom? Would Logan be able to mindspeak? Were all mindspeakers from that place, then? The place between realms?

I mounted my horse, and Logan followed, slipping onto his back behind me. With my hands wrapped in Starling's mane and Logan's arms around me, I had an overwhelming sense of belonging.

We rode through the pines, through a thin mist that revealed swaying boughs, cracking embers of flame dancing off them like candles. His canter was quick, but I felt like I was moving slowly.

I leaned forward and stroked the horse's mane. *"When the thin space is open, will you remain with me?"*

My horse did not answer immediately, but his words were thoughtful when he spoke. *"I promised you I would. I'm your guardian. Will you want me to stay?"*

I did not hesitate. *"I want you to be free."*

I thought back to all my dreams of the beast and the times I had awakened to the sound of faraway hoofbeats on the forest floor. I remembered the way I had panicked when I learned he had been trapped within the charred remains of Raina's house.

He would never be chained again—to me or this realm.

"I am free when I'm with you," Starling replied.

It sounded right and true. Knowing he was free was all that mattered.

We approached the wall. I couldn't see it through the smoke, but I heard the commotion of shouting voices and galloping horses.

I extended my arm before me, the branded **13** glinting in black swirling script. When Logan and I ran through those gates, the entire village would see me for who I truly was.

The cursed thirteenth child approached them.

Logan's grip around my waist tightened, and he spoke directly into my mind this time. *"Starling isn't the only one who'll stay with you."*

I nodded, knowing it was true. The locked gate came into view, but we didn't need a key this time. Starling leaped into the sky, allowing his wings to beat close enough to the wards for Logan and me to swing our legs onto the wall.

The horse huffed into the air before he flew away from the wards and disappeared. I stared after him for a moment, unwilling to turn back into the village, wondering if some part of me had been more at home in the Barrens all along.

The top of the structure was only a foot thick, just enough that we could catch our balance. We were at the western gate, only a short distance from the barracks, and from our perch atop the wall, I steeled myself to look behind me.

Masses of people had gathered in the quadrangle.

Dread rose in my chest as Logan jumped from the wall. He fell with the finesse of someone who had practiced the move before and extended his hand. The crimson skirts of my dress billowed around me as I jumped. I hit the ground less gracefully than Logan, but he didn't let me fall.

If any guards had been near the gate, they might have feared that a demon had approached the wall and successfully scaled it.

Their assumptions wouldn't be far from the truth.

Logan ran, and I followed him, taking the now-familiar path to the barracks. A crowd surrounded the stage near the wall, and the dread in my chest exploded as we approached. My feet failed me, and I stopped short, unable to continue.

Logan and I took our place at the back of the crowd, but nobody seemed to notice our presence. They were too enthralled with the prisoner before them.

Jacob was chained and locked on the gallows. His ebony waves spilled forward on his slumped head, and his clothes were torn. My brother hadn't gone into those gallows without a fight.

Good.

The scripted number *12* shone in the eerie glow of the lamp light.

Villagers shouted at one another in heated arguments. Someone threw a stone, and it plinked against the wood and bounced off the chain. The way my twin didn't move in response to the assault made me realize it hadn't been the first stone thrown at him.

I scanned the crowd for my father, but he and his brothers were nowhere to be found. Indeed, the only member of the Ledes family among the crowd was Mira. She stood beside a guard, her hands on her hips, and her forearm turned so the light shone off her branded *6*.

"We need answers!" one of the villagers shouted.

"Ever since he arrived, the mist has been thickening," a woman yelled. "Did he come here to rally the demons?"

Mira inclined her chin. "When the lords return from the Barrens," she said, projecting her voice with authority, "we will start his trial. I've been assured we will not sleep tonight. We will not rest until we have answers."

"Until we have justice!" a man shouted.

The crowd grunted their assent, and my twin's knees buckled. Fear rose in my throat, but I swallowed it and let it churn.

Churn into a rage that burned through my veins. Mira had tied my twin to the gallows and allowed villagers to harass him. She had stood idly by as they threw stones at him. Jacob Miller—no, Jacob *Ledes*—was as much a noble of this town as she was.

And he was mine to protect.

My brother, my *twin*.

Abject fury surged through me, boiling my blood and heaving through my magic until the lamps illuminating the stage flared. Strength fueled by my magic swelled, shattering the glass over the cobblestones of the barracks.

Men and women screamed, and panic set in. I was sure some expected to see the Devil himself standing in their midst.

Instead, they turned and found his daughter.

"Release him," I commanded.

A hush fell over the crowd as they beheld me in my blood-red dress. The Devil was not within the wall, but I was.

I stepped forward, and the villagers cleared a path. Logan trailed behind me, true to his word.

Logan unsheathed his weapon, and the only sound I could hear in the hushed crowd was the scrape of his iron over leather. Not to fight the monster.

To protect her.

I ran to the front and climbed to the stage where, earlier that night, I had presented my mural to the triplet Lords of Galloway. I took Jacob's head in my hands.

His eyes fluttered open just long enough for me to see a flash of blue and gray. It was like looking into our mother's eyes, but in an instant, they were closed again.

His face was bruised, and a trickle of blood was dried upon his lip.

The fire swelled in the lamps flanking the stage, and in my heart, I knew it was surging in the woods behind the wall.

Good. Let this whole place burn to the ground if this is how they would treat my brother.

I turned and found Mira. She was still perfectly coifed, not a brown curl out of place as she stood before me, fixing her stare on the freshly scripted brand on my arm.

She did not wither or shrink away as I stepped toward her.

"Perhaps you didn't hear me. Release him," I growled.

My cousin only inclined her head and gestured to the crowd. "It isn't enough to have a liar in our midst." She gripped my wrist and raised my forearm above my head. "The thirteenth child has come to free her twin brother, the criminal Jacob Miller."

I shook out of her grip. "His name is Jacob *Ledes*, and he's just as much a member of this family as you are."

Mira's eyes flared with rage. "How dare you? Your entire life has been a lie, Harper. I was the only one who could see through it from the beginning." She scoffed. "So fitting that your twin would come to this town wrapped up in his own deceit. He's no more of a Ledes than you are."

I wanted to let the fire seep out of my blood. I wanted it to sear her skin. I had always been told I was *less*. Not branded. Not part of the family. Strange and dark and different.

Mira had planted these thoughts in my mind, and I would rather be dragged out of this realm for good than let her plant them within Jacob's.

Her eyes widened as I let my magic snake into her mind. There was no wall around her thoughts, and I entered her brain like a knife through a bar of lye.

"If you don't put this to a stop, I will make your life a living hell," I said. *"Just like you did mine."*

She projected back to me. *"You've already done that, haven't you? Everyone in this family is wrapped around your little finger. They always have been. Harper is so smart. She's so witty, so talented."*

In the corner of my eye, I saw Logan's sword come down on the gallows chain, cleaving it open.

Mira laughed. "You have it all, don't you? The family, the magic. Finally, you have your brand. You even got the man."

I opened my mouth to argue, but my words were cut short. Gasps and cries erupted from the crowd as a figure materialized, perched atop the wall.

"A demon," they cried. "They've come to breach the wall."

"They've come for the thirteenth child, just like the mystic said."

But the shadow atop the wall was not a demon. Her snowy white hair was unbound, twirling around her in the breeze as though she were a part of the mist. She stood atop the very part of the wall where I had painted my mural of fire.

Jacob scrambled to his feet beside me, held up by Logan. My twin's eyes moved to the wall, his face flush with horror.

It was not a demon who had breached the wall of Galloway.

It was the midwife.

CHAPTER

FIFTY

"Raina!" Jacob's voice was raspy, barely audible over the panicked voices of the crowd.

Logan gripped Jacob by the elbow. "If you go out there, they'll turn on you. Stay back."

He was right. If Jacob ran to Raina, it would damn him. If the crowd didn't tear him apart, he would surely be sentenced to death in the trial. Logan and I knew it, and I prayed Jacob would realize the same and hold back.

Jacob strained against Logan, attempting to shake him off, but Logan's grip held.

"It's the midwife," someone shouted. "Lady Sarah's murderer."

The unspoken rule about mentioning my mother had fizzled into ash. I jumped from the stage and prepared to push to the front, but the crowd parted for me.

Nobody, it seemed, wanted to be in the path of the thirteenth Ledes child.

Emotions and thoughts of the villagers bombarded me as I pushed to the wall.

372

The devil's daughter.
Touched by demons.
Cursed.

A nauseating mix of fear and disgust flooded my mind, and I cursed my magic at that moment.

At the front of the crowd, some villagers had lit torches, and the shadows cast upon Raina's face made her pallid, almost as translucent as a ghost.

"Please," I yelled up at her. "Get down." I didn't know what she planned, but I had an overwhelming hunch that the outcome would be dangerous.

When the midwife's eyes found mine, she smiled softly. "Harper Ledes, branded the thirteenth child, do you have a message from my master?"

Realization hit me in the chest.

She was going to take the fall. For Jacob. For me. She had come to the wall to become the villain so we wouldn't have to be. All I could do was gape at her, unsure of what to say to convince her to come down.

Jacob had asked me to protect Raina. I had promised him.

She went still, and she blinked as if she were listening. I knew then that Jacob was projecting into her mind, begging her to stop. I turned back to face the stage, but the crowd had filled the space, edging closer yet dripping with hesitancy.

I was separated from the stage and pushed to the front of the crowd.

Raina turned back to me with tears in her eyes. "Tell me what the Devil told you." She raised her hand at the crowd, sparking with magic, and some of the villagers shrank back at the sight of it.

"Get down from there," I called, pleading. She would be taken into custody, her distraction tactic would help Jacob, and we could convince the lords of her innocence.

This woman had saved Jacob. I could do her the same favor now. I needed Starling. I screamed his name into the Barrens, and from beyond the wall, I heard a frenzied whinny.

He was on the way. I could ask Starling to fly to Raina, to pluck her from the wall the same way he had deposited Logan and me without breaking the ward.

Before I could plead with her again, the drum of horse hooves echoed from this side of the wall, and a company of men edged their way to the front of the crowd.

My father and his brothers gaped at the wall, their brows furrowed in confusion. The men stopped their horses before the frenzied villagers, and the mass of people reeled back.

Cade Ledes did not turn his attention to the wall itself.

No. My father immediately scanned the crowd, and when he saw me there, my red dress like a burning wick in the sea of gray and brown, his shoulders slumped in relief.

His eyes did not stop scanning until he found my twin, and when he beheld the gallows on stage and Jacob's hunched and battered form, the fire in the lamp lights flared again.

No matter what Jacob had done or how many lies he had told, he was a part of this family now. He held as much Ledes blood as any of us. Jacob Ledes was a walking, breathing reminder of Sarah's sacrifice, and if I knew anything about my father, I knew he would honor that sacrifice until his dying breath.

At that moment, Cade Ledes bellowed over the crowd. "What is the meaning of this?"

A hush fell over the villagers at the uncharacteristic temper of their youngest triplet lord, but a man beside me spoke up and pointed to the woman on the wall. "The midwife has returned, my lord!"

Uncle Bain reeled to the wall. Shock was swiftly replaced by rage as Bain unsheathed his sword. "How dare you come back to this place?" Bain growled at her.

He motioned to his men, who then unsheathed their weapons beside him.

"Take her!" Uncle Aaron bellowed.

The militiamen swarmed the wall, their weapons drawn.

I opened my mouth to scream, and I yelled in my mind for Starling to make haste, but no sound came out. At that moment, the panic from the crowd gripped me.

I was again within that realm of light and shadow. My feet were not on the ground. Everyone around me was shouting.

Terror and anger swelled from the frightened mass around me—emotions infused with magic so profound that it penetrated my skin like a needle.

People began to move, surging with the militiamen on horseback to the wall, but I was a statue among them. They moved around me as wisps of light, so swiftly they were slowed to nothing but a blur.

All I could see was the shape of the woman standing on the wall. She stared at me, locking her gaze to mine with an otherworldly stillness amid the chaos around us.

Raina's voice projected into my mind, soft and sure. *"Did the Devil ask you to take down this wall, Harper?"*

My heart leaped into my throat. *"Yes, but—"*

"I can feel the wards within the stone," she replied. *"I can feel the magic the mystics used to erect it. When the stone*

crumbles, the wall will explode, and the magic will vibrate into the Barrens. The demons on the periphery of the wall will feel it, and they will flee. What's left of the wards will hold through the night without the stone to support the magic. This will buy you time, Harper. It will buy Jacob time."

It was futile. Even if time were the thing we needed most, one night wouldn't be enough. Jacob needed a fair trial. I needed to explain everything to my father. The lords would need time to prepare the village, strengthen their arms, and allow people to ward their homes.

But I didn't get to say any of this to Raina.

The midwife was the only thing moving as I watched the horror unfold around me. Despite the surging mass of villagers and the horses approaching her, she was the only thing I could see.

The hum from the wall was deafening, as if it knew its fate, and the throb overcame me, drowning out all sound.

Raina raised her arms, magic sparking in her fingertips. Her lips moved, and with them, the wards' humming intensified into a palpable buzz.

I screamed, but there was only silence as Raina's magic crackled into the stones. Ropes of light twined through the structure before us, and the villagers reeled back. The light spread from the source, snaking through the wall and extending beyond us.

Past the limits of the quadrangle, through the western gate in a massive circle surrounding Galloway as the wards were dismantled within the wall.

"I can crack the wards, but only you can bring them down," Raina projected to me. *"These wards were made for you, Harper. Use everything you can to break the wall in your own mind."*

The sound of the crowd returned with sudden intensity, and I lifted my hands to cover my ears. The town was awash in light, and the ground vibrated as the wall crumbled.

There was no salt circle here. The humming would only spread as it fell. How many innocent villagers would perish if the wards fell directly upon them?

I concentrated every ounce of rage I had on the wall, using my mindspeaking magic.

The unfairness of being ripped away from Jacob. The fear of losing my father. The feeling of the Devil taking his hand in mine. How I would never know the sound of my mother's voice. How I had wanted my brand—wanted it so desperately—until the moment I had it.

Someone screamed, and the people around us began to flee as the wall crumbled.

Because I crumbled.

Because I forced every ounce of fear that swirled in that courtyard to break my own walls down.

The humming died, and the magic of the wards died with it.

In the distance, bells rang.

Galloway's wall had dissolved to nothing but stone and dust, and demons screamed beyond it as the magic of the wards seeped into the Barrens like a tidal wave, pushing them back and away from the town.

At least for now.

The militiamen reared back, their horses bucking as they, too, fought the urge to run from the scene unfolding at the wall.

Only one person was running toward the wall as it fell.

My twin.

Jacob called out to Raina. Logan ran after him.

But Jacob did not reach the wall. He stopped, clutching his chest, and I knew he was calling out with his magic to her.

My feet carried me to him, even though I still could not feel the ground beneath me, and when I came to his side, I gripped his hand.

Raina was upheld by nothing but wind. She fell to her knees and gripped the stone under her feet as the final pebble fell. A cloud of dust blanketed the quadrangle, intermingling with mist—a mist that arrived with such urgency I could taste the Alister's fear.

Only one segment of Galloway's wall had remained intact, and through the smoke, the crimson flames of my mural stood out in the blackness.

Only one part of the wall was left.

The part the thirteenth child had branded. Atop the remaining structure, the midwife had fallen, along with the wards and the stone that had held this town together.

And as my twin fell to his knees before the wreckage, I knew she would never rise again.

CHAPTER

FIFTY-ONE

The humming was so loud it had become a part of me.

Until the sound snuffed out completely.

Beside me, Jacob's gasping breaths were the first thing I heard when I regained my senses. I fell beside him, and he leaned against me, melting onto my shoulder as he lost his strength.

A pair of boots materialized in the dust, and a moment later, our father was beside us, kneeling in the rubble. He stared at Jacob for a long while, like he was an apparition from some long-forgotten dream.

Our father studied Jacob's face, marking the slope of his jaw. So like James. The hue of his eyes. So like mine. So like our mother's. Father's hands braced on my brother's shoulders, his eyes continuing to move over him, inspecting the man for any damage.

"She saved me," Jacob said, choking on the words. Tears streaked down my brother's cheeks, making trails in the dirt and dried blood on his skin.

Father released Jacob's shoulders and grabbed his forearm, tracing the branded *12*, the number that used to be mine.

"It wasn't supposed to be this way," Jacob said through ragged sobs. "This wasn't the way I wanted to tell you. I've dreamed about it my whole life. What I would say. Where we would be."

Our father shook his head. "You have Sarah's eyes," he said. "Harper's hair. James's jaw."

Jacob's eyes widened. "I lied to you. I lied to my cousins. Paxton and Brannon trusted me. I should have told them. I set this whole thing in motion. I stole the irons. Harper didn't know. I was trying to keep the demons away from her. I was trying to keep her secret. I was such a fool..."

Father shook his head. "I chose your name. Before you were born, Sarah chose Harper for a girl. I chose Jacob for a boy. I had forgotten. It hurt too much to think about it, so I had forgotten."

My twin's head snapped up, and he met our father's stare. "Raina's dead because of me. She wouldn't have done this if I hadn't stolen the irons."

"Even your voice—" Father said. "How did I not see it before? You were in our home. I should have known who you were. I should have sensed it."

"I stole the irons and forced Harper to help us solve a crime I committed. Because I needed to get close to her. I needed to tell her about the horse and the mist. What kind of man am I if the only way was to threaten her?" Jacob turned his gaze on me.

"Now I know," Father said. "We all know."

My father's attention snapped to me, his face full of devastation. He pulled my hand into his and traced the branded *13* on my forearm. "Oh, Harper. How could this be? How could this be real?"

Jacob put his head in his hands again.

In the distance, more boots clopped on the pavement, fast and purposeful. As they neared, James's voice rang out. "Harper!"

He came to a halt before us, and when he took in the scene, he also fell to his knees to meet us.

Aaron and Bain watched from a distance. In the dust, they stood over us like sculptures. Our family was united for the first time, in truth, and my uncles were there to witness it.

We sat silently for a moment, tears streaming down our faces, until Uncle Aaron's voice interrupted.

"We'll move Raina's body to the infirmary for the night," he said. "The blaze has been extinguished. We should ride the perimeter to make sure."

Figures appeared in the haze, approaching us cautiously.

"What do we do without the wall?" Axel asked. "Will the demons come into the village?"

Aaron shook his head. "The wall's collapse sent the wards out into the Barrens. The demons will flee. For now. But this village existed many years before that wall was built. Every home in Galloway has iron shutters on the windows and doors. The citizens are safe as long as they seek shelter before what's left of the wards melt away."

We were covered in a blanket of air so thick we could barely see. As Aaron spoke, iron gates and shutters creaked throughout town, metal clanging against stone.

Bain and Aaron unsheathed their swords as a figure materialized in the mist. I saw Logan first, leading Starling, apparently too strong to be affected by the collapse of the wards, with a hand on his muzzle.

My horse strode to me with easy, majestic steps, and the triplet Lords of Galloway reeled back.

I stood and ran to him. I scanned him to ensure he was not injured, put out my hand, and stroked his mane.

"This is why Captain Miller stole the irons," Logan said. "To capture the horse that had plucked Harper from the fire when she was born. When Jacob arrived, he worried the horse would come for Harper when her identity was revealed. Now we know the creature is our ally. He only exists to guard Harper."

My breath hitched.

Our father peeled his stare away from the beast before addressing my twin. "Is this true?"

All Jacob could muster was a weak nod of affirmation.

Logan continued, "Raina saw the horse carry Harper from the burning rubble of her home when she was a newborn. Jacob had every reason to believe the horse wanted to bring Harper to the Devil."

Aaron spoke up. "We found you at the gate, Harper. Bain and I. There was no explanation as to how you got there."

Bain nodded. "Patrice had seen Sarah talking to herself on long walks in the final weeks of her pregnancy. We were terrified she had gone mad. The midwife was gone, the house burnt to the ground."

"The horse brought me to the gate," I said. "He—Starling is my horse. When I was born, he was born in the realm of fire. A gift to me for fulfilling the Devil's promise. My guardian."

The triplet lords shared a wary glance.

"Starling reports the fires have been extinguished, and the weaker demons near the wall have fled into the pines, seeking shelter when the wards fell," Logan said.

"How do you know what Starling said?" Jacob asked.

Logan cleared his throat. "He's the beast that scarred me. His venom runs in my veins." He tapped the silvery blue scar on his brow, and his eyes darted to me.

My guard did not mention our trip into the place between realms, and I could have kissed him then and there for it. Instead, I asked my father, "What do we do now?"

Aaron and Bain also looked to their brother.

Father straightened. "James, where is Maggie?"

"At the manor," James said. "Safe and sound. Bess and Emelia are there, as well. I escorted them personally."

Father nodded gratefully. "Jacob will return to the manor with me. No son of mine will spend another night in that prison."

Jacob's eyes widened. "I haven't yet had my sentencing. The villagers will not look favorably on that, my lord."

Fire danced in our father's eyes. "I am not your lord. I am your father. You will come back to our quarters. The healer must tend to your wounds."

Father inclined his chin to his brothers, daring them to challenge him, but Aaron and Bain nodded.

James spoke up. "Lieutenant Greer and I will escort Harper back to the townhouse." Then he spoke into my mind. *"There is no way you're returning to the manor tonight."*

I clenched my jaw. No. There was no way I could be under the same roof as Mira right now. I tried not to fantasize about what it would feel like to squeeze her neck between my palms. She would pay for what she did.

One way or another, she would pay.

Uncle Aaron must have been thinking the same. "I assure you, Cade. My daughter will be..." His lips pursed. "Dealt with for how she acted this evening."

Paxton and Brannon's dark expressions mirrored my rage.

I turned my attention to my horse. "*Where will you go?*"

He huffed into the dusky air. "*Where would you like me to go?*"

I knew where I wanted him. Beside me.

But I had a feeling the presence of an enormous, winged demon beside our townhouse would set pitchforks against us.

"*Will you keep to the Barrens?*" I asked him. "*Tomorrow, we will need to...*"

He didn't let me finish my thought. "*Most of the demons fled into the Barrens when the wards came down. By tomorrow, they will return. The stronger demons may already be within the village. They will turn to you to open the thin space. Tomorrow, we will set them free.*"

I turned to my uncles. "Draw up a correspondence to the villagers. Explain everything. Tell them to seek shelter for now. Tomorrow, I'll begin working on sending the demons away. Nobody should leave their homes until it is done."

"How do you know it will work?" Bain asked, his brow furrowed.

I shook my head. "I don't know."

How could I explain to him that I didn't have a choice? This was what I had been born to do. I was the thirteenth child, an amplifier of their magic and all the magic tied to this place. My father and his brothers couldn't help that their birth closed the gap between realms.

I couldn't help that my birth provided the opportunity to open it again.

How would I explain to this village that the fires they had once been so terrified of would need to return? How could I explain that the absence of the fire was shackling this village?

The Devil had shown me how to restore balance to the Barrens, but how could I put my faith in a being like him? A being who kept monsters as pets and delighted in destruction.

I shook my head again and repeated, "I don't know."

But it was all I could do.

My uncles nodded at me as Father helped Jacob to his feet. Paxton and Brannon mounted their steeds, and Bain helped my twin climb astride his horse.

My cousins gave Logan a nod as we walked away, back toward the townhouse. The streets were eerily silent. The citizens of Galloway had indeed pulled their shutters closed. No lights came from the windows, but I was grateful for the streetlamps.

We walked silently, Starling at our side until we reached our street. A frantic man ran to us, and my brother ran to meet him.

"Ben?" James pulled him close. They shared a frenzied kiss, cupping each other's faces.

Ben pulled away. "You didn't return. I panicked."

James ran a hand through his hair. "So, you left the manor to walk the streets alone? The wall is down. You could have been killed."

Benjamin's brow furrowed. "Which is exactly why I came looking for you. You said your magic would afford you no protection against the demons. Your nobility in this town doesn't make you immune to them, James."

My brother stared at Benjamin for a moment before he pulled him into another kiss, this time soft and pleading. Their lips pulled apart, but James didn't let go. "I cannot fathom the idea of losing you."

Benjamin's eyes began to tear. "Then don't actively try."

I spoke into my brother's mind. *"Stay here with Benjamin, James. You two need some time alone."*

James turned to me. *"What are you saying, Harper? You need somewhere to stay. Don't be insane."*

"I shouldn't stay here, anyway. What if the villagers come for me? I don't want you caught up in their witch hunt."

I wanted to run into the Barrens and hide beneath the boughs.

I glanced at Logan. "I'll return to Logan's residence near the barracks. We'll be perfectly safe, and no one will seek me out there. You two can watch the townhouse. If anyone comes for me, tell them you haven't seen me."

James furrowed his brow.

"My residence is adjacent to the West Gate Park," Logan explained. "Starling can hide there beneath the willows. He can hear us if we call for him and would be there instantly."

I nodded, knowing I wouldn't need to call for him. Starling would know if Logan or I were in trouble.

James nodded before speaking into my mind. *"If anyone found out you spent the night with him, it would be a scandal."*

I laughed aloud. *"I'm already a living, breathing scandal. Nobody will care if the Devil's child is sleeping with the arms lieutenant."*

"Stop calling yourself that," James said. He cleared his

voice to speak aloud. "I trust you to keep her safe through the night, Lieutenant."

Logan pulled out his watch. "Yes, although it's nearly morning."

It was nearly two o'clock. It was hard to believe I had been dressing for the mural presentation ten hours ago. It seemed like a lifetime had passed.

"I'll change, and we'll leave you," I said.

Logan waited downstairs while I changed out of my crimson dress. I smoothed the fabric, wondering if there would ever be a time that I would wear something so beautiful again.

I pulled on a pair of riding pants and a black linen tunic. I swept my hair into a simple bun. I washed the dirt, sweat, and remnants of makeup off my face and studied myself in the mirror.

Is this what a daughter of hell looked like?

I painted my lips with a red-tinted balm and swept a gray shadow over my eyelids. My handiwork was sloppy compared to Maggie's steady hand, but I felt a little less naked.

When I returned to the foyer, Logan was waiting for me. We set back out into the deserted streets of Galloway.

The daughter of hell, her winged beast, and her scarred knight.

CHAPTER

FIFTY-TWO

Logan closed the door and locked the bolts.

I had been reckless the last time I had been in Logan Greer's private quarters, and I tried to push away the memory of his hands on me.

"I don't want to risk a fire in the hearth," he said, "or more than a lamp or two."

I nodded, setting a lamp alight with my magic. Logan went to the window and turned the sash lock. He slid the pane down, giving him access to the iron shutters. The bars pulled down after a forceful tug.

The window gates hadn't been fastened in many years. The locking hinge creaked a weary screech into the court-yard below.

"Good," he said. "I'll check the rest of the room. We should be safe as long as those bars hold."

I stood in the middle of the room, watching him pull out his dagger and search under furniture, in cabinets, anywhere even the most miniature demon could hide.

Logan said nothing as he searched, and I said nothing as

388

I watched him. When he was satisfied with our safety, he was at my side, rubbing a thumb over the angle of my chin.

I lifted my face as his fingers swept over my skin. He was searching me now, inspecting for damage. His brow furrowed when he found a small abrasion on my neck.

He took his hands in mine, turned them over in his own, and rubbed his fingers over the cuts and cracks in my skin.

Logan brought my hand to his lips and kissed the sensitive skin on my wrist, and I shivered.

His kisses trailed over my palm, and he turned over my hand, exposing my brand.

"Exquisite." He traced the numerals with his lips. "Everything about you is perfect, Harper Ledes."

My lips parted, and I almost started to tell him how wrong he was. But that gleam in his eyes. It gutted me.

Because he believed what he said.

Logan loved me. He knew every truth, and he still loved me. Despite all the insults I had thrown at him, the lies and half-truths, my self-deprecation, the darkness in my mind, my insane family, and the link I had to the Devil and the demons in this town.

This man knew every demon within me, and he still loved me.

So, I didn't argue with Logan. At that moment, I realized that if this man could love me, then maybe—just maybe—I could give myself the same honor.

If he could love me, I could love myself enough to love him back.

And I could give him everything he deserved.

I began to study him in return. The silvery blue scar over his brow warmed to my touch, and it sent shivers through me that settled over the scar on my spine. My fingers slid over his skin, tracing his ordinary scars. I rubbed a smudge of dirt off his chin with my thumb. I pulled pine needles from the golden strands of his hair.

He leaned into my touch like the softness was not enough for him. I leaned back, allowing my finger to tangle into the strands of his hair.

"I think you're perfect, Logan," I said. "I always have. Even when my words were sharp, my heart was softening to you. And I'm sorry if I didn't make it easy, but I love you, too."

His lips crashed into mine.

It was as though we had left the realm again. Only this time, he was the light, and I was the darkness. I wanted to pull him close enough that he would become a part of me.

I wanted everything that illuminated him to shine through the inky blackness in my heart.

Logan pulled me closer, and his gentle, exploring touches melted into firm sweeps of his hands over the curves of my back.

My cloak fell to the floor as he unbuttoned the straps of his leathers. I needed his skin on mine. A gasp escaped my lips as he kissed my neck, scraping my skin with his teeth.

I pulled my tunic over my head, and his eyes widened.

My mouth trailed over his chest, and I ran my tongue over his skin. He was salty and sweet, he smelled like pine and leather, and I wanted to breathe him into my lungs for the rest of my life.

He lifted me, and my legs wrapped around him.

Logan released a soft growl as he carried me to his bed, and it rumbled through me.

"I want everyone in this damned village to know, Harper." Logan lay me down and pulled off my riding pants.

This man set me on fire, and I was liable to burn down every tree in the Barrens.

He slid his hand over my spine. "I want everyone to know who you belong to. No matter what number is branded on your skin, you're mine, and I'm yours."

My words came out breathless. "I belong to no one."

He laughed, sending a vibration through me that made my head arch into his pillow. Logan crawled up my body until he was looking directly into my eyes.

The way he leaned over me, caging me between his thick arms—I did not feel trapped. I did not feel caged in.

"I belong to you," he said. "My lady."

I pulled the belt from his pants and slid them down. I grasped him and slid every inch of him through my palm.

He shivered and urged my legs apart with his knees.

"Tell me who you belong to," he said.

He slid into me, and I arched my back. He gripped my hips and filled me so completely, I thought I would never be able to breathe again. I would never recover from the weight of him.

Logan moved inside me like perfect torture.

"I will never get enough of you," he said into my ear.

"Logan." I was threatening to melt away. "I belong to you."

He held me tighter, and I wrapped my legs higher on his back, deepening him. I would never get enough of this man. There would never be a time when I wouldn't want him.

It didn't matter what I had to do next. As long as he was beside me, it didn't matter. He had proven he would follow me, and I would let him.

Maybe this iron-willed lieutenant with the infuriatingly perfect face who always had a smart answer for everything was the person I was meant for. Even if I were damned to the fire realm, Logan would be the only person stubborn enough to follow me into the flames.

I called his name as I unraveled, and he gripped me harder.

"Yes. Say it," Logan said. "Let everyone know who you belong to, Harper Ledes. You belong to no devil but me."

His body shook as he fell into me, and I never wanted to move from this place—never wanted to leave the safety of his arms.

His forehead came to a rest on mine. I counted his breaths and let him curl his body around me. My guard's name was the last word I uttered before exhaustion took me.

CHAPTER

FIFTY-THREE

Logan was already awake when I opened my eyes.

"What time is it?" I pulled him closer, hoping that if I buried my head in his chest, I wouldn't have to face this day.

"It's just before dawn," he said, rubbing my shoulders.

We had only slept for a few hours.

"I wonder what happened at the manor last night," I said. I hoped Father had kept Jacob isolated in our chambers.

I cringed at the thought of him walking through the halls unaccompanied, but I knew there was no way Cade Ledes would let that happen.

There was no telling what kind of lies Mira had been spreading around the manor about my twin. My jaw clenched reflexively at the thought of my cousin, the sight of her at the gallows with her head held high like she had achieved some sick victory.

Villagers would likely tout her as a hero. Meanwhile,

Jacob and I would be the pariahs that Mira had always wanted.

"He's in good hands," Logan said. "Lord Cade will keep him safe. It will give us time to do what we need to do."

A chill skittered over my skin.

"Can we lie in bed for the rest of my life?" I asked.

I allowed my mind to wander to another version of reality where I was a regular lady with no magic, lying in bed with a lover who didn't need to risk his life or reputation to be with me.

Logan smiled against my cheek. "There will be many mornings in the future when we can take our time. Today is not one of them. I'll get through it by fantasizing about what it sounded like when you screamed my name last night."

I blinked away the tears that welled in my eyes. Many mornings in our future?

"I think my future likely entails living in some haunted cottage in the pines away from whispering villagers," I admitted.

"Good," he said. "I hate people anyway. The more isolated, the better."

I scoffed. "You don't hate people."

He turned me in his arms. Logan was grinning at me, his dimples on full display. "How do you know?"

"I can mindspeak, remember? You love attention. You ate up being at those family dinners and getting fawned over by my aunts."

He raised a brow. "The only thing I *ate up* at those dinners was your eyes on me. Your attention is the only attention worth having."

My throat went dry. "Well, all the attention today is going to be negative. Are you ready for that?"

"Negative?" His brow furrowed. "Harper, one day, the people in Galloway will realize you saved them. Do you really think they'll exile you to the woods when they understand the truth?"

I barely understood the truth.

"Unless the Devil is lying," I said. "What if he's playing games with us?"

Logan shrugged. "He's the Devil. Known for trickery and mischief and all that."

I burrowed into the thick wall of muscle that was Logan Greer's chest. "Not helping."

He laughed. "We'll find out soon enough."

There was still so much about Logan I didn't know. "What will your family think?" I asked.

He cocked his head. "What do you mean?"

"What will your family think about you helping the cursed Ledes cousin?"

What would they think of him having a relationship with her?

He laughed. "What will they think about me solving the iron theft and helping Michael get his promotion away from the shore? When they learn I helped banish demons from the Barrens? Marrying into a noble family? I think they'll be pretty happy, Harper."

My eyes widened. *Marrying*? It was the first time that word had even entered my mind.

His gaze and his insufferable smirk slinked over me as I rose to get dressed. Logan loved to get a rise out of me. That would likely never change.

I pulled on my riding pants and tunic and smoothed my hair into a braid. I clasped my cloak around my shoulders.

My face was wan in the wavy glass of Logan's mirror.

"*Starling?*" I called out in my mind, softly beckoning.

"*I'm close. In the park,*" he replied.

It was nice to have him in range like this. Having him inside Galloway settled me in a way I'd never thought was possible.

"*How is the village?*" I asked.

"*Quiet,*" he replied. "*Iron gates are pulled closed. Not a soul to be found on the streets. I did see a few guards patrolling near the remains of the wall.*"

I turned to my guard and watched him put on his boots. He began tightening the leathers of his uniform. A baldric over his shoulder held the sheaths for his weapons, and he carefully strapped a dagger and a sword onto each side.

I tilted my head in appraisal.

Logan was primed for anything. He was a knight, a soldier preparing for battle. I glanced back at my reflection—shadowed eyes, pale skin, waves of hair already escaping my braid.

"Logan," I said. "Can I ask you a favor?"

The leather of Logan's militia tunic was loose around my shoulders, but the sword's weight was a comfort, nonetheless.

He had helped me tighten the straps and adjusted the sheaths so the sword's hilt was flush with my thigh. I couldn't carry an iron if I planned to ride on Starling's back, so Logan had found an alternative.

"It's copper," Logan explained. "When I trained as a smith in the armory, we used it to practice our shaping. It's softer than iron, and it won't harm Starling." His eyes swept over me as we walked the deserted path to the park. "It makes me feel better to know you're armed with more than just magic today."

I nodded, swallowing a lump in my throat. Starling was exactly where he said he would be, tucked under the willow tree. To anyone passing, he would have been a mere shadow through the boughs, but there was no one in Galloway brave enough to walk the park this morning.

I mounted Starling and stared past the tree line to the area where the eastern gate had stood mere hours ago.

"What next?" Logan asked me from his place on the ground.

"The manor."

Starling's hooves clapped over the stones as we rode through town. Galloway was a skeleton, all bones with no flesh or life to cling to. Shutters and gates had been pulled on every window and door, and as we passed the shops around the tavern, I noted items abandoned on the streets.

A wagon, a barrel, a box of tools. All had been hastily thrown down in an attempt to flee when the wall crumbled and bells began to toll.

It made me wonder if some other version of Galloway, in some other realm, was full of life at this moment. Perhaps the people could see the shape of us in their own windows as we passed through the streets in the early dawn light.

We went to the stable first, so Logan could retrieve his own horse. The mare bucked when she saw Starling, but the demon bowed his head to the animal and huffed a foggy breath into the mist.

I wasn't sure if he was able to speak to her in some other, more primal way, but Logan's horse allowed him to mount, and she seemed perfectly at ease to canter beside us after a few moments.

If the town of Galloway were a skeleton, the manor was her heart, still beating with life, trying to cling to a false hope. Guards had been stationed along the entryway, and when they saw Logan and me approach, they began to shout.

"It's Lieutenant Greer," one of them barked. "And Lady Harper. You know the orders, fetch the generals."

Paxton and Brannon were on the steps within moments, followed by all three triplet lords. Bain wore his armor, but Father and Aaron wore simpler leathers. My cousins wore the Ledes crest over their iron maille.

I dismounted, ran to Father, and allowed him to fold me into a hug.

"Is Jacob all right?" I asked.

He sighed into my hair. "He's safely tucked away in our chambers. James and Patrice are with him. Maggie and Bess are fussing over him like an orphaned kitten."

This made me smile. I pictured Maggie shoving coffee and biscuits down my twin's throat. At least she had someone new to worry over now.

Raina's death would be a scar he would hold forever. I glanced down at the brand peeking out of my leather sleeve.

Father's gaze trailed to the numbers as well. "What's the plan, Harper?"

My heart rose into my throat. I glanced at the company around me. My cousins and my uncles were mounting their own horses now, all strapped with irons. Each one turned to me with steady eyes.

"You're all asking me?" I asked.

Paxton laughed as he crossed his arms. "You're the only one who can speak to the demons, Harper. Our job now is to banish them. They fled when the wall fell, but I have no doubt they're creeping back toward Galloway."

I blinked up at Starling, but the beast merely stared at me. "Yes, but—"

"Our job is to secure this village," Bain said. "We can't do that without your instruction."

I studied the men before me, the leaders of this town, the protectors. One by one, my magic swept over them. Uncle Bain, stern and appraising. Uncle Aaron, his brow knitted with concern. Paxton and Brannon, both waiting with inclined chins and sharp, interested stares.

I looked to my Father last. His face was soft, and he considered me the same way he always had. It was almost like I was back in his study, a child with a childlike concern. A scrape on my knee or sharp words from my cousin were not what was weighing on my mind now.

I couldn't lead these men. I was the unbranded one, the youngest. My place in this town was in the back row. I was a daughter, a painter. At family diners, I was the one with my head hung low, listening to the words in everyone else's minds.

I had not been meant to lead a military mission, but my father and his brothers did not falter. My cousins did not stand down.

No, they stood beside me, despite it all.

Cade Ledes gazed up to the sky, and I wondered if a part of him could see the sun gleaming over the horizon.

"You know," he said. "When the mist started to thicken over town, I welcomed it. I had lost your mother, but the mist felt true. It mirrored the shroud over my heart."

My breath caught. I was still so unaccustomed to having him speak so freely.

"Your mother could mindspeak," he continued. "Just like you and your brothers, she could sense every one of my emotions. When she was gone, I was only glad for one thing.

My heart broke for me and me alone. She couldn't feel it. Only I could bear that burden."

Tears welled in my eyes, and I shook my head. "You never deserved to be alone."

My father reached out a hand and squeezed my shoulder. "And neither do you. You're my daughter, and I won't leave you. This will not be solely on your shoulders."

I peered up through the haze of building tears. The expressions on my uncles' faces had softened.

Starling nuzzled my neck. *"We should ride the wall's perimeter on the side of the Barrens and search for the creatures. If we encounter fire there, the lords can hold it at bay."*

I nodded. My horse knelt, and I mounted, relaying the message to the men around me. We agreed to move as a unit outside the border of town.

Paxton and Brannon relayed messages to the men nearby.

With a pat on Starling's back and a promise, we trotted to the bones of the wall.

CHAPTER

FIFTY-FIVE

"*Where are they?*" I asked the Alister.

We had been riding for hours and had looped the remnants of the eastern gate twice now. Each time, we set a wider reach, but no demons lurked within the pines.

"*They bide their time,*" he answered.

The sound I projected to him was as close to a sigh as I could make in my mind. It made sense that a demon made of mist could only speak in half-truths and riddles, but this would have been a good time to get a straight answer from him.

If the demons were keen to claim me, they sure as hell weren't showing it.

"Do you think any of them have snuck into town?" Brannon asked.

"If they had, they would meet nothing but iron," Bain said. "The village is built for them, even without the wall."

"I know you don't remember a time before the wall,"

402

Aaron said, addressing his sons. "You were children when it was built, and you never ruled the militia in its absence."

"Did the residents lock down their houses at all times?" Paxton asked.

Cade shook his head. "No. Demons were present but rare in those times. They only dwelled in deeply uninhabited areas of the pines. Doors and windows were only locked when there was known activity. Or during certain times of the year, like the solstices or the equinoxes. Always on a full moon."

Bain nodded. "But some refused to lock windows, regardless."

Aaron laughed heartily. "Yes, remember Sergeant Caldwell?"

"We used to say the old man was part demon," Bain said. "He had more scars than anyone in the militia. He used to claim he had wrestled a cryptid."

Aaron huffed a laugh. "Most of his scars were small, like pixies had inflicted them."

Beside me, Logan laughed, no doubt remembering his run-in with the pixies in the Barrens, which had earned him his scar—and his bond to Starling.

Suddenly, Starling halted. The rest of the horses stalled in tandem as though they had taken a verbal order from him.

"Raina's house is beyond these trees," Starling said. *"I sense a presence there."*

Logan turned. "Starling says there's activity at the midwife's home."

Bain raised an eyebrow. "You can hear the beast, Greer?"

Logan straightened his spine. "I can only hear him, no other demons. He's the one who bit me all those years ago."

Paxton and Brannon stared at Logan with gaping mouths.

"Does the venom open a line of communication to them?" Bain asked.

I cleared my throat. "There was no line of communication open until Logan and I went into the place between realms to speak to the Devil."

Logan's eyes flared. "You don't have to—"

I shook my head. "It's okay. They're here. They deserve to know."

My father's face was pale. "The Devil took you out of this realm?"

"Logan followed me. It's why I trust what the Devil told me," I explained. "If he wanted to take me, he would have done it then."

Cade Ledes turned to Logan, pulling the reins of his horse to stare at him eye to eye. "You followed my daughter out of this realm?" he asked.

A muscle ticked in Logan's jaw. "I should have stopped her. I know. But we didn't get pulled into hell. It was an in-between place—"

My father dismounted, and Logan followed suit.

"I know I was supposed to guard her," Logan said. "There was no other choice."

I held my breath as my father took slow, measured steps toward Logan, and the color drained from my guard's cheeks as the youngest triplet lord approached him.

Char filled the air like my father's magic had simmered to boil, threatening to light the tinderbox of pine needles at our feet.

My father's eyes swept over Logan with an intensity I had never seen from him. "You didn't know where she would be pulled. For all you knew, you were following her into the gates of Hell itself."

Bain and Aaron dismounted and stood behind their brother. It was so unlike my father to lose his temper. I had no doubt his brothers would do anything he told them to do at that moment.

Logan squared his shoulders. "My lord, there was no other way. And there was no way in hell—or any other realm—I would let her go alone. I followed her, and I would follow her again. I would follow her into the Devil's arms if I had to. My assignment was to guard her at the wall, but the wall can't protect her now."

Paxton and Brannon came to stand behind Logan, their feet set in a soldier's stance. Fear gripped me, and my throat dried. Were they truly going to hold him accountable for my actions? It had never been Logan's choice to leave this realm. He was following their orders, even though I had made it impossible for him.

I pictured Logan in the jail cell Jacob had inhabited, and a part of me cracked open. I opened my mouth to speak. To scream at them, but my father's voice cut me off.

My father inclined his head. "I don't think the rank of lieutenant is appropriate under these circumstances, do you, Bain?"

Uncle Bain nodded at Paxton and Brannon, a ghost of a smile on his lips. "I'll see to it when we return. The path is too overgrown for the horses. We'll need to travel on foot to the house."

The triplet lords turned and started down the path. Logan gaped after them.

What just happened?

Paxton clapped Logan on the shoulder twice before following the lords through the brambles.

"When this is over, we can plan your promotion ceremony, Captain Greer," Brannon said.

"Congratulations," Paxton said over his shoulder. "You think he's insufferable now? Wait until he adds that second bar to his chest. Be careful not to trip on the roots, Harp."

Logan was fixed to the earth as he watched my cousins disappear into the overgrowth.

"Would you like me to carry you above the trees, Harper?" Starling asked.

"No, thank you," I said aloud.

"What about you, Captain?" Starling asked. The way he stared at Logan made me wonder if the beast was making fun of him.

Logan shook his head. "You should guard the horses, Starling."

I raised my brows. "You were promoted less than a minute ago, and you're already bossing people around."

"I am not a people," Starling huffed.

I took Logan's hand and followed my cousins. I was grateful not to be wearing skirts as we walked through the thorny vines. Unlike the last time I had walked through the Barrens, I heard traces of wildlife—the call of a bird in the distance and the hooting of an owl from above. When we reached the clearing with the burnt house, the mist thickened.

The Alister was ever-present, even when my cousins had their irons in the fire.

They were not only drawn but held at the ready. Behind me, I heard Logan's blade rip free from the sheath.

Above us, perched on the remains of the roof, a curled

tail as thick as a grown man's leg wrapped around the wood beam. I followed the scales of the tail up to the furry body of the wolf torso it was attached to.

An aamon.

The monster hissed at us, and I reached for it with my magic. There were no words for me, but I sensed the beast's glee when the rest of his pack emerged from the ruins.

CHAPTER

FIFTY-SIX

Birds flew from the trees as the demons appeared in the clearing, fluttering through the canopy in a frantic scatter.

There must have been at least ten aamon around the burned house's foundation. We were outnumbered, but I did not doubt my cousins and Logan could take down multiple beasts.

We risked an injury if we didn't use magic. But would magic in the air strengthen them somehow?

"Let me speak to them," I called, projecting my voice over the snarls and growls.

"Make a circle," Paxton commanded, forming a protective ring around me.

"*Why have you gathered here?*" I asked. "*What do you want?*"

The aamon on top of the building spoke for the pack. "*We come for you, the one who can speak to us. Magic clings to this house. Fire magic. Mindspeaking. A mystic dwelt here once. Do you not feel it?*"

The aamon's voice crackled through me like ashes from a burnt log. Bile rose in my throat. I tried to recall everything Logan and I had learned in our research. The aamon were lesser demons, and based on the way they'd attacked Logan, I didn't suspect they had good intentions.

I racked my brain, trying to remember what notes I had scrawled in our research, but could not recall any way to attack or repel them. What I distinctly remembered was that aamon sucked the life force from their prey. They also sought out victims who held magic. It was no mystery why the Devil had sent them here.

He must have known the triplet lords would be with me as I came to face my reckoning.

"*What is it you seek?*" I asked, doubting they could even understand me.

"*You've brought down the wall,*" the aamon replied, and his wolfish maw widened into a terrifying grin. "*We can taste the human meat again.*"

I gritted my teeth, my desire to cut into this beast rising. Right now, there were children locked up in their houses, restricted from playing and walking the streets.

"Okay," I said aloud. "These are not friendly demons. They need to go."

A low growl erupted from Paxton's throat, and Brannon unsheathed an axe from the hook on his belt with a fluidity that gave me the impression that this was not the first time they had taken on a pack of aamons.

"When I banished the cryptid," I said in ragged breaths, "I used fire, but I don't think I can summon enough of it alone."

"Does it have to be your fire?" Aaron asked.

I squeezed my eyes shut. "I don't know."

"Summon what you can," Father said. "We can feed your flames."

I nodded, and my skin began to heat, like my power was sizzling to the surface in anticipation.

"When she banishes them, it will open a hole between realms," Logan said. "Hold strong, and don't get sucked in."

My eyes flew open and locked onto Logan. He was right. The Devil had said to bring down the wall. Without the presence of the wards, any banishing I did would tear holes in the fabric between realms. The thin spaces that previously connected the fire realm to our own would reappear.

And unlike when I banished the cryptid, the space wouldn't close. These rips would remain like thin ice over cedar water. What if we were sucked into it? What if a child or an innocent villager in the woods came across this place in the future and never returned?

"*Trust*," the Alister whispered into my mind. I let the word echo through me.

Trust.

Trust my magic.

Trust the people here with me.

Trust that I didn't need to do this alone.

I was the thirteenth Ledes child, the amplifier.

For the first time, I understood what the Devil had meant. My magic would grow in the presence of those who fed me. I reached out a tether of my mindspeaking power to the men standing around me, and I let my fire flare to the surface as I addressed the pack of aamons.

I let their emotions wash over me. My father was waiting, stilling his mind. Paxton was counting them. Brannon was tracking the ones on the periphery. Aaron was scanning for signs of flame. Bain was channeling his rage into his power.

And Logan was tracking the aamon closest to me, ready to pounce.

I projected my magic to the demons, splitting myself into raw pieces. *"If you've heard about me, then you know I will not allow you to harm my people."*

I didn't do it on purpose, but I projected my words to the demons and the men in the clearing. A silent shout into the misty air. Pure grief roiled off my father as I mindspoke. The last time he had experienced the sensation, what had my mother said to him?

The aamons began to pant at my words, and deep growls echoed from the house's structure. At least a dozen more beasts appeared from the walls.

Terror struck me. I needed to banish them before they encircled us. If they got too near, we would be sucked out of this realm for sure.

More fire, I needed more fire.

I let my anger rise to the surface, and with it, an ember appeared at the structure's base.

"Good," Bain said through gritted teeth. "Give us more."

I channeled every strong emotion I could summon, closing my eyes and picturing the sound of the stones pinging off the gallows. The blood that dripped from Jacob's knuckles as he hung his head. Mira's painted lips as she stood above him.

"Yes!" Father called. "It's working. Keep channeling that energy. Remember what I taught you, Harper. Open your heart to it."

I squeezed my eyes shut and remembered. I remembered Logan's hand closing over my wrist the first night I met him. My mind churned around the way I had wanted to strangle him. I tipped my head back and sucked in the misty air, recalling the way it felt when the Alister's voice had first slithered through my head at the wall.

"Open your eyes," Logan called out over the crackle of the flames.

So I did.

The flames were engulfing Raina's house, and it was not lost on me that I was about to rip into the thin space in the very spot where I was born, bathed in fire the same way I had come into this realm.

I stepped forward, past my uncles and out of the circle they had made around me.

I leaned forward and placed my hand on the ground before speaking directly to the pack.

"I am Harper Ledes, the thirteenth child of the triplet lords, daughter of Sarah and Cade. I am here to fulfill the promise made to your master. I send you back to where you belong."

The demons began to howl, and the sound ripped through me, threatening to pull me apart.

Somewhere deep below, the ground vibrated, and the composition of the earth changed.

A streak in the soil was blurred. Colors were not solid but made of darkness and light.

I remembered being in the space between realms, where I had witnessed beings jumping in and out of the fabric of existence, and I fought the pull to return there.

Because a large part of me wanted to feel that weightlessness again.

Aamon began to fall, one by one, into the ground. They were mere wisps of light, as though the rip in the fabric of the realm had turned them into ghosts.

They were phantoms, no longer in their corporeal form, and I beheld them in awe as the creatures on the periphery stopped howling and began to sniff the ground.

The aamon were not melting into the rift I had created. No, they were jumping in. They were leaping into that darkness and light like Logan and I witnessed when we spoke to the Devil himself.

My hand threatened to singe the pine needles as I pressed into the ground, and when the last aamon jumped in, I forced my hand from the earth. For a moment, I didn't think I would be strong enough to lift it. I jumped when a pack of pixies emerged from behind the trees, making a beeline for the rip in the earth like cockroaches scrambling for a crack in the floorboards.

They, too, turned into smoky light and shadow as they descended into the fissure I had made.

My hand couldn't move. It wouldn't move. I closed my eyes and heard the familiar ghostlike sounds of my past. A scream. A wail of a baby over the crackle of fire. The heavy beat of hooves on the forest floor.

Mist swirled around me like water around a whirlpool. It surrounded me, and all at once, I was a part of it.

The only air I wanted to breathe was that mist, sinking into the ground, into the rift I had opened. The Alister had been there since I took my first breath.

Cloaking me in alleyways.

Carrying the sound of voices from the wall.

Drifting around the strokes of my paintbrush.

All these years, I had outwardly resented it, cursing the

absence of the sun, but in my heart, I had reveled in his presence. I wanted to be shrouded by it forever.

The last thing I heard before I followed the mist into the space between worlds was the Alister's horrified scream.

CHAPTER

FIFTY-SEVEN

I was dead.

My eyes were wide, but I couldn't see. I didn't blink, partly because there was no air, but mostly because my eyes were no longer part of me.

If my heart was beating or if I was taking breaths, I would have counted them to mark the passage of time.

But there were no beats. No breaths.

Only mist, silent and soothing.

I was surrounded by nothing and everything.

After what could have been a second or an hour, a light appeared, shining like a beacon.

It was only as large as the head of a pin at first, but the light grew. Slowly, steadily, it became a tunnel, and it was clear now that I was in a place made of only light and shadow.

What is mist, after all, if not light and shadow?

Just as it had been in the place between realms, only now, I was completely and utterly alone.

Alone, yet surrounded.

415

I didn't have legs, but I walked to it. And the light grew brighter and more brilliant, and if I had eyes, it would have blinded me. As I neared it, I heard voices.

"Let this one be a devil," a desperate woman cried.

"Almost," another voice said soothingly. "Almost there."

Agonized gasps of air escaped before a baby wailed—the same sounds as my dreams. The child gasped and cried, maybe forever, maybe for less than the time it would have taken to draw in a breath.

It was me.

But it wasn't me. This child was some other version of me. I was not this child, but I was her, and the more she cried, the more my dead heart cracked open.

Horse hooves pounded through the light, the same sound from my dreams, so real they were palpable, yet so distant that I lurched toward it, trying to hold it in my heart.

"Let this one be a devil," the voice said again, and the horse whinnied in protest as the baby cried and cried. If I had a hand, I would have reached for it, desperate for touch.

I was on the edge of another realm. A version of my story that was true yet false. I realized then that every being is forged in infinite layers of words and emotions.

I took a step back on phantom legs.

The light began to shrink back with me. I was not moving toward it. Another step, and the baby's wails began to soften. Something in my chest fluttered.

Perhaps I was not completely dead. So, I reached for the one thing I always did in times when I was lost.

My magic.

I let it snake around me as it did in a crowd, seeking something to cling to. It reached behind me, and as I took another step backward, it hooked into someone's mind.

I was too far away to read thoughts, but emotions swelled through the tether. Sorrow, pleading, aching emotion so raw it gutted me.

Another step back, and the anguish grew, urging me back and back. The light before me had shrunk to the size of a small coin. It was receding into the blackness as I lurched along the string that pulled me.

Nothing else mattered outside of this gut-twisting sadness. I needed to go to it.

I need to go back.

The words had only just left my mind when a breath hitched in my chest, and I was yanked back through the rip I had created, back to the solid ground of the Barrens.

When I opened my eyes, the air was clear, and the sun blanketed my skin.

The sunlight was brighter than anything I had ever seen, and I couldn't focus my eyes. A horse's hot breath tingled my skin as Starling's wet nose nudged my arm. *"I saved you from this place once,"* he said.

"I saved you from this place once, too," I said.

"I will never need to save you from it again." His voice was sure in my mind.

I was in someone's lap, pulled against a broad chest. When my eyes adjusted to the light, my father's face was the first thing I saw, drawn in nearly identical expressions of concern with my uncles.

Paxton knelt beside me and took my wrist in his hand. "Her pulse is thready," he said.

A shadow slid beside him, Brannon's shadow. "She's breathing."

The arms holding onto me tightened, and the broad chest heaved. I held my ear to the leather, listening to Logan's heartbeat in between pulls of air.

His hand petted my hair.

"You left," he said. "I promised I would follow you. Never do that again. Don't you dare go someplace I can't follow you."

My father's hand wrapped around mine. "She needs a healer."

Logan slid his arms under my knees and lifted me, and as I drifted off to sleep in his arms, I watched the way the sun filtered through the pine boughs above.

CHAPTER 58
SIX MONTHS LATER

The triplet lords did not rebuild the wall around Galloway, but they did build a fence around the burnt remains of the house in the woods.

Logan stood beside me, his shoulders stiff. Sun gleamed off his newly appointed captain's badge, and I marveled at his beauty. I would never tire of admiring my guard. His golden hair was always neat, even after I ran my hands through it. I would never get over the way his eyes gleamed like aquamarines.

His dimples still made my blood boil, but not in a way that made me want to punch him.

"Don't go too close," he said. "I don't want your soul to slip through the cracks."

I laughed.

The last time I stood in this spot, I had left this realm. I still wasn't sure where I went—or why I went there—but I had no desire to leave Galloway to find out.

I squeezed his hand, reveling in the brilliance of the sapphire gleaming on my left ring finger.

419

"I don't feel anything, do you?" I asked him.

He shook his head. "Should we? Feel something?"

I shrugged, running my hand over the smooth stone pillar of the fence. There was no iron in this gate, no hum of magic, no wards to keep out the demons.

Because this fence was not built to keep the demons out.

It was built to welcome them in.

Humans were the ones we wanted to keep away from this spot in the Barrens. Unlike the previous wall, an imposing structure around an entire village, the fence merely encircled the ruins of Raina's house.

The fence had one job: keeping humans away from the thin space between realms that I had opened. Guards were stationed here morning and night, and demons were occasionally spotted, wafting in and out like ghosts through a mirror.

Now that the demons had freedom, they didn't enter the village. In fact, there had been very few sightings of them throughout the Barrens. The iron gates hadn't been removed from the windows, but it was rare that I would hear them squeak closed.

What the villagers did occasionally see was a winged horse. Some had seen him in the air, between the tops of the trees. Others had seen him swoop into clearings.

Logan ordered his officers to file official reports when they spotted any demons, including Starling. But his officers were unaware that Captain Greer saw the beast much more often than he admitted, specifically in the paddock we had built for him behind our cottage.

Occasionally, mist would thicken enough to whisper to me, and I would risk a ride.

Footsteps crunched behind us, but I didn't need to turn around to know who approached.

"I thought I would find you here, sister," Jacob spoke into my mind.

"I had a feeling you'd be here, as well, brother."

My twin held a small parcel in one hand and a bouquet of wildflowers in the other. He held out the parcel to me.

"Happy birthday," he said. Jacob's face was so much like Father's, and when he smiled at me, it reached all the way to his eyes.

I took the package and fished a small box from the pocket of my cloak. "Happy birthday to you, too."

I handed him the box. We had missed out on twenty-one birthdays together, and I vowed to make each one thereafter count.

Jacob placed the bouquet at the base of the fence, a tribute to Raina and the house where she had delivered all thirteen Ledes cousins into the world.

"Open yours first," I urged, bouncing on my feet.

He shrugged and swept a wave of ebony hair from his eyes. "James warned me about your gift-giving tendencies. Should I be worried?"

I rolled my eyes. James had especially loved the stuffed squirrel I had gifted him the previous year, after he had griped one too many times about their abundance in the townhouse courtyard. He'd even named it after me. Squirrel Harper. He had put it in the window.

"This is not a gag gift," I said, sighing. "It's an important birthday."

"I'm a little disappointed," Jacob said. "I was looking forward to a laugh." He unwrapped the paper, and his lips parted when he beheld what was wrapped in the parcel.

The bronze badge with the Ledes family crest gleamed in the sunlight. Within the crest, the number *12*, his brand, was engraved in Raina's handwriting, just as it was on his arm.

"It's a lord's badge," I said. "It's just like Paxton and Brannon's, only the engraver said it was much easier to fit their brands into the crest. Only one number each for them, two for you. I know you have the captain's badge, but I thought you could add this to your—"

Jacob held up his hand. "Harper, I love it." He pulled me in for a hug, and I wondered if I would ever get used to how this man had become an extension of me.

He gripped my shoulders. "Your turn," he said. "Logan, you should benefit from this gift, too."

Logan arched a brow. "I'm intrigued."

"It's nothing dirty, is it?" I asked. "I know you're my twin, and you can mindspeak, but I don't think you should be privy to my taste in undergarments."

Logan shook his head as Jacob punched my shoulder. "Don't be gross," he said.

"Save the dirty thoughts for later," Logan said.

Jacob pretended to gag as I unwrapped the gift. I turned over the wooden box in my hand and opened the latch.

"Watercolors!" I held them up to the sun, delighting in the shimmering blocks of paint inlaid into compartments.

Jacob beamed. "I asked Emelia to bring them back with her from York."

Emelia had finished her first semester of midwifery school just in time to prepare for the wedding this weekend. Father and Bess had dived into the preparations for their own wedding with the same vigor they had shown for their children. Emelia would be our sister soon enough, not through her own marriage, but through the love that had grown between our parents instead. She had only been back for a week but had already settled into a steady rhythm at the manor with Bess.

I was looking forward to having her back at family dinners.

Logan slipped his arm around me. "I was just thinking we could use some new paintings for the cottage. This is perfect timing."

I settled into his arms. We certainly needed some homey touches at the cottage. Aunt Bea and Aunt Pat had been hiking into the Barrens to visit our new home several times a week.

I didn't think they would ever forgive me when Logan and I married without telling anyone. It wasn't until I agreed to let them decorate our new home that they began to speak to me again. The least I could do was let them fuss over curtains and wallpaper, even if our home was in the "cursed woods," as Aunt Bea liked to say.

Thankfully, Mira had her own betrothal for my aunts to worry about now. Although it hadn't been a match of my cousin's choosing, her engagement to a wealthy merchant in Chatsworth ensured she would get out of Galloway. Somehow, a forced betrothal didn't seem like punishment enough. She did get what she wanted in the end, after all: a marriage to a powerful man.

It wasn't until I learned from Paxton and Brannon that her future husband was a cantankerous man, ten years her senior, that I began to feel a sense of justice. Perhaps a lifetime of being married to an old grump was a fitting punishment for Mira, but I doubted anything would ever feel like enough to me.

"I think the first thing I'll paint with my new watercolors is a wedding gift for Father and Bess," I said.

The image floated into my mind, and now that I knew the palette of flickering sunlight in the Barrens, only the most vivid colors would do.

Logan and I bid farewell to my brother and began to walk the path behind Raina's house back to our new home. We strode by the cedar water pond, and the stream that fed into the creek, and past the clearing where the first summer fire had singed the earth, allowing wildflowers to creep from the soil.

I climbed the brick steps, quiet and tucked in the shadow of the pines, and allowed my gaze to sweep over the garden Aunt Pat had planted on the side of the house.

When the sun dimmed low over the creek, a cloud swept in from the darkest part of the woods, wrapping over the garden like a warm blanket. A comfortable chill settled over me, blissfully warm yet cold, the air fresh and full of promise, a comforting whisper across my cheek.

I took in the expanse of the Barrens as the light reflected behind the boughs hanging over our cottage, and I studied the colors in the sky.

Impossibly bright, somehow even more so as they reflected in the mist.

Made of shadow and light.

THE END

Acknowledgments

The Pine Barrens are very real and very special to me. I wanted to paint them in a way that felt fantastical. Anyone who knows the area knows that the woods are incredibly haunting, but I always wondered if the monsters our families warned us about weren't monsters at all.

I want to thank my readers, especially those who have been on this ride with me since *The Elemental Realm*. My gratitude overflows for my beta readers: Mickey, Elizabeth, Jessica, Trisha, Sam, and Charlene.

Claire, your editing and faith in this project inspired me so much. To the incredible artists, JD and Rami, thank you for bringing this story to life with your artwork.

This book was already nearly finished in April 2025 when I tragically lost my father in a car accident. It felt impossible. How was I supposed to move on? I couldn't open the Word document for months, but when I did, it brought me an unexpected comfort.

While I was writing, I had no idea how much I had modeled Cade Ledes on my own father. From his patient, easy way of parenting Harper to his foot nervously bouncing while he worried, my dad was there with me. That's why I dedicated the book to him. He was my biggest fan. Even though he never read my books, he proudly displayed *The Gray Prophecy* in his office.

So, to any reader who has suffered through grief, I hope that Cade Ledes—and Tommy—made you feel seen. And for any reader who has ever been told they are less or that they don't belong, I hope that Harper inspires you to rise above the voices in your head.

THANK YOU!

As an independently published author, I cherish every reader to the ends of the earth!

Your thoughtful review or rating helps to get my books into the hands of like-minded readers. Thank you for taking the time to support an independent author.

–Maria

instagram.com/maria_a.eden_author

amazon.com/author/mariaedenbooks

ABOUT THE AUTHOR

Maria A. Eden is an author of paranormal and fantasy romance, including the award-winning *Elemental Realm Duology* and *Daughter of the Pines*.

Follow along by joining her mailing list for freebies, news, and first looks at upcoming releases:

ALSO BY MARIA A EDEN

The Gray Prophecy

A Vision of Lights